"If you knew me a little better, you'd know that I'm hardly ever disappointe

"What if I disapp

He was going to k̲̅ ̲̅ ̲̅ ̲̅eel it in his touch and hear it in ̲̅ ̲̅ of his voice, and though she wanted it, there was a nagging voice in the back of her head that kept telling her how stupid it would be to let him. If he kissed her, the rules of their game would change. Their roles would be compromised. Her job would be compromised. Heck, even his future could be jeopardized.

"You won't," she said, as his lips grew nearer, so close that she shut her eyes and readied herself to feel his lips press against hers. "And we…can't," she said, nearly breathless.

But he didn't stop. And she didn't pull away.

MS DEMEANOUR

BY
DANICA WINTERS

HarperCollins
PUBLISHERS
Since 1817

First Published in Great Britain 2017
By Mills & Boon, an imprint of HarperCollins*Publishers*
1 London Bridge Street, London, SE1 9GF

© 2017 Danica Winters

ISBN: 978-0-263-92940-9

46-1217

Danica Winters is a multiple award-winning, bestselling author who writes books that grip readers with their ability to drive emotion through suspense and occasionally a touch of magic. When she's not working, she can be found in the wilds of Montana, testing her patience while she tries to hone her skills at various crafts—quilting, pottery and painting are not her areas of expertise. She believes the cup is neither half-full nor half-empty, but it better be filled with wine. Visit her website at www.danicawinters.net.

To Mac.

No matter what comes our way,
we will always move our story forward.

Acknowledgements

This series wouldn't have been possible without a great
team of people, including my agents and editors at
Harlequin—thank you for all your hard work.

Also, thank you to Suzanne Miller and the crew at
Dunrovin Ranch in Lolo, Montana. Suzanne is the
inspiration behind one of my favorite characters in this
series, the fantastic Eloise Fitzgerald. Just like Eloise,
she always greets you with a warm smile and an
open heart.

I'm proud to say that all proceeds from the events in
honor of this series shall go to the Missoula, Montana,
Girls Using Their Strengths (GUTS!) program. This
program empowers and promotes leadership in girls
aged nine to eighteen. It is my belief that we must
support and help empower young women so someday
they can run the world.

Chapter One

There was nothing quite like the rush he'd felt when he had tried to kill his father. It had been like a charge running through Rainier Fitzgerald, shooting up from his toes straight through his body and escaping in one ill-advised and perfectly placed punch. One hit, one single punch had cost him more than three years of his life, thousands of dollars and nearly all his relationships.

There were times he wished he had really killed his biological father. Just a little bit harder or just a few more punches and he could've watched the life slip from the man's body. If he had died, maybe then Rainier could've felt guilty about what he had done to him; as it was, the only regret he held was that he hadn't punched him sooner.

The prison's chain-link gate vibrated; metal ground against metal and made an ear-piercing squeal as the gate opened. Rainier had been dreaming about this day, the day of his release, since the moment he'd entered this hellhole.

He took in a deep breath. The cold air carried the heavy and earthy scent of concrete, dirt and broken dreams, but he didn't care—for the first time in years, he was free.

The only hint it was nearly Christmas was the thick layer of snow on the ground and the black sedan in the parking lot complete with a set of felt reindeer antlers poking out of its passenger's-and driver's-side windows.

They looked ridiculous, but a hoarse chuckle escaped him, the sound so foreign that it caught him off guard.

In the corner of its windshield, the car had a parking decal for the Montana State Prison. Whoever it belonged to must work at this place, or was here enough that it was deemed necessary for them to have quick access—which made the Christmas fare seem even more asinine and somewhat obscene. It was as if the owner celebrated the fact that they could enjoy their freedom, even if it meant buying cheesy holiday decorations and displaying them from their cars for the inmates to see— and hate them for.

He looked around the parking lot, hoping to see Wyatt in one of their father's ranch trucks or maybe his patrol vehicle. Rainier smirked as he considered the irony of being picked up from prison in a squad car. Only in his life would something so ridiculous be possible.

But the only truck was an old beat-up Dodge at the far end of the parking lot. The pickup was empty and a film of ice covered the windshield as if it had been parked there for days.

His brother had left him in the lurch. He shouldn't have been surprised, but a promise was a promise.

Rainier sighed, rubbing his hands together as he tried to stave off the cold; though, if someone would have asked, it wasn't the chill of winter that caused him to shiver but rather the icy reception from his family.

On the other hand, he could hardly blame his brother

for not coming here to pick him up after everything he'd put the family through. It was the same reason he hadn't asked his mother to come get him—he hated her seeing him in this kind of place. All she'd ever done was take care of him and shower him with love, and yet he repaid her by being sent to a place where meals were given on a tray and people told him what time he could take a shower. In some ways, he felt like the bastard child he'd always been—thrown into foster care and finally picked up by the Fitzgeralds. They'd always made him feel like one of them, just another one of the adopted sons. Yet now here he was, alone and adrift again.

The door to the black sedan opened, the reindeer antler on the driver's-side door jiggling wildly, like a hand waving him down, as a woman stepped out. To say she was beautiful was an understatement. No, she was far more than that. Her ashy-blond hair was pulled tight into a no-nonsense bun, a pair of tortoiseshell-framed glasses teetered on the top of her head and her legs were long, and he couldn't look away from the round contours of her luscious hips. She turned, bending over to get something out of her car, forcing him to stop midstep as her pencil skirt hugged the curves of her ass. His mouth watered as he stared at the diagonal lines her panties created as they pressed against the fabric.

Maybe he had been imprisoned too long, but she might just be the sexiest woman he'd ever seen. She was dignified, classy and clearly the kind of woman who wouldn't have a damn thing to do with him. She was a far cry from the type of women whose pictures decorated most inmates' cell walls within his unit, as most of the pictures had been ripped out of men's magazines.

She stood up and patted her jacket pocket, searching

for something. He was pretty sure he saw her mouth form a collection of profanities, which seemed in direct opposition to the lines of her skirt and the straight-edged look on her face. It made him only want her that much more.

Yep, he had definitely been behind bars way too long. He'd never have a chance at a girl like that, not being the man he was, but that didn't mean he wasn't the kind who wouldn't swing for the fences.

She reached into her purse, rifling through its contents as he made his way toward her.

"Can I help you, ma'am?" he asked. "You lose something?"

She jerked as though she hadn't noticed him. She lifted her hand, motioning for him to stop. "I'm fine. Just fine," she said, then cleared her throat as though she were trying to collect her nerves. In fact, from the way her eyes widened, she looked almost scared of him.

He should have anticipated that this was what his life was to become when he got out—people fearing him, the feral Fitzgerald.

"I'm sorry, I didn't mean to bother you. Just thought, ya know…" His voice came out hoarse and tattered, befitting the man he had become. He turned to walk away.

"Wait." The woman's heels clicked against the pavement behind him as she rushed to catch up.

He swiveled back, and for a split second he could have sworn her gaze had been locked on his ass—or it could just be wishful thinking.

"Yeah?" he asked, cocking a brow.

"You're Rainier Fitzgerald, correct?" She lifted a phone he hadn't notice she'd been carrying, and was met with his mug shot from the day he'd been booked.

He stared at the picture. His green eyes looked nearly black. The only thing that gave away his fear over heading to jail was the slight quirk of his lip. He always looked like he was about to smile when he was nervous. Reaching up, he touched his lip and realized he was making the same face now—except, unlike in the photo, a new set of fine lines surrounded his mouth, thanks to his years of hard living.

"Is this you?" she asked, flipping the phone so she, too, could look at the picture.

"Did Wyatt send you to be my welcoming committee? If he did, I'm going to have to thank him." The words came out wrong, sounding far more crass than he had intended.

"Excuse me?" she asked. "I don't know what you're implying, Mr. Fitzgerald. And while I'm sure you would love a warm welcome, I'm far from being someone who is available or willing to supply you with such a thing. Plus, it might be in your best interest to steer clear of women who would be interested in *welcoming* you."

He hadn't been out of prison for five minutes and he was already in trouble with a woman and, in an upper-crust way, being told exactly where he could stuff his feelings for the opposite sex.

About right.

"Hey, I'm sorry for thinking maybe you were here to welcome me to the real world. I guess I just hoped, you being as beautiful as you are and all…"

It could have been the cold, but her cheeks seemed to take on a darker shade of pink as she readjusted her suit jacket and cleared her throat again. "Mr. Fitzgerald—"

"Call me Rainier."

"Let me guess, *Mr. Fitzgerald* is your father?" she

asked, her tone laced with distaste, as though she had heard that failed line more than a time or two.

"Actually, I wasn't thinking that at all. No one calls my father that, either." He motioned toward his hot pink Hawaiian shirt the prison had given him, one he was sure they had gotten for pennies on the dollar at the nearest thrift shop. "Does it look like I'm the kind of guy who should be called *mister*?"

There it was, her elusive smile flickering over her features. He was breaking through her icy exterior.

"Mister or not, *Rainier*, you need to watch yourself. I'm your parole officer. The name's Laura Blade."

He instinctively glanced down at the packet of papers he'd been given on the inside. Now her cool attitude made all kinds of sense. Of course she was from the other side of the law. "I thought I was supposed to report to your office tomorrow?"

"Your brother is a friend of mine. He requested we meet and you hear the terms and conditions of your release as soon as possible."

"Are you kidding me? My brother sent you to meet me at the door? Did he really think I was going to find myself in trouble so fast that I needed you to come here and warn me to toe the line?"

She tapped at her phone as though she was texting. "Actually, I had other errands to attend to, as well. You are hardly the only parolee I get the pleasure of seeing. Plus I'm always there for my brothers in blue."

"I bet Wyatt laughed his ass off when he set this up. Is he going to leave me here to figure out my own way home, too?"

"You must think little of your brother." She waved him off as he opened his mouth to argue. "Don't worry,

I offered to escort you. I need to perform a home visit, anyway, so I can make sure you will not find yourself returning to Montana's famous legal system."

"You mean infamous?" he said, snorting.

"It's hardly as infamous as you," she said, motioning for him to get into her car.

He stared at her. "Are you serious?"

"What do you mean?" she asked, swinging her car keys around her finger.

"Are you really offering to take me—a convicted felon—on a road trip all the way to Mystery?"

"I'm not your father, so I think I'm safe driving you home," she said. "Now hurry up and get in. It's not getting any warmer out here." She walked around to her door and the reindeer antlers jiggled as she sat down. She continued to tap on her phone as she waited for him.

He stood still for a moment, staring at the blonde before he got in next to her. She had done her research about him, but that didn't mean he wasn't dangerous. When it came to her, he could think of several things that he wanted to do—most of which involved kissing her pink lips and hearing her moan his name.

Then again, he'd always been the kind of guy to want what he could never have.

Maybe this tightly wound woman was more like him than he'd assumed. Maybe she liked to live life on the wild side.

Chapter Two

Laura had always thought it was just some stupid saying, but it was true that no good deed went unpunished. She'd thought Wyatt's request to help his brother would be easy and quick, and yet it had turned into her sitting next to a far-too-handsome convict for one painfully long and awkward road trip.

She glanced over at Rainier. His hair was flecked with bits of auburn and copper, and when the sunshine struck it just right it almost glowed like precious metal. His eyes were the color of emerald sea glass, their hue dulled and muted by the many years he'd spent behind bars. She wondered if, with time, their color would brighten and energy and light would return.

Her palms were sweaty as she gripped the steering wheel. The Dunrovin Ranch wasn't that much farther. She tried to nonchalantly glance at the clock on the dashboard to get an idea of how much more time she would be trapped in the car, but she noticed Rainier watching her and so she reached over and flipped on the radio. An old country song by George Jones filled the space between them, telling of broken hearts and destroyed lives. It was a bit ironic—the two of them were far too much like the song, she being the keeper of a broken heart, and his life destroyed.

She slipped Rainier a smile, trying to hide her thoughts before he could read them upon her face. Maybe she had it all wrong, or at least backward—her life had been destroyed in just a matter of minutes, as well.

Maybe the song was really just about her.

The country singer's twang grated on her nerves and she flicked off the radio.

"Do I need to go back over the rules and conditions of your parole, or do you think you understand them?" Laura asked, pushing a wayward strand of hair back into the tight bun on her head.

Rainier answered with a chuckle and lifted the manila envelope for her to see. "Between this ream of paper, and instructions you've been going over for the last hour, I think I've got it."

"I just want to make sure you fully understand that at any point we can revoke your parole, and you can be sent back to prison. Under no circumstances are you to violate any of the conditions I've given you."

"All right, there will be no drinking in excess, no hanging out where drugs are distributed or taken. I shall not leave my geographic limits without written permission. I shall see you between the first and third of each month..." He looked over at her and gave her a sexy half smile, and she tried to diffuse her nervousness by shifting in her seat. "I will not violate any law," he continued. "I won't associate with people who have criminal records, will not possess firearms or any dangerous weapons, and...well, we know the rest."

"Just so long as you do." She tapped her fingers on the steering wheel.

It was going to be a long year, seeing him every month, if this was the way he made her feel simply by sitting next to her and smiling.

Long ago, she had sworn off relationships, as the only thing they had ever brought her was heartache, thirty pounds that had now collected solidly around her thighs and ass, and what she'd learned later was a raging case of crabs. Not that she ever told anyone she'd had crabs, but she could think of no better reason to call an unwavering hiatus on all things men than a hundred little bugs making her itch like a madwoman. Looking back, she realized they weren't half as annoying as the man who'd given them to her.

"Laura—"

"Call me Ms. Blade," she said, interrupting.

"Sorry. *Ms. Blade.*" He said her name as if it were as sharp as the object it implied. "I was just gonna ask how you got into the parole officer game."

The last thing she needed was to exchange pleasantries with her assigned parolee. It would send the wrong message if Rainier thought for one minute they were anything that resembled friends. He had been assigned to her by the state, and her one job was to make sure he didn't find himself back in trouble. It was her job to save him from himself, even if that meant drawing a hard line.

"Being a parole officer isn't a game, Mr. Fitzgerald." She could feel her butt clench. "I take my job very, very seriously."

"Very very," he teased. "I guess you do. I haven't heard anybody say that since high school."

Just like in high school, she wanted to reach over and punch him in his arm for his cheeky manner. Under a different set of circumstances, she could've lightened up and they could've been friends. But he was the one who had chosen to nearly kill a man. Now he would have to deal with the consequences—not that missing out on her friendship was really a consequence that he needed to worry about.

"I'm surprised you didn't get into more trouble in prison, with a mouth like that."

He laughed, tilting his head back with mirth. "If you think I have a mouth, you clearly haven't been a parole officer very long. What are you like, thirty-two?"

Oh, they were so off on the wrong foot.

It was never okay for a man to guess a woman's age, especially if he was guessing too high. If he had said twenty-four, things may have gone more in his favor, but it was too late. He had fallen from her grace.

Thankfully, they ascended the hill that led to the ranch, and the tin roof of the Dunrovin barn came into view, letting him off the hook about erroring at her age.

It had been only about a week since she'd come to the ranch for their annual holiday party, the Yule Night festival, and it felt strange coming back again so soon. Yet even with all the drama that surrounded the place, a sense of calm came over her. She could almost imagine what it would be like to live there, walking through the spring pastures with her feet splashing in the mud, or her fingers touching the heads of the summer grasses that they would cut and bale for hay, or feeling the nibble of the crisp fall air while they moved the animals from their summer pastures.

She sucked in a long, deep breath, hoping that some

of the ranch's clean air had somehow slipped into the car. She could smell the faint aroma of horses, hay and diesel from the tractors. It was a heady mix, beckoning memories of her childhood spent daydreaming about horses and ranch life while her father whiled away the hours at his law office.

"I bet you're glad to be home," she said.

He glanced out the window, and she could swear that his green eyes turned a shade darker as he looked at the ranch. It didn't make sense how she could love this place so much and he could seem so disconnected.

"I'm glad to be out of prison," he grumbled.

"That doesn't mean that you're glad to be here."

"Oh, I'm glad to be home, but you gotta understand that I ain't gonna be welcomed with open arms. I screwed everything up. My brothers were so pissed, by now they have to have convinced everyone that it would be best if I just hit the road and never came back."

"I doubt your parents feel like that."

"They didn't come visit me. Not once when I was behind bars. They made it real clear they think I'm nothing but trouble."

"If you feel like your return to the family is going to inhibit your success in staying out of trouble, perhaps I can help you get settled elsewhere."

He grimaced as though she had just sentenced him to solitary confinement. "Nah, I ain't gonna run away. I'm just going to have to face whatever is coming my way."

She wanted to reach over and grip his fingers and give them a reassuring squeeze, but instead she gripped the steering wheel harder. "No matter what, I've got your back. I'm your ally."

"Well, at least I got one," he said, the sexy smile returning.

She pulled to a stop, parking the car in the gravel lot, which was covered in patchy snow. The ranch carried the warmth and feeling of Christmas, with its strings of lights, poinsettias and an abundance of wreathes that hung from every post. It looked like something out of a Norman Rockwell painting, including the older woman who was standing on the porch of the main office looking out at them.

She recognized Ms. Eloise Fitzgerald from passing and the occasional hello, and as they unbuckled, Eloise smiled and waved. Yet it was the congenial, halfhearted wave of a near stranger and a far cry from what Laura would have expected a mother to give her son.

Rainier's features darkened as he looked at his mother, having noticed her chilly reception himself.

"Don't worry, she probably just doesn't see you or something," Laura said, trying to soften the blow for him.

She stepped out of the car, Rainier following suit. Eloise shaded her eyes, casting shadows over her face as she looked toward them. Her mouth opened as she must have finally recognized Rainier when he stepped around the front of the car and made his way toward the office.

She smiled and her curved back straightened as she stood a bit taller. "Rainier, sunshine, is that really you?" Eloise asked, excitement fluttering through her words. "I can't believe it!" She rushed forward and threw her arms around her son's neck. "Your father and I didn't think you'd be here until tomorrow. Wyatt said…" Her words where muffled against Rainier's chest as she tightened her arms around him.

The reunion made a lump form in Laura's throat. Thank goodness it wasn't the chilly reception that he had expected and she thought had come to fruition.

In the history of hugs, this one may have been the longest, as tears collected in the corners of Eloise's eyes and slipped down her cheeks. "I'm so glad you're home," she repeated over and over.

Rainier gave his mother a kiss on the top of her head and finally she stepped back, releasing him from her grateful hold. For the first time since seeing her son, she seemed to notice Laura.

"Laura, I can't tell you how thankful I am in having you bring my boy back to us." She reached over and gave her hand a warm squeeze. "You have to come in. The girls and I just made a batch of cookies and there's fudge cooling on the counter."

Fudge and cookies. Laura pulled at the waistband of her skirt. This time of year, the pounds always seemed to jump onto her thighs at the mere nearness of fudge and cookies. In fact, if she closed her eyes and thought about it, she could almost feel herself expanding.

"I'd love to, but first I need to make sure that all will be well with you and your family regarding your son's parole." She tugged on the hem of her skirt, lowering it. "Is Rainier going to be staying with you and working here on the ranch? Is he welcome?"

Eloise gave her a disbelieving look. "Are you kidding, dear? Everyone is welcome at the ranch. My son made mistakes, and he's paid for them. I don't want things for him to be any harder than they already are. I would do anything for him."

Her admiration for Eloise grew. It wasn't every day that a convicted felon was treated with such kindness, even by family members or loved ones.

Laura looked over at Rainier as Eloise took them both by the hand and led them toward the main house and the waiting smorgasbord of sweets. He sent her a brilliant smile, his white teeth sparkling in the winter sun. He was so handsome; it was easy to see how someone could forgive him for his mistakes and trust him with their heart.

Chapter Three

The house was a flurry of motion. Gwen and Eloise were rushing around the kitchen, pulling together a meal reminiscent of the epicurean lifestyle of ancient Greece. Every countertop was filled to the edge with food. There was everything from cold cuts and cheese to spritz cookies and rosettes. His mouth watered. The food was a far cry from what had been ladled onto his tray in prison and the little packs of chips he bought at the commissary. Dang, it was good to be home.

His mother handed him a plate full of food, and another to Laura, as though she was just one of the gang and not someone with the ability to put him back in prison. He couldn't decide whether it was a part of his mother's plan that she overwhelm Laura with kindness in hopes it would keep him out of trouble, or if it was just his mother's way. Regardless, he loved her for it.

His adoptive father, Merle, walked into the kitchen while thumbing through a stack of mail. In all the excitement his mother must have forgotten to tell him that Rainier was home. When he finally looked up from the letters in his hands, a wave of recognition and pure joy overtook his face.

"Son, what are you doing here? I thought you didn't

get out for another couple of days?" His father gave a questioning glance to his mother.

"Oh, dear, I'm sorry. I meant to come get you. I just wanted to make sure that Rainier and Laura were taken care of. I'm so sorry," she said, throwing her hands over her mouth. "I can't believe…"

"It's okay, Mother," Merle said, giving her a quick peck on the forehead before turning to Rainier. "How long have you been home?"

He shrugged. With all the activity and questions his mother had been throwing his way, he wasn't sure if he'd been home five minutes or five hours. He wasn't used to this kind of attention, as if the world revolved around him. He both despised and loved it, but it was almost too much.

Even though he'd said nothing, his father seemed to understand and gave an acknowledging tip of his head.

"We haven't touched your room, Rainier. It's waiting for you if you're tired. This week we can go get you some new clothes," his mother said, coming over and pinching the pink Hawaiian shirt between her fingers and pulling it as if she wished she could throw it away then and there. "And we can get you anything else you need to get on your feet, as well. Waylon, Christina and Winnie will be coming home later this week." She grinned with excitement. "It's just going to be so wonderful to have the entire family here to spend Christmas. And Laura, you'll have to come, too."

Laura gaped as she glanced from his mother to him, almost as though she was checking him to see what exactly her reaction should be to that unusual invitation. "I…er…"

"You are more than welcome, Laura," his father said,

jumping in. "You don't have to answer us right away. I'm sure you've got your own family plans."

She looked a bit relieved, and it made Rainier's chest tighten as some part of him wished she had agreed to spend more time with him and his family. He took a deep breath as he tried to make sense of his body's reaction. He barely knew this woman, and their conversation had been limited mostly to business. Yet he couldn't deny there was something, a spark, between them. It was so strong he could have sworn he felt it in his fingertips.

Maybe it was just that she was the only person who had any real understanding of what his life had been like behind bars. She was his ally, and seemed to be the only one who could understand why he had changed.

"I… Y-you…" he stammered, trying to say something that would be as effectual as his father, but no words came.

Merle smiled. "Rainier and I are gonna head outside. I need to get to work on that broken spigot before the pump burns out." His father handed him a coat, and he shrugged it on.

He couldn't have been more relieved and thankful for his father's interference not just with the jacket, but with helping him to get out of the swirl of activity that made him feel so out of place.

Laura's face relaxed as she glanced over to him and gave an approving nod.

"If he's going to be home, you know we're gonna be putting him to work," the older man continued.

She gave a light laugh. "That's exactly what I was hoping for, Mr. Fitzgerald. If you don't mind, while you all are working, I'll take a quick look around, a brief home check."

"That's fine, but please call me Merle." His father frowned at the formal moniker.

"Thank you, *Merle*," Laura said.

"That's better," his father said. "Only Mother calls me Mr. Fitzgerald, and she only does that when I'm in deep trouble." He turned to Rainier. "Let's get going. We're burning daylight."

He followed his dad outside, and the moment the door opened and he breathed in the cold winter air, Rainier was thankful to be out of the kitchen. He loved his mother and the rest of his extended family, but he needed a minute just to be with himself in the quiet of life—an existence that wasn't framed by steel bars.

His father led him out to the tractor and, handing him the keys, motioned for him to take a seat. "Sometimes the best thing we can do when our world is a mess is bury ourselves in work in order to clear our minds. There are no prisons worse than the ones we impose upon ourselves."

The man was right. No matter how bad the nights had been when he'd been inside, the worst of them all had come when Rainier had thought about what he'd cost his family. There were so many things he wanted to say, but one in particular came to the front of his mind. "Thanks for everything, Dad."

It didn't seem like nearly enough, but emotions and expressing them had never been his strong suit. It was just so much easier to bottle everything up—although that was exactly the kind of attitude that had gotten him into trouble in the first place.

"Which spigot needs tending?" he asked, afraid of

things taking another emotional turn. He'd had more than he could handle for one day.

His father's stoicism thankfully returned, his face taking on the smooth and patient coolness that Rainier had always loved about the man. Since he'd left, however, his father's face had seemed to age. In fact, he noticed a new darkness in his eyes and it made a deep sadness move through him. Undoubtedly, he had played a role in those changes, and there was no going back or making things right. There was only moving forward.

"It's the one in the pasture. If you want to start digging, I'll grab the piping," Merle father said.

His father tracked through the snow toward the back of the house. Climbing up onto the tractor, Rainier could see a dark patch of grass and soot where the toolshed had once stood.

The tractor chugged to life and he moved the old beast toward the well as he thought about all the things his family had gone through when he'd been away, and what all else could have happened that his mother hadn't told him.

The earth was hard with the freeze as he set to digging up the piping around the frost-free spigot his family used for watering the animals throughout the year. The tractor's bucket broke through the top of the dirt, and as he dug deeper, the frozen soil turned into a muddy mess of gravel and clay as the water from the well spilled from the leaking pipes and saturated the ground. Water poured from the sides of the bucket as he moved the earth, piling it to one side.

It felt good to be working again, to be contributing to his family and the ranch. If he could work here for the rest of his life, he would die a happy man—he didn't want a job like Laura's, some nine to five.

He scraped out another bucketful of dirt from the hole. As he emptied it onto the pile, something white protruded from the sticky, brown earth. The object looked like a long stick, but its end was round and knobby.

An uneasiness rose up from his belly as he shut off the tractor, the bucket lowered midway. He stepped down from the machine and made his way across the sticky mud.

As he grew near, the thing lurched slightly, settling with the dirt around it. Based on the grooves and speckles on the surface, it was definitely a bone. He swallowed back the nerves that had tightened his throat as he reminded himself that, even though it was a bone, it was probably nothing—just some animal remains or detritus of days gone by.

He picked up the bone, scraping away the mud as he turned it in his hands. It was stained brown from the tannins in the dirt, the long shaft darker than the round ball of the joint. He wasn't absolutely sure, but it looked terrifyingly similar to a human femur. He laid the bone down near the base of the hill.

Turning back to the pile of dirt, he looked through it, hoping not to see another piece of bone. He scratched at the cold earth, the dirt and gravel tearing at his fingertips as he frantically searched for anything that could help him make sense of what he had found. His wet fingers grew icy as he worked away, then stopped abruptly when he touched something hard and even colder. His hand closed around something L-shaped and, as he pulled it from the mud, he gave a small, muffled cry. In his grip was a gun.

There was the clang of metal on metal as pipes hit the ground and bounced behind him. He turned to see his father and Laura looking at him. Merle gasped in shock.

Rainier dropped the muddy weapon, letting it fall to his feet as he looked at Laura's pale face.

"What are you doing with a gun, Rainier?" she asked, disgust and horror filling her voice as she stared at it, and at the bone lying beside it. "You—you haven't been out of prison for five hours and yet here you are, back to your old ways."

"I swear…it's not what you think," he argued, raising his dirty hands, palms up. "It… I didn't know it was a gun when I picked it up."

She shook her head. "You can take it up with the judge. In the meantime, you can kiss your parole good-bye."

Chapter Four

He couldn't go back to prison. For a moment, Rainier considered running, just grabbing one of the old ranch trucks and hitting the highway. Thanks to the many letters his mother had sent him when he'd been away, he'd learned all about the murder at the hands of his former sister-in-law Alli and her escape from persecution. It seemed that law enforcement in Montana was usually two steps behind. Then again, thanks to his own experiences, he wasn't sure he could rely on that to be completely true, or he would have never found his ass in prison.

"Laura—"

"Ms. Blade," Laura interrupted, as she typed something into her phone.

"My apologies, *Ms. Blade*," he said, careful to use the same sharp tone. "It's just that I don't... I can't go back to prison. That wasn't my gun. Hell, I didn't even know it was a gun until it was in my hand. You have to believe me, I never want to waste my time behind bars again."

She stared at him for a long moment, and from the set of her jaw and the look in her eyes, he could tell she was struggling to believe him. He had no idea what else to tell her. No doubt, as a parole officer, she would have learned by now that very few people in this world told the truth—and even fewer who were ex-cons.

He'd long ago given up the idealistic notion that anyone would take anything he had to say at face value ever again. The moment the judge's gavel hit the block and he'd been delivered the sentence, Rainier had known he'd forever wear a scarlet letter for his crimes. Part of that sentence would be always being thought of as less than and dishonorable—no matter how justified he felt in committing the crime.

"Can't we just look past this, Ms. Blade?" asked his father. Merle held his hands together almost as if he was silently praying that Laura would honor his request.

Rainier could've told him a long time ago that that kind of thing had a way of blowing back on a guy.

"Mr. Fitzgerald, I know your family's been through a lot in the last month, but that doesn't mean I can just ignore what's going on here." Laura frowned. "I made it very clear to your son that there were certain conditions associated with his parole—conditions he absolutely could not violate. And yet here we are. I can only imagine the kind of trouble he would find himself in if I *wasn't* here."

"I can assure you that my son has always been a good man."

"Let me guess—he's *just misunderstood*?" Her lips puckered as she spat the words out like watermelon seeds.

"I'm not going to make any excuses for my son's behavior, but you have to know that he wouldn't intentionally find himself in trouble. Especially not like this."

Her gaze swung to Rainier and he nodded, hoping that she would listen to both of them.

"Ms. Blade, it's not like I'm asking for a second chance. I'm just asking for any chance at all." Rainier hated the note of pleading in his voice. He'd never been one to beg, but he'd never been given his freedom and then had it rescinded on the same day.

"The police are on their way." Laura pushed her phone into her back pocket. "I won't tell them about the gun in your hand and the remains at your feet, but you have to promise me that this was just a case of you being at the wrong place at the wrong time and nothing else."

A sense of relief washed over him, but faded away again as the piercing sound of sirens echoed in the distance. He looked in that direction, but in the bright afternoon light couldn't make out their source. Hopefully, his brother wasn't on duty. The last person he needed to see right now was Wyatt.

"Do you promise, Rainier?" Laura pressed.

"Of course," he said, trying to sound earnest.

"And you won't find yourself in any more trouble?" she continued.

"You're welcome to stick around and be my wingman as long as you like, Ms. Blade," Rainier said, giving her a cheeky smile he hoped would ease some of the tension between them.

The parole officer looked away, making him wonder if his smile had worked, after all.

"Son, it may not be a bad idea for you to go inside and get out of the spotlight," his father said, motioning toward the house.

On the drive back to the ranch, Rainier had told

Laura he wasn't afraid and that he wouldn't run away from whatever life would bring him. But now, facing the possibility of seeing his brother after all this time, the urge was strong to tuck tail and run on back to the house. Heck, he could even pretend that when his brother questioned him about the remains and the gun that it was the first he was hearing about the findings. Wyatt would probably think nothing of it, and he certainly wouldn't jump to conclusions like he would if he arrived and Rainier was standing by disarticulated remains.

His brother had always been like that with him—always thinking the worst. Rainier couldn't blame him for the trouble he himself got into; he'd always been a little bit of a rebel and the family's black sheep. But his brother's condescending attitude certainly didn't help. It was like every time he screwed up, Wyatt was there to let him know he had seen it coming.

Once, when they had been young boys, their parents had sent them out to collect eggs from the henhouse. Gathering eggs soon turned into Rainier picking up rocks and pitching them to see who could throw the farthest. Colter and Waylon had joined right in, using different size rocks and different throwing techniques until they had found the one that suited best. But not Wyatt. Wyatt had stood to the side and kept warning them about how much trouble they were going to get into if their parents found them, or if something went wrong.

Of course, the other three didn't listen, and it wasn't five minutes before Rainier pitched the perfect pebble straight into the back window of their father's old Jeep. If he closed his eyes, he was sure he could still hear the crackling sound of the splintering glass, almost like someone stepping on the thin crust of ice on a lake.

Breaking that window had been his first lesson in keeping Wyatt out of his affairs and away from anything fun, as well as how much work it took to raise two hundred dollars to pay for a new window. His father had been understandably angry at the time, but just like now, he'd seemed to understand that sometimes bad things happened. A person could go about living his life between the lines, or as Merle put it, "living between the mustard and the mayonnaise," but even then couldn't avoid trouble. Or maybe Rainier wasn't really the kind who avoided it; maybe he was just as bad and destructive as people expected him to be.

"Rainier, are you listening?" asked Laura.

He hadn't heard a single thing she said.

"Sorry, what did you say?" he asked, blinking away images of him and his brothers playing around the ranch and causing trouble when they were younger. What he would give to go back to those days, when they'd all still got along and had truly lived for each other.

"Why don't I walk with you inside—you know, be your wingman?" she repeated, holding out her hand as if he was some kind of wayward toddler.

He was unsure if he should be excited or offended by the way she was treating him, but he had to admit the look she was giving him was far more comforting than the one from a few minutes before, when she had found him holding the gun.

He slipped his hand into hers, and she jerked, almost as if she hadn't expected him to take her up on her offer. She let go again at once, but not before his father gave him a look of surprise. Rainier was sure his own expression mirrored his dad's.

This woman continually surprised him. He'd heard so many things about parole officers when he'd been behind bars. From the stories that got filtered down to him, most sounded like real hard asses, but not Laura. Sure, she had a hard edge to her and she was a no-nonsense kind of lady, but there was something equally soft, almost maternal about her. That softness made him wonder if she had a child.

He wasn't sure if he should ask, especially now that she had agreed to take his side and cover up his role in discovering the remains. He didn't want to compromise her emotionally any more than necessary. More than that, from the second they had met she had made it clear to him that there was going to be nothing more than professional civility between them.

She walked ahead of him, leading the way back to the house as the sound of the sirens grew louder. As they approached the door, his mother and his brother Wyatt's fiancée, Gwen, stepped outside.

Rainier glanced down at his mud-covered coat as he tried to wipe the dirt from his hands.

"What's going on?" his mother asked, peering out in the distance toward the approaching police cars.

Laura smiled, but the action was forced and tight. "No worries, I just jumped the gun—" Her mouth gaped open for a moment as she must have realized what she had said.

"We just found something a little odd, and Ms. Blade thought it best if we got a crew out here to investigate it," Rainier interjected.

"Investigate what?" Gwen asked. "And where's your father?"

Rainier turned and looked toward the barn. "He was going to greet the deputies when they arrived. You don't think it's gonna be Wyatt, do you?"

Gwen frowned. "He wouldn't come roaring out here with the sirens on. He's been coming out here enough lately that he would know not to create any kind of scene for the neighbors. It's gotta be somebody else," she said, motioning toward the SUV hurtling their way. As it drew nearer, Rainier could see there was a patrol unit without its lights on following in its wake.

The SUV pulled to a sudden stop, skidding on the ice in the parking lot. A woman, her dark hair pulled into a tight ponytail, jumped out of the car and made her way over to them, with Merle hurrying after her.

"There's Wyatt," Gwen said, ignoring the woman and motioning toward the vehicle just pulling into the lot.

"Who's she?" Rainier whispered.

"New recruit. Her name's Penny Marshall." Gwen frowned, and the look on her face held a trace of jealousy, but he wasn't sure why his soon-to-be sister-in-law would have anything to worry about. Wyatt, above all things, was a good man.

His brother stepped out of the second car. "Penny, wait up. Jeez, woman, you seriously need to slow down. This is my family."

The patrolwoman turned around. "Hey, if you want to drive like some old fart, that's on you. For all you knew, someone's life could have been in danger out here, and you were driving like it wasn't some kind of emergency."

"If someone's life was in danger, Penny, we would have been told about it. That's what dispatch is for. I've told you before, there's no good reason to put our lives at risk when a situation doesn't dictate it."

"Okay, Deputy Fitzgerald," the woman said, but from the tone of her voice Rainier could tell that she was just playing along and fully intended to keep living her way with or without Wyatt's approval.

Rainier liked Penny already. From the looks of her, she was in her early twenties, and from the sound of his brother's exasperated voice, straight out of the academy.

Wyatt's lips puckered and his face darkened as he looked up and noticed him standing there. "So you made it back to the ranch?" He slammed his car door with a little too much force, clearly pissed off. "Is your homecoming the reason for our appearance?"

Rainier swallowed back the growl that percolated up from his core. He had known this was going to be the closest thing to a welcome he was going to get from his brother, but his expectations paled in comparison to the reality.

Or maybe it wasn't the lack of welcome he was upset with, but rather the reality that his brother had been correct in his assessment—he was in fact the reason they had been called. But Rainier would never give Wyatt the satisfaction of once again being right in assuming the worst about him.

"It's good to see you, too, brother," he said, trying to temper his disappointment before it had the chance to pepper his voice.

"Wyatt, Penny," Laura said, giving each an acknowledging wave. "Thank you so much for coming on such short notice. There was no reason for you to rush. In fact, if you have somewhere else to be, you are welcome to come back later."

From the stress in her voice, even Laura had to have known how futile and ridiculous she sounded. If there was somewhere else for the deputies of Mystery to be, they would have been there, but it wasn't a town that was usually fraught with crime.

"Laura, you know if you're calling we're going to come running." Wyatt chuckled as he came closer and gave Gwen a quick peck on the cheek. "Though I have to admit, I did drive a little quicker knowing that my fiancée would be here waiting for me."

Gwen smiled, the jealousy disappearing from her features.

It was nice to see his brother in a relationship, but it was strange to see him act so smitten. Wyatt had always been the serious kind, and watching him loosen up in his presence made Rainier wonder if there was still hope for them to fix their relationship. Then again, Gwen and Wyatt loved each other, and he wasn't sure he could say his brother loved him.

"The dispatcher reported that there was some kind of disturbance, something about a parole violation?" Penny asked, looking directly at Rainier.

"No, no. Everything's all right," Laura said with a bit too much indifference. "Actually, it had nothing to do with parole violation. Your dispatcher must've gotten it all wrong."

"Wyatt," Merle exclaimed as he came walking around the side of the barn. "What took you so long?"

Wyatt laughed. "We were worried you fell down or something. Didn't want you getting hurt," he teased.

Their father answered with a long laugh. "Nah, I

just found something behind the barn Laura thought you and your friend would want to check out. It's probably nothing, just some old animal bones. In fact, if you guys want to get going, I'm sure we can sweep this right under the rug."

"Why does everyone want us to leave all of a sudden? We just got here," Penny said. "Is this always the way you guys greet one another?"

Eloise's cheeks reddened. "Oh, dear, Penny, don't start thinking that. We're nothing like that around here. We love our boys. We just understand how busy you all can get, being the pillars of this community and all."

"Laying it on a little thick, Mom, aren't you?" Wyatt asked, raising a brow. "Dad, why don't you go ahead and show me those 'old animal bones.'"

Merle glanced over at him, as if trying to decide exactly what to say or not say to Wyatt about their discovery. Rainier shook his head ever so slightly, reaffirming their decision to keep his role in the findings quiet. It wasn't that he was being selfish, no. It was just clear that his brother had so much resentment toward him that if he caught a single whiff of his involvement, Rainier's hope for a life surrounded by family again would be as good as over.

Chapter Five

Laura wasn't sure she really believed that Rainier was as innocent as he and his father proclaimed him, but if she sent him back to prison, it would be an all-time record for the shortest turnaround. In her department, her friend Jim held the current record of three days before his parolee was sent back, after he'd been found in possession of a large amount of heroin. It was a running joke that the parolee had turned back to drugs after spending a day with Jim.

She could just imagine what the guys around the office would say if they learned that after only a matter of hours she'd found her parolee elbows deep in mud, holding a weapon with human remains at his feet. And that was nothing compared to what her father, the high-powered attorney Dennis Blade Esq., would say if he found out Rainier and the Fitzgerald clan were once again in trouble. He'd made it clear to her that he had nothing good to say about the Fitzgeralds.

She couldn't understand her dad's dislike of them. Though things were tense between Wyatt and Rainier, she could still feel a resounding warmth. And the fact that Merle would go to such lengths to help his son keep out of more trouble spoke volumes about his character.

Laura's father hadn't told her why he held such animosity toward the Fitzgeralds, only that they weren't to be trusted.

Then again, she'd never been very good at following her dad's advice.

Hopefully, this time it wouldn't come back to bite her, but the knot in her gut told her there was a very good chance it could.

Wyatt and Penny disappeared behind the barn, following Merle. Maybe that was what the knot was all about—what they were about to find. No doubt the place would be filled with their investigation and forensics team, and the coroner would soon arrive. Then the questions would start. She'd have to keep her story straight, and she'd never been one for lying.

"Laura, how about you and I go ahead and step inside." Mrs. Fitzgerald motioned for her to follow her into the house. "Unless you need to get running."

The word *running* echoed in the air, almost as though someone had struck a bell. No matter how badly she wanted to leave the ranch and resume her normal life, she couldn't go anywhere. They would have questions for her about her involvement, and if she left, she would only fall under further scrutiny.

"I could go for a cup of coffee," Laura agreed.

"So could I," Rainier said, but not before darting one more glance after his brother.

They made their way back inside. Though it hadn't been that long since Laura had been in the kitchen, with everything that had happened in the last hour, it felt as if days had passed. As she made her way through the living room, the sparkle of silver bows atop colorful presents under the Christmas tree caught her eye. There were piles of wrapped gifts—red, green, blue and even a stack of pink ones adorned with Disney princesses.

"Do you have grandchildren, Mrs. Fitzgerald?" she asked, gazing toward the princesses in her best attempt to mask the elephant in the room—the coming investigation.

Eloise beamed. "Just one for now, a beautiful little girl named Winnie. She, Christina and Waylon should be home in a couple of days. He's in the army, working as an MP, and they've been living at the base. I couldn't be more proud of them."

"I'm sure. That's something to be quite proud of," Laura said, but as she spoke she noticed the way Rainier's entire body seemed to tense as they mentioned familial pride and accolades.

"They're going to get married soon." Mrs. Fitzgerald reached over and gave Gwen's hand a quick squeeze. "Just like my Gwen and Wyatt, and Whitney and Colter. I was hoping that we could have one big wedding over the holidays—you know, put everything bad behind us and use it to start the New Year off with something to really celebrate. Whitney and Colter have been in Spokane, getting everything they think they're going to need. She sent me a picture of her dress the other day. It's just beautiful."

So all the brothers were engaged, except Rainier. Laura had an idea how he must be feeling. Both her sisters were spoken for, but not her. Her mother had made talking about her failing love life into one of her favorite pastimes. And she loved nothing more than giving Laura regular style hints. Last week's had been that she should dye her hair, as she was starting to, as her mother put it, "get a little less shiny…you know, that happens as we ladies age."

Laura had no idea how dying her hair would make it shinier, but she doubted her mom had meant it as anything other than another jab at her aging-spinster lifestyle. She was the same with her sister—which was part of the reason the three of them rarely had anything to do with one another. Recalling her mother's words nearly made her groan aloud, but she checked herself. Whether her mother knew it or not, Laura had no intention of living a life completely devoid of love from the opposite sex. She just had no desire to have a relationship her family knew anything about. She hadn't forgotten how poorly it had gone the last time she'd brought a man around.

The other ladies made their way into the kitchen, while Rainier walked over to the Christmas tree and ran his fingers reverently over one of the boughs, rolling the needles between his fingertips. His simple action made Laura smile.

He had missed so much in the last couple years. The closest he had probably been to a Christmas tree had been seeing them in pictures in the magazines that had been passed around his unit.

"Did you miss this?" she asked, gesturing around the room at the holiday trappings.

She suddenly realized how alone the two of them were, and it made her feel something almost like attraction toward him. She tried to stuff the feeling away. There could be none of that nonsense.

Maybe she'd identified her feelings incorrectly. Maybe it was just that she pitied him. If that was the case, she couldn't fall into the trap of letting her empathy for him morph into something it shouldn't be.

"You know, growing up, I used to love Christmas," Rainier said. "We always had a tree like this one—spruce. Those and ponderosa pine grow all over in this area. It was such a big deal to go pick one out. We'd spend all day in the woods, Dad pointing out what he thought was the perfect tree and my mother inevitably shooting each and every one of them down. It was like a game between the two of them, and it would only come to an end when the daylight faded and they were forced to compromise."

That was a far cry from her family's out-of-the-box trees that they had thrown together each year in just a matter of minutes. One year they had even plastic-wrapped the tree with the ornaments still on, so they wouldn't have to bother decorating it again the next year.

"We would have hot chocolate and s'mores that my mother would warm up on the heater on the dashboard," Rainier continued, as he picked up a red ornament that had fallen to the floor and rehung it on a branch.

"That sounds really special," Laura said, not quite sure if she should interrupt his reminiscing.

He nodded, but she could tell from the distant look on his face that his mind was in the past.

"It really was." He turned to face her, and she could see a glistening in his eyes that hadn't been there before. "I just can't believe that I'm at risk of losing them all again."

Oh, so that was what this was—some veiled attempt to pull at her heartstrings in order to make sure she wasn't tempted to change her mind about his fate. She wouldn't let him play that game, either.

"You have it all wrong if you think you can make me your mark," she said, taking two steps back from him.

"Huh? What are you talking about?" he asked.

"You can't try and manipulate me to get what you want. I know all about your kind."

"*My* kind?" He spat the words. "You mean convict, or do you mean orphans?"

He was trying to pick a fight. It was a good diversionary tactic from the real issue at hand, but she wasn't going to let him pull that one over on her, either.

"I'm just saying that you're not the first ex-con to think he's smarter than me."

Or hardly the first man who thought himself smarter than me, either, but she bit her tongue before she let the words slip from her. She didn't want to come off like some scorned woman. She wasn't anything of the sort, but Rainier needed to remember his place—and his place, right now, was under her thumb.

"If I was smart, the last place I'd be right now is here." He stared at her.

"If push came to shove, if a deputy found out I'd lied for you, I would likely be charged with accessory after the fact," she whispered, just loudly enough for him, but not the women in the kitchen, to hear. "That would mean we would both be headed to prison. Have you thought about that?"

"I know what you did back there was a gamble," he said, tipping his chin toward the barn outside. "Your sacrifice doesn't go unnoticed. You can trust me when I tell you that I had nothing to do with that body."

He moved toward her, and she carefully stepped back

until her legs pressed against Mrs. Fitzgerald's '80s model velveteen sofa. The little hairs of the couch upholstery jabbed into the back of her calves, but it was nowhere near as uncomfortable as Rainier was making her when he looked at her like he was now…a look of compassion, respect and maybe something more.

"You have to know that I would never compromise you like that," he added. "Though I've only known you…what? A couple of hours? I believe you're a good person. You're not the kind of woman who would risk everything if she didn't think a person was telling the truth."

The little zing she had felt for him returned, making her wonder if she would ever be able to control her body's responses whenever Rainier said something that made her want to smile.

He moved so close that the only way she could get away from him was by sitting on the sofa, so she plopped down in a most unladylike fashion—complete with a little *oomph* as the air rushed from her lungs.

"I've been wrong before, Rainier," Laura said, gripping her hands in her lap so as to not reach out and touch him.

Thankfully, he stopped his advance and glanced back at the tree. "We all make mistakes, Laura. No one more than me."

"So you agree that what you did to your father was wrong?"

"It wasn't wrong to do what I did. My biological mother and father may have been the worst parents on the planet. I don't even know how I made it out of there alive." He sighed. "How much do you know about my real parents?"

She had done her research on Rainier Fitzgerald, but it seemed that all his records had started when he'd been about sixteen and had gotten his first speeding ticket. His file had been dotted with a few misdemeanors, just the odd fine here and there that often came with a rambunctious teenager; that was, until the assault on his biological father in some low-end beer joint on the south end of town.

"Not much," she said, shaking her head.

"That night in the bar, when the assault happened, it had been a long time coming." Rainier turned away from her and went back to studying the tree. "My birth father was an evil man. He did things that should have sent him to prison and kept him there until his dying day, but instead, he got off scot-free… And in the end, I was the one sent away. Life has a wicked sense of humor."

She wanted to ask what exactly his father had done, but before she could, there was a knock on the door.

Mrs. Fitzgerald came shuffling out of the kitchen, a white apron tied around her waist and what looked to be fresh flour on her hands. She smiled at them as more knocking reverberated through the room.

"Be right with you," she called, wiping her hands on her apron. "I don't know why they bother knocking. If the police are done, I would hope that Wyatt would know to just come right on in," she said, more to herself than to them.

She opened the door and her hands dropped to her sides and she stumbled backward. "What are you doing here, William?"

There, standing in the doorway, was a sour-faced man in a business suit. As he looked inside, he smiled, and the action was as crisp and polished as the rest of his exterior.

"I thought it was high time that I stopped by the ranch and said hello," William Poe said. He nodded toward Laura. "How goes it, Ms. Blade? Your father mentioned that you were going to be poking your head in at the ranch from time to time, thanks to the family jailbird. You know, if it were up to me there would be more than one Fitzgerald prison bound."

The man looked as out of place at Dunrovin as a fox in a henhouse, and just as predatory.

"What are you really doing here, William?" she asked, getting up from the couch. As she did so she made sure to pull her skirt just a bit lower on her knees. The man had a reputation, and she didn't want him leering at her.

He opened his jacket and withdrew a letter. On the front, in big bold red letters, were the words *Final Notice*.

"Something was incorrectly sent to my house. I think it belongs to you all." He flipped the letter toward Mrs. Fitzgerald, but she didn't bother to try and catch it, and it fell to the floor at her feet.

"Why would you be getting our mail, Mr. Poe?" Eloise asked, her voice taking on a dangerous edge that Laura wouldn't have imagined the woman capable of unless she had heard it for herself.

"Well, Mrs. Fitzgerald, I would hardly know," William said, a sleazy smile spreading over his face. "But from that note on the front, I thought it better make its way into your hands." He nudged the envelope with his shoe, leaving tread marks on the paper. "I'd hate to stand in the way of justice being served. You know me. I've always tried to be helpful."

"We know you to be a thorn in our side," Mrs. Fitzgerald retorted.

Rainier walked over to the man. "Why don't you just get the hell out of here?" he said, pushing him back out the door.

"How dare you touch me," William said, his tone filled with hatred.

"What was that old commercial… *Reach out and touch someone*?" Rainier asked with a wicked laugh. "You're lucky all I did was touch you. The next time you set foot on this ranch, you are going to wish that *all* I did was touch you."

"You are going to wish that you never laid your hands on me." William readjusted his suit jacket in what Laura assumed was his best attempt to save his ego. "I'd threaten to sue, but based on what you're about to learn, we both know that you and your family wouldn't have the money to pay me if I won, anyway." He laughed, the room filling with the foul sound.

William turned toward Laura. "You know, if you were like your father, you would save yourself some time and just arrest Rainier now."

Her stomach clenched. Had he seen something? Had he witnessed her lying for Rainier?

"There's no way that man is going to stay out of trouble. In fact, I bet that's why the police are outside, isn't it? Are they just waiting to arrest him?" William continued on, seemingly unaware of the questions raging through her. "It wouldn't surprise me. This family is nothing but trash."

"You know what, William? I think Rainier was

right," Laura said, as she walked over to the doorway. "You need to get gone and stay gone." She slammed the door in the man's face.

As she did, she knew it would come back to haunt her. But right now she didn't need anyone to tell her who or what the Fitzgeralds were. To her, they were just another family that needed her help.

Chapter Six

The affection Rainier felt for Laura had grown tenfold in a matter of seconds. The last thing he had expected was for her to stand up to William Poe, his family's arch nemesis.

He watched as she leaned over and picked up the envelope from the floor, her skirt pulling tight as she moved, making him want her just that much more.

He forced himself to look away. His family didn't need any more drama right now. Since he'd gotten home today they'd found a body, he'd nearly been sent to prison and now William. Rainier hated to imagine what was coming just around the corner. Though, admittedly, if it somehow turned into having Laura in his bed, he wasn't sure that he would mind so much…as long as no one found out. If his mother ever discovered that they were sleeping together, it would probably be the thing that would push her over the edge.

She walked back to Eloise and handed her the letter.

His mom stood still, staring at the door as if she was just waiting for it to open and William to come strutting back inside. The letter in her hands trembled.

"Mom," he said gently. "Mom, why don't you sit

down?" He walked over to her and, taking her by the arm, led her to the couch and helped her settle there.

Her gaze never moved from the door.

"Do you mind if I take a look at the letter?" he asked.

She lifted her hand, motioning for him to take it, but said nothing.

He'd never seen her like this, at least not since the day he'd been sentenced. The memory of her sitting in the wooden stands of the courthouse made shivers run down his spine. He'd vowed he would never make her feel like that again, yet here they were…although this time he wasn't entirely sure it was his fault. William's appearance at his family's home had to simply be a coincidence—at least he hoped so.

On the other hand, William had mentioned that he'd known Rainier was being released. Maybe he had planned his arrival to coincide in hopes that his homecoming could be ruined. Maybe it was William's hope that they'd never be happy again. Little had he known that their day had already been ruined.

Now it was up to Rainier to fix what he could, and help them all to move past what they couldn't.

He took the envelope from his mother. It was addressed to the ranch, care of his parents. When he tore it open, a letter fell out, with the same red lettering as on the envelope. It read *Final Notice*.

He pulled open the letter and saw it was from the county. As he read the words on the page, they seemed to blend together into a jumbled mess of lines and swirls as he tried to understand how "back taxes" and "working ranch taxation rates" had resulted in "Payment due on or before December 31. If not paid in full, a lien will be placed against the property for $150,489."

The number rolled around on his tongue like a sour grape. His family couldn't owe that much. There had to be some kind of mistake. Where would they get that kind of money?

According to his mother's letters over the last few months, they had been barely scraping by, and it was only because of the Yule Night festival that they had managed to pay their bills for the month. Now this?

He looked to his mom, who was still staring at the door.

Was it possible that she had known what was in the letter? Had she known this day was coming, and that was why she had turned in on herself as she had?

He glanced back down at the page. There had to be a way to file for an extension—something, anything they could do to give themselves more time.

The taste in his mouth grew more putrid as he read the last line of the body of the letter:

"...an auction will occur if owners fail to remit all sums due by above date."

"What does it say?" Gwen asked, leaning against the doorjamb that led from the living room from the kitchen.

Rainier wasn't sure how he should handle things, but somehow telling Gwen the truth didn't seem like the best option. In fact, telling anyone what he had just read seemed about as much fun as chewing off his own hand.

"Do you mind taking care of Mother, Gwen?" he asked, motioning toward the couch. "Mom, do you want a cup of tea or something?"

She nodded, finally pulling her gaze away from the door. "Earl Grey, please, Gwen." She gave a half smile as she returned to the land of the living and false strength.

"I'll give her a hand in there," Laura said, taking Gwen by the arm as they made their way into the kitchen. "That way you two can have a moment."

He gave her an acknowledging tip of the head and sat down beside his mother on the couch. He moved the letter so she could see it. "Did you know about this?"

She took it from his hands and, opening the reading glasses that hung from a cord around her neck, she slid them on and started to read.

Eventually she tried to speak, but the words came out in a smattering of syllables and garbled sounds, until she finally stopped struggling and simply shook her head.

"What about Dad?"

She shook her head again.

"Is this even real? How could you be getting a final notice of something due next week if you didn't even know about this?"

"I'm sure it's real," she said, her voice filled with cold resignation. "If I've learned anything about William Poe, it's that he's capable of whatever he wishes. He has and will do everything in his power to try to tear the family and this place apart. He's not going to stop until he succeeds."

Rainier pointed to the letter. "But something like this had to be in the works for months. Why now? Why is he coming after us with this?"

"He's never been a fan of ours, but I don't know why. For the last few years we managed to keep him at bay, but once he became the county tax appraiser, we knew that our days might be numbered. Then with everything that's happened…it's only gotten worse. I told you about his brother, Daryl, and the fire in my letters, yes?"

He nodded.

William had to have some kind of vendetta—something that must have gone deeper than his wife dying at the hands of his crazed former sister-in-law, but Rainier could only guess what was behind it.

"I have to put a stop to this, to him." He stood up and made his way to the door.

"No, Rainier, you're not going to do or say anything that will stop him. William is like a dog with a bone right now. All we can do is hope…"

"And get a goddamned good lawyer, someone who isn't afraid to take the bastard down," he said.

"I'm sure we'll try. But Rainier…you have to know that this may be the end of Dunrovin. We are all getting so tired of fighting. Maybe this is just the world's way of letting us know that it's time to move on. To get a new dream."

"No, Mom, don't talk like that. You just have some asshat who thinks he can do and say what he wants without repercussions." He opened the door. William was standing beside his Mercedes, talking to Penny.

"Officer Marshall, I hope you are planning on escorting that man from our property," Rainier said, charging toward the two as Wyatt and his father made their way back from behind the barn.

"Actually, Rainier, Mr. Poe was just asking me a few questions about my job."

"Nothing about why you are here?"

Penny slid William a look that made it clear that was exactly what he had been pressing her about. And knowing about the kind of man William was, Rainier was sure that he was making a solid effort at making a pass on the twenty-something woman, as well.

"Something going on here?" Wyatt asked, coming closer and sensing the tension in the air.

"I was just making sure that William here got in his car and left. He ain't welcome," Rainier said, pointing toward Poe like he was something a horse had left behind.

"If you think I want to spend my free time in this hellhole, you have me all wrong. I have much better things to do. There's money to be made. I told you, I was here as a personal favor. That will be the last time I try to do something nice for you people," William said, adding an edge of pitifulness to his voice in what Rainier assumed was his attempt to play the victim.

"You and I both know what was in that letter, and you took great pride and enjoyment in bringing it here. You did it for yourself. You wanted to witness the results of that bomb firsthand."

William laughed, the sound echoing through the evening. "You must think that I'm the epitome of evil. I can assure you, Rainier, that I'm not the villain you and your family seem to have made me out to be." He reached down and took Penny's hand and gave it a quick peck. "I'm sorry you had to witness all of this, Officer Marshall. On the other hand, it is good that you know exactly the kind of hatred that this family seems all too capable of."

Penny pulled back her hand, but not before Rainier noticed a little flush in her face.

He really couldn't understand what women saw in this guy. He was clearly nothing but a selfish, lowlife con artist.

William walked away, giving Penny one more tip of the head before he got into his car and drove off. As the light from his taillights disappeared in the distance, Wyatt turned toward Rainier. "What was all that about?"

He looked to Penny, hoping his brother would take the silent cue that they shouldn't be talking about William in front of what could possibly be one of his many love-struck followers.

Wyatt gave him a small, almost imperceptible nod.

"What did you guys find back there?" Rainier asked, thankful for his brother's understanding. "Are they human remains or animal?"

"Definitely human. And the gun has been in that ground for a while. We got the area cordoned off and tomorrow we'll get our team out here to start excavating the crime scene."

"Crime scene?" Rainier asked, a cold chill running through him.

"Any time there is an unwitnessed death—no matter how long it's been since it happened—we have to treat it like a crime scene."

"Do you have any idea how long the bone has been there? Or who they could have belonged to?"

Wyatt shook his head. "Like I said, we'll have to go over the entire scene with a fine-tooth comb and send in our findings to the medical examiner. But until then there is nothing I can say as to what the findings will be." Wyatt stared at him for a moment. "Is there some reason you are so inquisitive?"

So there it was; his brother's true feelings toward him were rearing their ugly head once again.

"I just want the best for everyone and everything involved here, Wyatt. Can't we call some kind of truce or something?" Rainier waved in the direction William's car had gone. "He's our real enemy…not members of our own family."

"I'm not your enemy, brother, but I do care what happens to this family—and I care when someone, even someone in our ranks, does things that are outside our best interest." Wyatt turned to Penny. "I want you to stay here, retain the chain of custody on this crime scene until Lyle and Steve can come in and conduct their investigation. Don't let anyone, especially him—" he pointed at Rainier "—close to the scene."

His brother stormed off to his patrol car, slamming the door as he got in.

Rainier had no idea how he was going to fix things with his brother, only that he had to, not only for his own sake, but for the sake of his parents. They didn't need to deal with his brother's petty drama, not now.

"If you'll excuse me," said Penny, "I'm just going to get going…" She gave him a look that was half apologetic and yet still held an air of skepticism as to the kind of man he was.

"Yeah, no problem. And don't worry, no matter what my brother thinks, I have no intention of messing around with your crime scene or anything else. In fact, if you need anything—food, whatever—let me know and I can get something to you."

Penny smiled and some of the reservation she seemed to hold for him slipped away. "I appreciate that, Rainier. I'll let you know."

He nodded, and he and his father watched as she walked off. As soon as she was out of earshot, Merle turned toward him. "Now, what was that with William? What was in the letter?"

Rainier cringed. The last thing he wanted to do was break the news to his father about the back taxes. "I think you should talk to Mom. She's pretty upset."

They made their way into the house. Rainier was happy to get in from the cold. He hadn't noticed how it had crept up on him, stealing his heat until his fingers and toes had gone almost completely numb. He squeezed his fists, forcing blood back into his extremities as they made their way into the dining room. Everyone was sitting around the table, and it reminded him of their traditional family suppers, except in this case, no one was smiling.

This was all a far cry from what he had expected to come home to. He couldn't help wondering, as he looked around at the tired and haggard expressions, if maybe everyone would have been better off if he had simply stayed behind bars.

Laura stood up and made her way over to him, just out of earshot from the rest of the family. "Is everything okay outside? Is William gone?"

"You know it."

"Where's Wyatt and his team?"

"His team isn't going to come in until tomorrow. I think they feel a body this old doesn't need a team to come out this late in the night. I think they are planning on hitting it at first light."

"So they don't need to interview us?" A look of relief washed over her.

He shook his head. "No, and don't worry. Everything is going to be fine."

"Even with the letter? Are your parents going to be

able to afford this?" she whispered, looking around to make sure no one else could hear her.

He looked to his mother. "I don't think so. Their best hope is to find a good lawyer. They're going to have to fight...and fight hard. But there isn't much time. According to the letter, they have to pay by the end of the year. And by now—you know how the government works—everything is shut down for the year. They're going to have a hell of a time getting in touch with the right people...people who can put a stop to this, or can help them figure out how they should go about fixing it."

Laura nibbled at her lip. "Do they have a lawyer on retainer?"

He shrugged. "I don't think so, but with everything that's happened here, it would be a good idea if they did. Hell, I bet by now they would have some kind of punch card started."

She gave a little laugh, but bit it back. "If they need someone, you know my father...he's a lawyer."

"And apparently a friend of William Poe's?" He gave her a questioning look.

"They work together. You know how it is in small towns—everyone in the county runs into each other, and it's best that they remain civil. We all just end up using each other." She shifted her weight as if she were trying to rid herself of the burden of what she had just accused the government officials of. "My father is a tough man to get along with, and he may not take on the case, but if you want I can talk to him about all of this."

From the fatalistic but determined look on her face, Rainier could see that this was an offer she never made, and it helped him appreciate her favor that much more.

"If you wouldn't mind…maybe you and I can go tomorrow and I can talk to him, as well. Make him understand all that is happening."

"I'm sorry, Rainier." She looked down at her hands. "But I'm not sure that's the best idea. My father knows about you…what happened. He's not one of your biggest fans. And if we are going to have him as an ally, maybe it's better if someone else comes."

Merle cleared his throat, as though reminding them that they weren't alone. "Laura, if you'd like, Mother and I would love to go and talk to your father."

Laura blushed. "I'm sorry, I didn't mean for you to hear—"

Merle waved her off. "No worries. I… I mean, we appreciate all the help we can get."

"I'll meet you at his office in the morning." She reached over and touched Rainier's upper arm. Having her hand on him felt as good as it felt wrong, but neither of them pulled away. "Why don't you come with us, after all? Even if you're not in the meeting, I'd like to have you there to support your parents…and me."

He smiled. For the first time all day, something was going right.

Chapter Seven

She'd had an inbox full of emails when she'd gotten up this morning; most were about parolees and questions from potential employers. Laura made quick work of them and made a few phone calls, but all she could think about was seeing her father, the ever terrifying Dennis Blade, Esq.

There were many who thought her father charming, service-oriented and willing to go the extra mile. But she had known the other side of him much better—his need to control, to manipulate and use people, and to do whatever it took to get what he wanted. If someone were to ask her if he was a good person, she wasn't sure she could say yes; rather, she would have told them that he was simply a man. He was both good and bad, giving and taking, and though he had faults, he'd always loved her.

Even if that love meant him being a constant source of anxiety in her life.

That anxiety had always been associated with family, which was why the Fitzgeralds were like an enigma— with Rainier's parents' open arms and open minds, the self-sacrifice and generosity of spirit. The only tension came from Rainier and Wyatt, but even she could see that beneath the hurt feelings and animosity was a deep well of love.

It wasn't a long drive to her father's office building in the city, and when she arrived, Rainier, Merle and Eloise were already there. They were standing beside their car, huddled in a little group while they waited for her. She glanced down at her watch and saw she was fifteen minutes early.

She parked beside them, and as her eyes met Rainier's she couldn't help the little jolt of excitement she felt at seeing him again.

"Hey," he said, holding out his hand to help her step from her car.

Though it was in the single digits outside, his hand was warm, making her wonder if his body was reacting to her being near, just as hers was to his presence.

"Hi," she replied, but even to her ears she sounded like an enamored teen, and she chastised herself. She cleared her throat as she tried to collect her emotions, and reminded herself there was nothing between them. "Mrs. and Mr. Fitzgerald," she said, giving his parents a quick wave as she pulled her other hand from Rainier's warm grip.

"Please call us Merle and Eloise," his mother said. "I think we've moved past formalities."

"Absolutely, Eloise." Laura smiled and gave the woman a slight, appreciative nod. "Been here long?"

Rainier shook his head. "Only about ten minutes. We wanted to make sure we had enough time to talk before we went inside."

So he had been outside long enough for his fingers to grow cold. The thought made her grin. Maybe his attraction to her wasn't just something she was imagining. But it was still silly to get her hopes up—or to have any hopes at all, for that matter.

"Did you have something on your mind?" Laura asked, trying to stop herself from thinking about anything that wasn't directly involved with their mission.

Merle and Eloise looked at each other as if they could speak in some silent code after so many years of marriage.

"We just wanted to say we know you're going out of your way to help us," Eloise said. "We appreciate everything you're trying to do, with Rainier included. Yet we understand what a long shot it's going to be, getting us out of trouble with the county."

"I'm sure everything will be all—"

"No, that's it," Eloise interrupted. "It may not turn out how we all hope. We don't want you to be disappointed and feel like you failed if this doesn't work out."

Laura wanted to hug her for being so understanding even in these hard times. It took a higher class of lady to think about others and put their feelings first, when so much was going on in her own world.

Laura wanted to comfort her and tell her that she was wrong, that they would make everything come together and all their troubles disappear, but she couldn't bring herself to lie. Eloise was right, the chances were low, but that didn't mean they had to lose hope. If anything, it was in times like these, when everything seemed so bleak, that having faith and hope was most critical.

"Let's talk to my father first and see what he has to say. He tends to know the right people, at least the kind of people who can make something like this disappear." She wasn't sure if she should tell them about his penchant for being mercurial, especially when it came to his daughter and her requests for help.

Eloise sighed, the sound speaking volumes of relief that Laura's words must have given her. They made their way inside, through the elaborate curly maple doors that led to her father's office lobby. With each step, her nervousness grew, forcing her to wipe her sweaty palm against her skirt. She glanced down at the little wet mark left behind. No doubt her father would notice; he was nothing if not detail oriented.

"Why don't you guys wait right here?" She pointed to the leather sofa and chair set in the reception area, and the family sat down. "I'll be right back."

She walked over to the secretary's desk and was greeted with a smile from the woman sitting there. "Hello, Ms. Blade, your father is expecting you. Would you like me to let him know that you and your friends are here?"

"Please."

She waited as the woman made a call to her father's inner sanctum, and they spoke in hushed tones. From the look on the secretary's face, her father must have been giving her what-for, making Laura's anxiety grow.

"I'll head on in," she said, not waiting for the woman to get off the phone. "I'll come get my friends in a moment. I just need to speak to my father alone."

The woman held out her hand for her to stop, but Laura didn't heed her warning and she strode down the hall and tapped on her father's door. She could hear the phone slamming down on the receiver through the heavy wooden panel.

"Come in, Laura," he said, his baritone echoing through the empty hallway.

She swallowed back her fear and shook out her hands, then made her way inside, careful to close the door behind her.

"Father," she said with a nod. "Thank you for finding time in your schedule to talk to us today."

"Where are your *friends*?" he hissed. "I would think if they were coming here to request representation they would have the decency to at least show up."

"Oh, the Fitzgeralds are here," she said, gesturing toward the lobby. "They're just outside. Before bringing them in, I wanted to speak to you for a moment."

"What about? Them or some other harebrained scheme of yours?"

She wanted to stand up to her dad, to tell him he had no right to be so demeaning toward her, but right now, when she'd come here for a favor, it didn't seem like the right time to start a fight.

"I was hoping we could talk about them and what I would like to see happen with this taxes mess."

"I got the general idea, thanks to your late-night phone call. Don't you remember that I have to get up every morning at 5:00 a.m.?"

So that was the reason he was in such a foul mood today.

"I'm sorry to have disturbed you. That wasn't my intention. I just knew that this all had to be handled as quickly as possible. Though I would think you get phone calls at night quite regularly."

He gave her a heated look that told her she had made another mistake. "I have a call service for a reason. And you know, Laura, there are at least a hundred other things I could be doing with my morning besides dealing with more of your nonsense."

Hopefully he wouldn't go so far as to actually talk about Tanner, they had been down that road a thousand times and she didn't want to rehash what had happened with her ex.

She gritted her teeth. She couldn't be insolent.

"I appreciate you taking the time…as I said. I understand you're busy, but as you know, this is about William Poe. You have to stop him."

Her father chuckled. "William couldn't have done something like this. He doesn't have the power."

"But he knows the right people to make this happen. And explain to me how he could've gotten their mail. It just doesn't seem legal."

He tented his fingers in front of him on his desk and turned slightly in his chair. "That is odd, and as much as I respect William, it is suspicious that he would involve himself in something like this. Either he got sloppy and is playing more of a role than I'd assumed, or he really is innocent."

"I think we both know the answer to the question if William is innocent or guilty."

"You're naive if you think that we're not all a little bit of both. To be successful in life and at business means being able to make choices others aren't capable of, and William certainly is good at his job. But that doesn't necessarily mean that he is guilty of any wrongdoing."

"But you'll take the case?"

"What you're asking is far more complicated than you can possibly know." Her father put his hands down on his desk. "And we both know that you have a tendency to get wrapped up in things like this—things that you have no business including yourself in. It's just like that mess with Tanner."

Of course he would go there. Whenever she asked for something, and he wanted to say no, he would always go to the subject of her former boyfriend, Tanner.

"He has nothing to do with this, Father."

"He may not, but it's a perfect example of your weaknesses. You always waste your time on losers."

"The Fitzgeralds aren't losers."

Her father snorted. "If they're going against William Poe, then that's exactly what they're setting themselves up to become."

If this was what it was going to be like to work with her father, maybe they would be better off getting another lawyer. But if she went out and faced the Fitzgeralds now, it would deal them a hard blow. They'd rested all their hopes with her and her ability to have a civil conversation with her father, a conversation that could make or break their future.

"Besides, right now public opinion is starting to turn against the family, and that makes it even harder to take this all the way. Especially with this new finding on the ranch—that set of remains is going to be the straw that breaks the camel's back when it comes to the public being on their side."

"How do you know about the remains?" she asked, shock riddling her voice. Wyatt and his team were out at the ranch now, and they likely hadn't even finished up yet—and her father seemed to know all about it.

"Something like that isn't going to stay a secret for long. You and I both know how living in western Montana is. All gossip is just a phone call away. And it's my job to keep a close tab on what you are choosing to do with your life. You can't really think that I'd let you work with convicted felons all day long and not check up on you."

"So you're spying on me?"

Her dad shook his head as if he was growing tired of her. "Laura, I'm your father. No matter what you think of me or my choices, I'm always going to do what I feel is best for you. Even if you don't like it."

She couldn't stand him sometimes. "Dad, I'm old enough to take care of myself. I don't need you constantly looking over my shoulder. I'm an adult."

"If that's true, then take your friends and figure this out yourself." He pointed toward the door. "Mark my words, the Fitzgeralds are in a situation from which there is no coming back. If they are implicated with this body—if they had anything to do with this person's untimely death—and you are associated with them, everything you're fighting for is going to come to an end. You will find yourself in trouble right next to them. You need to go."

"They had nothing to do with this person's death," she said, ignoring his order for her to leave. "For all we know, the person has been dead for years. Long before the family owned the ranch."

"From what I heard, that may not be the case. Regardless, you need to stay away."

Her father had this all wrong. No matter what he had heard or what he assumed, the Fitzgeralds weren't the antagonists here. No, this family hadn't done anything wrong. Eloise and Merle had gone above and beyond in their attempts to take in foster kids, adopt Rainier and his brothers and run a guest ranch that brought smiles to their guests' faces. They weren't murderers. They weren't tax evaders. They were always trying to do the right thing, and she had no idea why her father couldn't see them for who they really were.

"If I show you, if I can prove that the Fitzgeralds had nothing to do with do with this fiasco with these human remains, would you agree to help them?"

He sat quietly for a moment. "We'll see what you're capable of. But let me say it again—you need to get off the boat before it sinks."

That was as close to help as she was going to get with her father for now, and the only thing sinking was her stomach. She turned and started to make her way out of his office.

"And Laura, be wary of William Poe. He's got his fingers in a lot of pots."

She gave a cynical laugh as she thought about William's reputation for seducing women. She was sure that was not what her father was referencing, but she couldn't get the image out of her mind.

Her laugh echoed down the hall, and as Laura made her way to the waiting room, Eloise stood up at the sound and looked toward her.

"So everything went well in there?" She smiled. "Is he ready for us to come and talk to him?"

Laura wanted to tell Eloise the truth, that they were barely hanging on by a thread to the hope that he would involve himself in their case, but she couldn't bring herself to do it.

"Actually, he's up-to-date on the situation. I'm hoping he's going to start looking into things."

She felt okay as she skirted around the truth. What she had said wasn't a bold-faced lie, rather a twist on words. For now, that would have to work.

"In the meantime, we need to make sure that Dunrovin focuses on clearing its name and restoring its place as a premier guest ranch."

"We can do that. Isn't that right, Merle?" Eloise said, joy speckling her voice and making Laura feel even worse about keeping the truth from them.

As they turned to leave, Rainier walked with her. As soon as they were out the doors, he took her hand and slowed her to a stop, while his parents walked ahead of them to the car.

"He isn't going to help us, is he?"

The blood drained from her face. There was no way he could have heard her and her father talking, so how could Rainier possibly know what had happened behind those closed doors? "I… He…he doesn't think there's a way to win the case—no matter if he or another lawyer takes this on," she said, letting the words pour from her. "And he's worried that the body is going to make the law come down on your family even harder, regardless of your brother's role in the department. The only way we even have a fighting chance of sorting this all out and getting any lawyer to take this case on is if we can prove that you all had nothing to do with those remains."

Rainier sucked in a long breath, as though composing himself before speaking. "Okay." He nodded. "You said I needed a job as a condition of my parole. From this moment on, my job is going to be to help Wyatt get to the bottom of this. Come hell or high water, my family is going to get the help they need."

Chapter Eight

When they made it back to the ranch, Wyatt and his team of investigators—which consisted of Lyle and Steve, who looked oddly like Andy Griffith and Barney Fife—were screening dirt that they had dug up from around the spigot. From the looks of things, they hadn't found anything else, which made a profound sense of relief wash through Rainier. If they couldn't find any more bones, that meant there wouldn't be a whole lot for the medical examiner to study, which hopefully meant the case would go cold and soon be forgotten.

If only they could get that lucky.

He looked over at Laura as she got out of her car, thankful that she had agreed to come back to the ranch after she'd made a few phone calls to make herself available. He couldn't believe how helpful she was being, or how many risks she was taking in helping him and his family. He doubted that she was normally this involved with her parolees, but maybe he was wrong. Maybe this was just her way—giving, selfless and filled with the spirit of altruism.

He couldn't deny that he'd gotten lucky in being assigned a parole officer like her. She wasn't anything like what he'd expected—some middle-aged, balding guy with a chip on his shoulder and a heavy drinking problem. Rainier chuckled at the thought of how far from the stereotype she was.

She closed the door to her car and turned to him. "Did you talk to your brother yet?"

He shook his head. The entire drive home from the city he had been trying to come up with a way, or something to say, that could mend the fences with his brother. Yet he had nothing, and the closer they got to the ranch, the more his nervousness had amplified. "Everything is going to be okay, Rainier," Laura said as she walked over to him. "Your parents told him what was going on, right?"

He looked toward the ranch house, where his parents had disappeared when they had gotten home. They had talked at length on the ride back, including about how thankful they were to have Laura's help, but the one thing no one had spoken of was what they had said to Wyatt.

Rainier cringed as he thought about the possibility that they hadn't mentioned the back taxes to Wyatt, and what would happen if he had to be the one to break the news. It would only give his brother more of an excuse to despise him.

"I dunno," he said.

"Let's just talk to Wyatt and see how it plays out," Laura said. From the way she wrung her hands in front of her, Rainier wondered if she was even more nervous than him.

He watched her as she walked toward the barn and the crew. Lyle was standing over the screens, pushing a clod of dirt through the mesh. He looked up as they approached and wiped his gloved hand over his brow, leaving behind a line of dirt complete with bits of rotting grass.

"Hey, Lyle. How's it going?" Rainier asked, trying to make ground with his brother's team.

"Slow and steady," he said, sounding every bit as stoic and relaxed as he looked.

"With something like this, I'm sure that you are going about it right." Rainier gave an approving nod. "You guys find anything interesting yet?"

Lyle glanced toward Steve, who was standing in the water-filled hole. A thin layer of ice had collected around the edges during the night and Steve lifted his hands and blew into them in an attempt to stave off the cold. He was wearing a pair of neoprene chest waders and a coat, but from the blue hue of his lips, the only thing the man probably wanted to do was get out of the freezing water.

"Steve, you know where Wyatt is?" Lyle asked.

The half-frozen man shook his head. "He disappeared a little while ago. Not sure where he went."

Rainier tried to tell himself that it wasn't strange that his brother would leave these two men alone and not tell them where he had gone. He could have been doing any number of things, or maybe he was talking to their parents or something, but there was a part of Rainier that went on high alert. Wyatt was always the kind of guy to see things through to the end.

"If you see him, would you let him know that we're looking for him?" Laura asked.

Lyle answered with a nod and went back to pushing another piece of dirt through the mesh.

They walked back around the barn. "That was odd, wasn't it?" she asked in a whisper.

"Either they found something and they didn't want to tell us, or Wyatt had warned them not to speak to us about anything," Rainier said.

"To be honest, I'm a little surprised that your brother is even heading this investigation. I would think it would be some kind of conflict of interest for him to be involved. You know, this being the family's ranch and all," Laura said.

"Well, you know how it is. His department isn't all that big. If people walked away from investigations just because they knew someone vaguely involved, every case in the entire town would have to be outsourced." Rainier chuckled. "And maybe that's why he brought Penny along. That way there's another set of hands in case he is ever scrutinized for his role in the investigation."

"You know, if you guys are gonna talk, you should talk a little quieter," Wyatt said, walking out of the barn and wiping his hands on a dirty rag. "The reason I'm heading this investigation is that, unlike you, people trust me. Just because I have some tie to this place doesn't mean that I won't do what is right, or prosecute those that need to be prosecuted—even if it's my own brother."

Rainier tried to control the anger that started to roil within him at the veiled accusation. "Look, I don't have anything to do with this body. I don't know why you think you need to keep threatening me. I'm sorry for what happened with my father. I know that it screwed everything up—probably for you more than anyone else in the family."

"You got that right. Do you know the kind of crap I

have to take from the guys at the station? The questions I've had to field about having a felon as a brother?"

"Wyatt, I've done my time. I've paid for my crime. Why do you think I need to keep paying?"

"It's not about wanting to make you keep paying. We both know it's not that simple. I know what kind of person you are, Rainier. We both know that you have a hair-trigger and it's going to get you back in trouble in no time."

"Can't you see that I've changed?" he countered. "If I was still the man I used to be, do you think I'd be standing here and just taking it as you talk to me like you are?"

Laura reached up and put her hand on Rainier's arm, calming him. "Wyatt, I understand that you and your brother have had a lot happen between you two, but don't you think that you should start fresh?"

Wyatt peered at her, a look of confusion and disbelief on his face. "Are you serious? You should know better than anyone what the return rates are for prisoners. People don't change. They are who they are."

Laura hand slipped down Rainier's arm, releasing him and making him wonder if Wyatt's words were making her question her approach. The anger within him grew, threatening to spill out. He wanted to tell his brother to go to hell, that it didn't matter what he thought, and to chastise him for screwing up the only thing he had going for him—Laura's belief that maybe he was worth helping. It had been a long time since he'd had an advocate besides his parents; and yet Wyatt thought it best that he stand in his way.

On the other hand, maybe his brother was right. Rainier could check his anger now, but how long would he be able to? And what if he saw his birth father again or he was put in a situation like before? He couldn't honestly tell himself, or anyone else for that matter, that he would make a different decision than the one he had. Maybe he really hadn't changed, after all.

"Wyatt," Laura said, "you're right. I have learned a lot on my job. I have learned that some people are incapable of change, but I know that your brother is different. He has a chance. But he won't if he has to fight against the people who are supposed to love him the most. When people don't have a soft place to land after prison, if they aren't given the tools to succeed, that's when they find trouble. You want your brother to succeed, don't you?"

The tight, ferocious lines around Wyatt's lips softened and he seemed to relax. He sighed as he glanced at Rainier. "Look, I don't want to stand in your way. You know I don't. You know I love you. And you have to know that I understand that we all make mistakes. Given, mine haven't been the same caliber of yours, but—"

"You're putting him down again," Laura said. "You're not helping."

"You're right," Wyatt said. "Rainier, I'm sorry. That wasn't intentional. It's just… It's going to take me some time to get over this."

Rainier couldn't believe the words that came out of his brother's mouth. No matter what he would have said to Wyatt, it wouldn't have been nearly as effective as Laura's cool, calm and logical approach. He was impressed with her, and it made him wonder how her parolees tended to fare compared to those of other parole officers.

"Thanks, man. I totally get it. And know that I truly am sorry for making you go through crap. I didn't realize… I *hadn't* realized how much it had affected you."

"If you want me to get past this, you need to promise me that you will do everything in your power not to get into trouble again," Wyatt said.

Rainier's thoughts moved to the investigation and the lie that he and Laura had told. He could only imagine what his brother would say if he learned the truth. "I promise, from this moment on, I'll do my best."

Laura smiled, and it made him wonder if she had thought about their lie, as well, or if she was smiling simply because she had heard his careful maneuvering around it. Or if she wasn't thinking like he was at all, and was simply happy that the brothers were once again back on square footing. Whatever was making her smile, he was glad to see her do it. She was so beautiful when she smiled. Even her blue eyes seemed to sparkle a little bit more when she was happy. He stared at her, unable to look away. It wasn't that she was just breathtakingly beautiful on the outside, with all of her wonderful and luxurious curves, but her soul was equally as intoxicating. She truly was the most enchanting person he'd ever laid eyes on.

And yet she was completely untouchable.

Wyatt threw the dirty rag over his shoulder and ran his hands down his face as he let out an exasperated breath. "By the way, Gwen told me about the letter."

"Good," Rainier said, relieved. "I mean not *good*, but I'm glad she told you," he said, trying to make up for his mistake.

"How did the meeting with your father go?" Wyatt asked.

Laura gave Rainier a look that made it clear she wasn't exactly sure what to tell him.

"I think it's best he knows the truth, even if our parents don't. He's the only other one who can really help us," Rainier said, urging her on.

"Wait. What are you guys talking about? What happened?" Wyatt pressed.

"Let's step into the barn," Rainier said, suddenly all too aware that Lyle and Steve may have been listening.

They followed Wyatt into the barn, and Rainier walked over to the first stall, where his favorite horse, Clark, stood with his head sticking out in greeting. He ran his hands down the horse's cheeks and scratched under his chin. "How's it going, old boy?" he asked as the horse sniffed at him, taking in his scent.

"So what did the lawyer say?" Wyatt pressed.

Rainier turned back. "He feels the same way about me that you do, or *did*. He thinks that Laura is making a mistake getting wrapped up with me and this place. And, well, he doesn't think that he can help us go up against William Poe with everything that's stacked against us."

Wyatt leaned against the table at the front of the barn. "So, we can get another lawyer."

"When it comes to tax law," Laura said, "there's no one better in the state than my father. His firm is fantastic. They can make anything go away. You want him. And besides, according to him, no one else is going to touch anything that goes against Poe. You know what kind of pull he has in the county. No one wants to go toe-to-toe with him."

"That man needs to disappear…" Wyatt said, half under his breath.

Rainier laughed. "Don't say that too loud. People around here are already questioning us. If Poe died… you know every law enforcement agency, including yours, would be down here and taking us all into custody. And even if he did *disappear*, that wouldn't mean that our tax problem would."

"I suppose you're right. We need to fix one major catastrophe at a time," Wyatt said, crossing his arms over his chest.

"Let's start with this body. Do you think we can just sweep it under the rug?" Rainier asked.

"Not after today…" Wyatt paused. "This morning we found the person's skull. From what I know about forensics, it looked like a man…a man with a gunshot wound to the head."

The breath seeped out from Rainier. No. This couldn't be happening. Not now. Not when they needed to put this behind them.

"If he had a gun with him," Laura said, "couldn't it be possible that the guy committed suicide?"

"Or the killer threw the gun into the hole when he buried the body," Wyatt said. "I mean, a person couldn't bury himself. There had to be someone else involved."

His brother was right. Rainier couldn't believe he had missed such an obvious thing.

"Did you find anything else? Anything that could date it?" he pressed, though he knew he was grasping at straws.

"You want to take a look? I was just bagging it up to send it to the lab," Wyatt said, motioning toward the bag that was sitting on the workbench.

"Sure," Laura said, surprising Rainier with her willingness to see something that could potentially be gruesome.

Wyatt grabbed the bag and, opening it, carefully withdrew the skull. Parts of it were covered in a thin layer of mud, which made it look like something from a movie and less macabre than Rainier had anticipated.

"So if you look right here…" Wyatt turned the skull and pointed to a small hole near where the right ear would have been. "See this?"

Rainier nodded. It was about the size of a dime and the bone around it had been stained an ashy black.

"I'm no expert in forensics, but from what I know about gunshot wounds, I would say that when the gun was fired it had to have been close. I mean, look at these margins," he said, indicating the edge of the wound. "Look at this internal beveling." He turned the skull so they could peer inside the cranium. He pulled out a flashlight and, turning it on, shone it into the empty space where the man's brain had once been. "And if you look here, see this collection of fracturing? That's from the increased pressure that occurs when the bullet moves through the skull."

"What does that all mean? As far as the shooting goes?" Rainier asked, staring at the hairline fractures.

"It's all proof that whoever did this was standing close. Very close."

"So someone executed the guy?" Laura asked, motioning toward the skull.

Wyatt shrugged. "It's hard to say. But what I do know is that if this story gets out to John Q. Public, your father is going to be proved right. People are going to be in an uproar. We've already had enough death at the ranch lately. This is going to push people over the edge. It's going to be hard to prove that we've just been going through a string of bad luck and nothing more sinister is going on."

"Let's not get ahead of ourselves," Rainier said, mostly in an attempt to stop himself from going off the rails. "We still have to wait on the report from the medical examiner, right?"

"Sure," Wyatt said. "And who knows, she'll probably see something I missed. Maybe she can help us make sense of this guy's death. At the very least, she can probably give us a time line."

"How long do you think it's going to take to hear back from her?"

Wyatt shook his head, turning off the flashlight and putting it back into his belt. "It's hard to say. She has the femur and the gun, but until we give her this…" Wyatt shrugged as he set the skull back in the bag. "To be honest, we're hoping to recover more before we go to her. If we do, we'd have more evidence to go on— maybe even find something to point in the direction of anyone else who was involved."

Now all Rainier could hope for was that if someone else was involved in what could have possibly been this man's murder, it wasn't anyone in his family. If it was, they would never clear the Fitzgerald name and there would be no going back.

Chapter Nine

Laura and Rainier walked out of the barn and toward the parking lot. She felt as though she was in a daze after Wyatt's findings. This place and all the people in it seemed to be cursed—and not just over the last month, as she had assumed. From the looks of the human remains, the curse had been looming over the place for years.

It seemed as if no matter what they did, they were never going to break free from the bad luck and torture that the world wanted to put this family through.

She thought of the old saying "You won't be given more than you can handle," and wondered if it was really true. Was this all just a way for Rainier's family to be tested? Was it some ethereal plan put in place to make the family come together? Or maybe it was nothing more than a string of bad luck. No. There had to be a reason behind the madness. This all couldn't be due to some cosmic randomness, but had to be happening for something greater—something that would bring the family joy and happiness in the end.

Or maybe, as her father was always happy to point out, she was being naive.

A white truck with a Dunrovin brand on the driver's-side door pulled into the parking lot. A man and woman she recognized as Rainier's brother Colter, and his fiancée, Whitney, from the ranch's Yule Night festival were inside the extended cab, and as she looked at them they each gave her a warm smile and an excited wave. Rainier stopped and stared.

"You okay?" she asked, seeing the way his eyes seemed to darken thanks to his brother's arrival.

Rainier nodded. "I'm just hoping he's a little bit more welcoming than Wyatt. I don't know if I have any more apologies in me."

She reached over and took his hand. "No matter what happens, I'm here for you. And from their smiles, I'm thinking they're more than happy to see you." As the words slipped from her, she second-guessed them. If Colter had been happy Rainier was home, he wouldn't have been MIA for the last day and a half.

From the scowl on Rainier's face, he must have been thinking along the same lines.

"Let's go say hello," she said, hoping against all hope that this would go better than he was assuming.

He said something unintelligible under his breath, but she pretended not to hear him grumbling and instead led him toward the truck.

Whitney was getting out as they approached.

"Hey, Whit!" she exclaimed.

Whitney's smile widened. "Heya, I'm so glad you're here. I could use an extra set of hands." She glanced down at Rainier's and Laura's entwined hands with the raise of a brow.

Rainier slipped his fingers from hers. Laura tried to ignore the awkwardness that suddenly seemed to fill the air.

"Hey, man. Long time no see," Colter said. He walked over and gave him a quick hug, complete with a slap on the back, almost as though Rainier had simply been on a long vacation. "Whitney, do you know Rainier?" he asked, letting go of his brother and turning toward her.

She stuck out her hand. "I've heard lots of good things."

Rainier looked at his brother as a surprised laugh escaped him. "Really?"

Colter slapped him on the shoulder. "I always got your back, brother," he said with a heartwarming smile.

Standing there and looking at Colter's and Whitney's mirrored expressions of joy, Laura could see why the two were getting married. As Colter moved, Whitney shifted closer to him, almost as if they were connected by invisible strings that drew them toward each other. She wanted that same kind of love. The kind that was far more than lust, and ran deeper and made silent promises that would last a lifetime.

A new sense of longing filled her as she looked at Rainier. Perhaps he could be the man she needed. Maybe they could have a relationship just like Colter and Whitney's—if they were lucky.

"I'm sorry we weren't here to welcome you home," Colter continued. "We had to run to Spokane to do some wedding shopping. Did you know that there are hundreds of different shades of blue?" He gave Whitney a teasing smile. "And our color is Bondi blue, to be exact."

"Bondi blue?" Laura asked. "What is that?"

"Exactly. You make my point for me," Colter said with a laugh, just as Whitney gave him a playful jab.

"No. Don't get them mixed up in this," she protested. "Technically, Bondi blue is kind of a blue-green color."

"Oh, that sounds beautiful. Is it your only wedding color?" Laura asked.

"That and a gray called—"

"Metropolis," Colter said, finishing Whitney's sentence. "And did you know that they are not always called the same name? It changes with the brand and the designer. So depending on the store, our gray was also called Ash." He turned to Rainier. "Holy crap, I think I just felt my man card rip itself from my wallet."

Rainier laughed as Colter waved for them to step around the side of the truck. He opened the back door and pulled out a stack of garment bags. "Here, take this," he said, handing Rainier four of them. "We'll take 'em to Whitney's office." He motioned toward the main office with his chin.

Laura stepped up, and Colter handed her a box of what looked like the entire contents of a craft store, complete with fake white and blue hydrangeas. For a moment she simply stared at the glittering petals. They were a far cry from the skull that she had just been looking at, and it struck her how, even in moments of peril, there could always be something beautiful just around the corner.

She walked with Rainier toward the office, and after he opened the door for her, made her way into the back and set the box on the table in Whitney's office. "I don't think they have a clue what's going on. Should we tell them?"

Rainier peered out the window of the door as if checking how far behind them they were. "They are going to learn soon enough. Wyatt's there now," he said, gesturing toward the truck.

Glancing outside, Laura could see the evidence bag

in Wyatt's hand. Colter's and Whitney's smiles disappeared as they spoke. She couldn't hear their exchange, but from the way Wyatt lifted the bag she had to assume he was telling them what Rainier had feared.

"Should we go out there?" she asked.

He stared out for a long moment. As Wyatt continued to speak, Whitney's face grew more and more stoic and she set the box in her hands down on the hood of the truck.

Rainier turned away and closed the door with barely a click. "No," he said, shaking his head.

He didn't need to explain himself further. After everything that had already happened today, Laura couldn't blame him for turning away from more drama.

"When were they planning on having their wedding?"

Rainier shrugged. "I know my mother said something about them doing it around Christmas, but I don't know when exactly. And now…with everything that's happened while they were gone, I wouldn't be surprised if they called it off."

She nodded, but she thought of the excited look on Whitney's face and the way the two had seemed so invested in something as simple as just their wedding colors. She could only imagine how devastated they would be if they had to cancel it. Yet to go ahead with a party on that scale seemed just wrong—almost as if they were trivializing the family's struggles.

"Maybe if we can get to the bottom of this, it's just another thing that can be made right," she said, her words sounding far more hopeful than she felt. She moved toward the door that led to the yard.

"How is that?" Rainier asked, staring out the window in the door.

"Well, if we can solve the murder, my dad can help us solve the tax thing, and then they wouldn't need to postpone anything. We could turn this into the party your mom always wanted and that they badly need."

Rainier ran his hands over his face as he turned away from the door and pulled down the shade, as if by being unable to see them it would keep him at arm's length from all the issues that came with their return. "Do you always look on the bright side of everything, Laura?" He gave her a serious glance, but her name rolled off his tongue like it had tasted of honey.

Him saying her name made her body clench. "I always try to be positive. It's better that way."

He stepped away from the door and closer to her. His nearness made her skin feel as though an electric current was racing through it, and that if he touched her they would both be at risk of getting hurt. Yet she doubted it was electricity, but rather something rarer—something that resembled love.

"Why?" he asked, and he gave her a look that made the current in her intensify.

"Huh? Why what?" she asked, only half-aware that there were even words coming from her mouth, as all she could think about was the way he smelled of winter air and Irish Spring soap.

"Why are you always so positive? How is it better?" he pressed, but this time his voice was softer, deeper.

"Like attracts like," she said, staring at his lips and the way they were pulled into a sultry grin. "So if I was pessimistic all the time, I'd bring in the results I expected."

"But isn't it better to expect the worst and be happily surprised when the good happens, instead of hoping for the best and constantly being disappointed?"

"If you knew me a little more, you'd know that I'm hardly ever disappointed." As she said the words, she knew they weren't entirely true—her father disappointed her all the time. But by and large most of the other areas of her life were marked by their greatness.

He reached over and cupped her face in his hands. She basked in the warmth of his callused palms against her skin.

"What if I disappoint you?" he asked, moving slightly closer, so close that his breath brushed against her face and warmed her cheek.

He was going to kiss her. She could feel it in his touch and hear it in the lilt of his voice, and though she wanted it, there was a nagging voice in the back of her head that kept telling her how stupid it would be to let him. If he kissed her, the rules of their game would change. Their roles would be altered. Her job would be compromised. Heck, his entire future could be jeopardized.

"You won't," she said as his lips grew nearer to hers, so near that she closed her eyes and readied herself to feel his lips press against hers. "And we…can't," she said, nearly breathless.

But he didn't stop. And she didn't pull away.

His lips met hers. All the desire she had been feeling poured through her, and the only thing she could think about was the glory and excitement of his kiss. The ways his lips moved reminded her of him, the way he walked, the rhythm of his speech and the gentle strength that seemed to characterize him. In a way, it completed him and the way he made her feel. As their mouths moved together, giving and taking as they tasted one another, she could only imagine that having sex would have been even better.

She wrapped her arms around him, running her fingers through his hair. It was softer than she had expected and she rolled it around her fingertips as his kisses moved from her lips to her chin, and finally her neck. She exhaled and it came out as a gentle moan, and at the sound his muscles tensed.

He pressed his body into her as he walked her deeper into the back office until she was backed against the far wall. He moved between her legs, lifting them around his waist as he kissed her neck. He was as hot as his kiss.

"Rainier." She said his name as though it was the last time she'd have the chance to whisper his name. "You… We… Mmm…" She moaned as he met her heat.

"I'll go back to being a good little parolee, I promise. No one has to know."

The nagging voice in the back of her head screamed that those were famous last words that would inevitably come back to bite her, but she pushed the thought to the side. Maybe no one would find out. It wasn't wrong to follow her heart, not when her feelings for Rainier were stronger than anything she had ever felt before. This was right. They were right. And his kiss… Oh, his kiss…

His hands moved down her sides as he held her against the wall. She rolled her hips, letting her body show him exactly how much she wanted this.

He reciprocated, matching her movements with his own. The world around them disappeared and all she could think about was the pulsing need between her thighs and the fulfillment that his body promised.

She was pulled from her reverie when a man cleared his throat.

She opened her eyes to find Merle Fitzgerald standing at the open back door. She pushed against Rainier, who was still kissing her neck. He didn't seem to notice.

"Hey, Rainier," she said, wiggling out of his arms and lowering her feet to the floor.

Merle turned away slightly, giving her a chance to recompose herself. She stepped out of Rainier's arms and readjusted her skirt, then patted her mussed hair.

Rainier turned and, seeing his father standing in the doorway, grabbed a book from the shelf and carefully placed it over himself. "Dad…" He looked at her and mouthed the words *I'm sorry.*

There was no possible way that he could be sorrier than her. The voice in her head had been right. His promise to keep this their little secret and "no one has to know" had already gone out the window.

Rainier ran his hand over his hair, flattening it where she had pushed her fingers through it. "Dad, what are you doing here?" he asked after clearing his throat.

Merle turned toward them. "I just wanted to take a look at the books and see how many reservations we had coming up," he said, motioning toward the computer in the main office area.

Something about his posture and the way he said the words seemed off, almost as if he was lying to them. Yet right now Laura felt hardly capable of judging the situation. After what Merle had just seen, it would be strange if he wasn't just a little bit off.

"Oh, okay," Rainier said. "Can't you look at that on the computer in the house?"

Merle frowned. "Yeah, but well… You know, I thought maybe this had a different schedule than ours. I just wanted to check."

Once again there was something about what he was saying and how he was saying it that made her wonder what Merle was hiding.

"No worries, though. I'll just look into it later," he continued. "By the way, did you hear anything about what your brother found? Looks like Lyle and Steve are wrapping things up back there. I asked them about it, but they wouldn't tell me anything. What do you guys know?" he asked, almost rambling as he spoke.

Something was definitely amiss with Merle, but Laura tried to tell herself that it was just because of the circumstances in which he had found them.

Rainier gave her a questioning look, almost as though he was hearing the same things.

"You'll have to ask Wyatt. He didn't tell us much," Rainier lied.

His father wrung his hands as he walked to the front of the office and peered outside. Wyatt, Colter and Whitney were still standing in the parking lot, talking.

Laura couldn't understand why Rainier had kept the truth from his father, but now wasn't the time to question him.

Merle turned back to them and let the shade fall back in place in the window. "If you hear anything, tell me. I have to know. It can make the difference between the life and death of the ranch."

Chapter Ten

Whitney's eyes were red from the tears she had been shedding for the last hour, after they'd learned of the events that had taken place at the ranch while they were out of town. The entire family was huddled around the dining room table. Even Wyatt was there, holding Gwen's hand. It felt a bit odd to have Laura sitting at his side during a family meeting, but Rainier couldn't deny that something also felt very right about having her there. Everyone had been so welcoming to her, perhaps even more than they had been to him. It was almost as if she was already a member of the family.

He was getting ahead of himself. Just because they'd had one quick make-out session that had been rudely interrupted by his father didn't mean that it was ever going to happen again, nor that it should. He wished it was easier to control himself around her, but every time they were near one another it was as if the world ceased to exist and all the rules and regulations that dictated their behavior were nothing more than suggestions.

He was tempted to reach over and take her hand, to make her feel even more welcome and supported by him, but he resisted the urge. No one in the family needed to know what was going on. Based on his father's reaction, it wouldn't be prudent to tell anyone what was happening between them—it would only put Laura and her job at risk.

"I won't hear of it," Eloise said. "This will all settle down. You know how things go here—there's always something that comes up, some hurdle that we have to overcome. We always find a way. It's what makes us Fitzgeralds. The second we give up and roll over is the second we really lose."

"Mom," Wyatt said, his voice soft and filled with concern, "we need to face the facts. If we can't find a way to get out of paying these taxes, this ranch is going to go up for sale. All the people here and you and Dad—you'll all be without jobs. For once, you need to do what's best for *you*. And I don't think that hosting a wedding right now is even close to being in your best interest."

Whitney and Colter were gripping each other's hands so tightly that Rainier could see the white tendons in the back of Whitney's.

Wyatt looked over to them. "You know I love you guys, and I want the very best for you," he said, squeezing Gwen's hand. "And your love isn't going anywhere. It's not going to lessen if you wait... I mean, look at me and Gwen. We wanted to get married as quickly as possible, too, but after we discussed it, we knew it wasn't the right time for the family."

Rainier glanced at Laura, trying to gauge her response to Wyatt's proclamation, but her face gave nothing away. He couldn't tell whether she agreed or disagreed. In fact, she'd been silent ever since they'd followed his father out of the office. Maybe she was feeling as conflicted over what had happened as Rainier was.

He wished he could take her out of here and they could just finish what they'd started. Though, admittedly, he would have been almost as happy to finally have a chance to just sit and talk with her. So much of their time together had been spent focused on the world around them, the taxes and the investigation. He wanted to know so much more about her—like if she was a sweets or salty eater, if she liked football, or any sports, for that matter. And he wanted to know more about her family. Maybe her family was more like his than he even realized. Maybe that was why she didn't seem to react to his brother being so protective.

"Wyatt, you're a smart man, and a lot of the time I think you're right. I've never thought of you as having anything other than a great head on your shoulders," his mother said. "But right now, you're being an idiot. This is about so much more than a wedding. This party could show the world the kind of family we are."

Wyatt leaned back in his chair but kept his mouth shut.

"Think about it," his mother continued. "If we only have a few more weeks at this place, I want them to be the best weeks ever. I don't want our memory of this place, of Dunrovin Ranch, to be destroyed by an evil man…a man with a vendetta. William may win. He may get his way. Bullies sometimes do. Yet he can only win if we quit fighting and give up the things that make us great. Let's have this wedding. Let it be a symbol of our greatness. Even if we lose our home, we can still win, because we will have lived our lives to the fullest and have stuck together."

A tear rolled down Whitney's cheek unchecked. She

stood up and, walking around the table, wrapped her arms around Eloise's neck.

Rainier couldn't hear what Whitney was whispering in his mother's ear, but it had to be what they were all thinking…that his mom was an incredible woman. If he became half the person she was, he would consider himself lucky. She always had the right answer. She always had the right perspective. He couldn't imagine a better matriarch.

"Mom, I agree with you," Wyatt said. "But you are forgetting that we are dealing with human remains out there."

Eloise nodded, putting her hands up, shushing his brother. "I know, but whoever those bones belonged to is long gone. They're not going to know whether or not we have a wedding." She gave a slight smile. "I mean, we should have some sort of memorial for him, but it may be months before we even learn who he was. In fact, we may never know. Those remains are the epitome of a cold case. Wyatt, do you really think Lyle and Steve are going to solve this?"

His brother's features tightened, but Rainier couldn't tell if it was because of anger or the fact that their mother was right in assuming the lead investigators on the case were probably not up to the challenge.

Laura looked over at him. She scrunched her face and it made her look cuter than ever. "Think we should go?" she whispered.

She must have thought this was going to lead to a fight. He wondered if this was just a unique set of circumstances, as it was his family that was on the brink of disaster.

He nodded and reached to take her hand, but she drew away from him.

She stood up and he followed suit. "I'm sorry to interrupt," Laura stated, "but I don't think I should be involved with this—it seems like a family matter."

His mother glanced at the two of them, looking as though she wished Rainier would voice his opinion on the matter. Truth be told, he agreed with Laura. Everything about the situation was complicated, but ultimately it was not his decision to make, but Whitney and Colter's.

"I'm sorry, Laura," Eloise said. "I didn't mean to be rude. And I didn't mean to drag you into this. Thank you again for everything you've done for us. Knowing that your father is looking into things is a huge burden off my shoulders."

Laura twitched. "It's an honor to help." She leaned down and gave his mother a quick peck on the cheek.

Eloise reached up and gave her a hug, and as he watched, Rainier could have almost sworn that through déjà vu or something, he'd seen it before—or maybe it had been in a dream. For that was what Laura was to him—something sent to him in a dream, and just like a dream, she wasn't permanent, but would dissolve into nothingness if he tried to hold on. Loving her was futile. They could never be. No matter how badly he wanted to see his dream become a reality.

Rainier grabbed her coat, which she'd hung near the door, and helped her slip it on. He followed her outside to the parking lot, where her car waited. Their footsteps crunched in the inches of freshly fallen snow. It had been snowing almost constantly for the last few hours. Lyle and Steve were smoking cigarettes beside the barn, their backs turned to them. Laura didn't say a single word, and it wasn't until she unlocked her car and opened the driver's-side door that she finally turned around and looked at Rainier.

She nibbled at her bottom lip nervously, as if she wanted to say something to him but didn't know how.

"I know," he said. "I know what you're going to say and you don't need to worry about it. I know what happened back in the ranch's office was a onetime thing and it's not going to happen again, so you don't need to feel bad about it. I'm just going to consider myself lucky that I even got the chance to kiss you."

She glanced over at Lyle and Steve as if checking to make sure they couldn't hear them speaking. "Why don't you get in my car? We can talk in there."

He walked around the side of her black sedan, but before he got in he ran his fingers down the felt reindeer antler that protruded from the top of the door. The thing really was ugly, and he couldn't understand why she would've done something so silly to her car. Yet its tacky cheerfulness made him smile. He liked that she was willing to break from the stereotype and be the one parole officer who wasn't afraid to let a little joy into her life.

He got in and closed the door. This wasn't going to go well, but then he couldn't say anything in his life was going very well at the moment.

She was staring out the windshield as fat snowflakes fell from the sky and stuck against the glass.

"Do you think it's ever going to stop snowing?" she asked after a long moment.

He wondered if this was her attempt to relieve some

of the tension between them, or if she was simply trying to ignore what he had said outside.

"You're from Montana, right?" he replied.

She nodded as she started the car, and cool air poured out at them from the vents.

"Then you know how it is. We can get all four seasons in a single day. Though," he said, glancing over at the thermometer on her dashboard, "at thirty degrees, it may be fair to call today a winter one."

She laughed and the sound made some of the tightness in his chest relax. "I always tell myself that as soon as I retire, I'm moving to Arizona."

"So you want to be a snowbird, eh?"

She smiled. "You can't tell me that thirty and snowing is better than seventy and sunny."

"If you don't like it here, why do you stay?"

Laura looked at him, then reached up and grabbed the steering wheel a bit harder than she had to. "Do you want to get out of here?" she asked, pointing at Lyle and Steve, who were now looking at the car.

"Where do you want to go?"

"I don't know. You hungry?"

They had eaten their fill; his mother had made sure of that when they had all come in, before they'd had their family meeting. Yet if going for another dinner meant that he got to spend more time with her, Rainier was willing to gorge himself.

"Sure, sounds good."

He could tell from the look on her face that Laura had the same thought about his mother's food. But she didn't say anything and, putting her car into gear, made her way out of the parking lot and down the dirt road.

It was awkward as the silence filled the space between them, interrupted only by the occasional jolt as the car hit a rut or frozen cow pie. It wasn't until they reached the main road that she finally turned to him.

"You know, I have a couple of steaks I've been meaning to cook up at my house. I bet you haven't had a good steak in a long time. Interested?"

He couldn't believe that she was asking him back to her place. If this was some attempt for her to show him that they needed to distance themselves from one another, she was failing.

"I'll never turn down a steak. I'm a dude."

She chuckled. "Me, neither, and I'm not a dude. What does being a dude have to do with anything about enjoying a good steak?" she teased.

"I don't know," he said, trying to match her playful demeanor. "I guess I always thought it was guys who were the steak and potato type."

"Have you dated a lot of women?"

"Are you asking because you think I'm inexperienced, or are you checking on my dating history?"

She laughed. "I'm just doing my due diligence. As your parole officer, it's my duty to be fully informed."

"About my sex life?" he asked with a quirk of a brow.

Either the heat had finally kicked on in the car or he was warmed by embarrassment; either way, he reached up and unzipped the top of his jacket to cool himself off.

"Are you blushing?"

He snorted. "Absolutely not. Must've been all that talk about steak, just me getting hungry."

"Uh-huh, I'm sure," she teased.

He was so confused. She was being flirtatious with him, but it was the last thing he had expected after they had been caught by his father. Had she not thought about what it would mean if their relationship came to light? It was always his belief that women were the brakes in a relationship and men were the gas pedal; but that was not how she was acting, and he didn't know what to make of it, or if he should even bring it up. Maybe this was just her attempt to sweep their kiss under the rug, like it never happened. That made the most sense.

"I think you're confusing hungry with hot," she said.

Maybe he was all kinds of wrong. Clearly, she wasn't pushing him back into the friend zone. Was that why she wanted him to go back to her place—so they could have sex? Oh, to be that lucky.

He fanned himself. "You're right, I guess I am kinda hot, and I don't mean just my looks."

"Oh, my God, I can't believe you just said that. You're ridiculous." She laughed again. "Humble much?"

"Oh, I'm humble, but when you've got a body like mine," he said, running his hands down his abs in a failed attempt to be sexy, "you just gotta flaunt it."

"If that's the only move you've got, I'm gonna turn this car around and take you back home," Laura declared with a giggle.

It would be smarter to have her take him home, of that he had no doubt. But he couldn't walk away from this—regardless of the consequences.

Chapter Eleven

Laura had never considered herself adept at flirting, or at the relationship game for that matter, but she was profoundly proud of herself as she parked her car in her garage. She had done it. She had made her feelings toward him known, and instead of playing some kind of coy game, had just let things be real between her and Rainier.

She walked through the back door of her house just outside of Mystery, Rainier close behind her. The place smelled like cinnamon sticks and pine, thanks to her Christmas tree.

"Wow," Rainier said, walking into her kitchen from the garage. "You are really into Christmas, aren't you?" He glanced over to the window ledge above the sink, which was covered in a variety of snowmen.

She glanced around and, for the first time, noticed the place for what it was—an homage to all things of the season. Every surface had at least one Christmas decoration, from stuffed reindeers to expensive gold-rimmed china.

"It's my favorite season," she said as she walked by her kitchen table and ran her finger along the edge of the gold charger plates she used to decorate the space.

"I actually own an online store. I supply handmade Christmas decor to sites like Amazon."

He laughed. "Well, now those reindeer antlers on your car make a little more sense."

"How's that?"

He gave her a sexy half grin, as if he didn't want to fess up to what exactly he was thinking.

"Hey now," she teased, "don't go bashing my antlers. It took me a lot of hours to get those patterns right. Now they are one of my company's best sellers."

"Reindeer antlers for your car?" he asked, sounding a little shocked.

"People love them. Though it seems like the most sales are coming from the South. It's all marketing and targeting your demographic."

He gave her a look that suggested she had just lost her mind.

Laura took off her jacket and hung it on a chair, right over a decoration that made the back of the chair look like Santa's face. She smiled as she thought of what the place must look like to Rainier. Hopefully, it wasn't a turnoff—like walking into a house full of cats if you didn't love felines.

Though she did have three: Albert, Einstein and Sappho. Sappho always had a habit of running off to Laura's office and hiding atop her bookshelf.

The empowerment she had been feeling started to slip as she thought of all the reasons Rainier wouldn't want to have a relationship with her now that he had more of an idea what her private life looked like. And that was to say nothing about the conflict of interest that came with dating one of her parolees.

A groan escaped her.

"Are you okay?" he asked as he tugged off his jacket and laid it over hers.

"Yeah," she lied.

This had been a stupid idea; she shouldn't have brought him here. She shouldn't have kissed him. They couldn't be alone. If someone else besides his father found out what they were doing, she could lose her job.

At the thought, she realized that deep inside her the thought of being unemployed didn't strike fear; instead, it was just a void. It was almost as if she didn't care, but that was just as idiotic as her bringing him here. She couldn't *not* work. She had bills to pay and a life to manage. Besides, she wanted to make a difference and help people. Not to mention what her father would say if she quit her job. He was the reason she was doing what she did. He had made sure that she had a *real* job, as he called it.

She walked toward the fridge, inadvertently brushing against Rainier as she passed by. That familiar feeling, that charge she felt when they touched, raced through her body. The feeling was so foreign and pleasantly uncomfortable, and the urge to touch him again was undeniable.

Her fingers found his, almost as if they had a mind of their own, and their hands entwined. He brought them up to his lips and gently kissed the back of each of her fingers, taking his time as he did so. His breath was warm as it caressed her skin, mimicking the softness of his lips.

She wanted him.

Stepping closer, she leaned into him, her hips leading her to the place she most desired to be.

"Laura, we have to talk," Rainier said as he stepped

back from her and bumped against the wall near the bar. "I don't want to, but—"

"Then let's not talk." She wanted to move to him, but stopped herself. She couldn't be the one to do all the chasing, and she knew he wanted her. His desire was evident in the way he kissed her and the way his body responded.

"No," he said, shaking his head. "And trust me when I say that I don't want to talk about anything other than to tell you all the things I want to do to your body. But I think...after what happened in the ranch office and how close we are to getting found out..."

"Your father won't tell anyone, right?"

"I don't think so. My dad has always been one to respect people's privacy, but I haven't had a chance to talk to him alone to make sure. For all I know, he's going to be angry. I'm sure he's wondering what the hell we are thinking. Just like I am."

"You don't like what we're doing?" She ran her fingers along the edge of her blouse, popping open the top button in her best attempt to be sexy.

"That," he said, moving toward her and taking her hand again, "has been just about the only thing I've been able to think about ever since the moment I met you. But we both have to be careful here. This isn't smart."

"I've always done what is right and what is smart. It's the reason I became a parole officer. But you know what I *really* want to do?" She reached down and slipped her fingers inside the waistband of his jeans.

He brushed a strand of hair behind her ear, his fingertips grazing her earlobe, and instead of letting his hand drop back to his side he moved to her lips.

"What?" he asked, staring at her with such intensity that she swore she could feel herself melting in the heat.

"I want to stop talking. I want to stop thinking and just *feel* for once."

"You need to know that feelings always have a way of getting me into trouble," he said.

"I normally am not one for trouble. I try to play by the rules." She drew his thumb into her mouth as she unbuttoned his pants. "Well, usually."

If this was what it felt like to break the rules, then she could finally understand why people chose to find themselves sitting in her office. Standing there, her fingers tracing the elastic band of his boxer briefs, and knowing that what she was doing was wrong...it was hot. Hotter than anything she could ever have imagined. She could only dream of what it would feel like to have him between her thighs, driving himself inside her.

He lifted her up and she threw her legs around him. "Which way to the bedroom?"

"It's upstairs. First door on the left." She pointed toward the stairs across from the living room. "If you don't want to go that far, there's always the couch." Or the floor, or the wall, or in front of the fireplace... She'd make love to him anywhere.

His body hardened against her as he shifted her higher in his arms.

"The bedroom it is."

Either the man had the willpower of a saint or there was some other reason he wanted to hold off. From the feel of him, he couldn't have been worried about disappointing her in the bedroom. In fact, she wouldn't be surprised if she'd be well satisfied, if not a little sore in the morning.

"Why wait to go upstairs when we can have fun right here?" she asked, moving against him.

He looked her square in the eyes. "If we are going to do the wrong thing, I'm at least going to do it the right way."

"And the right way is the bedroom? Are you some kind of sexual fundamentalist? You know, the kind that has sex in only one position—missionary style?" If he was as plain as vanilla in the sack, he could put her down right now—she had made a mistake.

He laughed so hard that she shook in his arms. "Oh, baby, you couldn't be more wrong." He buried his face in her blouse as he kissed the skin of her chest, licking along the edges of her bra.

They stumbled as he bumped against the couch, but he didn't take his mouth from her until they reached the bottom of the stairs.

"If you want, you can put me down. I'm perfectly capable of walking."

"I know you are," he said, slowly making his way upward. To his credit, though she knew she was a bit on the heavy side, he didn't make a single sound—and it only made her like him that much more. "But there's something you may not know about me. When I am with a woman, especially a woman as wonderful as you, I'm going to give the relationship everything I've got."

Her gut tightened. So he thought this was going to turn into a relationship instead of just being a one-night stand. She should've wanted that, she should've been thankful he wasn't like every other guy who just wanted to use her for sex and then move along.

He constantly surprised her as a man, and he was nothing like the other parolees she had worked with.

Which only made what the two of them were doing feel less taboo. Rainier wasn't like a normal con, blaming the world or acting like he had done no wrong, or otherwise trying to rationalize his actions. He owned his mistakes.

Why did she have to think about that right now? It wasn't helping the growing wetness between her thighs.

This was her moment…no, their moment, and she had to enjoy. In the morning, everything would be different.

In the morning they would have to go back to their normal roles, even if he didn't know it yet.

They couldn't have a relationship. At least not until one of their situations changed. Yet they could have tonight, one secret night of passion that she could carry in her heart for the rest of time.

As he carried her into the bedroom, she looked over at her bed and giggled with embarrassment at the pile of Christmas-themed teddy bears atop her holly-accented quilt. If only she had known this was where the day was going to take her, she would have hidden them away and not let this sexy man see what a single woman did when left to her own devices. Not that she was admitting she needed a man's touch around the place, but it would be nice to have someone who was a little bit taller put ornaments on the tree, or to have occasional help putting up a curtain rod. But for the most part, she didn't need a man—not when there was YouTube to teach her how to do things.

"Why are you laughing?" she asked, as he slowly sat her on the bed. "Are you about to say something about my collection of bears?"

He smiled. "We are all allowed a quirk or two. If

yours are Christmas stuff and teddy bears, I think that's far better than a woman who collects machetes."

"Is that right? Are you sure you wouldn't be more into a girl with a little bloodlust?" she teased.

"The only girl I want is you."

That look of his, the one that made her want to melt into a puddle, returned. That look, in conjunction with his oh-so-perfect words, made her rethink her stance on a relationship. Maybe they could make it. But now wasn't the time or the place to think about anything other than the way he looked standing in front of her.

He pushed her back gently until she was lying down. Leaning over her, he undid the rest of the buttons on her blouse. He moved to her skirt, and for a moment just stared at it as if it was a Rubik's cube.

"Here, let me help you," she said, reaching down to the zipper on the side.

"No, no, I got it." He bent and ever so gently grabbed the zipper with his teeth and dragged it open, making her heady with lust.

He tugged at the edges of her skirt, pulling it free of her legs and dropping it to the floor. He didn't wait for her to undress him. Instead, as though suddenly in a hurry, he pulled off his pants and yanked his shirt over his head. He threw it behind him, laughing as he moved atop of her.

"Wait," she said, "do you have a condom?"

"Do you?" he asked.

Of course she did, but she wasn't sure she wanted to admit it—or the fact that they could have expired, even though she had never used any. She wiggled out of his embrace to open her nightstand and grab the black box. She checked the expiration date—they were good, and she sighed with relief. Pulling one of the foil-wrapped condoms from the box, she turned back to him.

He wiggled out of his boxers. She had been right; he was everything she had hoped and assumed him to be.

"Do you want me to put it on?"

He looked a little bit surprised that she offered, making her wonder if he hadn't slept with many women. She liked the idea, as Rainier was definitely a man who would've had his choice in women.

She ripped open the foil and threw it to the floor. Gently, she unfurled the latex down his length. He was hot in her hand, and as she came to the base, he moaned her name and his voice dripped with desire.

She was still wearing her bra and panties, but it didn't stop him. He folded down the cup of her bra down, taking her nipple in his mouth and sucking, hard. It made a wet, popping sound as he released her and moved to the other side. There was something so sensual about the warm, soft feel of his tongue compared to the scratchiness of her lace bra as it rubbed against her skin.

Maybe the man knew what he was doing, after all.

"Please," she begged.

"Mmm," he murmured, not taking his mouth from her.

"Let me feel you."

He made a sound that was half groan and half growl as he pushed her panties to the side and drove himself into her. She cried out as he filled her, heavy and deep. There had never been a better sensation in the history of mankind. There couldn't have been or they would have died from the thrill of ecstasy.

She took hold of his ass—it was stronger and more muscular than she had realized—and as she held him still inside her, her muscles contracted around him. He felt so good.

Laura moaned, though she had meant to find words to tell him what she was feeling...that she wanted more...that she wanted to be his forever.

She moved against him, letting him pound against her again. Harder. Faster. Then he stopped and, rolling her over, picked her up by her hips and set her on all fours. He moved back into her, pressing her face into the bed. The sheets rubbed the skin of her cheek.

"Oh... I'm close," he said, his voice barely above a whisper.

He hadn't needed to warn her, for she was already there.

Chapter Twelve

Rainier hadn't had to do the walk of shame since before he'd gone to prison, and in the years that had passed, it hadn't gotten any easier. He walked quietly up to the front porch of his parents' house. The lights were on inside even though it was early. Ranching hours. He had nearly forgotten.

He glanced toward the barn, where the door stood slightly open and light from within streamed out and lit up the snow.

"Are you okay?" Laura asked from behind him. "Are you sure you want me to go inside with you? I could just go back home. Come back later or something."

He shook his head. By now everyone had to know that he'd gone home with Laura and she hadn't brought him back. Well, until now.

He couldn't help but think that everything about their relationship was a flip on traditional gender roles, but he didn't mind. Actually, it was a turn-on to have an empowered woman taking an interest in him. Especially since she could be doing so much better for herself. She could be with anyone she chose and yet she wanted to be with him—an ex-con.

There was no denying that he wanted to be with

her in every way, but now that it had happened, everything had changed between them. Sure, he could pretend that nothing had occurred and they could try to slip back into their assigned roles, but pretending was all it would be. Beneath it all, everything was muddied and conflicted, now that feelings were involved. They had made a mistake in getting involved with each other, but now that it had happened, he didn't want it to end just because it was inconvenient.

As they walked into the house, they found Rainier's father in the living room in front of the fireplace, setting about lighting it for the day. The room was filled with the familiar scents of struck matches and blazing kindling.

As they approached, Merle turned around and gave them an acknowledging smile. "Good morning, you two. Have a good night?" To Rainier's surprise, the awkwardness of the day before had disappeared from his father's demeanor.

"Uh, yeah. How's it going? I see the sheriff's department team is gone. Did they button up their investigation?"

Merle nodded. "Yep, and Wyatt and I finally got the chance to fix the pipe. With any luck the pump will be okay, but with as much as it was running it may have burned out."

Was his dad really talking about piping and how long the pump would last? Maybe his awkwardness had just taken on a new form and had become avoidance.

"Did Wyatt's team find anything else?" Rainier asked.

His father shook his head. "Thankfully, no."

"What do you mean, *thankfully*?" Rainier pressed.

Merle twitched. "Nothing. You know, just that I'm glad they're not still out there tearing through the pasture. At least now we can get back to worrying about more important things, and this can just disappear."

"You don't think finding a body on the property is at all concerning?" Laura asked.

"No, no. You're getting me all wrong. I just mean that there are so many other things we need to worry about. The dead are dead."

Something was definitely up with his father, but Rainier wasn't sure talking about it in front of Laura was a great idea. She seemed to be firmly on their team, but at some point would have to start putting her work first. Last night she hadn't seem to care about her role as his parole officer, but that was in the privacy of her own home and the comfort of his arms. Yet if his father had anything to do with the murder, or whatever had happened to this person whose body they'd found, then it was going to become more than just a simple distinction between ethical and unethical—it would be a question of legal versus illegal.

Merle Fitzgerald wasn't a murderer, and he wasn't the kind of guy who would ever do anything that would put his family in jeopardy—even if it meant putting himself at risk. In fact, selflessness seemed to be the personality trait his parents had most in common. To them it was always family first.

And maybe his father was right, and the last thing they needed to do was dredge up some cold case. On the other hand, whoever this person might be, he was someone's brother, father or son. The victim's family deserved to know what had happened to their loved one—even if it meant they had to go through an even harder time in order to get closure.

"Dad, I hear what you're saying. To some degree, I think you're right, but we have to see this through. It's not going to just disappear. And I'm not assuming anything, but if you know something you aren't telling the police or Wyatt or whomever…you may want to come clean. It's better to do it now than to wait and have it come out later."

"What are you talking about?" Merle's angst sparked in the air.

He had clearly struck a nerve, which meant he must have struck a nerve or touched on a secret his father was trying to hide.

"Why don't we go get some breakfast?" Laura suggested as though she was as uncomfortable with the situation as he was.

"Great idea. I'll cook us some eggs." He looked back at his father, who had turned away and was stoking the fire. "Dad, are you hungry?"

"No," he said in a clipped tone.

Merle Fitzgerald, in addition to his selflessness, was also known for his stoicism and his ability to control his temper. They had been through a lot over the years, and the only time he could remember seeing his father this upset was when Rainier had been kidnapped by his birth mother when he was a child. The day he had been returned, Merle had been yelling at the police, telling them they had to go after the real person responsible— Rainier's father, the one who had put his wife up to it.

Rainier had been young when everything had happened. He could barely remember most of those fateful days, but the one thing he recalled vividly was the way his adoptive father's face had looked…the way the wrinkles had suddenly appeared around his eyes, making him appear much older than he had just days before. Those lines had never disappeared, but simply deepened with age.

And Rainier remembered the phone call they'd received to let them know that his biological mother had been killed. Everyone knew that his birth father had killed her. Yet when it came time to prosecute, the case had fallen apart and the man had never gone to prison. Some people had gone so far as to say his biological father's evasion of justice was due to political corruption, while others cited ineptitude on the part of the police department—but Rainier had called it just plain wrong. His father had deserved to pay for his crimes, and then and there in front of his father, Rainier had vowed to seek revenge.

It was in that moment that he had last seen Merle Fitzgerald look as he did now, with that same expression of deep-seated anger with an edge of fear. And that look, in addition to the way his father was acting, made Rainier's blood run cold. Nothing good could come of it.

Rainier and Laura went into the kitchen and he set about making breakfast, pulling eggs out of the refrigerator and getting the pans ready. He moved automatically, and as he waited for the electric stove to heat up the pan, he realized that in the years he had been gone, nothing in the house had really changed. All the things he had left behind could still be found as they had been when he'd left—every pan was still in the same cupboard, they used the same cups and plates, and even the ingredients in the fridge were nearly the same. It was as if life had been on hold.

None of that mattered. What mattered was his father and what Rainier was going to do about him.

If he turned to his mother, it would only upset her.

Laura stood beside him, cracking the eggs and dropping them into the pan. "What's going on, Rainier?"

"Huh?" he asked as she pulled him from his thoughts.

"With your father. I don't know him that well, but I can tell that something is wrong. Is he going to be okay? Does this have anything to do with us?"

This was such a departure for her, when she had found him with the bone she had followed the requirements of her job and called the police, yet now it seemed that she was putting their relationship first and he loved it. "Do you mind if I just go talk to him for a minute?" he asked. "Could you maybe take over cooking for a bit?"

"Take all the time you need." She nibbled at her bottom lip.

He turned to walk out of the kitchen.

"You know," she said, stopping him, "I could just head back home. I don't want to make things harder for you and your family. I know you have a lot going on."

He should have agreed and let her go, but every time he was around her, she reminded him that he wasn't alone, and of what life could be. The thought of them being apart made a deep, nonsensical loneliness creep through him. If she left, he was sure she would come back, and they could pick up from where they'd been.

It may have been selfish, but he couldn't let her go.

"No, it'll all be okay. I'm sure he's just stressed. I just need to talk to him," he said, forcing himself to smile in a way that he hoped would lighten the mood and wordlessly assure her that everything wasn't as bad as he was thinking.

He walked over to her and gave her a long, hungry kiss. Her lips carried the saltiness of sweat and the flavor made him long to be back there, making love with abandon. He could have lived and died in the moments they had shared, and he would have died a happy man.

She ran her hand down his face as she leaned back from their kiss, and when she looked into his eyes, he was almost certain he could see love in them.

No. She couldn't love him. It had to be just some momentary reaction like his, some desire to bring back the night in each other's arms, and how carefree they had felt in the moment.

She let go of him. "Go. Go talk to your father. He needs you."

She was right, but Rainier couldn't help the thought that his dad wasn't the only one who needed someone.

It had been a long time since Rainier had been in a relationship, and even longer since he'd thought he'd been in love. Maybe this was just their honeymoon phase, when the other could do no wrong, and as soon as their infatuation was over, they would really see each other for who they were. Not that Laura was anything other than what he assumed, but he…he was far from an angel. Over time, if she came to see him for the imperfect person he was, he doubted she would continue to be with him.

Everything would change. Undoubtedly, she would walk away. And he couldn't blame her.

He had made his choices. He had always told himself that he was ready for the consequences and reprisals for the decisions he had made. He had just never considered the possibility of losing her, especially because he hadn't thought he would get her in the first place.

"Go," she said, motioning him out of the kitchen. "I'll make you some eggs when you are done."

He nodded, but as he looked at her, sadness filled him. Perhaps he was just being pessimistic, and his fears of her dismissing him wouldn't be realized. He couldn't make her choices for her, or change the way she was feeling.

As he turned away, she gave his buns a squeeze. "I'll be waiting."

"Hey now," he said with a laugh. "It's only fair if I get to do that to you."

She waved him toward the door. "Turnabout is fair play…in fact, I'd be disappointed if you didn't come back in here and feel me up when you're done."

Her simple action made some of the roiling ball of emotions within him calm. They'd get through this. If they were meant to be together, they would be…

His father was staring into the flames that licked up the logs in the grate. "How did you know?" he asked, turning around as Rainier closed the door to the kitchen with a quiet click.

"Know what?" Rainier inquired, walking over and standing beside him.

"That I'm not telling you something?" Merle looked at him, his eyes reflecting the fire. The effect was unsettling.

"I've known you my whole life, so I'm surprised you'd even have to ask. Wouldn't you be more worried if I didn't know something was wrong with you?" The only thing that truly surprised Rainier was that no one else in the family had seemed to notice the change in

Merle, or at least they had failed to mention it. "What's going on, Dad?"

His father ran his hands over his face, and left behind a smudge of ash on his cheek in the process. That, along with the light in his eyes, made him look as though he was in the middle of hell.

"I thought I'd never be back here again. I feel so stupid. So ashamed. So relieved. So *everything*."

Rainier was shocked by the man's admission. It had been hard to get his father to confess when he had a headache, even. He'd always been a pillar of strength in the family, so to hear him talk about his feelings was even more unsettling than the way he looked.

"Back where, Dad? What do you mean?"

"I… I just never thought I'd have to deal with this mess again. The body… The man's disappearance…"

"You knew about the body?" Rainier couldn't move. He could barely breathe under the weight of his father's words.

Merle fell to his knees in front of the fire and dropped his head in his hands. "I'm so sorry, Rainier."

"Did you…did you kill the man?" The words seemed like grains of sand scraping against his tongue.

No. His father could have never done something so destructive…not when so many people depended on him. He'd never pull the trigger. Rainier had met many convicted murderers in his time behind bars. Even though many of them proclaimed their innocence, there was always something about those who had ended another person's life—a deadness that filled the convict's eyes, as if a piece of them had died along with their victims.

His father had never had that look. He didn't have the eyes of a killer.

"I may as well have," Merle said, his words muffled by his hands.

Rainier didn't understand what he could possibly mean.

"If you didn't pull the trigger, then you are not responsible." He paused. "You didn't pull the trigger, did you?"

His father looked up at him with a jerk. "No. I'd never."

"But?"

"But I knew he…his body…was out there somewhere," he said, waving in the direction of the pastures. "I should have called the police."

Chapter Thirteen

The front door slammed. Laura wasn't sure what she should do—stay in the kitchen and ignore whatever was going on between Rainier and his father, or go and make sure that the two men were all right. She waited for a moment, hoping to hear something, but the only sound was the sizzling of the oil in the pan as she waited to put in another egg.

Certainly things between the two of them couldn't have gone so badly that one had stormed out. Besides, Rainier wouldn't have left her standing alone in his parents' kitchen without so much as letting her know where he was going, or coming to get her before he left. Though he had his issues, he wasn't thoughtless.

Yet if it was his father who had gone, it didn't explain why Rainier wasn't coming to tell her what had happened—not that she needed to know. No, whatever had been said between father and son could stay between them. She was an interloper, an outsider in the tightly woven Fitzgerald clan.

She turned off the stove and removed the pan from the heat.

It was eerily quiet.

Unable to stand it any longer, she opened the kitchen

door and looked into the living room. Standing beside the Christmas tree were Merle, Rainier and Wyatt. Wyatt was in his uniform and had his thumbs hooked into the armpits of his bulletproof vest as he stood talking.

He looked over at her and frowned. "Laura, what are you doing here?"

She should have stayed in the kitchen.

"Good morning, Wyatt."

He dropped his hands as he glanced at his brother. "Why is she here?" he asked, his voice cracked with accusation.

"I… I was dropping him off. I was just about to leave," she said, heading toward the front door in hopes that she could get out of there before Wyatt had another chance to interrogate her.

He didn't have to know anything—in fact, he was the last person who needed to know what had gone on between her and Rainier. Though he and his brother had called a tentative truce, if he learned that they were sleeping together she was sure it would all come to a head once again.

"You don't need to go," Rainier said. "Wyatt, you don't have any right to ask about my guest."

"Your *guest*?" Wyatt gave a contemptuous chuckle. "Oh, I see."

"You don't see anything," Rainier said, jumping to intercede. "Why don't you just stop busting my chops and tell us all why you are here, Wyatt?"

"Whatever. To make things clear, Laura, I like you, but whatever you two want to get mixed up in…that's your mistake to make. I just don't want to get wrapped up in your mess."

"Why are you here, Wyatt?" Rainier asked again.

He gave her one last look. "I came here to let you all know that we got our report back from the medical examiner. As we assumed, it was a male. Turns out he was fifty-two years of age, five foot nine, Caucasian, brunette. Cause of death was a gunshot to the head."

"Murder or suicide?" Rainier asked.

Wyatt answered with a cynical smile. "Hard to tell."

"How do you know so much about what the man looked like, based on just a skull and a femur, but can't tell me who pulled the trigger?" Rainier asked.

"Good question," Wyatt said, slapping his brother on the shoulder. "The ME also managed to pull some dental records. They got a match."

Merle walked to the couch and sat down. He glanced over at her, and there was a look of terror in his eyes. It was so frightening that Laura was tempted to turn away, but she forced herself to stand her ground. She had to be reading him wrong. Merle had nothing to be frightened of…unless…

"The body belonged to Paul Poe." Wyatt gave a long exhalation, like he was working up the courage to finish talking. "Paul was William Poe's father."

Rainier stared at his dad. "You have to be kidding me."

"'Fraid not," Wyatt said. "Their findings were conclusive."

"Have you told William yet?" Laura asked.

Wyatt glanced at her, but the distaste that had marked his gaze now seemed to be gone—as though he had bigger fish to fry than what was happening between her and his brother. For once she was thankful that someone had died. Well, perhaps not thankful, but grateful that the discovery of the identity could cover up what she wished to keep discreet.

"Are you here in a private or professional capacity?" he asked her.

She looked to Rainier, hoping he would supply whatever answer best suited their needs. "I, er…"

"She's here as a friend. Isn't that right, Laura?" Rainier interjected, but the way he said her name made her wonder if they were even that.

"Yes, I'm here as a friend. Why?"

"Then you will keep my little secret?" Wyatt asked. She nodded.

"Good." He turned slightly to face them all. "Under normal circumstances, I would first have to notify the next of kin—William. However, given the situation, I wanted to tell you all first."

"William is going to be out for blood—even more than he already is," Merle said, his voice worn thin.

"Is there anything we can do…to keep us safe from any kind of reprisal?" Rainier asked, dropping down onto the couch next to his father.

Laura could hardly blame him for needing to sit down. Even her knees were weak at the thought of how William was going to react when he received the news. He was already trying to take the ranch out from under them.

"Wait," she said "With this new break, maybe I can convince my father to take the case."

"What do you mean, *take the case*?" Merle asked. "You said your dad was already working on it."

Laura nibbled at her bottom lip. "That may not have been entirely true… Let's just say he's been a bit resistant. But I didn't want to burden you with that, along with everything else you'd been going through."

"I see." Merle gave a thoughtful nod. "It may be best if we don't tell Eloise about this. She's been so thankful to your father. She thought he would wrap this all up."

"And he may, but it's going to take a little more convincing to get him to come to our side with this."

"Do you really think he will? We both know that your father is William Poe's friend." Wyatt crossed his arms over his chest.

She shook her head, and raised her hands in an attempt to stop him from getting ahead of himself. "Wyatt, you of all people should know how politics work. My father and William are civil—they have done favors for each other in the past. That doesn't mean they are friends."

"Why would your dad want to take on this case?" Wyatt asked.

The truth was she didn't know. All she could do was hope that her father would see the desperation in her eyes and be unable to refuse her when she begged for help again. At least this time when she talked to him she would have information.

Her father was a hard-edged man, and controlling, but maybe she could convince him that he had been wrong—and that the Fitzgeralds were a family worth saving.

THINGS WITH HIS father couldn't be left as they were. Rainier had so many questions, and yet now he wasn't sure that he could get him alone to hear the answers he so desperately needed.

Merle had been so vague. What had he meant, the

man had just *disappeared*? Did he think Paul Poe had left of his own free will—or something else? Something far more sinister? His father had seemed convinced that he was complicit in the man's death, but why? There had to be more to the story than what he had told him.

Yet such was life, and Rainier suddenly found himself deep in the situation at hand—dealing with the revelation that the man in question was William's father. The one thing Merle had made clear was that William would be out to take the Fitzgeralds down. And the only thing he could do right now was prepare for war.

War. The word rattled through him. He would have to do everything in his power to keep his family safe—and Laura, too. What if Poe went after her? He certainly had enough power to get her fired, or at least mess with her career. Hopefully, he wouldn't think to target her. There was no way for him to know about their relationship. Now more than ever it was vital that they kept their feelings under wraps.

Rainier glanced over at Laura, who was putting on her boots. Even though the tension in the room seemed so immense that it pressed against him like some invisible hand, he couldn't look away from her. She was so beautiful. If William saw them together, Rainier would have to do everything in his power not to give his attraction to her away. It would be one of the most challenging things he would ever have to do.

He walked over to her and lifted her coat so she could slip her arms in the sleeves.

"Thank you," she said, giving him a tired smile.

His father and Wyatt exchanged glances, but he pretended not to notice. They could think what they wanted, just so long as William never found out.

Hopefully, Rainier's family was still as strong as it had once been, and when push came to shove they would come together instead of turn on one another. Yet the only way that would happen was if Wyatt was truly over his animosity toward him, and Rainier wasn't sure. Wyatt had said he liked Laura, but he clearly didn't approve of her choices.

Rainier opened his mouth, hoping that he would think of the right things to say to convince his brother that he wasn't making the wrong choice by following his heart when it came to Laura, but no words came out. It could be he himself wasn't sure that what he was doing was right, putting her in danger the way he was.

No, they were both adults. They had both made the decision to fall for one another—and they both knew what was at stake. Besides, he couldn't deny the way he felt when he was near her, or the way he could imagine their future—two small children, white picket fence, him working at the ranch and her following her dreams of making Christmas special for the world.

Love wasn't something that could be controlled or denied. It was one of those mysterious forces that was greater than them, greater than any sort of argument they could make against it. It was just…meant to be, regardless of the obstacles that stood in their way.

At least for him.

Laura stepped away from him as she grabbed her purse. "I hope my father is going to be okay with us just dropping in. He may be busy when we get there."

She couldn't have known what Rainier was thinking or feeling, but the way she had moved away and seemed a bit distracted made him worry. God, he was so confused. He didn't remember love being this hard.

Fighting for survival in prison was easier than dealing with feelings.

Though it was a bit of a drive to her father's law office, thanks to her company, it didn't feel as though it took very long.

When they arrived, there was a young couple seated in the lobby, the man looking distant, as though consumed by thoughts of what they would face once they went in to see their lawyer. Rainier couldn't help but wonder what they were there for, and if he looked like them—full of concern, and half ready to run.

He looked over at his dad as he walked into the lobby, having just arrived. Even though he was adopted, with the exception of the gray hair at his temples and the collection of wrinkles on his face, they mirrored each other.

He'd do anything to make that look on Merle's face disappear.

Laura walked over to the secretary's desk. "I was hoping to see my father. We don't have an appointment, but I thought he could squeeze us in."

The secretary smiled. "I'll let him know you're here, and see what we can do. If you'd like, please take a seat."

As Laura turned back to Rainier he noticed that she, too, was wearing that look of concern. He couldn't blame her. The last time they'd been in this place, his family had been on the losing side and her father hadn't been afraid to let her know exactly what he thought about the case. Hopefully, they had done enough to convince him that they had a case worth taking. If nothing else, maybe he could give them a few answers or suggest a direction they could take to make things right.

The secretary made a quick call, and within a matter

of seconds, Mr. Blade was standing in front of them. Rainier had never seen the lawyer before, but even so, he would have known he was Laura's father. They had the same aquiline nose and the same haunted blue eyes. Unlike his daughter, however, the man wore a dour expression, and as he looked at them, Rainier was certain he saw a look of disdain flash over his features.

"Why don't you all step into my office?" Mr. Blade said, waving them down the hallway. He glanced at the couple sitting in the lobby and his expression darkened.

The way he looked at them reminded Rainier of the day he'd gone to trial for his birth father's assault. The prosecutor had worn that same expression, as if no matter what he said or did, the man knew he was guilty as sin.

Rainier followed the others along the hall and into the office.

When he'd been in prison, he'd promised himself that he would never find himself sitting across from another attorney like that, one with hate in his eyes, and yet here he was.

Everything about the lawyer's office, from the mahogany desk to the books that lined the walls, and even the leather chairs, screamed power and prestige. It was no wonder that this man and William Poe were connected; from what Rainier could make out about the guy, they were both consumed by image and politics.

Mr. Blade closed his office door.

Laura didn't wait for her father to speak. "Dad, I don't know if you heard the latest development in the case with Dunrovin." Her hands were shaking, and as she spoke, she balled them in her lap in what was likely an attempt to get them under control.

"What development?" Mr. Blade asked, walking around the side of his desk and sitting down in his leather chair. He motioned for the three of them to take a seat.

Rainier sat between his father and Laura. From where they were, they had to look up slightly, probably some psychological maneuver on the lawyer's part to remind them that he was the one controlling everything that went on in this office.

"We were made aware that the remains discovered on the property were those of Paul Poe. William's father," Laura said.

Merle twitched.

"My family and I are in desperate need of legal counsel, sir," Rainier said, hoping that would take some of the pressure off Laura.

The man nodded. "After Laura was here last time, I had my people do a little digging. So far we haven't found much, but I can tell you that there is a way you can work with the state and the Department of Revenue and create a payment plan that could help you pay your back taxes."

Merle leaned forward and put his hands on the edge of Blade's desk. "This isn't just about what we owe—this is about justice. You, me and everyone involved here knows that this isn't really about taxes or money. This is about William Poe's desire to destroy me and my family. If you don't see that, you are just as bad as he is."

Though Rainier agreed with his father's sentiment, attacking the man who was possibly going to help them seemed like the wrong approach.

"What my dad means to say, Mr. Blade, is that we are truly grateful you are looking into things. It is appreciated," he said, nodding to Merle in hopes that he would get the message that he needed to keep his temper under control. "We would like to move forward with figuring out a payment plan. However, we would also like to get to the bottom of this thing with Poe. Are you willing to take this on?"

Mr. Blade gave him an approving smile. "I can see you learned some things while you were away."

The man's words grated, but Rainier wasn't sure they had been meant as a jab.

"Dad," Laura said, affronted.

Mr. Blade waved her off. "I'm just commenting that he has moved past his crimes. A man should be proud when he can learn and move forward from his mistakes. It takes great strength to make a blight on a record into something more positive."

She sank back in her chair, but mouthed the words *I'm sorry* to Rainier. He gave her an acknowledging tip of the head, but she hadn't needed to apologize for her father—he felt the same way. All he could do was move forward from his past and try not to fall into the trap of resentment and anger it could have generated.

"Thank you, Mr. Blade." He wanted to reach over and comfort Laura, but held himself back. "Now, about my family…"

The attorney stared at him for a long moment as if weighing his options. Tenting his fingers in front of him, he tapped his chin. "This case is going to take a lot of man hours. It could get quite expensive."

Of course his next concern would be their ability to pay.

"Dad, I'll help them," Laura said.

Mr. Blade's mouth gaped open for a moment. "Laura—"

"No," Merle said, interrupting. "We don't take charity. Mr. Blade, regardless of the outcome, we will pay you and your staff for your time. But we want to win. We have to bring William Poe to his knees. I don't want him to use his prestige to go after another family like ours ever again. He cannot be allowed to think his power is absolute."

"As Lord Acton said, 'Power tends to corrupt, and absolute power corrupts absolutely.'" Mr. Blade sent them a sly smile. "If his guilt is as abundant as his hubris, I believe that we may just have a case."

Chapter Fourteen

The next morning it was as if a renewed sense of freedom had taken over the house. From the scent of frying bacon and the sound of women's laughter coming from the kitchen, Rainier guessed everyone was up and busy.

As he made his way down the hallway, he stared at the couch where Laura had spent the night after the long drive back to the ranch. He would be lying if he said he hadn't thought about her out there and wishing she would have come to his bedroom in the night. Several times he had nearly gotten up to go and get her, but he'd decided against it. If she hadn't wanted to spend the night in his arms, then that was her choice.

He peeked into the kitchen, where his mother, Gwen and Whitney were chopping and stirring. Laura stood at the stove. She was fresh-faced, her blond hair hanging long around her shoulders, and she was wearing a sweatshirt complete with an iron-on calico cat. It must have been one of his mother's, and the thought was even more unsettling than the sweatshirt itself. Though, admittedly, Laura would have been cute in anything she chose to wear—even if it was feline inspired.

"Good morning, ladies," Rainier said, winking at

Laura as she looked up from frying bacon. "You all need any help in here?"

"Good morning, sunshine." His mother pointed to the gray, cloud-filled dawn outside. "Isn't it a wonderful day? They said it's going to get up to the high teens today."

If he could name a day that wasn't particularly glorious, it was one in which they had to worry about freezing their fingertips off.

"Waylon called. He and the girls are going to be here sometime today." Eloise bustled across the kitchen, grabbing the loaf of bread and putting two slices into the toaster. "I can't wait to see little Winnie. I know it's only been a week or so, but the place has been so quiet without my little sweet pea around. You know, she's going to be turning three this spring. How time flies!"

From his mother's letters, he had heard much about the little girl that his brother Waylon had only just found out was his. From what Eloise had written, Waylon's ex-wife, Alli, had kept the secret of who Winnie's father was from Waylon in hopes that he could live his life and find a passion that didn't revolve around the ranch. But Rainier saw it for what it really was—his family's unparalleled ability to keep even the biggest of secrets.

He thought back to his father's revelation. From the way he spoke, he and his mother had learned about Paul around the time they were adopting Rainier and his brothers—starting twenty-five years ago. It was incredible to think that they could have known about a man's body buried on their property for twenty-five years and never mentioned it.

However, Rainier could have it wrong. His father hadn't come right out and said that they knew Paul Poe was dead—rather that he had disappeared. But then, with all Merle's talk about pulling the trigger…he had to have known Paul Poe had been killed. Which meant it was possible that he knew who had pulled the trigger and why.

Rainier had to talk to his dad. Today. He had to get to the bottom of this. This was one secret that was just too big to let lie. It impacted them all.

"What's the matter, sunshine?" his mother asked. "You seem awful quiet. Aren't you excited about everyone being here for the holidays? And that's to say nothing about Ms. Laura and what she did for our family." She gave Laura a brilliant smile.

"It was the least I could do. I only want the best for you all," she said, sending him a longing glance.

He was right, it did impact them all including Laura. And for her well-being, maybe it would be better for him to let his father's secret lie dormant. If Mr. Blade learned that they were all keeping secrets, ones that put his daughter at risk, he would undoubtedly drop their case. They could hire another attorney, but then they would be starting over at square one—and time was quickly running out. Not to mention what her father might say to her for getting involved with his family. Judging by their interaction yesterday, her relationship with her dad was nothing like what he had with Merle. Everything between the lawyer and his daughter was tense and wrapped up in what he could only assume was years of hurt feelings.

"Why don't you and Laura go check on the horses? We can handle things in here, can't we, ladies?" his mother said as she took the spatula from Laura. "We'll eat as soon as your father and brothers come around, but you two can eat whenever you please, once it's ready. For now, just go out and enjoy the fresh morning air."

This was by far the happiest he had seen his mother since he had gotten home, and from the way excitement seemed to radiate from her, he could tell it had been a long, long time since she had felt this carefree. It was as if a blanket of worry had been lifted from her, a shroud that had been in place for years.

He hadn't spent any real time in the barns since he had gotten home, and he couldn't wait. Like the rest of his family, he'd grown up riding, roping and enjoying the lifestyle to which he had been introduced as a child. He had missed the feel of a horse's gait and the scents of hay and sweat. Not only could he finally get back in touch with a part of him that had been missing for the last few years, but now he also had someone to share it with.

They each grabbed a coat and slipped it on before they made their way out to the barn. A black mare stood in her stall, looking out at them as they entered. The animal took in a long breath, taking in their scents and, not recognizing them, gave a high-pitched whinny.

"Looks like I'm going to have to introduce myself to my mother's other children," he said with a laugh. "You spend a lot of time around horses?"

Laura shook her head. "I wanted riding lessons and I begged my mother and father to get me some when I was younger, but my father always thought they were too dangerous. One of his attorney friends had a case where a young girl died after a horse rolled on her on the way back to the barn. It ended up costing the man's client hundreds of thousands of dollars to settle with the family."

From the way she spoke, Rainier wondered if her father had cared more about the girl or the legal case that had come from the tragedy.

"From what I can get, you and your dad aren't very close, are you?"

"We talk a lot. He's always been really involved in my life and my choices. He always wanted the best for me."

"Do you mean *involved* or in control?"

She grabbed a handful of pellets from a galvanized bucket and made her way over to the mare. The horse smacked her lips as she chomped on the treat.

"You don't have to answer me if you don't want," he said, knowing he had pushed her too far in asking her about something that clearly made her uncomfortable.

"No, you're not wrong," she said, but her voice was filled with indecision, as if she wasn't sure whether or not she should speak about this. "My father is not like your dad. He's always been the kind of guy who finds comfort in routine. Even when I was a child everything we did was on a schedule. To this day my family sits down for dinner at six thirty on the nose. Once, I was playing high school volleyball and practice ran late. My parents waited for me until I got home. My sisters were so angry."

"Why were they upset?" he asked.

"We were expected to be home on time at all costs. According to my parents and my sisters, I should have left my practice in order to be home for dinner. They felt it wasn't my coach's fault, but mine because I didn't put the family first."

Her story reminded him of being behind bars and what had been expected of him. He had been forced to live by just as restrictive and regimented a routine as she was describing from her childhood. Which made him wonder if he wasn't the only one who had been living in a prison, even if his prison was of a different kind.

"Are you close with your sisters?"

She shrugged. "My eldest sister went to law school and is practicing family law in LA. My other one went to med school and is now an ob-gyn at Kaiser Permanente in Baltimore. To say the least, I'm the black sheep. To my father I've been nothing but a source of disappointment. He thinks I should have gone to law school or med school or some Ivy League college, and he has made it a point to tell me more than once that he thinks I've wasted my life."

"By being a parole officer?"

She ran her hand down the mare's cheek. The horse nudged her hand, urging her to feed her another pellet. "I never wanted to become a parole officer. My father got me this job." She said it like it was a touchy subject.

"Do you like it?"

She looked over at him and smiled. "There are parts of it that I love."

He stared at her. Had she meant that she loved him?

"But there are definitely days I wish I hadn't let my father push me into this line of work. Most parolees and ex-cons aren't anything like you. So many are truly evil. I read their files and I see the things that they've done, and I know that out in the civilian world they're probably going to become repeat offenders. It's so disheartening."

"You don't think that some of them can be rehabilitated?" The question was more self-centered than he had intended.

"Like I said, I'm not talking about you, Rainier. I don't know what happened between you and your biological father, but I can tell just by being around you that you are not like many of the convicts I work with. Some of these men are capable of killing and thinking nothing of it. They don't feel things like most people do—don't have remorse for the mistakes they made."

He didn't know if he agreed with her. "I heard so many stories when I was inside. You know the one thing they all had in common?"

She shook her head.

"All the men I knew felt like they had been unjustly persecuted. I never heard one man say, 'I got what I deserved.' Most of them felt like victims."

"Is that how you felt about what you did?"

"You may hate me for this, but I might have more in common with those ex-cons than you think." He walked over and took her shoulders, then turned her to face him. "I don't regret what I did. I don't regret hitting that man. To this day, I know that if I was put in a similar situation I would act the same way. My father was evil."

"So you don't think you're guilty? You think you're the victim?" All the softness in her face disappeared and there were tears welling in her eyes.

"As an adult, I'm not a victim. I knew what I was doing when I chose to act the way I did. I deserved to be sentenced like I was. But as a child…as *that* man's child… I was victimized."

She stepped closer and wrapped her arms around his middle, pressing her body against his. Her hair smelled of lavender and sage.

"I… I don't know what to say, Rainier. 'I'm sorry' just doesn't feel right, like it's somehow not enough to make up for all the things I assume you must have gone through." She looked up at him. "Do you want to tell me about it?"

He didn't want to talk about it. In fact, he never really wanted to talk about his biological parents with anyone. They were like the demons that lived inside his head and, though it was illogical, he was afraid if he opened up and told her about them, they would haunt her, as well. But if she was really going to be a part of his life, she needed to know about his past—everything about his past, and not just the part from police reports.

"The night my father and I got into a fight…it was just the climax of all that came before. He and I had no business ever being in the same room, but yet…there he was, standing like a cock in a henhouse, smack-dab in the middle of the old bar downtown."

"Yeah, I heard about what happened." She nodded. "Was your father from Mystery?"

"After my mother died, my father wasn't really from anywhere. From what I heard, after her murder, he just hit the road and started traveling around the country like a nomad. His friends told me it was because he was lonely, but I know the truth—he was afraid that if he stayed in any one place too long, the community would figure out what kind of person he really was and work to prove that he had a role in my biological mother's death. It was his way of running from the law."

She frowned. "You told me he was an evil man, but what did your father do?"

The mare nickered from her stall and, stretching her neck out, gave Laura a nudge for another pellet.

"You better feed her or she's likely to bite." Rainier

gave her a weak smile as he let her go so she could return to the horse.

He didn't want to release her, but he was starting to sweat as he thought about all the things his dad had done to him in the years that he had lived with his biological parents. He glanced down at his arm, even though the burns his father had given him were covered by his coat sleeve.

Laura looked at him as if she knew he was trying to emotionally distance himself, but thankfully, she didn't point it out. Getting close to someone meant that he had to trust them, and trust was one thing he had always fallen short on—especially when his cellmate was just as likely to shank him in the night as he was to give him a piece of gum.

She held out her hand for the mare to take another pellet. "You said your mother was murdered?"

A flicker of anger moved through him. "Yeah, she died about a year after I came to live with the Fitzgeralds."

"How did you come to live with them?"

"My mother and father, they had always had their share of problems, but it all came to a head when I was about three. From what I know, we were coming back from Washington and my parents were pulled over by the highway patrol. My mother was driving."

Laura didn't look at him, and he was a bit relieved. It made telling her his truth that much easier.

"They searched the car. I was sitting in the back seat, asleep in the sun." As he spoke, he could remember the feel of the heat on his skin, but most everything else from that time was a blur. "They found several bags of meth and a collection of drug paraphernalia. From what

I could make out from the police report, my mother and father had been using all day."

Laura shook her head as she ran her hand over the mare's forehead. "What happened?"

"I was picked up by Children's Protection Services and they were arrested. From there, I was introduced to the Fitzgeralds. At that time, they were fostering kids and had already adopted Wyatt. They were in the process of adopting Waylon and Colter, too."

"Do you remember coming to the ranch?"

"I remember thinking that it was the most magical place on earth. You know…my version of Disneyland."

She smiled, but there was a deep sadness to it.

"No, really," he said, feeling like he needed to clarify. "It was amazing. Everything before in my life was just darkness, hunger and pain." He took off his coat. "The only real memory I have of my father from when I was very young was when he gave me these." He rolled up the sleeve of his plaid shirt so she could see the little puckered circles that were littered on the inside of his forearm. "He used to love to put his smokes out on me. Thought it was real funny."

She gasped as she took her arm in her hands. Her skin was oily from the horse, but even so her touch felt good.

"Who would do this to a child?" she asked, her fingers running over the scars.

"Like I said, my father was a cruel man. And what he did to me…it was nothing in comparison to what he ended up doing to my mother when he murdered her."

Laura leaned down and kissed the circles near the crook of his elbow. They were hard to see and she wouldn't have noticed them if he hadn't pointed them out and told her what they were. She laid her cheek to his skin and closed her eyes, as if she wanted to take away the pain he had experienced when he was a child. "Why didn't you show me these the other night?"

He shrugged, pulling his arm out of her grasp, then rolled his sleeve back down to cover his scars. Showing them to her made him feel more vulnerable than if he had been standing there naked for the whole world to see. Though she wasn't the kind of woman who would ever turn the truth against him, he couldn't get over the shame and embarrassment that filled him.

"This isn't something I have ever really talked about. I think you're the only person, other than my parents and brothers, who knows the truth about those scars."

Her fingers trembled as she reached toward him. "Thank you. I... I hope you know you can always tell me anything."

Her phone buzzed from her back pocket, reminding him that they weren't alone in the world and, no matter how badly he wanted to forget what stood between them, she had the power to put him behind bars if this all went wrong. If she was like the people in his past, she would use what he told her to explain to a judge why she believed he should be sent back to prison. She could tell them that he was too broken, too risky to be set free.

"Do you need to answer the phone?" he asked, but as he spoke even he could hear the harsh edge in his voice.

"Whoever and whatever it is, it can wait." She reached over and clasped his fingers.

He hesitated for a moment, not wanting to open himself up any more, even if that meant just holding her hand.

"Tell me...what happened to your mom?" There was

a kindness in her voice that calmed the fears bubbling inside him.

She wouldn't hurt him—not like his biological parents had.

"When my mother was released from the county jail, she came to find me. At that time, they were living in the next town over and word had made its way through the gossip mill that CPS had placed me at Dunrovin. It was only a matter of days before she showed up here. I was playing with Waylon out in the pasture when she took me."

"Your mother kidnapped you from foster care?"

"Yeah, but the police found me, returned me to the Fitzgeralds, and I've been here ever since—except when I was locked away." He squeezed her hand. "I later learned that when my biological father found out that my mother had kidnapped me, he waited for her to post bond, and when she got out, he was waiting and he put a bullet in her head."

"He…he *shot* your mother? Why would he want to kill your mother for trying to get you back?"

"From what I know, he thought she was stealing me to get me away from him. He thought there was still a chance that I would come back to them."

"So he killed her because he thought she was stealing you from him?"

He shrugged. "Drugs do strange things to the human brain—paranoia among the top of them. And who knows, maybe it was just an excuse to kill the one person who knew the real him."

"How did he not get sent to prison?"

"When the police arrested him, there was no gun on scene. Though he hadn't admitted to killing her, they knew that he was behind it, and in an effort to speed everything up, they planted a gun on him. During the trial it all came out, and he got off."

Laura opened her mouth to speak, but closed it before any words came out; instead she just stood there, shaking her head.

He didn't know what else to say, either.

Finally, she looked up at him. "I get it. I get why you would want to strike that man."

"Like I said, I have no regrets. I made no mistake in hitting him…but if I'd have known he was at that bar and would have been emotionally prepared to see him, I think I would have killed him. That way no one else in the world would ever have to suffer because of that man."

As HIS PAROLE OFFICER, Laura was required to report Rainier for what he had just said. He clearly wanted to kill his father. Yet as his friend and lover, she couldn't deny that there was legitimate reasoning behind his feelings. If she had been in his shoes, she doubted she would have felt any different. In fact, just seeing and feeling the scars on his arms made her want to find his father and put a bullet in his head herself.

Children deserved to be protected above all else. Sure, wounds inflicted on the skin would heal, but injuries inflicted on the heart would never completely mend. The darkness she had noticed in Rainier's eyes made sense now. He was a child who had spent his days in blackness, and something like that left a mark.

No matter what either one of them did, there would be no going back in time and getting justice for all those his father had hurt, or saving the little boy Rainier had once been. There was only saving the man he was now. And though she wasn't the only one who had a role in Rainier's welfare, she was one of the only people who could help him avoid going down a path that mimicked his father's.

"Rainier, you're right in hating him. I hate him, too, but murdering him isn't the answer. Murder is never the answer. Taking a life changes a person forever, even if it's self-defense. Each time you close your eyes all you'll be able to think about is the choice you made. And when all you see is death, you can't come back to a world in which life and happiness take center stage."

"So basically you're saying that I shouldn't kill because it will give me PTSD?" he asked.

"Don't look at me like that. PTSD is serious. Taking a life is serious."

"I know they are serious. That's not what I meant," he said, raising his hands in supplication. "It's just that it doesn't seem like enough of a reason not to take down a murderer. Don't you think he should have to pay for his crimes?"

"Just because he didn't go to jail doesn't mean that he isn't paying for his crimes. Unless he's some kind of sociopath, I'm sure he is haunted by your mother's death. He has to live with what he has done. And I'm sure at one time, even with all their problems, he probably loved your mom. Which has to make what he did all that much harder."

"You are assuming my father isn't a sociopath." He gave a derisive chuckle. "But you don't know him like I do."

"I may not know him, but I do know you. And I know that you don't want to be anything like him. And if you killed him, you would be doing exactly what he did to your mother. You'd become like him." The words tasted like salt water in her mouth and they burned as she said them.

He cringed as though they had burned him, as well.

"I just want what is best for you, both as your parole officer and as your friend." She wanted to reach over and hold him, but she resisted the urge. "You deserve to be loved and to have a life filled with everything you want. If you throw it all away in an attempt to sate your anger and your need for revenge, you are only going to hurt yourself in the end. Sometimes, Rainier, the best thing you can do is just let things go."

He looked at her. "Letting go is the smartest thing… but you and I both know how hard it can be to walk away when feelings are involved, good or bad."

He had to be talking about their relationship. Yes, they should have walked away, but it already seemed as if that option was too far out of reach. They had taken things to the point of no return and there was no going back to a time when they could simply let go. Not now.

But this wasn't really about them. This was about his father, his choices and his future.

There was a roar of an engine from the parking lot and the spray of gravel as a car must have come to a stop.

"Do you think that's Waylon and Christina?" Rainier asked, tilting his chin in the direction of the noise. From his tone, she could tell that he was relieved that he could hide from any more talk of feelings and the duality of right and wrong.

Admittedly, she was just as thankful for the interruption, for whenever they started talking about serious things it seemed they always took one step closer to deciding to give up on their feelings. And letting herself feel all she did for Rainier was the first decision she had really made in following her heart and breaking away from what everyone else thought was right or wrong.

She walked with Rainier to the barn door just as a car door slammed in the parking lot.

Looking out, she gasped.

Standing there in the red and green glow of the Christmas lights was William Poe. His normally pristine suit was fraught with wrinkles and his hair was disheveled. He looked over at them and, when he saw them, curled his lips in a punishing smile.

"Rainier Fitzgerald." He said the name like it was a curse. "You are a goddamn murderer. It's time you and your people paid."

Chapter Fifteen

Rainier sauntered out to meet his family's enemy head-on. Opening and closing his fists, he found the rhythmic motion both invigorated and frightened him. William Poe was a foolish man to think he could come here and talk to him that way.

"William, before you say one more thing you're going to regret, you should put your ass back in that car and drive away," Rainier said between gritted teeth.

Laura grabbed him by the wrist and tried to hold him back as he neared the tax appraiser, but he pulled out of her grip. She couldn't stop whatever was about to happen, and neither could he. There were moments in life in which things came to a head, and this was one of them.

William laughed as he looked down at Laura's hand and then back up at him. "You have no right to tell me what or what not to do. In fact, if you were smart, you would listen to your little handler and stay where you are."

"Ha," Rainier said with a snort. "So you're afraid. Good. You should be."

William pulled at the edge of his wrinkled suit jacket in a feeble attempt to straighten it, as though the action could give him a more dignified air. "I have no need to be afraid of you. You are just like the rest of your family—worthless."

Rainier ground his teeth together so hard that they squeaked.

"Rainier, you should just go inside. William is here for a fight." Laura rushed in front of him and put her hands up. "Do I need to remind you of what we were just talking about?"

Walking away was easier when a crazed man wasn't standing in his driveway slandering his family.

"I'm sure Mr. Poe isn't stupid enough to come here for a fight. Or are you, William?" He gave him a warning glance.

"I'm here to set things right. Is your brother Wyatt here?"

The door of the ranch house opened with an ominous screech and his father came walking out, followed by his brother.

"What do you want with me, William?" Wyatt asked. His hair was matted on one side of his head and there was a line on his cheek from where he had just been lying on his pillow, but he was wearing his uniform. Finding William there must have been one hell of a thing for his brother to wake up to.

"Did you really think you could get away with not telling me the body you and your family found on the ranch belonged to my father?" William asked.

Merle and Wyatt both stopped at the edge of the porch, and Wyatt leaned against the railing. For a moment he didn't answer William, but stared at him like he wished he would disappear.

"William, I think you've made a mistake in coming here."

"So you don't deny that you tried to hide my father's death from me?" William took a few steps toward Wyatt, then stopped and looked back at Rainier as though trying to decide whether or not he was a threat if he turned his back to him.

Maybe he wasn't as stupid as he looked.

"I wasn't trying to hide anything, William. I had every intention of notifying you today of your father's passing."

"And yet you were telling the rest of the world about it yesterday?"

Rainier jerked as he looked over at his brother. The only people who knew about the body being Paul's were family members, Laura and her father. Had Wyatt told other people on the force, or had someone else leaked the information before Wyatt could tell William?

"Don't talk about things you don't know or understand, William. It will only lead you deeper into trouble," Wyatt said.

"I'm hardly the one in trouble here." William laughed. "In addition to my father's mysterious death, do I need to remind you about your taxes?"

"We have that figured out," Laura said. "We're going to get the family on a payment plan…so whatever it was that you were hoping to accomplish by undermining this family, you are going to have to try a lot harder."

William sneered at her. "So I've heard. But if you think that the Fitzgeralds are going to be able to get their payments figured out before the deadline, then you are wrong."

Laura's eyes widened with shock and anger.

"What in the hell are you talking about?" Merle asked.

"Do I need to spell it out for you, you dumb red-neck?" William asked, smoothing down his hair. "No matter what you and your family try to do to save this little ranch from falling into the hands of the county isn't going to work. It's too late."

"We know you're behind all this, William, and as soon as we can prove it, we are going to have you fired. You are going to be in far more danger than we are," Merle said. But his voice wasn't filled with the same conviction that was in his words.

William leaned against his car. "You don't have a clue what you are talking about. Maybe if you could take your head out of your ass, you would see that your world is going to crash down upon you and your family. I will make sure of it, but that doesn't mean I'm the one at fault. If you want to know who is really responsible for all this, you should look in the mirror."

Merle turned around and walked into the house, slamming the door behind him. Wyatt gave Rainier a questioning glance, but he couldn't have told his brother what William was talking about or what he seemed to be accusing their father of, because he didn't have a clue.

"You need to get your ass out of here and off this property. Or I will arrest you for trespassing," Wyatt said.

"You enjoy that power and authority while you can, Wyatt, because I'm coming for your job next."

"I'm not afraid of you, William. You are nothing but an overinflated, egomaniacal prick who thinks he can control and manipulate everyone around him into giving him what he wants."

William straightened up and walked toward Wyatt.

"Don't you dare take one more step toward my brother," Rainier said, moving around Laura and making his way over to the man.

William turned. He looked him up and down as if sizing him up and then lifted his nose in the air. "I don't know who in the hell you think you are, Rainier Fitzgerald."

"I'm the man who is going to stop you. I've heard all about you."

"Oh, what have you heard? Aside from your brother's colorful analysis of my character?"

"I know that you think you can control women, that they are nothing more than playthings to you. You were an embarrassment to your wife, Monica. And whether you want to admit it or not, you are the one who was behind her death. If you had just kept your dick in your pants, she would still be alive today."

"You don't know what the hell you are talking about," William growled, moving so close that Rainier could smell the dank odor of his sweat and the stale scent of his hair oil. "We both know you're the murderer here. You killed my father. How else could you have known where to find his body? And it's a little odd, don't you think, that on your first day out of prison you would come home and dig him up? I think you just wanted to get him out of here before anyone else had a chance of finding his body. And then, when your family found out, they all came to bat for you." He pointed toward Wyatt. "Even your fucking brother."

"That's the dumbest thing I ever heard, William." Rainier balled his fists in an attempt to control his rage. All he wanted to do was reach up and tear out the man's throat. "For knowing so much about your father's remains, I would think you would know that, according to the medical examiner, he has been dead for around twenty-five years. That means I was just a toddler when your father died. I couldn't possibly have been the one to pull the trigger."

William glanced over at Wyatt as if gauging his reaction, to see whether or not Rainier was telling the truth.

"Don't look at my brother. You look at me."

William did so, then took a step back.

"I… I didn't know it happened that long ago. But that's no matter," William said, waving off Rainier's point. "You probably planted his body and made it look like it'd been there for a long time. It's probably just another one of your stupid games."

The man was grasping at straws and everyone knew it.

"William, ever since you started poking around I've been hearing about you and what you're capable of. Thinking back, if I had to bet, you are the one who is responsible for us finding your father's remains here."

"That's asinine. I have never wanted to hurt my own father. Unlike you."

The dam inside Rainier broke. Before he knew what he was doing, he reached up and took William by the throat. His fingers dug into the soft flesh around his trachea and squeezed. The little tube in his hand would have been so easy to crush. One motion and his family's nightmare would be over. Everything could go back to the way it had been before hell, in the form of William Poe, had rained down on them.

"No, Rainier. Don't do it," Laura begged. "He's not worth it. If you hurt him, your life is over."

He squeezed the man's throat just a little tighter. He

was already violating his parol: if Rainier sacrificed himself by killing the man, at least he could say he had done something for his family—for the greater good.

"He isn't your father," Laura said. "If you kill him, it won't fix anything."

"But he's so goddamned evil. He has to be stopped," Rainier retorted, not looking away from William's eyes as they started to bug out of his head, thanks to the pressure he was creating by closing off the flow of air and blood.

"Let the judicial system take care of it, Rainier. We don't live in the Wild West anymore. Justice will come, but it's going to take time. We can't resort to violence or we're no better than animals, and you'd be no better than your father. Don't be like him, Rainier. If you love me at all, please…no…" she pleaded.

He let go of the man's neck, but there were impressions from where his fingers had gripped him. William slumped down to the ground, gasping and wheezing for breath. "Screw you," he whispered, his voice hoarse. "You're going back to prison if it's the last thing I do. Everyone in your family is going to pay for the mistake you just made," he said as he stood back up after regaining his breath.

Rainier looked at Laura. She had an expression of terror on her face, as if she knew that what William was saying was true. He had just violated his parole by assaulting the man.

If he was going to go back to prison, at least he would go for something he truly deserved to be punished for.

He leaned back and, with every bit of strength he possessed, struck. His fist connected with William's face. The scoundrel went flying across the snowy parking lot.

"Rainier! No!" Laura screamed.

Wyatt came running. "Goddamn it, Rainier!"

William lay on the ground, his back to them as he clutched his face. Blood speckled the snow, and Rainier watched a droplet melt the white crystals around it. He shouldn't have hit him, but he couldn't deny that it felt good to rain just a little bit of justice on the man who had wrought so much terror and tragedy on his family over the last few months. William deserved a hell of a lot more than just being punched in the face.

Leaving the man whimpering behind him, Rainier turned to face his brother and held up his hands. "Cuff me."

Wyatt reached down to his utility belt and grabbed his handcuffs. "I don't want to do this, Rainier. Why couldn't you just fucking control yourself?"

"That was control." Rainier looked down at his hands. Blood was dripping from his fingers, from where he had gripped his hands so tightly that his nails had cut through his skin.

Laura rushed to his side and threw her arms around him. "No. No. No," she repeated over and over, as if she just couldn't believe what had happened.

He wrapped his arms around her and smoothed her hair as he looked at her. "I made this choice. Good or bad, I have to pay the price. But know that I did this for my family, to make things right. It may seem stupid to you, and you have every right to be angry with me, but William had that coming."

"You wouldn't have done that if you loved me," Laura said.

His heart shattered under the pressure and weight of her words. "This doesn't have to do with the way I feel about you, Laura."

"Once again, Rainier, you're wrong." She let go of him and walked away toward the house. On her back was the blood from his hands.

Chapter Sixteen

After all they had talked about, and despite the consequences he must have known would follow, Rainier had still acted like he hadn't learned a thing in prison. He had failed and so had Laura. She couldn't save anyone—even those she had thought savable. He would never change. Her father had been right. Maybe she would have been better off just walking away.

She stood at the living room window and watched as Wyatt slipped the cuffs back onto his belt, unwilling to put them on his brother. Instead, he simply walked Rainier to his squad car and opened the back door, waiting for him to get in of his own accord. Watching him climb in was one of the hardest things she had ever witnessed. It was almost as if a piece of her was being sent back to prison with him—and in a way it was.

It had been a mistake to give him any of her heart.

Eloise walked up behind her and put her arm around her shoulders. "I'm so sorry, Laura."

Laura nodded.

"Are you going to go to the station with them?" Eloise asked.

"I… I can't. I can't watch him go back to that place."

She stared out at the back of Rainier's head as he sat

in the car. William and Wyatt were talking, and William had a piece of gauze stuffed up his nose. He was speaking animatedly, his hands flying as he made angry gestures. She was sure he was telling Wyatt how he was going to continue tearing away at the family.

He may have deserved what he got, but no matter how much she empathized with Rainier's anger, she couldn't understand Rainier's choice. And maybe that, more than anything else, was the reason they truly couldn't be together. She couldn't be with a man who didn't harbor some level of self-control. There were always moments and situations in life when it would be easier to throw a punch and resort to violence, but that didn't mean people could allow themselves to act that way.

More than anything, he frightened her. This wasn't like the man she had come to know over the last few days. The one she had just seen seemed far too much like the other convicts she had known over the years. All the memories of convicts who had missed meetings, threatened her, showed up drunk or high—they all came to her at once. It may have been a stereotype of the ex-con, but it was a stereotype for a reason—those things were grounded in truth.

She had been stupid and naive to think Rainier was different.

Laura turned away from the window and embraced Eloise. She buried her face in the woman's neck and just let her tears fall. She didn't care that she barely knew her, or that she was making a show of herself. All she cared about was the ripping sensation in her chest as her heart was torn to pieces.

"I don't know what to say that will make you feel bet-

ter, Laura," Eloise whispered. "Know that I'm hurting,
too. I never wanted to see any of my sons being taken
from me—and definitely not again."

She hadn't thought about how Rainier's mother must
be feeling. It would of course destroy her from the inside out, as well. The poor woman had thought she
would finally have her family all back together, and
yet her dream was never realized. And though Eloise
didn't know it yet, William had promised that their ap-
peal for a payment plan would fail, which meant they'd
be losing the ranch.

No matter how badly Laura's heart ached, Eloise was
going through something so much worse—losing her
son, her family and the chances of keeping her beloved
home, all in the same day.

The tears came more rapidly. As she hugged Eloise, Laura noticed faint shaking as the woman sobbed
in her arms.

Whitney and Gwen were standing by the Christmas
tree, their faces pale.

She wasn't going through this alone; she was going
through it with the whole Fitzgerald clan. It was strange,
but even though she had been around them for only a
few days, she felt more like a part of this family than
she ever had her own. They were all about love, support
and understanding, not about who could get what from
whom or how each of them could get ahead. It was just
about the family and how they could be there for each
other even when they didn't know what to say or do.

And yet her time with them was over; Rainier was
gone. Any hope she'd had of saving him had disappeared with one perfectly placed punch, and the future

that she had allowed herself to fantasize about for the last few days was just as unattainable as ever.

All she had was a houseful of Christmas decorations to go back to.

She pulled herself from Eloise's arms, trying to collect herself, just in time to see Wyatt and Rainier rolling out of the driveway. William Poe was already gone. It was over. Everything.

The smoke alarm started to beep and she glanced over at the kitchen, where smoke was billowing from the doorway toward the ceiling of the living room.

"Son of a—" Eloise said, charging toward the kitchen. "I must have left the bacon going."

"How much bacon did she cook?" Laura asked the two women by the tree, trying her hardest to focus on anything other than the tight pain in her chest.

"Oh, Eloise always does everything big. Everything," Whitney said with a smile as forced as Laura's words.

"I think she was really hoping that Waylon and Christina would come rolling in with Winnie this morning. And instead…" Gwen trailed off as she glanced out the window. "Do you think there's anything you can do, Laura?" she added.

Laura wanted to say yes, that she had the power to stop the train of destruction that was Rainier Fitzgerald, but she couldn't bring herself to lie to the woman. "I don't know," she said quietly.

Merle came into the house, and as he opened the door a cold, bitter breeze filled the living room, stealing all the fire's warmth.

"What are we going to do?" Whitney asked.

Laura was thankful she had spoken first, as she was afraid that if she had to ask about what had transpired she would dissolve into tears once again. She could fake strength for only so long before it would melt away and reveal the sensitive mess she was inside.

Merle closed the door and took off his coat.

She wasn't sure if he wasn't answering because he was afraid to tell them, or because he didn't want to tell *her*.

"You can tell us what happened, Merle. I'm sure I'll get a chance to read through Wyatt's report regardless of what transpires," Laura said, her voice cracking as she spoke. She coughed lightly, trying to clear the emotions from her throat.

He nodded. "William is obviously upset. He threatened to press charges, and well…we all know what will happen if he does." He laid his coat over his arm and stared at her as if there was something he wanted to say, but wasn't sure exactly how to say it.

He looked to the kitchen, where they heard the thump of a pan and the sound of running water. Thankfully, the smoke had stopped pouring through the doorway.

"Did you tell Eloise what William said…about the taxes?" Merle asked.

Maybe Laura had been wrong about the family. Maybe they weren't as supportive and forgiving as she had assumed.

"Really? Your son gets carted away to be processed, and yet here you are, worried about your taxes?"

"No, Laura, that's not it. I just…" He stared at the kitchen door. "I just don't want to burden her with one more thing."

That she could understand.

"Sorry," she said, dabbing at a wayward tear that had escaped her. "I… I don't know what came over me…"

"You're fine. It's just a hard time. Trust me when I say that we are familiar with the strain," Merle said, sending her a soft, forgiving smile.

Gwen came over and took her hand. "No matter what happens, know that we're here for you."

Another unchecked tear slipped down Laura's cheek.

She had to stop crying. She couldn't be a mess like this over a man she had known for less than a week. She was a grown woman.

"Thank you," she said. "Really."

Gwen squeezed her fingers. "I know how much you love him. And I know what it's like to fall in love with one of the Fitzgerald men. They're wild and fiery— all of them. What Rainier did out there…it could have been any of those boys. They all love hard, and they defend even harder."

Laura wasn't sure how Gwen could say that any of the four sons could have assaulted William Poe. Wyatt wouldn't have. He had seemed to show incredible restraint when they had been outside, but then again maybe Gwen just knew him better.

She smiled in appreciation of Gwen's attempt to comfort her.

"I notice you're not denying the fact that you love him," Merle said. "I like that about you."

She opened her mouth to argue, to tell them all that they had her feelings toward Rainier all wrong. A few hours ago, she could have told them what she was feeling toward him was love, but now…she wasn't so sure.

Her phone rang. Pulling it from her pocket, she looked down at the caller ID. It was her father. Her chest constricted impossibly tighter, stealing her breath.

He couldn't have already heard what had happened. Or maybe he could have.

William had probably called him from Dunrovin's driveway.

She hit Ignore.

It rang again. Couldn't her father get the hint that she didn't want to talk to him right now? The last thing she needed was further castigation.

She hit Ignore again.

And once more it rang.

"What?" she asked, finally answering the phone, as she knew full well that if she didn't he'd just keep on calling.

"I knew you were there," her dad said, his voice as gruff as her own. "I don't know why you think you can just stop answering me. It's convenient how you're happy to talk to me when you need something, but when I want to talk to you you're too busy."

That wasn't it at all, and he had to know that. He was just being an ass.

"The last thing I need right now is to get into a fight with you. What do you want?"

"I want you to check your attitude," he said.

No matter how old she got, she was sure that he would always treat her like she was some sixteen-year-old with an attitude problem. It only infuriated her more.

"If you're just calling to pick a fight, I need to go. I have better things to do."

"Those *better things to do* are why I'm calling. William Poe contacted me a few minutes ago. He was seeking representation."

Her stomach dropped.

"Do you know anything about Rainier Fitzgerald hitting him in the face? He said you would be available to act as a witness in his case."

She couldn't believe how quickly William was at it. She had been right; he'd probably called her father as soon as he'd gotten in his car.

"Are you going to take his case?"

There was a long silence on the other end of line. "I need to know a few things from you first, before I decide on anything. I need to be well informed. Is Rainier the man William makes him out to be?"

"I'm assuming you mean that William tried to tell you Rainier is a typical ex-convict."

She wanted to go to bat for Rainier and tell her father that he was different, but she couldn't bring herself to utter the words, as right now she wasn't so sure.

"It would be foolish of me," her father continued, "to think he was anything otherwise. Based on the way I saw you looking at him the other day, I'm a little unsure of how to proceed with this."

So her father had noticed her attraction to Rainier, after all. She really needed to learn how to mask her emotions better.

"You know I'm not stupid, right?" she asked, in an attempt to maneuver around her father's question.

He wasn't really calling her about what he should do with William. No, he was calling to see where things stood between her and Rainier.

"What do you mean?" her father asked, an innocent inflection to his voice.

"You have taken on the Fitzgeralds as your clients. In such a case, it would be a conflict of interest if you were to take William on as a client, as well. So let's not beat around the bush."

Her father laughed. "Sometimes I forget how smart you are."

She wasn't sure how to take his backhanded compliment, so she ignored it.

"Why did you really call? Did you just want me to know that you knew about the events at Dunrovin?"

His laughter came to an abrupt stop. "That and to let you know that William Poe is gunning for them even more than he already was. I'm going to work at him from my side to see if I can get him to drop the charges against Rainier, but I don't know what I can do for sure. He seemed pretty upset when I talk to him on the phone a few minutes ago."

She was surprised by her father's willingness to lend a hand.

"What did William do to you, Dad? Why are you suddenly willing to fight him? And don't try to tell me that this has anything to do with justice or some altruistic need to help the Fitzgerald family."

Her father sucked in a long breath and exhaled into the phone. "Whether or not you believe me, I love you. Though I don't always agree with your choices, or the men you seem to be attracted to, that doesn't mean I'm going to let you find your way into trouble."

No matter what her father did, she would always have a habit of getting into trouble. But she appreciated the fact that her dad was stepping up and doing something for her for once, without some ulterior motive. At least she thought he didn't want anything from her, but she couldn't be sure. Only time would tell.

"You didn't answer my question about William. Did he do something to you, Dad? Something that you need retaliation for?"

"I don't know what kind of man you think I am, Laura, but you're wrong."

"After so many years of you showing me exactly what kind of many you are, I find it pretty hard to believe that you're doing this out of the kindness of your heart and because you love me. I'm sure you loved me a few days ago, when I first came to you about the Fitzgeralds' case, and then you weren't willing to take it on. I just want to know what made you change your mind."

"Let's just say that a few things came to light that I didn't know about before, a few things that have changed the way I feel about this community and the people within it. And let's leave it at that. But do know," her father added, "it truly is my love for you that is guiding me with all of this. And I have a feeling that it is your love that is guiding you."

Chapter Seventeen

He'd screwed everything up. His life. His freedom. His one chance at love. In a blink of an eye, he'd reverted back to the man he'd promised himself he'd never become again. He hated himself more than ever. And even more than that, he hated what he had done to Laura and the position he'd put her in. She'd vouched for him, she had gone to bat for him and she'd gotten her father to take on his family's case even when that meant putting herself in the path of her dad's wrath.

She done so much for him, and Rainier had repaid her by finding himself here, in the back of Wyatt's squad car.

He ran his hands over his face and let out a long sigh.

"I wish I could say I was surprised," Wyatt said, pouring salt in his wounds.

"You can just stop, Wyatt. Whatever you think you need to say to me, just don't. If it helps, know that I am already beating myself up for the decision I made."

Wyatt looked at him in the rearview mirror. "You know, brother, if you hadn't done something, I don't honestly know how much longer I could've gone on listening to him."

Rainier was taken aback by his brother's admission.

They hardly ever agreed on anything, especially not since he'd come home. It was an odd sensation to know that his brother felt in any way similar to him.

"So you're saying that you would've hit him in the face, as well?" he asked, a wicked grin on his lips.

Wyatt shrugged. "You know, in my line of work, hardly a day goes by without somebody mouthing off at me or telling me how I'm doing my job wrong. It takes a certain amount of willpower to not go off on every idiot who thinks he should open his mouth and say something stupid to me. Ninety-nine percent of the time I don't have a problem walking away and letting whatever they're saying roll off my back, but it's different when they're talking about my family and when they start dragging people I love through the mud."

He could only imagine the number of times over the years people had probably commented to Wyatt about what he, Rainier, had done, and how he'd ended up in jail.

"If that's true, I'm sure that you wanted to take a swing at someone many a time, thanks to me."

Wyatt chuckled as he turned the car down the main road that led into Mystery. "Right after everything with your birth father, things were a little rough. But once word got out about everything that led up to it, most of the community understood why you acted as you did. It probably didn't hurt that most people know and love our parents."

"I heard about Yule Night festival, and how the community came together to raise funds for the ranch. I can only imagine how hard it must be for Mom and Dad to be going through all this crap right now." He paused as he thought about how it had felt when his fist had connected with William. "I can't believe I made things worse."

"We'll see how this all plays out," Wyatt said. "Maybe if William is concentrating on taking you down, he won't be able to focus as much of his energy on going after the ranch."

Rainier tried to laugh, but the sound came out dry and forced. They sat in silence, letting the failed laughter die in the air between them.

It started to snow, and as the tiny flakes fluttered down from the sky, they caught the light and looked like glitter filling the air.

"What would happen if William didn't press charges?" Rainier asked, hating to get his hopes up. "You know, not that he won't, but just in case?"

"Didn't like my plan, huh?" Wyatt asked, tapping his fingers on the steering wheel. "Let's face it, we both know that William isn't going to let what you did slide. He's going to do everything in his power to make sure you are sent back to prison."

"What if there weren't any witnesses to testify on his behalf?"

"What, are you thinking of taking us all out?" Wyatt teased. "If they put us under oath, we'll have to tell the truth. You know how it is, perjury and all."

"I know. I guess I'm just grasping at straws. I wouldn't want to put any of you at risk like that, anyway," he said, blowing out a long breath.

There was no getting out of this. What was done was done. Once again, he would just have to face the consequences for his actions.

"I'm glad to hear it," Wyatt said, checking his rearview mirror again.

Rainier turned to see what he was looking at. William was behind them in his sedan.

"Do you think he's going to follow us all the way to the station?"

Wyatt glanced up again. "Technically speaking, he has yet to file charges against you. I told him that in order to do so, he would have to come down to the station and sign some papers."

"I'm sure he won't miss the opportunity." Rainier had an insatiable urge to turn and give the man the bird, but this time he resisted. "Wait…if he hasn't signed anything, then am I really under arrest or are you just taking me in?"

"I didn't read you your Miranda rights, did I?"

A tremor of excitement moved through him. Maybe he wasn't as screwed as he had assumed. Maybe there was a way around this, after all; the chances weren't in his favor, but at least he could still hope.

As they neared town and the police department, Rainier wanted to turn around to watch what William did. He felt stupid for hoping that along the way the man would just turn off, go home and forget about what happened. Such ideas and desires were ridiculous. Even without looking behind him, he knew William would still be there. In fact, with everything involving Dunrovin over the last month, it seemed he was always there. Rainier had a feeling that, no matter what happened in the future, William Poe wouldn't be happy until he ruined their family and the ranch—even if that meant they all ended up dead. The thought made chills run down Rainier's spine.

"Did you look in William's car when he came to the ranch?" Rainier asked.

Wyatt shook his head. "Why?"

"Doesn't it strike you as just a little bit odd that he would come out there, all by himself, and start harassing us? He had to have known that he wouldn't be welcome—that there was a hell of a good chance he wouldn't get out of there without getting his ass beat."

"He was provoking you. We already established this. So what does that have to do with his car? I'm not following."

"What if he was coming there to attack us?"

Wyatt sat in silence for a moment. "William Poe's many things, but stupid isn't one of them. And if he came after the family on our ranch with the intention of hurting us, that would be more than stupid. There's no way he would've walked away from something like that alive."

"Maybe that's why he lost his nerve," Rainier said. "Maybe once he saw us and got a chance to speak his piece, maybe he realized the error he was making."

Rainier couldn't stand it anymore. He turned around in his seat and stared out the back window. William was talking on the phone, and as he spoke his free hand flew in angry gestures. From the look on his face, he was yelling at someone.

They drew up at a stoplight. William and Rainier locked eyes, and the man stopped talking. Neither would look away, and even from that distance Rainier could see the distaste and hatred William held for him.

Wyatt started to drive forward as the light turned green, but instead of following them, William swung left.

"What the hell is he doing?" Rainier asked.

Wyatt peered out the window and watched as William's car disappeared down the road. "Who knows what that guy is up to."

They were only a block from the police department. If he was turning away, did that mean he wasn't planning on pressing charges? Or was he playing some kind of stupid mind game? Rainier wouldn't put it past him. He was certain he hadn't scared him away with simply a look. William wasn't that weak.

Wyatt parked the car in front of the station and opened the door for Rainier to get out.

As he stepped from the car, he took in a long breath of the cold winter air. For all he knew, it was his last breath of real freedom.

"What do you want to do?" Rainier asked.

"If he does show up and sign the documents, then it will be to your benefit if you stay here and prove to the courts that you didn't try to run, and you were trying to make the best of a bad situation. Maybe the judge will be more lenient and won't add more time to your sentence in prison."

He still had five years left on his sentence if he went back. Until now, he hadn't really thought about the fact that if William did press charges those five years could easily turn into ten. The realization made him nauseous. That would mean by the time he got out he very well could be thirty-six years old. He would have spent a third of his life behind bars. It would be such a waste.

"Then I guess we need to go inside," he said, but the words passed from him in the same way a judge would've passed a ruling—without emotion.

"Are you sure?" Wyatt asked. "If you wanted, the Widow Maker Ranch—you know, Gwen's family's spread—is buttoned up. They're about to put it on the market, and no one is living there. If you wanted to hide out for a little bit and let everything die down and see what happens, you could stay there and nobody would know where you were."

"You would know," he said, giving his brother a weak smile. "It would compromise your integrity if you had to lie for me. You can't get wrapped up in this. I can't let you put your career in jeopardy for me."

He appreciated what Wyatt was doing for him, and the offer he was making, but from the look on his face, his brother knew that it was unfeasible, as well.

"We'll get through this," Rainier said. "You just lead the way to where I need to wait for William. From there, I'll navigate this journey the rest of the way."

"No matter what goes down in there, I got your back. No matter what's happened in the past, you're my brother. I'll always be your brother," Wyatt said.

Rainier wasn't a hugger, but right now it was the only thing he could think to do that could express the way he was feeling toward his older brother.

"Wyatt, I don't know what I'd do without you, man," he said, his voice cracking. "And hey, for what it's worth, I'm sorry."

Wyatt shrugged as Rainier stepped back and they let go of one another. "Like I said, if you hadn't gone after William, I'm not sure that I wouldn't have. Maybe, if nothing else, you saved me."

This relationship would be one of the things he would miss the most.

"If they lock me up, I want you to look after Laura."

Wyatt nodded. "She'll always be welcome at my home, and I know Mom loves her almost as much as you do." He walked toward the front doors of the station and, opening it, waited for Rainier to walk in ahead of him.

"Mom *has* taken a shine to her," Rainier said with a laugh. "Can you believe she asked her to spend Christmas with us the first time she met her?"

"You know Mom. She knows from the get-go whether or not she likes someone. If I were you, I'd take that as Mother's official seal of approval."

"What do you think of Laura?"

They walked into the main office, and the secretary behind the glass smiled at Wyatt and gave them a little wave as they made their way past her.

"I mean, aside from the fact that we shouldn't be together, that is," Rainier said.

"I know I told you that I didn't want to get wrapped up in all of your drama, but we both know it's too late to stop whatever is going on between you two. And believe me when I say I know better than anyone how the heart wants what the heart wants. I mean, just look at Gwen and me."

"How did you guys end up back together?"

"It's a long story, but after her sister was killed…we both realized that we were just *meant* for each other."

"What about her mother? Didn't she have something to say about it? Especially after Gwen's father was killed on the ranch after his accident with the hay tedder?"

"Oh, her mother had plenty of issues with our getting together." Wyatt paused. "Come to think of it, our story ain't that different from yours—a lot of people didn't want to see us end up together. But if it made one thing abundantly clear, it's that we don't get to pick who we fall in love with. And when it comes to true love, nothing and no one should get in the way."

They turned a corner in the hall that led to Wyatt's office. Standing on the other side of his brother's office door was Mr. Blade, who was holding his briefcase.

Rainier came to a dead stop. "Shit. What is he doing here?"

"I was about to ask you the same thing. You think Laura called him or something?"

From where they were standing, Rainier couldn't see the lawyer's expression, but he wished he could so he'd have some clue as to what kind of hornet's nest he was walking into.

"You want to wait here?" Wyatt asked.

Rainier shook his head and then bulled his way into his brother's office. Mr. Blade looked a little shocked at his sudden appearance.

"Are you here to yell at me? Go right ahead. But know that whatever you have to say to me, it's not going to change my feelings about your daughter."

He shook his head. "No, my daughter is the reason I'm here right now," Mr. Blade said, raising a finger as if threatening. "Know that if you break her heart or if you continue to hurt her, I'll be far more dangerous to you than William Poe."

"I have no intention of hurting your daughter any more than I already have," Rainier said. But as he spoke to the man, he found that he couldn't look him in the eye, and instead focused on a forensics manual on his brother's bookcase behind him.

"I'm glad to hear it, but regardless of your intentions, it doesn't guarantee her safety."

Wyatt stepped forward. "No, but I do. If Rainier has to go back to prison, she won't be left out to dry."

Mr. Blade looked Wyatt up and down, weighing and

measuring him in a glance, then cracked a smile. It was almost imperceptible, but Rainier had a feeling that was about as big as the lawyer's smile ever got.

"Laura wasn't wrong about you Fitzgeralds. You're good people." Mr. Blade sat down in front of Wyatt's desk. "And that's why I'm here today. I already heard what happened with William."

"Did Laura call you?" Rainier asked, a bit surprised that she would've already reached out to her father.

"No, William did."

Apparently, being good people wasn't enough to keep them on good terms with her father.

"Sir, are you here to let us know that you've decided not to take our family's case?" Rainier inquired.

"Far from it." The little smile on Mr. Blade's face disappeared. "In fact, he asked my firm to help him file assault charges against you. However, due to recent findings, I had to decline. I may have mentioned to him that if he wished to pursue assault charges against you, it would force my hand in acting upon your family's case, and we would be moving to court more rapidly than I intended."

"What did you find? And does that mean he's not pressing charges?" Rainier asked, a sense of excitement moving through him.

Mr. Blade nodded. "I think he realized it would be in his best interest to simply put what happened between you two at the ranch behind him. However, I strongly recommend that you do not act on your impulses again. If you were dealing with any other parole officer besides my daughter, I am sure that by now you would have already found yourself behind bars. You're just lucky that she likes you, and you have a brother who is in law enforcement. Professional favors can go a long way, but they can't keep you safe forever."

Rainier was glad he was sitting down, as he feared his knees would have given out on him had he been standing. "Thank you so much, Mr. Blade. I can't tell you how much that means to me. How relieved I am. I'm so sorry that all this happened. I swear I won't let it happen again."

"See to it that it doesn't." Mr. Blade reached down to his briefcase. He pulled out a series of papers and laid them on Wyatt's desk. "Now, to the other business at hand and what we managed to find... Have you ever talked to your parents about how they came into possession of the Dunrovin Ranch?"

The brothers looked at one another questioningly, and Wyatt shook his head.

"I had a feeling that may have been the case." Mr. Blade tapped the paper on top of the stack. "We managed to find the bill of sale on the property. Did you know that Dunrovin Ranch was on the chopping block twenty-five years ago?"

"What do you mean, on the chopping block?" Rainier asked, peering at the stack of papers. The page on top looked like a jumble of legalese that only a lawyer could understand.

"I mean it was up for auction. From what I could find out from the paperwork, the family who owned the ranch before lost it in a situation very similar to that of your parents."

"That's impossible. William Poe has been a tax appraiser only for the last ten years. He couldn't have screwed anyone over twenty-five years ago," Wyatt said, taking his seat behind the desk.

"You're right," Mr. Blade said with a nod. "He wasn't screwing anyone out of their land twenty-five years ago. No, it was actually his family who had owned it before you and yours."

"No!" Wyatt dropped his hands down on the desk with a thump. "That can't be true. Mom and Dad said they had gotten it from a family who had decided they didn't want to be ranchers anymore."

Mr. Blade's eyebrows rose in surprise. "I think your parents may have been lying to you. From the looks of it, William's father, Paul, had lost the property due to a tax lien. When the place went to auction, the Poes had thought they would be able to buy it back. However, your parents came in and bought it out from under them."

"Does he think he can recreate the same chain of events? Is this some twisted attempt to pay my parents back for getting the ranch?" Rainier asked.

"I have no idea what William Poe is thinking," Mr. Blade said. "But if I can prove that he is behind these taxes and is doing it so he can buy the ranch, I think we have a really strong case, as we certainly have found a motive for his erratic behavior."

"Thank you, Mr. Blade," Rainier said. "We'll see if—"

"Wait." Wyatt interrupted with a wave of his hand. "What about the body? How did Paul Poe's remains end up on the ranch?"

"That's one thing I can't make heads or tails of," Mr. Blade said. "But we are going to have to hope that your parents had nothing to do with his death. If they did, everything we're working toward is going to go up in smoke."

Chapter Eighteen

He couldn't believe his parents had lied to him. Surely their lie had been well intended, and they had never thought it would come back to haunt the family, and yet here they were. Or maybe Merle and Eloise had been kept in the dark about the circumstances in which the ranch had gone up for auction. Since they had bought it before the days when a person could Google just about anything, perhaps they hadn't been told who the ranch had once belonged to. Rainier had to hope that his parents weren't involved in anything that would cast a bad light upon the family.

Wyatt turned the squad car down the road to the ranch, and as they drew nearer to home, Rainier's stomach tightened. He was more nervous now to face his mother and father than when he'd been released from jail. It was one thing for him to know he was guilty of wrongdoing, and another to think that his family may have been guilty, as well.

"Do you realize today's Christmas Eve?" Wyatt asked, looking over at him in the passenger seat.

"Damn." He had barely thought of anything beyond what they were dealing with and what was happening between him and Laura. Somehow the date had slipped through the cracks. He had no presents for anyone. Hopefully, the family wouldn't be even more disappointed with him than they already were. He was so tired of feeling like a disgrace. With every choice he made it seemed he was screwing up.

If this was what life on the outside was, he wasn't sure which lifestyle—his present situation or prison—was harder. At least in jail very little was expected of him. Yet he could never let himself go back to that place. It killed his soul. "I'm sure you haven't gotten the chance to pick anything up for Laura, but in my experience women tend to like what comes from the heart the most."

"So you think I should write her a love poem? 'Roses are red, violets are blue...'" he said with a laugh.

"That's not what I meant, smart-ass. But I'm glad you're feeling good enough to be your normal smart-mouthed self."

"It's amazing what not going back to prison can do for a man," Rainier said with a smile.

"Do you know if your birth father is still alive?" Wyatt asked.

Why was he bringing that up right now?

"Did you hear something?"

Wyatt shook his head. "No. I'm just thinking about what happened with you and him. If you saw him again, do you think you would do to him what you just did to William Poe, or would you do something worse?"

"You know how I feel about what happened with William. I won't make the same mistake. And with my father, if he's still alive and if I see him, I think I would turn around and walk away. One thing I did learn in prison is that the worst punishment someone can undergo is isolation. The mind does strange things when you're forced to be alone with it, and think about all the mistakes you've made. All I can hope is that my father, like William Poe, is haunted by his wrongdoings."

"You should make that into a Hallmark card, man," his brother said, giving him a soft punch to his upper arm, reminding him exactly what it was and how it felt to be brothers.

Wyatt parked the car next to Laura's and chuckled as he noticed the reindeer antlers on her doors. "Those are hilarious. Gwen would love something like that. She's all about Christmas stuff. Now that her mom's in rehab for her alcoholism, she grabbed all of their old decorations and brought them over to my place. It's like Santa's workshop in there."

"Laura's house is the same way. Heck, it might even be worse. Her house actually *is* Santa's workshop. She was telling me that she makes and sells Christmas decorations online."

"You mean like on Etsy or something?"

He had no idea what Etsy was, but he nodded. "She seems to really enjoy it."

At the thought of Laura, all that they had last said to one another and what had happened between them, Rainier stopped in his tracks and stared up at the front door. He glanced over at her car, surprised that she was still here and hadn't gone home.

"It's going to be okay, man," Wyatt said.

"No. I have a feeling that I'm not gonna have time to worry about a Christmas gift or lack of one for Laura. She must hate me. And she has every right to. I can't believe what I did to her. How she must feel. I put her in an impossible situation."

"You made a mistake, Rainier, and thankfully, you avoided trouble by the skin of your teeth. I think she's just gonna be excited to see you. I can tell from the way you two look at each other that you guys are in love. And when you love each other, I mean really love each other, you can get through a lot."

"But when is it too much?"

"*Too much* isn't really something that applies when you love. Because you can never really love someone too much. All that love equates to a lifetime of learning to forgive one another, and accepting the person for who they really are—stupid decisions, screwups, bad sense of humor and all."

"Hey, I'm not the one with the bad sense of humor," Rainier joked.

It all came down to this. If she loved him like Wyatt assumed, she would forgive him. And if she couldn't move past this, and it was *too much*, then what he was feeling toward her wasn't being reciprocated and he would have to take a few steps back. It would never work if they weren't in the same emotional place.

He and Wyatt made their way into the ranch house. His heart hammered away inside his chest as they walked into the living room. It was unusually quiet, so much so that the only sound he could hear was the erratic thump of his heartbeat.

"Hello?" Wyatt called.

No one answered.

"Maybe they're out in the main office. Did you notice if the lights were on or anything?" Rainier asked.

"It was dark out there."

"Weren't Waylon, Christina and Winnie coming

back to the ranch today?" Rainier asked. "Maybe they called and everyone ran to the airport to pick them up."

"Everyone? Even Laura?" Wyatt said. "No, something's not right." He reached down and put his hand on his Glock.

Rainier chuckled, trying to make light of the situation even though he was just as nervous about his family's disappearance. "I don't think you really need to take things there, do you?"

Wyatt dropped his hand, but Rainier could see his fingers twitching as if he wanted to reach back up and take hold of his gun once again.

"Let's take a look around and see if we can find them. Did you at least text Mom or Gwen?"

Wyatt got his phone and quickly tapped away, then slipped it back in his pocket. "You're right. I'm sure this is all nothing and everyone is fine. What can I say? I'm just a little bit jumpy after everything that's been going on at the ranch lately." He gave a light laugh.

"While we wait for them to get back to us, let's go check around the barn. Or maybe they're in the pasture or something. I'm sure we'll run across them."

They made their way outside and over to the barn. The door was partly open and Rainier was met with a thin shaft of light. Relief swept through him as his mother's voice filled the air.

"We didn't mean for anything to happen with your brother, your wife or your girlfriend. We never wanted anything bad to happen to you," Eloise was saying.

He looked inside the barn, but from where he was standing he couldn't see anyone. He started to walk inside, but Wyatt held him back and shook his head. His palm was back on his weapon.

"You're making a huge mistake," Laura said, her voice high and tense.

"You would know all about mistakes, wouldn't you, Ms. Blade? I can't believe you would be stupid enough to find your way into that lowlife Rainier's bed. You could've done so much better, and I know your father doesn't approve." William Poe's voice filtered down from the hayloft above.

"I don't care what you think about my life. As far as I can tell, you have no room to judge anyone else for their personal life," Laura said.

Rainier loved the defiance in her voice. She was so strong. Yet mouthing off to William was probably not the smartest thing she could have done. Then again, he had no right to judge another's approach to dealing with that man.

"Yes, I heard all about what your father intends to do. He is a fool if he thinks he can go against me. I always get what I want."

"Really?" Merle asked. "If that's the case, then why are you here? If you thought you really had a chance at having us give up on this ranch and letting it get taken by the state, then you wouldn't be standing here holding that gun."

Gun?

William had to be desperate. From everything Rainier had heard and everything his mother had told him, the man was conniving and smart, but he always sent other people to do his dirty work for him, whether it be Waylon's ex-wife, Alli, or someone else. He was always careful to keep himself out of the limelight. Which meant in this case, he didn't intend on letting anyone walk away to become a potential witness.

He and Wyatt had to get in there and help their family and Laura. They'd have to move fast. No doubt William was going to kill them and anyone else who stumbled onto the scene.

"You don't know what you're talking about, old man," William yelled. "I'm just tired of screwing around with you people. I'm tired of you all getting people I care about hurt or killed."

"We didn't have anything to do with your wife's murder or your brother's incarceration. You did all that, William," Merle said. "You don't get to point your finger at us because you had to deal with the consequences of your choices. You need to take accountability for your actions."

"I don't know who you think you are to tell me how I should and shouldn't act," William said. "You're not my father."

Rainier looked over at Wyatt and his brother cringed. No one spoke to Merle like that and got away with it.

"Besides," William continued, "it's your fucking fault that my father wasn't around. You are all nothing but murderers."

"We had nothing to do with your father's death, William," Merle argued.

"Then how did he die on this ranch? I'm sure it wasn't just some coincidence that after you stole the property from underneath us, he went missing, and then twenty-five years later his remains are found here. Knowing this family, he probably came out here and you all shot him."

"Why would we shoot him?" Merle asked.

William snorted in anger. "He probably realized that you guys were never going to let him win at that auction—no matter how high he went. You must've known in advance what his max amount was. You probably paid somebody off, and then when it came down to business, your underhandedness got you this place. He probably came out here in search of revenge for what you did. And you managed to pull the trigger first."

There was a click and slide, like the sound of a round being jacked into the chamber of a gun.

"But you won't get the drop on me," William continued. "Not like you did with my father. I'm going to get this ranch. And I'm going to get my revenge. My sweet, sweet revenge."

There were the sounds of a scuffle.

"Don't you dare touch me," Laura said.

William gave a mocking laugh. It was too much for Rainier to take. They had to get in there. Rainier motioned for them to move forward. Wyatt nodded and stepped ahead of him, pulling his gun from his holster.

Damn, he wished he could have a gun. Standing there, watching his brother take the point position, ready to face whatever firestorm they were walking into, Rainier felt ridiculous and ill-prepared. He had no way to protect the people he loved. The only thing going for him and Wyatt was the fact that it didn't seem as though William knew they had returned. The element of surprise was on their side.

Wyatt eased into the barn, and taking a low ready position, flagged the main area. A couple horses had their heads over their gates, peering out at them. One, a black mare, greeted them with a soft nicker.

Rainier lifted his finger to his lips, instinctively motioning for the horse to be quiet. As he realized what he'd done, he felt ridiculous. Laura would've loved to see him do that. No doubt she would have laughed at him.

He glanced up to the hayloft. Laura's feet were sticking over the side, her high heels hanging off her feet. From the angle of her feet, she must have been lying on her stomach, as if she were a prisoner who had been told to hit the ground in an officer's attempt to neutralize a possible threat.

William had his back to Rainier as he stood at the edge of the hayloft. He leaned against one of the support beams. There was a gun in his right hand, but it hung limp at his side.

At least they weren't in immediate danger. Yet Rainier had no idea how Wyatt intended for them to get up to there and take down William before he noticed them. From the main floor of the barn they would lose any gunfight.

They would have to outsmart the man.

He tapped Wyatt's shoulder and motioned for his brother to follow him outside. They retreated slowly, easing out of the door.

"You need to call backup," he whispered. "There's no way we can get the drop on him."

Wyatt took out his phone and tapped another message. "Done, but it's gonna take some time for anyone else to get out here. Most everybody's home with their families because of the holiday."

Of course. Rainier hadn't thought of the fact that the department would be running on a skeleton crew. Though it made sense, as they had seen very few other officers coming and going at the station.

As he thought about it, it struck him as a bit odd that Mr. Blade had been working. But maybe a man like him never really took a day off. Maybe he had more in common with his daughter than Rainier had originally assumed.

"In the meantime, we are going to have to figure this out ourselves," he whispered.

Before his brother had time to react, Rainier pushed Wyatt out of view from anyone inside the barn, and made his way back inside. The door screeched as metal ground on metal when he opened it wider.

"Hello? Anyone out here?"

There was the sound of footsteps on the wood floor above as William turned to face him, but the man kept his gun out of sight. "Rainier, just the man I wanted to see." There was a large cut along the arch of his cheekbone, right under his eye. It was puffy and his eye was so swollen that Rainier doubted he could see out of it. He chalked it up to advantage number two. Though maybe it was really number one, now that they no longer had the element of surprise.

"I see you're not gonna be winning any beauty contests in the near future, William," Rainier said with a dry laugh. "Then again, even without that shiner, I don't think you had much going for you in the looks department."

William produced the gun and aimed it at him. "Say hello, Laura. It may be the last chance you get to talk to your lover boy."

Laura gasped and he heard her as she rolled over and sat up at the edge of the loft. It looked as though her hands were tied behind her back, but besides her arms being immobilized, she appeared unharmed. "Rainier, what are you doing here?"

He smiled. "Turns out I had an unexpected ally who

helped keep me from going back to jail. You know, your father isn't half-bad."

"Did he know you were coming back—"

"Shut up, woman," William said, shoving her away from the edge until she was out of view.

Wyatt wouldn't be able to take a shot at William. Not from here. Not with everyone out of view and so close to the man. One stray bullet and someone else could be killed. He couldn't risk their lives.

"Don't talk to her like that," Rainier said, forcing William's attention back to him and away from the woman he loved.

"You really are stupid, man," he retorted, pointing the gun at him.

"I'm not the stupid one, William. I'm not the one who just took four people hostage with the intention of murdering them."

"Are you really going to think you're better than me? You think you can judge what I'm doing? You are trash. Your opinion is of no matter to me."

"William," Eloise called out, an edge of panic in her voice. "I know what happened to your father."

What was his mother doing? William was angry, and who knew what he was capable of. In a split second, he could point the gun and pull the trigger, killing her.

"What in hell are you talking about?" William spat.

"You were right," she continued. "Your father came out here to get his revenge. He was hoping, just like you are now, that if he killed us maybe he would get another chance at buying back your family's ranch."

"So you killed him?" William asked.

"No, nothing like that." Eloise's voice was soft, almost apologetic. "In those days, do you remember your family's old barn? It was about a hundred feet or so from where we are now. Your father was standing in front of it when I came out and found him. He was smoking a cigarette. You know, everyone smoked back in those days, but even so there was an unwritten rule that no one smoked near a barn. You couldn't put the animals at risk. I told him to put it out. Instead, he threw it back behind him, straight into a haystack."

"My father would never put animals at risk. No matter what you say, he wasn't a monster. He just had a run of bad luck, then more, when you guys moved into Mystery."

"I'm telling you the truth, William," Eloise said. "Everything caught on fire. It was an inferno in no time. Unfortunately, I was there alone that night. Merle had gone into town to meet up with an old veteran friend of his. Before I could run inside and call the fire department, your father was on me."

"Shut your mouth right now, you lying bitch. My father would never have touched you," William seethed.

"He put the gun to my head, but I struggled. I don't know what happened, but somehow in the fight, the gun went off. I swear I didn't pull the trigger. Your father's death was just a horrible accident."

William leaned against the support beam. He lowered the gun slowly, but it was still pointed in the direction Rainier assumed his mother was sitting.

"You're wrong. It doesn't make any sense. There's no way…" William said, stunned. "If that's true, that it was nothing more than an accident, why didn't you report his death to the police?"

There was a long pause.

"You have to understand, William," Merle said, "it

was around that time we were trying to adopt the boys. Adoption is a very tough process. If an agency caught wind of anything like that happening…we would've never gotten our sons. We would've never gotten the chance to help all those kids in need."

"My mother deserved to know. I deserved to know what happened to my father. Do you have any idea how many years I've been searching for him?" William asked.

"We're so very sorry," Eloise said. "We couldn't tell you. We couldn't risk everything. Our lie has haunted us for so long, and I'm sorry you had to find out like this. But you need to put your gun down. If you do, we can forgive you. No one has to know about this. You forgave Rainier and didn't press charges, and we will return the favor."

"Shut up," William said, running his free hand over his face. "I can't hear any more of your garbage."

"If it makes you feel better, William," Eloise said, "I was the one who buried your father. I made sure to say a few kind words and give him a little service out of respect for you and your family."

"You mean right after you killed him? If you did anything kind, it was out of guilt and not some selfless act." William pushed the gun into the waistband of his pants. "Get down there with your son." He pointed toward Rainier.

What was the man doing? Was he going to have Eloise climb down from the loft so he could have an easier target?

His mother slowly made her way down the ladder. Turning, she saw Rainier and threw her arms around his neck. "I'm so glad you're here. I hope you know how much I love you."

From the way she spoke, it sounded as if she was afraid they would be her last words.

"Get down here, William," Rainier ordered. "You don't get to stand up there and pretend like you're some big shot. If you are going to kill us, do it like a real man. I want to look you in the eyes when you pull that trigger."

William's laughter filled the air and the shrill sound spooked several of the horses. They squealed as they panicked and paced around inside their stalls.

William climbed down the ladder, watching Rainier carefully as he stepped onto the ground. "Not as much of a chicken shit as I thought you were." He pulled the gun from his pants and pointed it between Rainier's eyes. "I'm going to kill Laura last. I want her to watch as your family is wiped off this planet."

In a flash of movement, Rainier reached up and took hold of the gun, stepping out of its sights. It went off. The bullet lodged into the ground at their feet. The boom echoed through the cavernous barn as the scent of gunpowder thickened the air. The shot was so loud it made his ears ring. Yet he could still hear the cry of the animals as they panicked.

He tried to twist the weapon, breaking William's grip. But the man was stronger than he looked, or perhaps just as driven by rage and fury as he was. Rainier elbowed William in the chest and twisted the gun again, this time breaking his hold. Grabbing the weapon, he stepped back and pointed it at William.

All he had to do was pull the trigger. This would all be over. His family would be safe.

If he pulled it, his actions would be justified. It would be in self-defense. But he'd made a promise to his brother, and he couldn't compromise Laura again. He'd already gotten lucky once today in escaping the vise-like grip of prison.

William smiled nervously. "Just put the gun down. I know you don't have what it takes to pull that trigger. I was wrong about you before. You may be an ex-con, but you're not a murderer."

For once, the man was right. Rainier had no desire to take a life, not even William's, when push came to shove. He'd never be able to look at himself in the mirror again, knowing what he'd done.

He took his mom by the arm and slowly moved back toward the door. Leaning close, he whispered, "Wyatt's outside. Wait for the police."

If he could hold off William for just a little bit longer, he and everyone else in his family could get out of this without having to make a terrible decision—whether or not to take a life.

He let go of Eloise, and she disappeared into the darkness. Wyatt was nowhere to be seen. Rainier threw the gun away. It thumped down into the grass of the yard, but he couldn't have said exactly where.

It was better this way.

William laughed. As Rainier turned to face him once again, he found the barrel of a revolver pointed directly at him.

"No man goes to battle with just one weapon." William cocked the gun.

A shot rang out through the air.

William crumpled to the ground. Blood poured from the hole in his head. It spread out in a macabre crimson pool and started to leach into the muck and used hay that littered the floor.

Standing at the barn's side door, a few feet from the body, was Wyatt.

His brother had pulled the trigger. He'd saved Rainier's life.

Wyatt was still aiming his gun at the body as if he was worried that the dead man would rise again. But William Poe wouldn't be coming back. He'd never again terrorize their family.

Chapter Nineteen

The next morning, the ranch was quiet and still after a night of frenetic activity. There had been news trucks and cars of inquisitive friends and neighbors filling the parking lot until the wee hours of the morning. Every time Rainier thought about last night, all he could envision was William's body lying in a pool of blood as reporters' cameras flashed wildly, casting eerie shadows throughout the barn.

Rainier held Laura in his arms as they stood at the living room window, looking outside, as he thought about everything that had happened. Even though they hadn't stepped out-of-doors since last night, Laura still felt cold to his touch.

She had been through so much that he wasn't sure what he could do to help her get through this in as healthy a way as possible. When they had gone to bed, it was more symbolic than anything else, as neither had slept. Instead, they had lain there holding one another. It was cathartic and comforting to have her in his arms, and to listen to the calming sound of her breathing.

There was no longer any question in his mind or in his heart—they were meant to be together. When he was with her, it was as if he inherently knew everything would be okay. No matter what life threw at them, they would make it, as long as they were together.

"Heck of a way to spend Christmas Day, isn't it?" Rainier said.

She smiled at him, but didn't say anything and stepped out of his arms. She walked over to the windows and pulled the cord that released the drapes, shutting out the world.

"I have thought about it a lot, and every time, I come back to one thing—William Poe got what he deserved," Laura said. "He was crooked. And he had a hand in each of the deaths that happened over the last month. He thought he was above the law, and that if he just threw enough money and power behind issues and pulled enough political strings, he would get away with whatever he wanted. His only goal in life was to hurt other people."

"You're right, Laura. But don't forget about yourself. What William did to you was inexcusable. And as long as I live, I'll never let anyone lay their hands on you like he did."

She smiled, and some of the stress and exhaustion that had blanketed her seemed to lift. "As long as you live? That sounds like some kind of promise." There was an edge of playfulness to her voice.

"It would be, if you allowed me the honor."

She opened her mouth to speak, but a sudden patter of footsteps sounded in the hall. Winnie, Waylon's two-year-old daughter, ran into the living room. Her brunette hair was plastered against the side of her face and there were sleep marks on her cheeks. She must've slept hard after she, Waylon and Christina arrived on a midnight flight.

"Did Santa come?" she asked, her words the rushed and garbled ones of a toddler.

Laura walked over and squatted down at her eye level. "Did you look over there?" Smiling, she pointed at the hearth, where the mantel was covered in Christmas stockings. "But I think before you open any of the presents you should go get your dad and Christina. And I bet Nana and Gramps wouldn't want to miss all the fun, either."

Winnie looked over Laura's shoulder and stared longingly at the large stack of presents under the stockings, decorated with Disney princesses and shiny bows. "Can I just open one?" the little girl asked, and gave Laura a pleading look.

"No, little miss." She stood up and put her hand on the little girl's back. "You run along and wake everyone up, and I'll go get some hot chocolate ready. How many marshmallows would you like? Wait, I bet you don't even like marshmallows, do you?"

Winnie looked up at her as if she had lost her mind. "I *love* mushmellows."

"Well, I better give you a couple extra," Laura said.

The toddler turned and ran down the hall, banging on doors and calling out the names of family members as she rushed to wake them.

Laura laughed. "I guess I'm going to need your help finding the ingredients for hot chocolate in your parents' kitchen. Would you mind?"

"Whatever you need. Like I said, I'll always be there." Rainier took her hand and they walked together into the kitchen.

Seeing her with Winnie made him love her that much more. Laura was incredible. And it was incredible how well she fit into his family. It was almost as if there had always been a place for her. As soon as she'd walked into their lives, she had taken on the role she had always been meant to have.

"Do you think Wyatt is going to be okay?" she asked as she walked over and took mug after mug from the cupboard.

"As far as I know. He's on paid leave, just as long as it takes to investigate everything that happened and clear him of any wrongdoing. It shouldn't take long, as he did what any officer would have done."

Laura nodded and walked over to the refrigerator and took out the milk. "I'm glad to hear it. I know you and Wyatt had your problems, but just like you and the rest of your brothers, he's a good man. In fact, you have a wonderful family."

One he hoped she would join someday. If he was going to ask her to marry him, he wanted to do it once and he wanted to do it the right way. She deserved the very best. She always would.

"I'm lucky." He took the milk from her hand and set it beside the stove as he stood in front of her. He wrapped his arms around her.

"Are you now?" she said, smiling up at him. "How so?"

"Are you fishing for compliments?" he teased, rubbing his thumb on the small of her back.

"Would that be so bad?" she asked.

"Not at all." He pressed a gentle kiss to her forehead. She smelled of his fresh sheets and faintly of cinnamon and cloves. "I've never been luckier than when I walked out those gates at the prison and saw you. You took my breath away. It was like some kind of dream—me finding my freedom and you, all in the same seconds. And ever since that moment, all I've wanted is to be close to you. You were my Christmas miracle, and I want to be with you for the rest of my life."

Her arms tightened around him as she giggled. "You say that now, but are you going to be able to put up with all my quirks? I mean, you haven't seen me in craft mode. You know, felt flying everywhere, hot glue guns and sequins, the whole shebang."

He laughed as he imagined her with glue in her hair and a sequin stuck to her forehead. "I think that would only make you that much more lovable."

"Lovable?" she asked with a quirk of her brow.

"Well, I was going to say beautiful, but you are already the most beautiful woman I've ever seen. With or without sequins, you will always be stunning."

She smiled, and her whole face brightened. "Wow, you are quite the charmer this morning."

"Are you going to answer my question?" he asked, his hands becoming sweaty as he grew more nervous.

"What question?" she teased.

"You know darn well what question."

"If we do this I'm going to have to quit my job," she said, but she didn't look unhappy about the prospect. "Someone else would have to take on your case."

"If you want to quit, you could. I don't care about who has my case—I'm not going to cause any more trouble," Rainier said. "Think about it. You could focus on your business. I have always thought the best investment people can make is in themselves. You could follow your dreams. And I could go to work here at the ranch. They are starting to book up for next summer. I could be a handyman or something around here. So we have that figured out. Now, what do you say?"

She stepped back from him, her hands on his waist. "I don't see a man on his knees. I thought that was, like, a requirement. You know, if a guy was to make some kind of request that included something like marriage, or whatever."

From the way she spoke, he could tell she was just as nervous as he was.

"Gosh, you are so demanding. Are you always going to be like that?" He gave her a playful, inquisitive glance.

"Hey, take it or leave it, Mr. Charm. I'm always going to be the imperfect and wonderful me."

"And it is all of you that I love. I'd never want you to change." He slipped his hands into hers as he got down on one knee in front of her.

"You love me?" She smiled.

"More than anything in the entire world."

"Good, because I love you, too." She leaned down and kissed the back of his hand. "And if we're going to do this…if we're going to have a life together… I don't want to start it out on uneven footing. I want us to always be best friends, for us to walk side by side. I never want you to feel like you need to kneel to me."

"But you just told me—"

She laughed. "Welcome to my world. I guess I want what I want, but there's a part of me—the little girl who's always had a dream of this moment—who wants the tradition." She squeezed his hands. "How about this?" She got down on her knee, so they were face-to-face. "From this moment on, I want us to be equal partners."

Just when he thought he couldn't love her more, she did something like this.

"We can have any life you dream of, just as long as

you promise to be my wife. I don't have a ring, but if I did it would have a green emerald at its center and I'd have it in a red velvet box—all Christmas for you. More, it would be a symbol of how rare our love is." He kissed her knuckles and pressed their entwined hands against his chest, where he was sure she could feel his heart thrashing wildly. "Laura Blade, will you marry me?"

The door to the kitchen flew open and Winnie came rushing in, not stopping until she stood so close to him they nearly touched. "They ready," she said, breathless and unaware of her intrusion. "Dad wants two mushmellows."

Laura laughed at the girl and her cute mispronunciation. "Coming right up, sweetheart."

She moved to stand up, but he stopped her. "Please, answer me." He didn't care if he sounded like he was begging. He couldn't go another moment without knowing her answer.

Laura looked him in the eyes. "Rainier Fitzgerald, I would be honored to spend the rest of my days with you. You have brought me a happiness that I didn't know I could feel. I love you and I know that I will only grow to love you more and more each day that we spend together."

"You guys gettin' married?" Winnie said, but it was as much a proclamation as it was a question.

"Is that okay with you?" Rainier asked.

"Hmm…" She popped her thumb in her mouth and answered with a simple nod. Just as quickly as she had appeared, she turned around and ran to the door of the kitchen. "They gettin' married!"

There was the sound of cheers and clapping from the living room.

"I hope you didn't want to keep it a secret," Rainier

said with an apologetic tilt of his head. "With this crew, it seems like most secrets tend to come out. It's only a matter of time."

"Even those about dead bodies," Laura murmured.

He laughed. "You make a good point, but I'm hoping that kind of a secret was a onetime thing."

"I certainly hope so, but you're not allowed to go digging around anymore spigots. Deal?"

He stood up and held out his hand to help her stand. "You got it, my love. No spigots."

They finished making the hot cocoa and carried trays of drinks out to the living room. All three of his brothers and their fiancées were sitting on the couches, and his mother and father were in their chairs. Everyone looked up at them as they came into the room. His mother jumped to her feet and, as soon as he set the tray on the living room table, threw her arms around him and then Laura.

"Congratulations, you two! I couldn't be happier," she said, tears running in wild rivers down her face. But she didn't seem to notice or care. "With Wyatt and Gwen's wedding, and now this…all our boys are getting married!"

His father gave them each a hug. "Anything you need, you two. Anything at all. We're here for you." He turned to face the others. "And that goes for all of you. You are always welcome in our home and in our lives. You are the reasons we do what we do. You are the reason we fight. And no matter what the future brings, we will always fight for this family."

As Merle spoke, Rainier thought of the threat that still loomed over them. There was still the matter of the taxes. Just because William Poe was dead didn't change the fact that they still needed to pay what they could and get legal proceedings together to fight the state in court. The battle was won, but the war was far from over.

He couldn't let what he couldn't control destroy or tarnish Christmas. They had tomorrow and the next day and the next to fight, but for now all they needed was each other, and all *he* needed was Laura. The rest of the world could wait.

Winnie took a long slurp of hot chocolate from her Minnie Mouse mug. The sound made everyone smile.

"Hey, Win, why don't you help me hand out the presents and stockings?" Waylon asked.

She thumped down her cup, sloshing chocolate on the table.

As they handed out gifts, no one opened theirs except Winnie, who tore through the wrapping and bows and squealed as she uncovered trucks, Legos and a collection of plastic horses. Eventually, Waylon went to the front door, motioning for Rainier to stay quiet as he slipped outside.

A few minutes later a knock sounded.

Rainier walked over and, expecting Waylon, opened the door. "Need help?" he asked. But he stopped when he saw Mr. Blade standing there, an envelope in his hand.

"I hope you don't mind. I knew my daughter was here for Christmas, so I knew you all were home. I didn't want to intrude, but I have a gift for your mother and father."

"Come on in," he said, motioning for him to step inside.

"Mr. Blade, we're so glad you stopped by," his mom exclaimed, as if she had been expecting the man on Christmas Day.

"Thank you, Eloise." He walked over to her and handed her the envelope.

The front door opened again, and Waylon walked in.

"Winnie, girl, we know how much you love the ranch dogs, Milo and Lassie, and how much you were wishing for one of your own," he said, sending a smile to Christina.

In his arms was a tiny black ball of fur.

Winnie gasped and the little dog's head perked up. He gave a little yip of excitement as he spotted the girl. Waylon put the puppy on the floor and he ran straight to Winnie as though he knew how much the little girl already loved him. He wriggled into her arms and licked the dribbles of chocolate off Winnie's chin as she laughed.

"I love him, Daddy!" The puppy barked, as if he knew what she was saying. "Can we call him Mush? Like mushmellow?"

Waylon laughed. "We can name him whatever you like, sweetheart."

"Are you going to take him back to the base with you, Waylon?" his mother asked, curling the envelope Mr. Blade had given her in her hands. There were little smudges of moisture on the manila.

"Well, I was going to wait to tell you all, but I've decided not to reenlist. I have six more months, but then I'll be moving home. I was hoping to get a job—maybe with the sheriff's office, Wyatt?" He looked over at his brother.

Wyatt laughed. "Are you sure you want to come to work with me? You'd have to do real investigative work…and what did you call us? *Girl Scouts?*"

"What can I say?" Waylon said with a laugh. "I guess I'll start working on my merit badges."

Rainier glanced at their mother. The tears had returned and she sobbed into a tissue Merle had handed her. "Mom, are you going to be okay?"

She nodded.

Mr. Blade stepped back and gave Laura an awkward look, as though he wasn't sure if he should stay or go.

"Dad, here." Laura took him by the arm and had him sit on the couch next to her.

"I'm sorry…" Eloise said, trying to speak between sobs. "I'm just…so happy. I never thought this day would come."

"Then you may not want to open that envelope," Mr. Blade said.

All the laughter and voices in the room stopped. The only sound was of Mush as he hopped and crunched through the discarded wrapping paper around Winnie.

"No, it's not like that," Laura's dad said with a wave. "Inside, you will find a great deal of paperwork."

"About what?" Merle asked.

"Basically, my team I have been talking. We met with the DA about your role in covering up Paul Poe's death. As it stands, and because of the amount of time that has gone by since the man's death, the DA doesn't wish to pursue any charges."

Eloise clapped her hands over her mouth. "Oh my… Thank you… Thank you so much."

"That's not all," Mr. Blade continued. "We also went through a great deal of records to do with your property as well as county tax records. We found that William Poe had pulled something similar to what he was trying to do with your family's ranch once before—after filing a lien against a family, he bought their property. That was the house where he and his late wife resided. With your records, and those from that sale, we were able to prove that he had the intention of doing the same with this property. Having that, along with the police report and what he said to you all, I talked to a judge and we made a filing against the Department of Revenue. Simply put, and providing there are no extenuating circumstances, your case is already won. You owe no additional taxes, and as soon as we have everything worked out and in order, I believe we have enough evidence for you to file a strong a lawsuit against the DR, should you wish to. In fact, I have it from a reliable source that they would be likely to settle in order to make things right with your family."

"What do you mean?" Eloise asked.

"I think we could get enough money that you and your family would never have to worry about losing the ranch ever again."

"Oh, Dad," Laura said. "Thank you so much."

Rainier stared at the scene around him. In all the nights he'd been surrounded by cinderblock walls and iron bars, he had never imagined a future that could be so magnificent. Though the world would undoubtedly bring the unexpected, he and Laura had the things in life that made it complete—love, family and a future brighter than even the brightest Christmas lights.

They would have one another forever.

* * * * *

Can't get enough of MYSTERY CHRISTMAS?
Check out the previous titles in the series:

MS. CALCULATION
MR. SERIOUS
MR. TAKEN

Available now from Mills & Boon Intrigue!

"Alyssa, all you have to do is hold on to me and I'll get us out of this."

She shook her head. Her blue eyes didn't drop their stare. It finally clicked in place for Caleb. He should have realized why she was so terrified.

An overwhelming wave of feeling surged through him. Without a second thought he angled her face up. Then he met her mouth with his own.

The kiss was meant to distract Alyssa from her fear, to give her something else to focus on. Caleb also hoped it reminded her that he was there, down in the trenches with her. That, no matter what, he'd get her to safety.

Yet all thoughts and intentions fell away as the warmth of Alyssa's lips pressed against his. Those pink, pink lips aroused something almost primal in Caleb. He wanted it to last. He wanted her...

THE DEPUTY'S WITNESS

BY
TYLER ANNE SNELL

First Published in Great Britain 2017
By Mills & Boon, an imprint of HarperCollins*Publishers*
1 London Bridge Street, London, SE1 9GF

© 2017 Tyler Anne Snell

ISBN: 978-0-263-92940-9

46-1217

MIX
Paper from
responsible sources
FSC™ C007454

This book is produced from independently certified FSC™ paper to ensure responsible forest management.

For more information visit: www.harpercollins.co.uk/green

Printed and bound in Spain
by CPI, Barcelona

Tyler Anne Snell genuinely loves all genres of the written word. However, she's realized that she loves books filled with sexual tension and mysteries a little more than the rest. Her stories have a good dose of both. Tyler lives in Alabama with her same-named husband and their mini "lions." When she isn't reading or writing, she's playing video games and working on her blog, *Almost There*. To follow her shenanigans, visit www.tylerannesnell.com.

Chapter One

The rain slapped the windshield in such fierce bursts that Alyssa Garner almost decided not to go into the bank at all.

She moved her glasses up to the bridge of her nose and peered out the window, analyzing the few feet between her car door and the overhang of the Waller Street Credit Union's awning. If she used the two-week-old *Carpenter Times* she'd thrown on the back seat floorboard as a makeshift umbrella, she might not get soaked to the bone.

Alyssa looked down at her outfit. She worked at Jeffries & Sons Remodeling, and apart from being the only employee who was not a Jeffries, she was the only one who ran the day-to-day operations pertaining to the physical office. That meant she was the first person anyone saw when they walked through the front door. Even though she wasn't a Jeffries or a son, she played a big part in creating a first impression of the small business. Which meant she was currently wearing a finely pressed white blouse, a pencil skirt and black heels that boosted her height considerably. An outfit that didn't match with the downpour outside.

She sucked on her bottom lip, considering the option of forgoing the bank run until the next day. But just as quickly as she had the thought, she sighed, defeated. While corporations and bigger businesses might be able to push off making weighty deposits by just one day, places like Jeffries couldn't afford the delay. Alyssa took her cell phone out of her purse and slid it between the waist of her skirt and her stomach. Some women couldn't go anywhere without their purses. Alyssa was that way about her phone. She blamed her sister, Gabby, for that. Whenever Alyssa pointed out that Gabby always had her phone, her little sister would snap back with a simple, yet effective stance.

"The one time you don't have it is the one time you'll need it the most."

It was hard to argue with logic like that.

Alyssa adjusted the phone against her so it wasn't noticeable, put the deposit bag beneath one arm and grabbed the newspaper. Thunder crashed loudly overhead, but Alyssa crossed the divide between her car and the bank's front door without getting swept away in the storm.

However, her glasses fogged the moment the wet air pressed against her. She paused in front of the glass double door to take them off before walking inside. She hated waiting for them to defog, looking like some kind of klutz. She didn't need help in that department when it came to her vision. Alyssa was one of those people who couldn't survive without her glasses or contacts. That is, unless the world decided to orbit within an inch of her nose.

Further proving that point, no sooner had she walked into the lobby than she bumped shoulders with a man leaving.

"Sorry," she said quickly. He was too far away without her glasses on to be able to make out his face. But the blur responded all the same.

"It's okay," he said, before moving to the doors.

Alyssa smiled in his general direction and continued on to the closest teller line. By the time she was called up to a woman she knew as Missy Grayson, her glasses were clear again and had been replaced atop her nose. Now it was time for business.

"Deposit for Jeffries?" Missy guessed, already pulling up the account on the computer. That was a perk of living in a small town. Routines were noticed and information became common knowledge. Everyone knew Alyssa made the deposits.

"Yes, ma'am," Alyssa chirped, trying to match Missy's pep. "Then I think I'll take lunch at home so I can grab a warm pair of clothes and the umbrella I didn't think to take this morning."

Missy's face pinched.

"You know, I watched the news this morning and Carl didn't say anything about a storm coming at us," she said, nearing a full-out scolding for their local weatherman, despite the fact that he was not in the bank. "I told my husband he should even take the Jeep out with him to fish this morning. It has a soft top that's been off on account of it being summer, so I know he had one heck of a time with that. I bet I'm not going to hear the end of that any time soon."

"Hopefully he won't be too grumpy about it," Alyssa said. "When in doubt, blame the weatherman."

"You bet I am!"

The two laughed and started in on the technical parts of making a deposit. Alyssa was already imagining running back to her car and pointing it toward home. She had some leftovers from her night out with her friend Natalie on Saturday and could warm those up while she changed clothes. Her umbrella, though... Where was it? In the garage? When was the last time she'd seen—

A scream shattered her thoughts. Alyssa whirled around and found the source coming from a woman perhaps a few years younger than her twenty-seven. Aside from the scream, she was obviously distressed. Her expression was one of pure terror. It simultaneously confused Alyssa and put her on edge. It wasn't until the woman pointed toward the front doors that Alyssa understood.

And felt the same fear.

Two men and a woman, dripping wet, had come inside, the storm their backdrop. They wore matching gray jumpsuits, workmen's boots and, with her stomach plummeting to the floor, Alyssa realized, ski masks. Only their narrowed eyes and lips could be seen. Their hands were gloved too. Which made the fact that they were holding guns even more menacing.

"Anyone move and we'll start shooting," yelled the bigger man. He stood taller than his partners and looked like he had muscles beneath his getup. He was quick to move his gun and point it at the woman who had screamed. "Keep yelling like that and you'll be the first."

The young woman had backed up to one of the two desks on either side of the large open room. Ted Danfield, a loan officer in his fifties, had been standing in front of his desk talking to an elderly man. Now he reached out and grabbed the young woman's shoulders, pulling her the rest of the distance to his side. Her scream downgraded to a whimper.

"Don't you even think about it!"

Alyssa's attention moved to the female in the ski mask. She had stepped to the side and had her gun pointed at Robbie Rickman. Alyssa's stomach fell even more. He was the bank's lone security guard. Robbie had worked at the bank for years. Everyone who stepped through its front doors knew and loved him. He was kind, compassionate, and fiercely loved his wife of thirty years and three grown children.

So when the woman shot him, the ten or so patrons and employees of the bank collectively gasped. Alyssa went cold as Robbie dropped back on the floor. The gun he'd had in his hand hit the floor. Alyssa realized he'd been shot in the chest.

The woman quickly scooped up the gun and handed it back to the shorter of her partners. She kept her own gun held high. Her eyes skittered among them. Alyssa hoped the gunshot had been heard by the tenants next door, but as another loud crash of thunder sounded, preceded and followed by the hard rain, she doubted they knew the difference.

"Now that you know we're serious," said the bigger man, "let's get this moving along."

The two men shouted out orders left and right, swinging guns this way and that to help emphasize their urgency, while the woman stood silent, watching their every move. When they ordered everyone to the middle of the room, Alyssa had a hard time complying, thanks to fear that seemed to be trying to grow roots into the tile floor. But soon everyone except the other teller and the bank manager who had been taken to the back with the gunwoman were sitting in the middle of the room.

"Now," the bigger man started, walking to an elderly man and taking off his ball cap. He flipped it upside down. "Everyone put your cell phones, wallets and jewelry in here! If you have a purse, throw it next to our friend here who got shot!"

He didn't waste time letting that information set in. Moving quickly, the men and women of the bank put their phones, wallets and jewelry in the hat while others threw their purses near Robbie. When he got to Alyssa and shook the hat, she decided to do something risky.

She lied.

"I left everything in the car," she explained, holding her hands out to show they were empty. "I didn't want anything to get wet."

The man was close enough to smell. His scent was a

mixture of rain and smoke. But not from cigarettes. He smelled more like he'd been to a barbecue recently. Or standing too close to a fire pit. It was an odd thought that pushed its way into Alyssa's head when she really should have focused on how his eyes narrowed even farther.

"Yeah, righ—"

"She just swallowed her ring!"

Alyssa and the gunman in front of her turned to look at the other gunman by the door. He was pointing to someone behind them both. Alyssa turned back around just in time to hear Missy cough.

"Did you really just swallow your ring?" the bigger gunman roared. He swung his gun over to point at her.

"You're damn right I swallowed my ring," she yelled back, fire in her eyes. "That ring was my mama's and her mama's before then. So unless you plan to wait it out, it's staying with me."

Alyssa felt a flash of pride for the woman—Southern ladies take their heirlooms seriously—however, it was short-lived. The gunman struck out with the butt of his gun and hit Missy across the head so fast that she didn't even have time to yell. But Alyssa did.

She crawled over to the woman just as she fell back against the tile. Blood burst from her cheek.

"Did I say you could move?" the gunman yelled at Alyssa. She froze next to Missy, knees against the floor and hands in the air.

She didn't respond to him. Nothing she said would have made the situation better when he was so obviously itching for some violence. Just like his woman partner. Robbie bleeding a few feet from them on the floor was a good indication of that.

"Get the rest of their stuff," said his partner, a reminder that he'd forgotten his original task. The gunman sneered down at Alyssa, just long enough to have his dark eyes imprinted in her memory for the rest of her life—whether or not she wanted it—and moved on to the last two people in their group.

Alyssa dropped her hands and felt her adrenaline spike. Moving so her back was to the gunman near the door, she reached out and helped Missy sit up. The woman's fire moments before had been doused. She was in pain. But she was going to have to forget that for a moment.

"Are you okay?" Alyssa whispered. With one hand she touched the open gash on her cheek and with the other she grabbed one of Missy's hands. "It'll be okay," she said before Missy could answer her question. The woman looked confused as Alyssa pulled her hand to her lap. From anyone else's point of view, Alyssa hoped it looked like she was just trying to console the woman.

When in reality she just wanted the woman to feel her cell phone, tucked out of sight in the raised waist of her skirt.

"Now, everyone keep their mouths shut! You make a move, you die," yelled the taller gunman. He took the hat full of their goods and gave it to the other gunman. They whispered a moment before the bigger man went to the back.

The bank patrons and employees were alone with the man who, Alyssa guessed, was the most observant of the three. She wasn't going to be able to use her phone while he was there. This realization inspired another risk on her part. One Alyssa hoped wouldn't get her or anyone else killed.

Still holding Missy's hand, she slipped her fingers into her skirt and pulled out her cell phone. Missy, bless her, didn't flinch as Alyssa put the phone against her palm. When she felt the woman's grip tighten around it, Alyssa put her hand back in Missy's lap and patted it twice.

Then Alyssa turned, heartbeat hammering in her chest.

"Can I go over to him?" Alyssa asked, nodding over to Robbie. "Someone needs to put pressure on his wound to try to stop the bleeding."

The man seemed, thankfully, less angry than his partners. Still, he was resistant. "I don't think so. You stay right there."

"But look at all that blood," she tried again, her voice near breaking. "Please, all I'm going to do is put my hands on it. Nothing else. *Please*."

The man cast a quick look at the group as a whole and then adjusted his gun's aim to the young woman in front. She flinched back into Ted's arms. The gunman looked at Alyssa.

"If you try anything, and I mean *anything*, I'll shoot her in the face. Got it?"

Alyssa nodded, amending her idea that this man was any less violent than his friends. She got up slowly, giving Missy time to hide the cell phone, hopefully, and walked with her hands held high over to Robbie's prone body.

She hadn't been lying. There *was* a lot of blood. Since she had never been a part of the medical field in her life, she had no idea if putting pressure on a gunshot wound even worked. All she had to go by was TV shows and movies she'd seen. Still, she did as she said and dropped to the guard's side. Alyssa put one hand and then the other on top of the wound and pressed down. Warm blood squeezed out between her fingers. Robbie was still breathing, although the breaths were shallow.

The sound of rain and thunder continued in chorus for several minutes. Alyssa kept her eyes off Missy, since the gunman seemed to be looking in her direction every few seconds, but she prayed the woman had made the call to the cops. After another few minutes, Alyssa came to the conclusion that she hadn't.

But then Alyssa spied movement on the other side of the glass doors and several things happened all at once.

The gunman had started to turn toward the doors when she found herself speaking up again.

"He really needs a doctor soon," she said, drawing his attention toward her.

He opened his mouth to talk just as his partners came back into the lobby.

"Cops," the woman yelled.

The gunman at the door didn't hesitate. He whirled around.

Then the gunfire and screaming started.

All Alyssa had time to do was throw herself over Robbie and hope she'd live long enough to tell her sister that, for once, she'd had her cell phone right when she needed it.

Chapter Two

Caleb Foster cursed something awful.

"How do you even function out here in this?"

Deputy Dante Mills let out a laugh.

"You get used to it," he said. "Just one of those things."

Caleb, a man who'd spent the majority of his career—and life—in Portland, Oregon, might have been okay with the blanket heat that the small town of Carpenter, Alabama, was throwing at him, but its humidity was another problem altogether.

It was one thing to be stuck in the heat. It was another to feel like you were drowning in it.

"I don't want to get used to this," he said sourly. He didn't care if Dante heard him. Ever since his transfer to the Riker County Sheriff's Department had been approved one month ago, he hadn't been making it a secret he was unhappy. Not that he'd had much of an alternative option, though. "I want some air that doesn't make me feel like I'm swimming standing up."

Dante chuckled. "You city boys sure do complain a lot."

Caleb was about to ask what his partner's definition of "city boy" was when they came to a stop in the parking lot. He decided he'd ask that question later. Right now he was concerned about why the sheriff had called him in minutes after their shift started. He might not have wanted the Alabama weather, but he did want his job.

The Riker County Sheriff's Department stood between the local television station and the county courthouse, all three in the very heart of the town. With two stories and faded brick and concrete, the department faced one of Carpenter's main streets and was subsequently always busy. This was a familiar sight for Caleb, and while he wouldn't admit it to any of the other deputies, the busyness made him a little less homesick.

He followed Dante through the front doors and into the lobby. A pretty blonde dispatcher named Cassie, who was rumored to be as tough as nails when needed, was in the center of the room talking to another woman. Both had cups of coffee in their hands.

"Hey, guys," she greeted, cheer clear in her tone. "Happy Monday!"

"There's no such thing as happy Mondays, Cassie," Dante pointed out, though he smiled as he made the little quip. It seemed the whole of the department functioned like that. One person saying something, only for another to add on something equally clever or nice. Most of the time it was inside jokes or references beyond Caleb's knowledge. He tried not to let it bother him. He was the new guy, after all. Plus, once he was done with his time in Riker County, he'd go back home. So what if he wasn't in sync with his colleagues now? He hoped it wouldn't matter in a few months or, God forbid, a year.

"I'm going to go see the sheriff," Caleb said, nodding to the two women. "I'll catch you after."

"Good luck," Dante called after him.

Caleb hoped he didn't need it.

He walked out of the lobby and down the hallway where the offices were located. The sheriff's was smack in the middle, nameplate auspiciously brighter than the others. Caleb slowed, stilling himself. He knew he was more on the pricklier side of a good personality. Quiet too. So far he hadn't met anyone in the department with the same disposition. Again, he didn't mind if the rest of them didn't like him. However, he did want the sheriff to find him at least agreeable. He tried on a smile that felt forced before knocking on the doorframe of the open door.

"Come in."

The muscles in Caleb's smile tightened as soon as he saw the man hunched over his desk.

Billy Reed by no means should have been an intimidating man. From first glance he was too tall, too lean, and had dark hair that was too long. Maybe that was just Caleb's opinion bleeding through, though, considering he was the opposite of the sheriff.

At five-eleven, Caleb was a man who believed in the gym as much as he believed that anyone with a clipboard on the sidewalk ready to talk about political candidates or a chance to win a cruise was supposed to be ignored. With his solid shoulders, trim body and a hard jaw, the only thing that looked remotely playful about him—according to his sister—was his golden hair, cut close but still with enough curl to annoy him. He sported a goatee but had been playing with the idea of shaving it since he'd come to town, as it was just another thing that made him hot in an already hot-as-hell town. Luckily, he still looked his age of thirty without it. He knew the sheriff was on the young side too—especially for his position—but Caleb couldn't read the man to guess an accurate age. Billy Reed was a mystery, while Caleb was the kind of man who looked like "what you see is what you get."

It was apparent that everyone in the department not only respected the sheriff, but liked him. And just as quickly when the man gave an order, it didn't matter if anyone was his friend or not. Everyone listened without skipping a beat.

So when he told Caleb to take a seat, Caleb took the seat without arguing.

"I'm going to cut right to the chase," Reed started. He threaded his hands on top of the desk. "I'm pulling you off patrol and putting you at the courthouse."

Caleb opened his mouth, ready to complain—respect and authority for the sheriff be damned—but Reed stopped him. He held his hand up for silence. "When Chief Thomas called me and asked if I had a spot for you, I was skeptical. But I've known Thomas a long time and he's a good judge of character, so I looked past what happened and gave you a chance. But while you've done a good job so far, being new has its own set of demands." He thrust his thumb over his shoulder to point back at the wall behind him. "That includes pulling courtroom deputy when I need you to."

Again, before Caleb could protest, the sheriff handed him a newspaper. A picture of a storefront with caution tape across it took up a spot above the fold.

"Almost a year ago to the day, three armed suspects used a storm as a cover to try to rob a bank a few miles from here," he started. "There were nine hostages, including bank employees and a security guard who was shot when they entered. A woman inside was able to get a call out to us, but when we arrived the suspects opened fire. In total, three people were killed, including one of the gunmen."

Caleb could tell by the way the sheriff's expression turned to pain that the other two deaths had hurt. In a small town like Carpenter, he'd probably known the victims personally. Something Caleb was in no way used to. When he was a cop in Portland, he'd dealt with mostly strangers. Their indiscretions hadn't affected him outside of his having to deal with them as his job.

The sheriff seemed to collect himself. He pointed to the newspaper again.

"The trial takes place next week and it's going to draw a lot of attention," he continued. "I'm adding you as backup, along with the current court deputy, Stanley King."

"Wait, so I'm not even *lead* court deputy?" Caleb had to interject. It was bad enough he'd lost his reputation and his position in Portland. Never mind he had to be transferred to keep from being completely jobless. But now he was expected to go to the bottom of the totem pole to not even being *on* the totem pole?

Sheriff Reed didn't bat an eyelid.

"I'll be out of town during the beginning of the trial, as well as Chief Deputy Simmons and lead detective Matt Walker, or else I would be over there too. But as it stands, I'm looking to you," Reed said. "This may not be your dream job, but it's what you have and you can either complain about it or impress me. After what happened in Portland, any good marks on your résumé will help."

Caleb wanted to argue but knew he couldn't.

The sheriff seemed to realize he'd made a good point. He grinned. "And, hey, look on the bright side. Air-conditioning!"

ALYSSA WAS ANGRY. She was nervous too, but mostly angry.

Standing outside the county courthouse, she was dressed in her best and ready to finally testify against what locals had dubbed the "Storm Chasers."

After the gunfire died down a year ago, she'd thought the terror was over. She'd focused on moving past that day and trying for a happier existence because of it. But then the nightmares had started. In them she'd seen the dark eyes of Dupree Slater, the taller gunman, hungry for violence, peering down at her. No regard for life. Especially not hers. Thinking of him and his only living partner left, Anna Kim, she still felt a flood of fear beating against her mental dam of calm. That dam didn't always hold, despite the fact that both Dupree and Anna had been in custody for a year, but today she needed it to keep its place.

She shook her head, trying to physically get rid of the way Dupree's dark eyes seemed to try to eat her whole.

But then, just as quickly, thinking of him led to the image of his partner, a man named Kevin Bates, lying dead on the floor a few feet from her. Farther away one of the bank tellers, Larissa Colt, and a local patron, Carl Redford, lying in their own pools of blood. Gunned down before the deputies could save them. They'd all been so afraid. The fear lingered to this day.

And just like that, Alyssa's familiar fear was replaced with anger.

Alyssa hadn't known Larissa well and she hadn't met Carl officially, but she knew that they had been good people. Their deaths had been senseless and cruel. Both had rocked the community.

Alyssa took a deep breath and righted the purse on her shoulder. She was here for them, for herself and for Carpenter as a whole. Justice needed to be had. And it was now or never.

She walked through the double doors into the courthouse, knowing she was early but ready to get it over with. Her mind was tearing through a hundred different thoughts, trying to find a happy one to stave off her growing anxiety. So much so that she lost focus on what was right in front of her.

"Hey," a man said. The voice was deep and even and snapped her out of her own thoughts. She turned her attention to a man standing next to the set of metal detectors that visitors had to pass through to get into the courtroom. Alyssa did a double take.

His Riker County Sheriff's Department uniform and the belt lined with cuffs and a holster for his service weapon gave him away as a courtroom deputy. However, his job designation wasn't what made her mentally hiccup.

The first word that clawed itself out of her mind was *hot*. It was such a quick, unexpected thought that heat began to crawl up her neck.

With a tan complexion that reminded her of caramel, green eyes rimmed with gold, golden hair that looked ripe for twisting with her finger and a jaw that had been chiseled straight from a statue, the deputy wasn't what she'd expected to see in the courthouse. Or in Carpenter. Let alone addressing her directly.

"Excuse me?" she said lamely, hoping he hadn't somehow heard her thoughts.

In turn the deputy didn't seem to be distracted by her looks, to her slight disappointment, but was motioning to her purse with no real enthusiasm. She looked down at it, confused, until he explained.

"I need to look inside it before you can go into the courtroom."

The heat crawling up her neck made its way into her cheeks. She was half-certain she could boil water if you put a pot of it against her skin. It had been a long time since she'd blushed with such intensity, as if she were some schoolgirl.

"Oh yeah, sorry about that." She handed him the purse, fumbling a little in the middle, and watched as he opened and inspected the inside of it.

Alyssa averted her eyes to the doors a few feet from her. The deputy might have been unexpectedly attractive, but one look at those doors and that novelty was being replaced with nerves again.

"Are there a lot of people in there yet?" she asked the lone deputy.

He looked up from her purse, seemingly okay with it, and passed it back to her. He nodded. "More than I thought would show up this early. But I think a lot of them just came for the show."

There was distaste in his words and she agreed with it. Small towns equaled big reactions to anomalous events. Good, bad or otherwise. Plus, somehow the robbery felt intimate to her. An experience no one understood unless it had happened to them. She could understand the loved ones of those who had been inside the bank, but for the people who showed up for the basic need for gossip, she held no love.

Alyssa took her purse back and inhaled a big breath. She started to walk forward but found her feet hesitating.

"Dupree Slater isn't in there yet, right?" she asked just to make sure. The deputy's golden brows drew in together. "He was one of the gunmen."

The man who survived, she wanted to add.

"No. He won't be escorted in until the beginning of the trial."

Alyssa exhaled. At least she had a few more minutes to collect herself before she saw her own personal nightmare in person again.

"Are you a family or friend of his?" the deputy asked. "Of Slater's?"

Alyssa felt her face draw in, eyes narrowing into angry slits, before the heat of anger began to burn beneath her breast. Without giving her mind permission, she thought again of what had happened in the bank. Like a movie scene left on repeat. The spot on her back began to burn in unison with fresh anger, as if it had been lit on fire and she was forced to bear the flames.

No, she didn't want to be associated with Dupree Slater ever. Not as his friend. Not as his family. And most certainly not as his victim. That thought alone put a little more bite into her response than she'd meant.

"I am *not* a part of his family and certainly not his friend," she almost hissed. "I'm here to testify against him."

She didn't wait for the deputy to respond. In fact, she didn't even look for his reaction. Instead she pitched her head up high and marched into the courtroom. Ready to get the Storm Chasers and the damage they'd done out of her life. She wanted to move on and leave that nightmare behind.

No.

She *needed* to.

Chapter Three

Caleb was perplexed. Not a word he often thought about but one that fit the bill as he watched the courtroom doors shut behind the woman. He'd been at the courthouse since it opened, and she had been, by far, the most interesting part of his Monday. And he doubted she even meant to be interesting.

The analytical side of his brain, the skills in reading body language and social interactions that he liked to think he'd honed through his career, had locked on to her expression, trying to read her. To figure her out.

She had run a gauntlet of emotions across her face in the span of less than a minute. Fear, concern, anger, defiance and something he hadn't been able to pin down. A mystery element that snagged his attention. Then, as quickly as she'd shown up, she was gone. In her wake a taste of vulnerability that had intrigued him even more.

Who was she?

And why did he want to know?

"Was that Alyssa?"

Caleb spun around. He was surprised to see an older man dressed in a suit standing so close. Caleb hadn't heard him walk up. Leave it to a beautiful woman to break his focus so quickly. Though, if he was being honest, that hadn't happened in a long time.

It was Caleb's turn to say "Excuse me?"

The man pointed to the doors. "The woman you were just talking to, was it Alyssa Garner?"

"I didn't catch a name," Caleb admitted.

"Oh, I thought you two knew each other. I saw you talking when I walked in."

Caleb wondered why the man cared but still explained. "I asked if she was a family or friend of Slater's, one of the gunmen from the robbery."

It was like something was in the water in Carpenter, Alabama. As soon as the name left Caleb's mouth, the man's expression darkened. Unlike the woman, the man stayed on that emotion. If his skin had been lighter, Caleb would bet it would have been red from it. That was what rage did. Turned you raw. Caleb knew what that looked like—felt like too—and the man was suddenly waist-deep in it.

"You know, she had the same reaction," Caleb had to point out. Again the cop side of his brain was piqued. He wished he'd done more research into the robbery other than reading the newspaper article the sheriff had given him. Then again, it wasn't a necessity for him to research a case he wasn't a part of. Especially since he'd get a recap from the future proceedings.

"You'll find no love for that man in this town. Not after what they did. Not after what *he* did." The man touched a spot on his chest. "You know, his partner, Anna Kim, shot me, and I still hate Dupree more."

Caleb couldn't stop his eyebrow from rising.

"You must be new to town," the man guessed.

Caleb nodded and was given the man's hand in return.

"I'm Robbie," he said. "I was the security guard. A good lot of luck that did anybody. Less than a few seconds after they came in, I was down for the count. After I was shot they let me just lie there in my own blood, ignoring me as if I was some character in a video game or whatnot. They didn't care if I lived or died. And I would've died had

Alyssa there not been as crafty as she was." He pointed at the courtroom doors.

"Crafty?"

"She hid her cell phone until one of the tellers could call 911 and then distracted the gunman on watch by coming to my aid."

Robbie put his hand on his chest again and pushed.

"She kept me from bleeding out and got a front row view when the shooting started. She watched that…that *man* kill two people—two *good* people—in cold blood."

"The paper said they died in the cross fire," Caleb remembered.

Robbie looked disgusted.

"I don't believe that for a second," he said. "Dupree Slater is an evil sumbitch. Pure and simple. He wanted to kill us all and probably regrets he couldn't get the job done."

Caleb didn't know what to say. In his career he'd seen what he thought of as pure evil. Slater, although Caleb knew he was in no way a good man, didn't seem to fit his definition of it. He'd just been a man who'd robbed a bank and gotten in a shoot-out with the cops. He'd been a piss-poor shot and people had died because of it. If anything, his female partner had seemed like the worst of the two. It was common knowledge that the first thing she'd done was shoot the security guard in the chest, which apparently was the man standing in front of Caleb.

Maybe Robbie sensed Caleb's thoughts.

"Not convinced he's evil? You want to know something that they didn't put in the paper? Something that was kept out to try to protect her privacy?" Robbie lowered his voice. A group of people could be seen milling outside the front glass double doors. The residents of Carpenter were downright punctual. Robbie waited until Caleb turned his gaze back to him. When he spoke, there was no denying his anger again. His rage. "When the shooting started, Alyssa Garner threw herself over me—someone who could have been dead any moment—to protect me. She could have run and tried to hide like the others, but no, she covered me up like she was indebted to me. Like I was a good friend or even family. And by some miracle she wasn't hit in the process. But you want to know what happened after they surrendered?"

Caleb might not have known the woman named Alyssa past a minute ago, but he knew he wasn't going to like the answer already.

Robbie nearly bit the words out. "Before anyone could stop him, Dupree Slater walked over to us and shot Alyssa right in the back." He let that sink in. "Now, you tell me. What kind of man does that? What kind of man shoots an unarmed young woman who was just trying to save an old man like me *in the back*?"

"Not a good one," Caleb answered. He was surprised at the anger growing in him. It wasn't a good feeling. Not after what had happened back in Portland. He tried to distance himself from it, but then he pictured the woman who had stood before him only a few minutes beforehand.

Her light auburn hair had been pulled back, showing blue eyes, bright and clear and nice. They'd sized him up and then left him alone, traveling back to see what must have been the memory of Dupree Slater killing people before he'd tried to kill her too. He hadn't been able to see if her smile lit up the rest of her expression. Dupree had stripped her of it simply by her recalling a memory.

Caleb now felt like he needed to apologize to her, which was absurd. He hadn't known her name or what had happened when he asked about the bank robber.

Robbie, seemingly coming down off his emotional high, let out a long exhale. It dragged his body down. His expression softened. He gave Caleb a tired smile.

"You seem like a man who's dealt with bad before," he said, reaching out to pat Caleb on the shoulder.

The contact surprised and unsettled him. Another sentiment he wasn't used to from the general public in Portland.

"But know that just because we're a small community, it doesn't mean we're all good here either. There's bad everywhere. Even in a small place like Carpenter." The man gave another weak smile and then was gone.

Caleb went back to his job. He decided it best to keep his mouth shut as he manned the detector. Instead he tried to catalog everyone who walked into the courtroom with a new perspective. Now he felt a small connection to a case he hadn't even bothered to research. It was irrational to feel involved, or, as his sister would say, maybe it was compassion attaching his thoughts to the woman named Alyssa. He'd never met her before and doubted he'd have a chance to talk to her ever again, but still he felt anger for what had happened to her. That feeling made him question every person who filed into the courtroom and his or her part in the robbery.

So when a man dressed in a suit wearing a pair of horn-rimmed glasses walked toward him and stopped just shy of the metal detector, Caleb was already trying to figure him out.

How did he fit into that day?

Had he been one of the hostages?

Had he known someone on the inside?

Or was he just there to gawk?

"Has it started yet?" the man asked, motioning to the closed doors.

Caleb shook his head. "Not yet."

The man started to turn away.

"You aren't going in?" Caleb asked after him, surprised.

"No, I'm only here to wait for a friend," he said. "I'll do that outside."

The man smiled, adjusted his glasses and was out the front doors in a flash.

Caleb would later pinpoint that smile as the moment he knew something bad was about to happen. But in the present he would try to pretend everything was all right, dismissing the feeling in lieu of doing his job correctly. He'd already almost lost his career because he'd let himself get carried away once. Plus, like he'd told Robbie, he *was* new in town. That man, and his out-of-place smile, could have been one of the nicest locals he'd ever meet. Who was *he* to judge? Especially after what he'd done?

So he'd let his mind swim back to dry land and stood diligently at his post. This was just another job he had to do—and do well—to get back to where he should be. Back in Portland, away from small towns and their problems. Away from everyone knowing your name. Away from the humidity, droves of mosquitoes and copious amounts of sweet tea. He didn't have time for distractions. He needed to focus on the end goal.

But then no sooner had he gotten the thought than the fire alarms started going off.

THE JUDGE WASN'T even in the room before Alyssa and the rest of the courtroom were being ushered outside.

Just when I was getting up my nerve, she thought in the middle of the group. Together they all created a blob of people talking loudly to one another, to the point where even her thoughts became muddled. She tried to look for someone in charge to ask them if it was a false alarm or if the fire was real but couldn't see anyone other than her courtroom companions. At least there was a smiling one among them, looking right at her.

Robbie picked his way through the crowd to stop in front of her.

"It's always something, isn't it?" he greeted, motioning back to the building. The sirens screeched something awful. While Alyssa had been itching to get everything done with, she was at least thankful to be out of that noise. The beginnings of a tension headache were starting to swarm in the back of her head.

She snorted.

"We spent a year waiting for this day," she said. "What's a few more minutes?"

"Your optimism is always refreshing," he said, knowing full well she'd been sarcastic.

She smiled up at him.

In the last year, she'd grown close to Robbie and his wife, Eleanor. She'd made sure they both knew that they owed her nothing in trying to protect Robbie at the bank. Mostly because she hadn't done a thing to actually protect him. With or without her body covering his, he'd still almost died. But then they'd point out that if she hadn't been where she was, Dupree might not have shot her.

"Nowhere in that bank was safe as long as Dupree and Anna were inside," she had often countered.

They would quiet then, remembering Larissa and Carl had been shot too. And nowhere near where Robbie and Alyssa had been.

Still, Alyssa and the Rickmans had grown close through more than any sense of warranted or unwarranted life debt. Which made her feel more comfortable being candid around either of them. She lowered her voice and admitted something she wouldn't have said otherwise.

"I'm a little glad I get a break from seeing Dupree, though. Between the newspapers, the local news channels and the occasional nightmare, I'm tired of seeing him."

Robbie nodded.

"Even Eleanor can't stand to turn the TV on lately. But, like I tell her, this is our last hurdle and then we're done," he said. He reached over and patted her arm. "After this we can all move on and live happy, full lives with a completely rational fear of banks for the rest of those happy, full lives."

Alyssa gave him a smile for his attempt at humor and hoped that was true. Closure for her would be when the Storm Chasers landed behind bars for life, never to hurt her or anyone else ever again.

"Can I have everyone's attention?"

They turned to none other than Judge Anderson, the judge for this case. Her robes moved in the stiff breeze as she descended the entrance stairs and came to a stop in front of the crowd. Another courtroom deputy, an older man Alyssa recognized but couldn't recall his name, stood at her side. Alyssa wondered where the other man was. The golden-haired deputy with the muscled body in no way hiding beneath his uniform.

A little bit of heat started to swirl behind her cheeks at the thought of that muscled body. Why she never met men like him during the everyday routines of her life, she'd never know.

"I wanted to personally tell you all that we'll be taking a recess until this afternoon at one o'clock," she said, her voice carrying clear across the distance. "I am sorry for the inconvenience."

A series of groans erupted through the crowd, followed by the clash of everyone talking at once. Alyssa was one of them.

"Speaking of hurdles," she deadpanned.

Robbie let out a hoot of laughter.

"Why don't we turn that frown upside down and take my beautiful wife out for some coffee and cake?" he said with a pat on her back. "Because I know she probably needs some caffeine considering how late she's running anyways. My treat. What do you say?"

Alyssa felt her lips upturn in a smile.

"You had me at coffee," she said, nodding. "But isn't it a little too early for cake?"

Robbie laughed again. "According to my wife, there's never a wrong time for cake."

Chapter Four

Caleb was pacing. An action he actively tried to avoid doing.

For one, people who paced were *not* in control of their current situation. Hence the nervous movement edged with anxiety and uncertainty. His career—and his personality if he was being frank—had made his desire to be in control, well, desirable. So he wasn't a fan of walking back and forth trying to burn anxious energy. Second, pacing usually meant someone was waiting for *something* to happen, and patience was also not Caleb's strongest suit.

Yet here he was, moving back and forth just inside the entrance of the courthouse on repeat. Burning a hole in the lobby's faded carpet.

It had been three hours since the fire alarm went off. Since there was no fire in the building, or even smoke, Caleb had put his bet on the culprit being a punk kid or a disgruntled attendee. Someone who wanted to break up their day with a little excitement. That is, until he'd seen the alarm that had been pulled.

Smashed beyond recognition. Obliterated. It had been a miracle the sirens had managed to keep blaring after the alarm had been pulled and then destroyed. They'd had to wait for the fire department to shut it all down. One firefighter had whistled low at the broken shell of the alarm and asked what was the point of pulling it *and* breaking it.

Caleb hadn't had an answer. He'd officially gone on

alert, a feeling of foreboding lying heavy in the pit of his stomach. Hours later, that heaviness hadn't gone away. Not when deputies had come over from the sheriff's department next door. Not when they had gone through the entire building, room by room, looking for anything suspicious. And not when the security footage hadn't been helpful, thanks to a gap in the recording, which was due to poor funding.

"It happens sometimes," the other deputy had said with a shrug. "The courthouse isn't the only place in town waiting on funding to come through to get a better system."

"Sounds like an excuse," Caleb said beneath his breath. The deputy hadn't heard him, and he wanted to keep it that way.

Again, he didn't know how Carpenter, or Riker County, truly worked. He didn't know their struggles or their points of pride. Jumping to conclusions about a broken fire alarm at an underfunded courthouse wasn't something he needed to do. He certainly didn't need to overstep his job description by trying to investigate a situation that probably wasn't anything more than someone caught in the heat of the moment and deciding to break something.

At that thought, Caleb's body went cold.

His hands balled into fists.

His thoughts turned tumultuous in a fraction of a second. Memories of what he'd done flew through his head.

"Foster! Stop! Dammit, Foster! STOP!"

But Caleb hadn't stopped.

And now he was in Riker County because of it.

He began to pace again.

ALYSSA WAVED GOODBYE to Robbie and Eleanor. They drove away from the courthouse in Robbie's little red pickup, both smiling as they disappeared down the street. Alyssa couldn't help but smile too. There was nothing like spending a few hours at Danny's—a local café with the best cake, according to Eleanor—with the couple to get her back into a good mood. Them laughing and smiling at each other had been contagious. Being with them always reminded Alyssa she was missing something they had been lucky enough to find. A partner. A best friend. Someone who would buy her morning cake without flinching.

Being that close to such a strong couple brought out a sense of peace in her too. Like the sight of calm waters after looking over the edge of your boat.

It had helped that, despite it being the day of the trial, they had sidestepped any talk of the Storm Chasers. It was a groove that had become familiar with them over the last year. A rhythm that had become second nature. They talked about happier topics, even mundane ones. Anything that filled the time.

But now Alyssa was back, staring at the front of the courthouse.

How she wished she could go inside, tell the jury what she'd seen and then watch as Dupree and Anna were led away in cuffs. Forever.

Alyssa let out a long sigh. She still had a few hours to go before she could get her wish.

"I might as well go soak in a bath," she muttered to herself. If there was ever an answer to quell unwanted anxiety, a quiet, citrus-scented bath had to be at the top of the to-do list. She had started to walk around the building, mind already made up, when the sound of footsteps sounded behind her.

"Excuse me!"

Alyssa turned to see a man jogging toward her. He was brandishing a set of keys.

"You dropped these," he explained, motioning to where she'd been standing when she was dropped off.

"Really?" Even though they were clearly hers—the

wineglass pendant Gabby had given her was glinting in the sunlight—Alyssa still opened her purse to look inside and confirm they weren't there. "Wow. I don't know how I did that. I could've sworn they were buried in my purse."

The man pushed his glasses up his nose. Alyssa mimicked the motion on reflex. Gabby always made fun of her for the "nerd" move, but when Alyssa was around her own glasses-wearing kind, she was happy for the little inclusion.

"You must have been thinking of other things," he offered. "This Storm Chasers business has a lot of people around here distracted."

Alyssa took her keys and tried on a polite smile. Though she didn't like the way the man had said "here," she agreed with him.

"Yes, it definitely has the attention of the entire community. It'll be nice when it's all over." She jingled her keys, wanting to end the conversation. "Thank you for being less distracted than me."

The man grinned.

"No problem," he said. "Have a nice day."

The way he said the last part, just like the word *here*, was so odd that it caught Alyssa a little off guard. She hesitated a few seconds too long. His smile wavered.

"Thanks again." She tried to recover, heat exploding into her cheeks. She turned away and hurried to her car. When had she dropped her keys? And how?

She tried to mentally retrace her actions, and none of them included her opening her purse, let alone taking her keys out.

"Maybe I *am* way more stressed than I originally thought," she mumbled, unlocking her door with the key fob. The day was hot and twinged with growing humidity. She held the unlock button down a few seconds longer. The front windows rolled down in response. She waited a moment, still trying to puzzle out the question of her keys leaving her possession, as a wave of heat poured out. It pressed against her skin with a maliciousness she'd come to expect from Alabama summers.

And here she was, about to go get into a hot bath. She sighed, wondering how that made sense, and tossed her purse into the passenger's seat. She smoothed down the back of her pencil skirt and plopped down into the driver's seat.

Click.

Alyssa paused, confused.

Click.

"What?" she muttered, trying to find the source of the noise. Last time she checked, her car had never *clicked* before. "I swear if it's the AC crapping out…"

Alyssa didn't have to look far. "Oh my God."

CALEB'S PACING GAVE him a front row view of the woman named Alyssa Garner. He watched as Robbie and, presumably, his wife had dropped her off and then watched as she had started for the parking lot.

For a moment she had seemed happy, lighter than she had been that morning. Almost carefree. Her head was tilted up, lips in the same direction, and her shoulders were relaxed. At some point, wherever she'd gone, she'd even let her hair down. It cascaded over her shoulders and back, shining in the sun, more red than brown as it had looked inside. He wondered how she looked without her trendy black pair of frames on. Either way, he couldn't deny that he found her attractive.

Alyssa seemed to be a quiet woman with an equally quiet beauty.

But Caleb now wondered if that was true…especially after what she'd done at the bank.

That anger that had startled him before began to rise in his chest again just thinking about the man Dupree Slater.

Caleb wondered if she had a scar from him.

Surprised again, he caught his thoughts before they became even darker.

He didn't know Alyssa. At least not personally. He hadn't even known she existed until that morning. He wasn't close to her or, in fact, to anyone in Carpenter or Riker County. Having feelings for her like he was didn't make sense. And wasn't wanted.

You won't be here long, he thought, resolute. *Keep your head down, follow orders, and then you're back home.*

Caleb had started to turn away from the glass doors, giving Alyssa some privacy and his thoughts a firm shake away from her, when movement stilled his motion. A man ran up to her. He gave Alyssa something, but from Caleb's angle he couldn't see what it was. Or what the man looked like.

Could be a friend, he reasoned. *Or a boyfriend.*

No sooner had he thought that than he dismissed it. While he couldn't see the man's expression, he watched as Alyssa's changed. Her brow furrowed and she frowned. Then she was smiling, but in a flash that smile fell away.

She was confused or unhappy. He couldn't tell which, but it was enough to keep him watching as she left the man's side and went to her car.

The man watched her go. He must have known her, Caleb thought. Why else would he just stand there watching?

Maybe he was admiring her too?

Either way, Caleb didn't like it.

He left his post and stepped out into the heat. The humidity was suffocating. It amazed him that it still caught him off guard. And that people chose to live in it.

"Excuse me?" Caleb called out.

The man didn't move.

Caleb's gut started to talk.

And he didn't like what it was trying to say.

"Hey," he tried again, taking a few steps forward and giving the man the benefit of the doubt. Maybe he hadn't heard him. "Hey, buddy!"

The man, now a few yards away, turned around. It was a slow, lazy movement. He didn't seem surprised at a slightly agitated court deputy's appearance, but the same couldn't be said for Caleb.

"You."

The man with the horn-rimmed glasses grinned. "Hello, Deputy. How can I help you?"

Caleb hung back at the bottom of the stairs. His gut was full-out yelling now. It prompted him to *really* look at the man.

Over six feet and thin, the man wore glasses, but they had the opposite effect that Alyssa's had on her. Instead of giving the impression that he might be on the quiet side, they turned his sharp facial features and thinness into an overall look of aggression. The descriptor popped into Caleb's head so fast he realized he'd already had the thought the first time he saw the man. It didn't help that his body was seemingly speaking an entirely different language with how he was dressed—slacks, a dark red vest and dress shoes—and where he was.

He was comfortable *and* anxious. While he greeted Caleb with a grin, Caleb noticed one of his hands against his thighs, his fingers tapping out a rhythm. A nervous tic. An anxious activity like pacing but more controlled.

"What are you doing out here?" Caleb asked, acutely aware of the space between them. "Are you still waiting for your friend?"

The man's grin widened.

"You're good with faces," he said. "I didn't think you'd remember mine. But no, I've already seen my friend." He glanced toward the parking lot and then back to Caleb. "I'm on my way now. Have a good day, Deputy."

He didn't wait for a response. Putting both hands in his pockets, he moved away from Caleb to the sidewalk in front of the courthouse. Caleb thought about following him and demanding his name at the very least, but then his gut was twisting again.

He turned back to the parking lot.

Something felt off.

Alyssa's outline could be seen in her car in the middle of the visitors' lot, but she hadn't started it yet. Why she hadn't at least turned the ignition just to get the AC going, Caleb didn't know. Maybe Alabamians were made with more heat resistance than he was.

Still, the lot wasn't in the shade and the sun wasn't being kind. It beat down on the little Honda like it had been doing all morning.

The inside had to be hot as hell.

Caleb took a moment to debate whether or not he should check on her. Maybe she was having issues with her car. Or maybe the man with the glasses had said something that upset her. Maybe it wasn't any of his business either way.

Caleb adjusted his belt and turned back toward the courthouse.

Keep your head low, he reminded himself. *It isn't your place.*

Halfway up the stairs, his feet stalled.

No, it was going to be impossible to keep his head low when his gut was telling him to do otherwise.

IT WAS *SO* HOT.

Alyssa's muscles were straining to not move while sweat began to roll down her skin without any such constraints. While the windows were down, no breeze moved throughout the car. Her only company was a stifling, unforgiving blanket of wet heat. It was turning her situation into more of a nightmare. The hammering of her heart hadn't broken the silence, but that didn't mean it wasn't beating against her chest in terror.

Sure, there was a chance she was overreacting. *Paranoia*. But what if she wasn't?

She tried to take in another deep breath to help tamp down her nerves.

It didn't help.

Especially not when someone approached the open window.

"Excuse me?"

Alyssa let out a shriek and gave a small jump in her seat. It was enough movement to make her adrenaline surge higher.

"Sorry, I didn't mean to startle you," the man said.

Alyssa allowed herself just enough movement to look at the stranger. Although he wasn't just any man. The golden-haired deputy was staring back at her. She found his eyes, the perfect middle ground between golden and green, and felt genuine relief at his presence. However, she guessed her expression said something else entirely. His light brows drew together so quickly that she knew *he* knew something was wrong. "Are you okay?" he asked, voice ringing with authority.

Alyssa took a deep, wavering breath. "Have you seen the *Lethal Weapon* movies? You know, with Mel Gibson and Danny Glover as cops?" she asked.

The deputy raised an eyebrow but nodded. "Yeah…"

"Well, you know the one where Danny Glover's character is sitting on the toilet?"

"Yeah, that's the second movie," he said. "When he realizes there's a bomb strapped to it. Why?"

A chill ran up Alyssa's spine at that four-letter word.

"Well, this is probably going to sound ridiculous," she started, "but I think there's a bomb under my seat."

Chapter Five

The deputy squatted down on the other side of the door so that his gaze was level with hers. Under any other circumstances she probably would have been distracted by the proximity, but right now her mind kept going to what might or might not be beneath her seat.

"You're going to have to elaborate on that one for me."

Alyssa licked her lips. They were already drying out despite her lipstick.

"Okay, so when I sat down I heard something click," she started. "I hadn't turned the car on yet, so it confused me. Then I heard two more clicks and actually *felt* those coming from under me. Under my seat. And then I saw the light."

"The light?"

Alyssa moved her head to try to motion to the floorboard. She still wasn't about to move the rest of her body if she could help it. Her hands were on her lap, fused together with sweat and nerves. In the movie, once Danny Glover's character had gotten off the toilet it had exploded. And she was *not* about to blow up in a Honda.

"I can see the reflection of a red light blinking on the floorboard," she answered. "It's faint but it's there. And it hasn't stopped blinking."

The deputy didn't ask for permission, not that she was going to begrudge him for the invasion anyway, and moved his head in through the window to look toward her feet. Alyssa caught a whiff of either shampoo or body wash that smelled intoxicating as he moved into her personal space. Some kind of musk and spice infusion. Something she definitely shouldn't be distracted by at the moment.

"I know I could be overreacting, but I guess I've just seen so many movies and TV shows where clicks and flashing lights equals bombs," she admitted. The fear that had tensed her every muscle was now starting to feel a little silly. "And if it isn't a bomb, which it *probably* isn't, I'll just be mortified for life."

The man pulled out of the space and back into a squat next to the door. His expression gave nothing away.

"Can I open your door?" he asked, voice even.

Silly thought or not, the request scared Alyssa.

"If there's a bomb under your seat, opening the door shouldn't trigger it," he added.

"But if it does?" she couldn't help asking. A drop of sweat rolled down the side of her face. It was *so* hot.

The deputy's expression stayed neutral when he answered.

"Then, I promise you, we won't know the difference."

Alyssa felt her eyes widen.

"I don't know if I'm happy with that logic."

The man didn't apologize for it.

"I won't do it if you don't want me to," he said. "I just need to take a closer look."

Alyssa chewed on her lip but nodded.

"What's your name?" she tacked on. The man raised his eyebrow. "Just in case we do blow up."

"Caleb Foster."

"I'm Alyssa Garner," she introduced. "I would shake your hand, but I'm terrified that if I move I'll— Well, you know…"

Caleb flashed a smile. It didn't last long.

"Then let me do the moving for now," he said. Alyssa watched as his attention focused on the car door's handle. Her muscles tensed further.

Please don't let us blow up in my Honda.

But nothing went *kaboom* when the deputy opened the door wide.

Alyssa let out a breath she didn't know she'd been holding.

"Okay, well, if it's a bomb it's not connected to the door," he pointed out. He moved closer to inspect the space between the seat and him. "I can't see anything here." He met her gaze. "I'm going to try to look under your seat now, okay?"

Alyssa nodded, even though she was already trying to do the logistics of that in her head. She was on the shorter side and had her seat closer to the dash because of it. Which meant Caleb Foster was about to get really close to her.

He dropped to his knees on the concrete, braced himself with one hand on the inside of the door and then very slowly hunched over so that his head was near the floorboard. Alyssa felt his breath against her bare legs as he moved between them to get a better view.

The most irrational fear that she'd missed a spot while shaving flitted through her head. When Caleb popped back up after only a few seconds, she wondered if she really had. His expression was the definition of neutral.

"So, was I being ridiculous?" she asked, hopeful.

But that ray-of-sunshine feeling lasted only an instant.

Deputy Foster pulled out his phone, but he took a moment to look directly into her eyes.

"I need you to keep doing what you're doing a little longer, okay?" he said, tone calm.

"You want me to keep sitting still," Alyssa spelled out, just to make sure they were on the same page.

Deputy Foster nodded.

Before she could stop it, her breathing went off the rails. It was one thing to think there was a bomb beneath your seat while also thinking you were being a bit insane. It was another for a man of the law to tell you to keep sitting perfectly still.

It was real now.

"So there *is* a bomb under my seat?" she asked around two short breaths.

"There's something under your seat, yes," he hedged.

"But is it a bomb?"

"I don't know for sure, but—"

Alyssa sucked in a breath and had the deepest urge to grab the man by the collar of his shirt. "You answer me right now, Deputy Foster. Do you think there's a bomb beneath my seat or not?"

He seemed surprised by her outburst, but who could blame her?

This time the deputy didn't hedge.

"Yes," he said. "I do. Which is why I need you to keep calm until we can deal with this. Okay?"

Despite his answer Alyssa decided to panic. Or, at least, her body did. The heavy air in the car, the heat of the day and the sheer thought of having survived a gunshot to the back only to be blown up in a parking lot were all too much to take. Her heartbeat wasn't just galloping anymore—it was full-out trying to exceed the speed of light. Its pursuit was having a chain reaction on what was left of her calm. Her breathing was no longer erratic. It was rushed, clumsy and impossible to conquer. It was starting to make her vision blur.

The urge to swipe her glasses off and completely freak was escalating. She wanted to try to scramble out of the car and escape the heat and fear that were tripling at an alarming rate. If the deputy hadn't been between Alyssa and the door, she might have attempted an escape plan.

But the deputy *was* there.

And his eyes were enough to hold her in place long enough for his words to reach her.

"Alyssa," he said, moving as close to her as he could without making contact. "From what I've heard, you've handled a lot worse than this." His lips quirked up into a grin. "All you have to do right now is sit still, okay? You think you can handle just sitting?"

The way he said the last part, like he was looking down on her for her worry, made something snap within her. Like he was the parent and she was a child who was being ridiculous. She took a deep breath, exhaled and took another one before she answered.

"Yes, *Deputy*," she said with a little too much attitude. "I think I can handle it."

Deputy Foster's grin grew.

It made her feel better. If only for a moment.

"I'm going to take a few pictures and then I'm going to make a lot of calls," he said.

"You aren't going to leave, are you?" she asked, already panicked at the thought.

The deputy shook his head. "I want you to know one thing for certain, Miss Garner. I *will not* leave you."

Alyssa hadn't realized how good that promise would sound.

But, boy, did it sound good!

THIRTY MINUTES.

That was all it took for all hell to break loose.

True to his word, the deputy had made several phone calls after he snapped a picture of the *maybe-but-probably* bomb. He'd done it far enough from the car so that she couldn't hear what was said—no doubt, his intention—but not far enough that Alyssa felt alone. Because, also true to his word, he didn't leave her.

Not even when the bomb squad showed up and confirmed the *maybe-but-probably* bomb was in fact a *probably-and-definitely* bomb. Though the head of the squad, a towering man named Charlie, encouraged the deputy to clear the area while they assessed options.

Options.

That was a word that might have brought Alyssa a sense of hope, or even fear, if she wasn't baking alive. The day had gone from hot to hell and she was stuck in a vacuum of it. She no longer had the energy to panic. All of that had left her body in waves of sweat, adhering every article of clothing she was wearing to her like a second skin.

And yet the deputy kept coming back.

Along with Charlie, who was now suited up with a helmet and clear mask in front of his face to boot. He lifted it to address Alyssa directly.

"Miss Garner, how are you doing?"

"I'm okay," she lied.

Deputy Foster raised his eyebrow.

"Alyssa, how are you doing?" he repeated with a tone that reminded her of a parent. She managed a defeated sigh.

"I think I might pass out soon," she admitted. "It's getting really hard to breathe."

If this alarmed the deputy, he didn't show it. In fact, neither man did. Which meant she probably looked as bad as she felt and they had been expecting it. The cold water she'd had through a straw hadn't been enough. Just like the fan that had been set up next to the car. It had only pushed the heat toward her. In no way did it alleviate the temperature she was currently suffering through.

"Then why don't we get you out of here?" Charlie said.

"That would be nice," she responded. Picturing a bathtub filled with ice cubes with her name on it. Forget about citrus bath salts.

A man she didn't recognize walked up to the car and cleared his throat.

"Can I have a moment, sir?" he asked Charlie.

He nodded, flashed a quick smile to Alyssa and then walked off. Again, she couldn't hear what was discussed, but the movement brought attention to the far end of the parking lot. It was being cleared. The staff from the courthouse, and even some people from the sheriff's department next door, were moving farther away.

Alyssa looked back at Deputy Foster. She realized he was wearing a bomb vest. "So, do they think they can really get me out of here?"

The deputy followed her gaze to his vest. He straightened it and then lowered himself to meet her stare head-on.

"I'll be honest with you," he started. "I don't know them personally, but the sheriff and Captain Jones both say Charlie and his team are the best in the South." He cut another grin. "And they think they're going to get you out of this with all limbs attached, so I'm going to bet on a yes."

Alyssa gave the smallest of nods. Her vision was starting to blur a little. She tried to pull in a calming breath. The air was so wet she felt like she was drowning.

"Hey, listen to me," he continued, tone tough. Stern. "When they get you out of here, how about I take you out for a nice jug of sweet tea? That's something you guys seem to like around here, right? Sweet tea?"

Despite everything, Alyssa snorted.

"You must be from up north," she muttered, each word strained.

She watched as his look of concern seemed to grow. Then, altogether, he began to blur.

"Alyssa," he said, voice raised. "All you have to do is sit still. You got that?"

"I'm trying," she defended. To her own ears she sounded breathless. And not in that sexy Scarlett O'Hara way.

Charlie swam back into view a few seconds later. His mask was down now. He turned to the deputy. "I guess if your captain *and* sheriff can't make you leave, then I shouldn't try either."

The deputy shook his head. At least, that was what Alyssa thought he did. Either way, when Charlie was addressing her, Deputy Foster was still there.

It was comforting.

"Okay, Miss Garner, I'm going to very slowly try to replace your weight with this metal plate," he said, already going into the back seat, the only way to reach the bomb. Which made her a little happier, considering she didn't think her floorboard could accommodate the big man like it had the deputy. "When we've done that successfully, then Deputy Foster here will take you somewhere much cooler."

"O-Okay."

The world around her was becoming one giant blur. Alyssa wanted to watch what Charlie was doing. She wanted to ask questions. She wanted to tell Deputy Foster to go where it was safe. But the fact of the matter was, Alyssa was putting all the energy she had left into not passing out.

CALEB WAS SWEATING BULLETS.

He split his focus between Charlie trying to fool the bomb by thinking Alyssa was still sitting on top of it and the woman herself. Since the water and fan hadn't worked, she'd spent almost forty-five minutes being drained, and now he wasn't sure if she'd make it past another minute.

Her head was leaning back against the headrest, and her eyelids seemed to be fighting gravity. Caleb wanted to touch her, to remind her he was there, but he couldn't.

Not just because of the bomb. While he was starting to get an idea of her character, she still had no idea about his.

And he wanted to keep it that way.

"Okay. Here we go. Get ready to grab her," Charlie commanded. "I think I've— What the hell?"

Alyssa must have really been out of it. She didn't look alarmed in the slightest at the sharp tone the man trying to disarm the bomb beneath her took on.

But Caleb did. "What's go—"

Click.

"Damn," Charlie interrupted. "Grab her!"

Click. Click.

"Grab her now," Charlie yelled again, struggling out of the back seat in his uniform.

Caleb didn't have to be told a third time.

He threaded his arms beneath Alyssa's legs and back and hoisted her out in one quick move.

Click.

Charlie was already yelling, "Now run!"

Caleb tucked Alyssa against his chest and ran faster than he'd ever run before.

"Eight seconds," Charlie yelled out to anyone who could hear.

Like ants in the rain, everyone in front of or behind the blocked-off perimeter of the parking lot scurried this way and that, trying to get as far away as they could. The crowd that had formed was yelling while deputies and bomb squad alike were barking orders to each other and bystanders.

Two members of the squad in particular stood out. Instead of running away from the car, they were running toward Caleb, Alyssa and Charlie with two dark blankets. When the five of them finally collided, Charlie yelled to hit the ground.

Caleb dove onto his side so he would take the brunt of

the fall, and then just as quickly rolled over to cover the woman in his arms. The bomb squad men positioned themselves on either side of Charlie and Caleb and threw the blankets—which Caleb now realized were bomb blankets, made from layers of Kevlar—over each of them.

Caleb felt like he was being pulled every which way in the moments that followed. What-ifs sprang up in his mind like flowers in the spring—What if they hadn't cleared the blast area? What if the bomb blanket didn't help them? What if he never got to take Alyssa out for that drink of sweet tea he'd offered?—while his body seemed to be running on instinct. It created a cage around the woman, trying to make itself as big as possible to protect her at all costs. But then another part of him, one he didn't know where it was coming from, was looking down at her face—slack from the unconsciousness she finally had given in to—and thinking how beautiful she was. But then everyone was yelling and he remembered to fear what was about to happen.

Not for himself, but for Alyssa.

Chapter Six

They waited.

And waited.

And waited.

No explosion rocked the ground, filled the air or even disrupted the birds chirping in the distance. Caleb chanced a look over to Charlie, who gave him nothing less than a similar expression of confusion.

"When I slid the plate in, a counter slid out for ten seconds," he defended. "It started to count down instantly. It should have gone off by now."

Cautiously both men stood, Caleb scooping Alyssa back up and putting her firmly against his chest. "I'm getting her out of here."

Charlie didn't stop him and ordered one of the bomb squad with the bomb blankets to follow until they made it past the barricade.

"Thanks, man," Caleb made sure to say. The man nodded.

"No problem," he answered. "It's my job."

The simple statement was all it took to remind Caleb of his own job. If he still had one. As if he'd been summoned, Captain Jones was at their side.

"I told the EMTs to stay farther back, just in case," he hurried, pointing out the ambulance on the other side of the street. There was a news van a few yards from it, despite the blocks that had been put between them. A cameraman and a woman wielding a microphone were standing tall and ready. "Let me take care of them. You follow—"

Both men paused as a foreign sound filled the air.

"Is that—" the captain started, turning around to look in the direction of Alyssa's car. Caleb did the same. "—music?" he finished.

The world quieted around them. Bystanders, deputies and bomb squad alike became silent and listened. There was no mistaking it. Coming from the abandoned Honda wasn't fire and smoke but music.

A piano solo.

What was going on?

Alyssa stirred in Caleb's arms. It brought him out of his moment of wonder. "Time to get you out of here."

ALYSSA WISHED SHE'D worn a nicer bra. The one she had on now was off-beige, comfortable, did its job and was *not* supposed to be seen by anyone other than herself. Her panties—black, not beige, also comfortable and just as capable of doing their job—were on the same list of Things That Were Very Private. And yet, looking down at herself, there they were. Open to the hospital room around her just as they had been open to the EMTs who had deemed it necessary to strip her down in the ambulance.

Sure, they were trying to bring her core temperature down as quickly as possible to save her brain cells from dying off and, well, her dying off too. Yet there she was, all brain cells intact, remembering that it hadn't just been her and the EMTs in the ambulance.

Deputy Caleb Foster had been there too.

Fresh heat crawled up Alyssa's neck and into her cheeks. No one would count it as embarrassment, seeing as how she'd spent the last half hour being treated for heat stroke. Still, when someone knocked on the door, she tried to mentally restrain the blush.

"Hello?" a woman called. "My name is Cassie Gates. I'm from the sheriff's department. May I come in?"

The name was familiar to Alyssa, but she couldn't quite place how.

"You may," she responded, grabbing the thin sheet and holding it loosely over her body. Part of her treatment had allowed her to stay in her own undergarments but nothing else, minus several ice packs strategically placed against her skin. Which was a big reason Deputy Foster had excused himself. Though, she realized later, that was only after the doctor had said they believed she'd be fine.

A blond-haired woman around Alyssa's age came in and shut the door behind her. She was dressed in a pale pink blouse, khaki skirt and sandals. Not what Alyssa expected when she'd said "sheriff's department."

"I hope I'm not intruding too much," she greeted, coming forward with her hand outstretched. "They told me you were a bit indisposed until your temperature was back to normal."

"No, it's fine," Alyssa assured her, shaking. She motioned to a chair next to the bed. "There's already been quite a few people who have seen me today. I'll take good health over modesty any day."

The woman smiled and took a seat. The movement shifted some of her hair to the side. In the middle of her neck was a nasty, circular scar. Alyssa brought her eyes back up to Cassie's in a flash. She hoped her stray in attention wasn't noticed.

"So, you're from the sheriff's department?"

Cassie nodded. If she noticed Alyssa noticing the scar, she didn't comment on it.

"I'm one of the dispatchers," she explained. "Currently working night shift."

Alyssa still didn't understand why a dispatcher with the sheriff's department had come to see her.

"And you're probably wondering why I of all people am here right now," Cassie added with a laugh.

Alyssa joined in.

"Not to be rude, but yes, I was wondering that a little," she admitted.

"I don't blame you," Cassie assured her. She moved to the edge of her seat and clasped her hands across her lap. "I'm actually here because of several different reasons, the first being I'm a woman and Captain Jones thought it would be more appropriate if I was the one to check in with you." She held up her hand to stop whatever comment Alyssa had. "While there are several women throughout our department, I think he *actually* chose me because I was in your position somewhat last year." She moved her hand up to motion to the scar on her neck. "I think he wants you to be able to talk to someone who knows what it's like to be going about your day and then in a flash everything changes."

It finally clicked for Alyssa.

"The man who shot inside the department last year," she remembered. That story had been on all the news outlets for weeks after it happened, including the woman who had been shot in the neck. It had been because of a case the sheriff had been working then. Though the rest of the details were harder to recall.

"When I woke up that morning, I didn't imagine I'd be taking a bullet," Cassie confirmed. "Which is why I think Captain Jones thought of me to check on you."

"Because, not only did I not plan on sitting on a bomb today, I also didn't plan on taking a bullet last year either," Alyssa guessed.

Cassie nodded. "I may not be a therapist, but I am a fellow trauma survivor." She cut a grin. "I'm relatable!"

Alyssa couldn't help laughing. It felt good. She eased the sheet off her, no longer worried about the other woman seeing her exposed skin. "So you're here to see if I'm coping with everything that's happened?" she asked when both had sobered.

Cassie nodded. "Basically."

Alyssa had already spent her slight isolation in the last half hour wondering about that same thing. One person could only take so much, but she'd come to the conclusion that she wasn't at her breaking point. Not yet, at least.

"I'm doing okay," she answered. "I'm more confused than anything. I don't understand who would put a bomb in my car or why. Especially one that just played music, like Deputy Foster said. What's the point?"

Cassie shrugged.

"Some people don't think like we'd expect them to, but I assure you the sheriff's department will get to the bottom of the who at the very least." Cassie held up her index finger. "Which brings me to another bit of business. Sheriff Reed along with Chief Deputy Simmons wanted me to express their deepest apologies that they aren't here in person to help with the investigation. They are working another investigation that has become hard to break away from. But the sheriff wanted to assure you—and I do too—that Captain Jones and the rest of the department are more than capable."

Alyssa felt better at the sheriff's words, even if they were funneling through someone else. She had been one of the many residents of Riker County who had elected him to office. She was also a closet fan of his wife's because of the fund-raising event she and her business partner had put together to help the victims' families in the wake of the bank robbery. The couple's kindness, as well as the department's, had shone through during a dark time in the community. Alyssa trusted them, even if some of them weren't actually in town.

"Thank you," she said. "I just want the trial to be over and everything to go back to normal."

"It will," Cassie promised. She started to stand. Her demeanor flipped. Her smile turned mischievous. "Now, before I go to work, I wanted to give you a little advice." She walked closer and lowered her voice. Alyssa leaned in, curious. The ice pack on her stomach shifted. "Ask specifically for Deputy Foster to take you home when the time comes. If you want to help him out, that is."

Another thought Alyssa wouldn't share with the woman was how she'd already decided it would be his help she asked for. Considering that he had risked being blown up to save her, she wanted the chance to truly thank him. So far she hadn't gotten any alone time with him since she'd been brought in. Still, she wondered why Cassie had brought it up. "Why does he need help?"

Cassie's playful mood depleted. Her smile disappeared.

"He's new and not the easiest man to work with," she said. "His position wasn't helped when he defied several direct orders today."

"He defied direct orders?"

"To leave you and let the professionals handle the dismantling themselves," she answered, apologetic. "It sounds harsh, but it's protocol. And, well, that's not the first time he's overstepped his duties during his career."

Cassie's eyes widened and her face flushed. Alyssa had a feeling she hadn't meant to say as much as she had.

"Either way, I thought that maybe you asking for him specifically would remind everyone else that there are exceptions, even to protocol."

Her smile was back. She did a little nod to Alyssa and started to leave.

"Hey, Cassie," Alyssa called. The woman turned, face open and still smiling. "Getting shot…" Alyssa paused while she looked for the words she hadn't realized she needed to say, to relate with someone else. The spot on her back felt like it was burning again. Finally she settled on simple. "It sure does suck, doesn't it?"

Cassie didn't miss a beat. "It sure does."

"THEY'RE SAYING IT was a joke."

Caleb looked up from his chair and at the water bottle Deputy Dante Mills had outstretched.

Caleb was mad. "Then whoever *they* is has one hell of a sense of humor."

Dante shook the bottle again. Caleb finally took it. He'd already downed a few since they'd come to the hospital.

"I'm not arguing with that."

He quieted as Caleb took a drink. He'd noticed that Dante had often given him time to let his thoughts, and mood, settle while they were patrolling together. It was a much different situation than what he'd dealt with on the force in Portland. While he never had just one partner, it seemed that everyone he did get matched up with fought to keep the conversation going. Even when it was clear he didn't want it to. Either way, he was usually grateful for the quiet.

However, at the moment, it wasn't helping calm him down. Not after the morning he'd had.

"No one thinks that it's connected to the Storm Chasers' trial?" Caleb snapped. "I mean, it's one hell of a coincidence it happens after the fire alarm was destroyed. Which we conveniently don't have any security camera footage for, I might add."

"The last I heard, Captain Jones and Police Chief Hawser were discussing the possibility of a connection, but there's not enough to go on yet to make any real claim."

"Other than 'some people' think it's a joke," Caleb deadpanned.

Dante held his hands up in defense.

"Hey, man, I'm just telling you what people are thinking," he said. "You're not the most loved guy around here—seemingly of your own choosing, which is fine, you do you—so I'm trying to keep you in the loop here."

Caleb wanted to retaliate with a barrage of "you don't know me" and "I don't need your help or pity" sentiments, but for once, he let it lie. Because Dante wasn't exactly wrong. Instead the deputy's words rolled into a silence that he waited a few moments to break.

"Listen, I just wanted you to know what's going on," Dante continued. "And not just because I know you a little bit better than the rest of the department, but because of what you did today. Took guts."

At this, Caleb snorted.

"I don't think the captain or sheriff appreciate my 'guts,'" he mused. He'd been on the receiving end of some heated words from Captain Jones for disobeying a direct order.

Dante nudged Caleb's shoulder. "Well, I know one person who does."

Caleb followed his gaze down the hall behind him.

Captain Jones had his head bent and his brow pulled together as he talked and walked along with a woman.

Caleb wasn't sure what reaction he'd expected to feel when he saw Alyssa again, but whatever he was currently feeling he couldn't quite place. Even when she brought those startlingly blue eyes up to meet his.

However, that feeling went away when Captain Jones swung his stare toward him.

"Ruh roh," Dante said beneath his breath. They both stood tall and ready. Before Alyssa or Jones could reach them, Dante added an afterthought. "Remember to be nice," he whispered.

"Good to see you up and moving around." Dante greeted Alyssa before the captain could get his, no doubt, hit in at Caleb.

"Thanks," Alyssa said with a smile. It was amazing how much better she looked from earlier that day. Then again, the AC in the hospital was no joke. The silver lining, at least, to having to be there at all. "I still would love to shower and get some fresh clothes, but I'm not going to complain, since it could have been worse."

Her eyes flashed to Caleb's. He kept quiet. Jones did not.

"Which brings me to the what-happens-next," he began. "I've told Miss Garner here that the bomb squad has finished its search of her residence and come up empty. Still, I'd like to keep a law enforcement presence around her until we can find this man with the glasses you both have described or another lead."

Caleb felt his jaw tighten. He wanted to volunteer, but seeing as how his last conversation with Jones had gone, he was sure that he would only dig his proverbial grave deeper with the man.

"Miss Garner has agreed to this suggestion, and—" Jones took a noticeable pause to draw in a deep breath. Frustration. "—has requested that that deputy be you, Mr. Foster."

"If that's okay," she hurried to add. "You've already done more than enough, thinking you were risking your life to keep me, a stranger, company." Her eyes flickered over to the captain. "It was brave and selfless."

The captain gave a tight nod. His smile was tighter. A muscle twitched at his jaw. Caleb felt his eyebrow rise. Was she pleading his case in a not-so-subtle way to the captain?

"It was no problem," Caleb assured her. "And if it's okay with the captain, then that's fine by me."

Captain Jones brandished a forced smile. "Who am I to bench such a brave and selfless man?"

Chapter Seven

"I think my love for cars is now forever tainted."

Alyssa gave Caleb what she hoped was a humorous expression, not one that reflected the anxiety that had begun to well up inside her at the mere sight of his car.

"Or at least the seats," she added with a little laugh. Just beneath her surface, her already tired muscles were tensed.

Her car might not have been the most reliable vehicle—it was over a decade old and had the rust and wear to prove it—but at the end of the day it was hers. To have someone go plant a bomb, fake or not, inside it felt a little too intimate. She had, admittedly, felt upset when Captain Jones told her it had been transported to a different site where CSI and bomb squad could take a better look at it. Captain Jones assured her she'd get it back in a day, two tops. Still, with nerves twirling in her stomach like a majorette's baton, she knew her days of carelessly sliding into any car would be met with a good dollop of anxiety. Her car especially.

And she hated that.

Caleb settled in behind the wheel and looked through the opened door out at her. He motioned to the passenger's seat, unflinching. "Don't worry. When I came down to turn the AC on while you were talking to the captain, I made sure to look beneath all the seats. No bombs, real or otherwise, in this car. I promise."

She kept her fake smile in place and covertly let out an exhale of relief. Soon she was buckled in and they were pulling away from the hospital. The trip had been another unwelcome surprise to a day she'd never expected to live through.

Alyssa was glad to see the hospital move to their rearview as they drove toward her house. With close to no interaction with him, she pointed out which streets the deputy needed to take. The lunch traffic was tapering off, but it was still congested in some parts and slowed their progress. The quiet that had taken over the car intensified. It made her uncomfortable. Or, rather, the time it gave her to think did. By the time they hit the intersection that guided them toward her neighborhood and had to wait through two more lights, Alyssa was nearly out of her mind. So she tried to alleviate the heaviness of memories starting to weigh down on her by talking.

"I don't like hospitals," she admitted.

The deputy cut her a look. It made her feel silly for blurting out the first thought that had popped into her head.

"I think that's a universal truth," he said. "Show me someone who loves hospitals and I'll show you a liar."

Alyssa had to agree with that. "I suppose you're right. I guess I should say my last experience with one was…" She paused, looking for a word that expressed terror mixed with confusion but still polite for everyday conversation. *"…unsettling."*

No sooner had she said it than Alyssa realized she had no idea if the man next to her knew what had happened the year before. At least not to the extent of her personal injuries. While she was in the car that morning, they hadn't spoken about anything personal.

"I was hurt during the bank robbery last year and woke up in the hospital," she hurriedly explained. "Law enforcement referred to me as a victim, while the doctor and nurse referred to me as a survivor. And all I wanted to know was how I'd gotten there and how badly I was hurt. It was all very…" She paused to look for another word to describe such a heavy feeling.

"Unsettling," Deputy Foster offered. Alyssa nodded. "Was today the first time you've been back after the robbery? If you don't mind my asking."

Again, Alyssa nodded.

"At least this time I woke up beforehand," she said. A fresh wave of heat moved through her cheeks. "Though it was definitely an experience to wake up to my clothes being taken off in an ambulance. Again, definitely not how I saw my day going."

Deputy Foster kept his eyes on the street. Alyssa felt her blush cranking up the heat. Again she found herself wishing she'd worn a different bra and panty set.

"The EMTs were pretty quick with it too," he said, eyes still averted. "I turned away one second and in the next they were handing me your clothes." He shrugged. "But they assured me that they were used to dealing with heat exhaustion and knew what they were doing."

Alyssa patted the buttons on her blouse. "I am impressed they didn't rip anything. I already lost my favorite shirt last year."

The deputy chuckled but didn't respond past that. Alyssa decided to steer clear of any more hospital talk while silently saying a thank-you to the powers that be. At least this time she hadn't died in between the ambulance ride and the ER.

Carpenter was small but not small enough where there weren't a handful of heavily populated neighborhoods in and around the town. Alyssa lived in one named the Meadows, closer to the town limits. The houses were older and, at times, funkier than the traditional ones in other parts of the town. She liked to believe it was an infusion of character and not simply houses that were in desperate need of renovating.

"So, this is me," she said, pointing to her house at the end of a cul-de-sac. Again she thought of the word *character* as he pulled into the driveway of the two-story.

"Nice house," he said, not cutting the engine off. She wondered what his plan was but couldn't find the courage to ask. He was still a stranger, despite their shared morning.

"Thanks. My sister calls it the jigsaw house. It's a work in progress, on the inside, that is. I've been slowly remodeling it since I moved in. The previous owners had a hard love for 1970s-style wallpaper and green tile. Almost every room looks different from the others."

Deputy Foster switched his gaze back to the house and nodded. His talkative levels were plummeting. And she didn't know why. One of his hands rested lazily on the steering wheel, the other on his lap. He seemed bored.

"Okay," she rallied. "Well, thanks again for everything. I can't imagine how I would have handled everything without you there earlier."

Alyssa fumbled for the door handle. Her embarrassment made the space between them seem so small. She was itching to get inside the house.

"No need to thank me. I was just doing my job."

He turned off the engine but didn't move a muscle.

Alyssa hesitated. A part of her wanted to invite the man inside—it was the least she could do—but the way he was acting ignited her self-preservation.

"I'll be out here if you need me."

A new hardness edged its way into his tone as he said it. One that spoke of finality. Alyssa finally got a hold on the handle and let herself out. Her muscles whined at the quick movement, but her blush compelled her to keep the pace until she was at her front door. It wasn't until she was in the privacy of her bedroom that she wondered what the deputy was thinking.

Because the man she'd just left wasn't the same man who had promised he wouldn't leave her that morning.

NIGHT WAS CREEPING around the car before the porch light clicked on. Caleb had been listening to the frogs chirping like insects for the last half hour. Before that he'd focused on the birds. And before that he'd been thinking about him being an idiot.

If Alyssa hadn't requested him to guard her, Caleb would have volunteered, no doubt about that in his mind. Yet as soon as he'd seen the fear—the vulnerability—that had overtaken her outside his car in the hospital parking lot, he'd remembered his one rule while in Riker County.

Don't get attached.

So he'd shut down. Spoken only when spoken to and kept things professional. Yet he couldn't deny that he'd wanted to know more about her. And it was that feeling that had only strengthened his resolve to stay in the car.

Even though he'd wanted to go inside.

Now, after his resolution had hardened, Alyssa stepped onto the front porch and turned her gaze directly to his. She'd dressed down in the few hours that had passed since he saw her, wearing a white T-shirt and jeans. Her hair was wet and dark, pulled back at the nape of her neck, and her glasses were off. She was squinting. It compelled him to step outside his car.

"Is everything okay?" he asked.

Alyssa adjusted her gaze. It was still a little off. It made him wonder how blind she was without her glasses.

"Um, actually, this is kind of embarrassing." She shifted her weight from one foot to the other. "But could you give me a hand? I kind of…" She said the last part so low Caleb started toward her.

"Say that again?"

Alyssa shifted her weight again. She was embarrassed, that was clear. It intrigued Caleb even further. He was already at the steps when she spoke up.

"I kind of lost my glasses," she repeated. She let out a long sigh. "In the attic."

It was so unexpected that Caleb's rule of staying away from the woman took a back seat. "Okay, you're going to have to explain that one."

Alyssa's cheeks noticeably reddened. She motioned for him to follow her. "Remember how I said the inside of the house is like a jigsaw?"

"Yeah."

"The attic is more of an endless maze."

She shut the door behind him and motioned up the stairs. Just from where Caleb was standing in the entryway, he could already agree with Alyssa's sister's nickname for the place. The stairs were oak but had a thick green carpet runner, while the tile they were standing on was a multicolored mosaic design. Of what, he couldn't tell, but it was definitely different.

"The second story isn't as dramatic," she promised, guessing at his thoughts. "Just some *funky* wallpaper I've been avoiding. The shag carpet, however, officially died right after I moved in."

She led him up the stairs into a hall that opened up to one guest bedroom, one bathroom and he assumed the master suite. He couldn't help pausing at the open door to the closest bedroom.

"Well, you weren't lying about the funky part."

There was bright-orange-striped wallpaper as far as the eye could see. If he had a weekend, he could tear it all out, no problem. Then they could paint it something less intense and headache inducing.

They.

That had popped up out of nowhere.

"It's a work in progress," she continued, unaware that he'd just mentally coupled them. "The attic, though. It's stuck in its ways."

"And can I ask why you were up there and how you lost your glasses?"

He followed her to the ladder in the middle of the hallway. Instead of going up, she hesitated and turned to face him.

"Short story, everything that happened today got me feeling…" She paused, seemingly looking for the right words. Her eyebrows drew together and her lips turned down in a frown. Those lips. He'd noticed them while hovering over her waiting for a bomb to go off. Pink and bare.

"Nostalgic," she supplied, holding up her hands. "I know that sounds strange, but when I was in the hospital, right after what happened at the bank, my sister, Gabby, took a leave at work to help me while I recovered. We were really close growing up and she lives in Colorado, so it was the longest we had seen each other in a while. And it was nice." She smiled. Those distracting lips stretching wide. "Today got me thinking about what happened then, which got me thinking about Gabby and, well, that snowballed into thinking about my parents." She laughed and pointed to the ceiling. "And I was trying to get to a particularly difficult box with photo albums in them when my glasses dropped out of sight."

"And you're one of those people who *really* can't see without your glasses," he guessed.

It earned him a laugh.

"Blind as a bat," she answered. "I tried feeling around for them but for the life of me couldn't find them." That blush was back, showing up against her skin in a flash. It surprised Caleb.

And intrigued him.

"So I should probably go up first just in case," he said with a laugh. She nodded.

"If you don't mind. I'm not a fan of contacts and would really like to not break my current pair of glasses." She groaned, blush burning bright. "Because I kind of already lost my only spare."

Caleb couldn't help continuing to laugh.

It in turn grabbed a giggle from her. "Armed robberies and fake bombs? I can be smooth. Any other time? Not so much."

"Being good under pressure isn't a bad thing," he pointed out.

"But having your glasses fall off your face into oblivion isn't either."

He couldn't argue with that.

They climbed the ladder and began the great attic search, as Alyssa dubbed it after several minutes had gone by without any luck. The space was roomy and easy to stand up in, but thanks to boxes, old furniture and awkwardly shaped decorations, navigating around wasn't the easiest thing to do.

"I just have to ask," Caleb finally said, after pushing aside another box like he was directing a game of Tetris. "Do you have a box in here that leads to Narnia maybe? Because I—"

"Ah!"

Caleb shot up from the crouched position he'd been in just as Alyssa danced, twirled and then flung herself toward him. He met her halfway between their original spots just as she grabbed the hem of her shirt.

"Spider," she shrieked. *"Spider!"*

Without wasting any time, Alyssa yanked up on her shirt and pulled it clear over her head like it was on fire. She threw it across the attic. Caleb watched in awe as the

T-shirt soared through the air and fell out of sight through the open attic door. Still, the woman was not satisfied.

"Is it on me?" she yelled, flapping her arms in the air. Her terror had its claws in her so deep that she didn't seem to realize she'd just stripped down in front of him. Wearing a white lace bra, definitely not the beige one from earlier in the ambulance, she kept flailing around with fervor. The motion might have helped her with the bug problem, but it wasn't helping with his concentration.

"Hold still," he ordered, trying his best not to laugh. He reached out to grab her by the arms. It was the only way to keep her in place when it was clear she wasn't listening.

"Is it still on me?" she repeated, voice pitching high.

Caleb did a cursory look at her chest and stomach, actively trying not to scan too closely, before turning her around.

His stomach dropped.

Thoughts of spiders and lace bras and lost glasses were blanketed by a wide puckering of skin.

A scar.

The one that Dupree Slater had given her.

Caleb had seen his fair share of gunshot wounds and scars during his career with law enforcement, but this one was different. Angry. The scar *looked* angry. Violent, even. Just like the man who had left it.

It made *him* angry in turn.

During his lifetime, Caleb had learned to stop asking the motive of why some people did what they did. But right now, feeling the warmth of Alyssa against his hands and staring at her bare skin, he couldn't help asking that question.

Why would someone do anything to hurt this woman?

"Well?" Alyssa asked, voice still raised. It dislodged his anger. Though he had no doubt there would be a dark aftertaste for a while in its wake. "I'm still blind here."

"There's nothing on you," he answered. Even to his ears

his voice had gone cold. He tried to adjust it to something lighter. "I think your new dance moves shook it free."

Alyssa stopped her panicked routine and let out a deep, shuddering breath. She turned back to face him.

"I felt it drop on me and then just saw this blur against my shirt," she said, shaking her head. The movement once again shook the rest of her. Caleb made sure to keep his eyes above her chest. "I can't handle spiders."

Another shudder racked her body.

He lowered his hands from her arms. And tried to ignore how pink her lips still looked.

Caleb cleared his throat.

"Not that I'm complaining about the view—" he started. He didn't have to finish the statement. He couldn't help smiling as Alyssa finally realized what she'd done. Her arms slapped across her chest in a flash. A blush that put all the other blushes of the day to shame ran across her face in an instant.

"Oh my God," she breathed.

Caleb averted his gaze completely, already turning, when something caught his eye.

"Well, look at that." He walked a few feet away to an overturned box, one of a handful of casualties of Alyssa's panicked dance. "Too bad a spider couldn't have fallen on you sooner." He bent over and picked up her glasses. There was no telling where they'd been before she started flailing around.

"Thank goodness!" She shied as far away from him as she could while still grabbing the black frames from him. Once they were back to their rightful place, she tightened her arms around herself. She didn't meet his gaze as she looked around the immediate area. "Now, how about my shirt?"

Caleb laughed.

He was about to give her the news that it was no longer

in the attic when the ladder leading to the hallway beneath them creaked under someone's weight.

This time Alyssa met his stare.

One emotion was written clearly across her face.

Fear.

Chapter Eight

One moment Alyssa was standing next to the deputy and in the next he was in front of her, gun out and raised.

It happened so fast that she temporarily forgot her lapse in sanity that had led to her stripping off her shirt and then demanding the man take a look at her. That embarrassment was sucked straight out as another long creak sounded on the steps. Someone was definitely climbing up.

The deputy squared his shoulders, tightened his stance and waited.

A dark bald head popped into view, followed by a truly alarmed face.

"Robbie!"

Alyssa reached out and grabbed the deputy's shoulder.

"He's a friend," she hurried, but he was already lowering his gun.

Robbie's eyes were wide as he looked between them. The deputy holstered his gun and took a step back, blocking Robbie's view of her bare skin. Still, they all knew he'd seen enough to know she wasn't wearing her shirt.

A fact the man already knew, given that he was holding it in his hands.

"Do you always walk around unannounced, Mr. Rickman?" Caleb asked, tone dry.

"We knocked and when no one answered we got worried," he defended. "We used the spare key Alyssa gave us."

Eleanor's voice floated up, but Alyssa couldn't make it out. Maybe it was the mortification that was setting in.

"Could you throw me that?" she cut in, motioning to the shirt.

"I guess it's not my business to ask why it was down here?" Robbie tossed it over. Caleb caught it and passed it back without looking. Alyssa hurriedly put it back on.

"There was a spider," the deputy deadpanned.

Robbie held up a hand.

"Say no more," he said. "If she's anything like Eleanor when she sees a lizard, then you're lucky to be alive, son." Caleb's demeanor loosened. He snorted. "Okay, well, unless you kids are busy, we brought some food over for supper. And by some food I mean a lot of food."

On cue Alyssa's stomach growled.

Caleb thrust his thumb back at her. "I think that's her answer."

Robbie smiled. "What about you? We brought more than enough."

Alyssa couldn't see the man's expression but was surprised when he nodded so quickly.

"If that's okay with you, that is?" Caleb turned toward her and waited.

From one moment to the next, the deputy had shifted his demeanor. Blunt to compassionate to detached and empathetic to humorous and, now, polite. He was a hard man to pin down, that was for sure. However, Alyssa couldn't deny she felt a connection. Or maybe she just wanted one.

Another flourish of heat began to make its ascent upward as she shared a look with the handsome man. She managed to nod.

"You helped me find my glasses," she pointed out, avoiding bringing up any part of the fake bomb while

Robbie was within earshot. Once she had begun to normalize, Alyssa had called him and his wife to let them know what happened. Carpenter might have been a small town, but not everyone had seen the live news story when they were trying to get her out of the car. The Rickmans had been upset but promised to give her space. But now, standing in an awkward position with the deputy, she was almost thankful that their idea of "space" was waiting until supper to come over with food. "Of course you can stay and eat, Deputy."

"Why don't you call me Caleb?" he said, voice filling with a hint of grit. "I think we've both earned that, wouldn't you say?"

Alyssa felt the burn in her cheeks now. And she hated herself for it. She'd only met the man that morning and now here she was, wanting to know him.

In more ways than one.

ELEANOR DIDN'T HOLD BACK.

"Sweetie, if you keep that up you'll end up suffocating her," Robbie pointed out. "I'm pretty sure she needs to breathe."

Caleb watched as the older woman kept her arms tightly around Alyssa before finally relenting. He started to take a seat when Robbie stopped him.

"You might as well go ahead and let her get at you before you get comfortable," he warned, pointing to his wife.

Caleb raised his eyebrow.

"I didn't do anything," he tried, but apparently Mrs. Rickman wasn't having any of that. She detached from Alyssa and was on him within seconds. For a tall, slender woman she had a surprisingly viselike grip. It reminded Caleb of his mother. Which made him instantly like the woman more.

"You stood by our girl." Her brown eyes locked on his

after she pulled away. "Don't sell yourself short for that," she scolded.

Caleb nodded. "Yes, ma'am."

Eleanor smiled and then turned her attention to the dining room table. It was long and narrow but in no way looked prepared to hold the spread that the Rickmans had brought over. Robbie caught his eye and shrugged.

"We Southerners are big on comforting each other with food," he explained. "Some people like flowers, some like presents, we like overgenerous portions of mashed potatoes and gravy."

Alyssa motioned to a glass container half covered in aluminum foil.

"Which can be found in this particular dish," she said with a laugh.

Caleb didn't miss the smile that sprang up on Eleanor's face at the sound. It was clear Robbie and his wife cared about Alyssa. It was also clear that she was fond of them too. Helping Robbie during the robbery had made a stranger into a friend.

And now here Caleb was, getting hugged and fed by strangers while trying to protect another.

Don't get attached, he reminded himself. His stomach growled in response.

"Here, let me suggest this." Alyssa took a seat next to him and opened a plastic container with obvious glee. Eleanor handed out plates before taking her own seat opposite them and next to her husband. They started to talk among themselves as Alyssa continued. "This is Eleanor's famous green bean casserole. If you're as hungry as I am, then this should hit the spot just right." She leaned closer to him and lowered her voice to a whisper. Caleb caught the scent of citrus off her wet hair. "But make sure you save room. I spied a few slices of homemade apple pie in the kitchen. And you definitely don't want to miss that."

Alyssa gave him a coy smile.

His inner voice chanting out his one rule quieted.

The food was good, but with Robbie and Eleanor the company was better. It wasn't long before Caleb found out just how likable the couple was.

And just how polite they remained.

No one brought up the fake bomb or the trial or asked personal questions. Instead they talked about sports, the weather, and their suggestions on how to make Alyssa's house less like a puzzle and more of a home. On that particular topic Caleb kept his opinions down to nodding to the couple's suggestions. He didn't want to intrude more than he already was doing.

It wasn't until the pie was eaten—apple, as Alyssa had promised—that the conversation took a turn. Surprisingly, it was Alyssa who drove it there.

"So, no one has called me to update me on the trial," she started. "But last I was told, a lawyer is supposed to contact me today or tomorrow about it." Her stare found Robbie's. "Do you know why?"

Robbie put down his fork. His face pinched.

"Last I heard, they were talking about having you sit out the trial," he said. "At least as a witness."

Alyssa bristled at his side.

"Sit it out?" she exclaimed. "Why?"

"The trauma of what happened. Some think you're too emotional or might make the jury more sympathetic toward you and your testimony."

"Too emotional?" Alyssa nearly yelled. "Why? Because someone played a dumb prank on me or because I'm a woman?"

Robbie held up his hands in defense.

"That's only what I heard from Ted," he said. "I don't agree with it and I don't even know if it's what's supposed to happen. I'm assuming we'll all find out tomorrow when they announce what time the trial is rescheduled for."

"Is Ted the lawyer?" Caleb butted in. Again he wished he'd researched the case and trial more after being assigned to the courthouse.

"Ted worked at the bank," Eleanor answered. "He was there when…" She cut herself off and glanced at her husband. Caleb felt stupid for not realizing earlier that what had happened at the bank had affected her just as much as the other two. She'd nearly lost her husband.

"He was also supposed to testify after Alyssa," Robbie jumped in. "They thought it would be more powerful for her to start off, considering she saw the whole thing *and* was hurt."

That surprised Caleb.

"Wait, so you aren't just a witness," he said. "You're the first."

Alyssa nodded, visibly trying to calm down.

"I was, but if someone's already talking to Ted, then it might be him now." There was anger behind her words. It was powerful, potent.

Caleb understood it.

And wanted to help it lessen.

"From what I know of what happened, even *if* you aren't able to testify, there's still a pretty cut-and-dry case against Dupree and Anna," he pointed out. "And regardless of your presence on the stand, what happened to you will still be told. Probably several times depending on what's asked of each witness."

Alyssa took a deep breath.

"I guess you're right," she said. "I just— I want them to rot in prison for the rest of their lives."

Caleb fought the urge to reach out and touch her. There wasn't much space between them as it was. It would be easy to take her hand, balled on her lap, and let her know he was there. That he was on her side. That he knew anger and how it could destroy. But he didn't.

"In my experience, people like them get what they deserve," he said instead. "Plus, I may be new, but what I know of the law enforcement in this town, and the sheriff for that matter, is they do their best to make sure justice is served."

A small smile pulled up the corners of Alyssa's lips. She nodded.

The conversation veered back into a more comforting area as they took their plates to the kitchen and cleaned up. Caleb checked the clock several times, wondering what his next play would be. Since he had been requested by Alyssa for guard duty for the day and night, Captain Jones had put Dante in his place for guard duty at the courthouse the next morning. A move that had surprised Caleb.

Captain Jones was a desk jockey and a stickler at that. Unlike Dante, he and the rest of the department hadn't shown him any special treatment. He didn't blame them, but he'd been ready to ask for it anyway.

Until Alyssa had spoken to the captain before he'd had the chance. It was against protocol, he was sure, yet the captain had obliged.

Why? he had wondered.

But now, looking at Robbie—alive and well, thanks to the woman—he could make a guess. Small towns left no room for heroics to go unnoticed. Even the sheriff's department respected what she'd done at the bank.

It made the growing foreign feeling of *needing* to protect her that much greater.

"It was good to meet you, Caleb," Eleanor said as they all filed out onto the porch. She wrapped him in a hug before he could prepare himself for it. "We're going to do this soon, so don't think we won't see each other again."

Caleb laughed. "You keep feeding me apple pie like that and I'll have dinner with you anytime."

Eleanor beamed and turned to say goodbye to Alyssa while her husband clapped him on the back.

"Thanks again for everything," Robbie said. They shook hands, but the man didn't let go right away. Instead he spoke in a whisper so the women couldn't overhear. "She's a special woman and deserves nothing but the best. You keep a good eye on her, okay?"

Caleb was quick to nod. "Yes, sir."

"Good." Robbie gave one final pump. "And maybe next time there's a 'spider' you two could put a sock on the door or something." Robbie gave him a wink and a hoot of laughter before turning to his wife and taking her hand. "It's time to go, my dear," he sang. "Wave goodbye to the young'uns!"

"I can't wave goodbye to myself," she teased.

Robbie hooted again and the two walked to the car, caught in their own bubble of mirth.

Watching them, Caleb felt an odd twinge of emotion. Regret? Desire? Grief?

He didn't know. However, it put more weight on his current situation, standing next to Alyssa on her front porch.

"What did he say to you?" she asked, an eyebrow rising. "You're grinning."

Caleb shrugged.

"You know, just a little of this and that," he hedged. "Men talk."

She snorted. "Men talk?"

"You wouldn't understand." He felt the grin widen. It had been a long time since he'd had a good home-cooked meal. It had been even longer since he'd had even better company to share it with.

One look at Alyssa, baby blues focused solely on him, and Caleb thought he should tell her that. And thank her.

And ask when they could do it again.

Alyssa bit back a yawn.

"I'm exhausted," she said, eyes watering at the effort. Caleb ignored how that disappointed him.

"Which is my cue to get back to work," he said, already walking down the steps. "Let me know if you need anything."

"Wait, Caleb."

He should keep walking. He should go to the car and sit in it until the morning. He should ignore the pull he felt toward a woman he barely knew.

"If you're going to sit up in the driveway all night anyways, why don't you at least do it inside the house?"

Caleb turned and watched a new blush blossom across her cheeks. She scrambled to finish her thought. "I mean, I have a guest room and even a really great couch in the living room. It doesn't make sense for you to be scrunched up in a car for hours. Believe me, that's no fun."

Caleb hesitated.

He met those bright blue eyes head-on.

"You don't know me," he finally said.

However, Alyssa didn't hesitate. "I know enough." She gave him a smile. It was kind. "Please, let me do something nice for you."

He should have argued. He should have declined. He should have done a lot of things, but what he ended up doing was nodding.

And then following Alyssa Garner back into her house.

Chapter Nine

Despite being exhausted, Alyssa spent the next hour on the phone with her sister. It gave Caleb time to explore the downstairs without her by his side.

Apart from the aesthetics of floors that didn't match, walls that were covered in wallpaper from the '70s, and random bits of tile, the house was very much lived in. Books, magazines and knickknacks could be found everywhere he looked, while pictures were framed and hung with care. Caleb stopped at a few of these and tried to figure out who each person was in them, or at least, who everyone was to the woman.

The sister, Gabby, if he heard her correctly, was the easiest to spot. She made several appearances throughout the first floor. Her hair was lighter, but she had the same blue eyes. In every picture of them together, she had her arms around Alyssa. Their smiles matched too. It was contagious. It made him miss his own sister. He needed to call her soon.

Another person who was easy to connect to Alyssa was an older woman with brown hair and dark eyes but who shared the same expression as the sisters. Their mother, he guessed. She, however, wasn't in many pictures. At least not with the girls when they were older. His smile fell as he guessed she'd passed away.

Other pictures included Alyssa with people who must

have been friends. Always in groups and never one-on-one. It wasn't until he was examining the frames in the living room for the third time that he realized what he was really looking for.

A boyfriend.

The day had been a rush, crazy and unexpected. In the time he'd spent with her, she'd only mentioned her sister. He'd assumed that meant there was no man in the picture. But, then again, maybe she was being private about it. Or had her own reasons not to bring him up.

Caleb's eyes stopped to rest on a collage above the fireplace. In one of the pictures, a smiling Alyssa looked out at him while two men around their age stood on either side, arms wrapped around her waist. They didn't look like her brothers.

Jealousy sprang up faster than Caleb could track it.

"I see you've found my attempt of making photo collages."

Caleb turned, surprised he hadn't heard the woman come down the stairs. He was finding that when it came to Alyssa, he wasn't always on his game. Which could be dangerous. For both of them.

"I was trying to figure out who everyone was," he admitted. He tapped the picture with the men and tried his hardest to look uninterested. "Brothers?"

He already knew they weren't but felt another pulse of jealousy when she shook her head.

"Those are the sons of Jeffries and Sons," she answered. "That's where I work. It's a small remodeling company that's local. I'm sure you would have already met them if they'd been in town. The whole family does a big cruise every year. I was invited but the trial cut into it. So they shut down the shop and now I'm getting paid vacation. *But* they, the sons, are like brothers if that counts." That satisfied Caleb more than it should have. "They even do that 'don't you hurt my sister' speech when I start dating someone. The last guy got it the worst. They sat him down and threatened bodily harm after—" Something doused her humor on the spot. Her eyebrows knitted together. Her lips thinned. It alarmed Caleb.

"After?" he prodded. Anger was already starting to burn in his chest. If any man had laid a hand on her he'd—

"After he stopped visiting me in the hospital."

"He stopped visiting you in the hospital?" he repeated. "You mean after the robbery?"

Alyssa nodded. With the motion the rest of her body seemed to fall.

"I mean, I can't blame him," she tried. "We hadn't been dating long and then suddenly I was hospital-bound and in need of hours and hours of physical therapy. It was too much for someone who already had a busy schedule." She shrugged, attempting to play off the hurt at being left when she had been most vulnerable.

Caleb didn't like that, and maybe she saw it in his expression.

Hers softened.

"It's okay," she said. Kind despite the obvious hurt. Her pink lips formed the smallest of smiles. "Not everyone stays when you want them to."

Caleb almost did several things in that moment.

He almost reached out to touch her, to comfort her, to let her know *he* was here right now. He almost turned that touch into a kiss, giving in to his curiosity about those pink, pink lips and how they felt. He almost told her that he would never have left her.

But then he realized that was exactly what he was going to do.

When he found his redemption in Riker County, he would use it to take him home.

Away from the sweltering heat and unforgiving humidity, away from the built-in familiarity between every resident, away from a department that didn't know what he was capable of, and away from the beautiful stranger standing less than a foot away from him.

So, instead, he kept quiet.

"I guess it's time for me to try to sleep," Alyssa said after the moment had passed. She didn't smile as she turned away. It wasn't until she was at the stairs that she called back to him, "Good night, Deputy."

Like an idiot he stood right where he was.

"Good night, Miss Garner."

ALYSSA SLEPT LIKE the dead.

One moment her head was touching the pillow, and the next she was waking up to someone knocking on the door. Light streamed through a gap in the curtains as she tossed the covers off her and sat up.

"Yes?" she asked, fumbling for her glasses. In the process she got caught on the cord to her cell phone charger. It fell off the night table and became a blur on the floor.

"You okay in there?" Caleb asked through the door.

For one wild second she blushed, wondering why he was outside her door, when the night before came back.

"Yeah, I'm good," she assured him, still fumbling around for her glasses. Usually she left them on the nightstand next to her phone, but for the life of her, she couldn't lay hands on them. "What time is it?" she asked, getting out of bed and searching the floor by the sides of the little table. When that search was fruitless, she got onto her knees and looked beneath the stand.

"Eight thirty," he called back.

"Eight thirty," she exclaimed, sitting up. "I'm not missing the trial, am I?"

"It was officially postponed until one this afternoon."

Alyssa let out a sigh of relief. She reached under the bed and felt around. No glasses.

How did she keep *doing* this?

"Hold on a second," she said. She grabbed her robe off the ottoman at the foot of her bed and put it over her short nightgown before opening the door. Caleb's blurry form became focused into a well-rested man dressed down in a T-shirt and jeans. "You're never going to believe this," she started, already embarrassed. "But I've—"

"You lost your glasses again?" he interrupted. He was grinning.

She nodded.

"I had them on when I got into bed so I could read a work email, but they aren't on my nightstand." Caleb's grin grew wider. "Why are you smiling like that?"

Alyssa froze as the man took a step closer. He reached up to her hair.

"Probably because they are on top of your head."

He took them off her hair. She felt heat in her cheeks.

"I can count on one hand how many times I've put them on top of my head," she said, taking them from the man and slipping them on. "And of course you get to witness one of those times. I promise I'm much more of a capable human than I let on."

Caleb laughed. It was a booming, pleasant sound. She wished she could hear more of it.

"I believe you," he assured her. "But I also believe you're just really good at losing your glasses."

"I can't disagree with you there." Once her glasses were on and she was refocused, she got down to business. "No one called me last night or this morning—unless I slept through it, of course—about the trial. I assumed it was pushed back to the afternoon."

"The results from CSU came in about the fake bomb. Whoever made it was careful, precise, but it had nothing in it that could have physically harmed you. Who put it there is still being investigated, but since the act couldn't be linked directly back to the trial, the judge thought it was pointless to delay the proceedings."

"The entire town just wants the Storm Chasers behind us," she agreed.

"Which is what's going to happen," he said. "But until then, Captain Jones needs me back at the station. I volunteered to help with the investigation since Deputy Mills took my place at the courthouse. So I was wondering, is there anyone you could call over or visit until I'm done?"

Alyssa was caught off guard by that.

"Is it necessary to keep watching me?" she asked. It sounded more blunt than she meant it to. The man didn't seem perturbed by it.

"I think we'd all feel better about leaving you alone once we figure out who put that bomb in your car," he answered. "Fake or not, it took a lot of effort."

"Not to mention it was creepy."

"That too. So, until the trial, is there somewhere else you can stay? I would offer up a deputy, but the department is spread a little thin at the moment because of another investigation." His expression hardened a fraction. "And I don't know anyone I can trust in the police department."

He didn't trust them? To do what? Look after her?

Why did he care so much? Was this just part of the job? *Calm down, Alyssa*, she thought. *He's just being polite.*

"I'm sure Robbie and Eleanor wouldn't mind if I stayed with them for the morning. I could ride with them to the trial too."

Caleb nodded. He looked relieved.

"Do I have time to grab a quick shower first?" Alyssa was suddenly hyperaware of how crazy she must look.

"Yeah, that's fine. I'll wait outside."

"Do you have time to eat with me?" she asked on impulse. That heat—a heat she was starting to associate to the man and no one else—pushed up her neck and into her cheeks at lightning speed. "I mean, we have a lot of left-overs from last night and I think I even have some cereal and, of course, some coffee."

Caleb raised his hand and shook it.

"Not today," he said, voice hard. "I'll be out in the car."

There it was again. One second the deputy showed her compassion and humor, and the next, walls were up and he detached.

What happened to him to make him that way? she wondered.

Or was it just her that turned him off?

"HE EITHER HAD an affair with a married woman, killed a man in cold blood or stole drugs from the police department's evidence lockers." Alyssa looked up from her email filled with work orders. Eleanor sat across from her at the table, sipping her coffee. She shrugged and continued. "Those are the three most popular reasons for why Deputy Foster was transferred to the sheriff's department."

Alyssa felt her eyebrow rise.

"Most popular reasons according to the gossip mill?" she guessed.

Eleanor nodded.

"You have to love small towns and their gossip mills." Alyssa was all sarcasm. Said man had put her into a weird mood. Unlike the day before, they had driven in silence to the Rickmans'. It was like that night hadn't happened at all. Any familiarity between them was gone. Still, she had enough humor in her to roll her eyes at what the gossipers of Carpenter had to say about the man.

"I'm just repeating what I heard," Eleanor said.

"You know, a wise woman once told me that gossip

might pass the time, but putting any stock in most of it is a waste." Alyssa gave the woman a pointed look.

"Sounds like a smart woman, if you ask me." A sly smile picked up her lips.

"I like to think she is," Alyssa said, unable to keep her frown stationary. "When she isn't listening to gossip, that is."

Eleanor shrugged again. They quieted. It was always a companionable silence. It made Alyssa miss her mother. It had been almost ten years since she passed, and still there were moments when it felt like no time had gone by at all. Alyssa would have to resolve some of the ache of memory by giving Gabby another call after the trial was done.

"You know, there is one piece of gossip I heard that maybe wasn't as much gossip as I would have liked," Eleanor said after a few minutes had stretched quietly between them. She set down her coffee cup. Alyssa already didn't like what she was going to say. The woman was frowning. "No matter what the reason for the deputy coming to town is, everyone seems to be on the same page about his future plan."

Alyssa's stomach did a weird flip.

"And that is?" she asked.

"When he's done here he'll go—"

Eleanor didn't get to finish her thought.

The world exploded around them.

Chapter Ten

The entire house shook. Eleanor's coffee ran off the table, cup overturned. With wide, terrified eyes, both women looked at each other, paralyzed. Somewhere in the distance a woman started to scream.

That shook Alyssa out of her haze. She got up and ran for the front door. It was flung open before she could touch the handle.

Robbie's face was stone.

He didn't meet Alyssa's stare and instead searched over her head. A small look of relief crossed his face as he found his wife. Then he was back to stone.

"Stay here, Eleanor," he said. "Please."

She started to call after him, but Robbie turned around and ran back into the yard. Alyssa followed, nerves twisting up tight. It didn't take long to figure out what the noise had been.

"Oh my God!"

Robbie and Eleanor lived in a bigger neighborhood than Alyssa did. It was more of a community too. The houses were closer, the neighbors were friends—some even family—and there wasn't a time during the day when it was empty of everyone.

The Rickmans' street curved into a half circle where cute brick houses, colorful mailboxes and green, green lawns sat on either side. Those lawns were now dotting with the men and women who were still home on the weekday.

All of them were in various stages of anguish, fear and shock.

And every single one of them was staring at the house near the end of the street.

Or what was left of it.

"Mary, call the police and fire department," Robbie yelled out to the neighbor across the street. Being older than him and his wife didn't stop the woman from whipping back into her house in an instant. Then Robbie was in the street and running.

Toward the house that was currently in flames.

The one that had exploded.

With her nerves tightening to the point of forming one cohesive clump of fear, Alyssa found her leg muscles pushing her to follow him.

The sounds of her heels hitting the street were quickly drowned out by the chaos around them. Neighbors were shouting to one another while a few joined in on the sprint toward the house. Some stayed in the yards, hands over their mouths and tears in their eyes.

"St-stay here," Robbie yelled out after they made it to the front yard. Alyssa was breathing hard, but Robbie was breathing harder. Both had spent a good chunk of the last year rehabilitating from their gunshot wounds. Robbie's journey had been more difficult.

"No, *you* stay here," Alyssa retorted, adrenaline giving her a strong second wind. She stood tall.

The house was two stories. Or had been. The explosion seemed to have happened on the second floor, and now the yards were covered in brick, wood, glass and debris of what she guessed had been a bedroom or two. Alyssa just hoped whoever owned the house hadn't been in one of those rooms. But a car parked in the driveway didn't give her much hope.

"He's—he's home," Robbie bit out from behind her.

Alyssa didn't wait for permission or for one of the other neighbors running toward the house to brave the house to see if anyone had survived. The fire department was on the other side of town. It would be at least ten minutes before they showed up.

You've been brave before, she thought, bolstering her courage up. *What's one more time?*

The front door's glass had been shattered like the rest of the windows.

"Is anyone in here?" she yelled into the entryway. The roar and crackle of fire made it impossible to pinpoint if anyone was calling back. She stepped through the middle of the broken door. Her heels cracked already broken glass beneath her feet. She slid on a chunk of it as she ran straight into the kitchen.

"Hello?" she yelled, as loud as she could. Smoke was starting to fill up the open-concept floor plan. She wouldn't be able to yell much longer. "Is anyone in here?"

No one responded.

Alyssa put her arm across her nose and mouth and moved deeper into the house. She didn't stop at the stairs. No one was getting up those. Or down.

She hurried to the backside of the house. The smoke moved in faster, became more aggressive. She summoned up her middle school knowledge of when the firefighters had demonstrated what to do if the house was on fire. Obviously, she would have already failed the lesson, since she'd run *into* the house instead of away from it for safety. But as she couldn't leave without checking the rest of the rooms on the first floor, she ducked low.

A small hallway led to two closed doors. Alyssa tapped the doorknob on the first and, when she found it wasn't hot, opened it. The laundry room was empty. A small window over the washer opened up to the backyard. On the other side of the fence was another house. A man and woman stood in it, gaping at the destruction.

Alyssa hoped Mary had called the cavalry in.

She turned tail and moved to the second closed door, also pausing to test the temperature of the doorknob. It was cool to the touch. She put her hand around it, ready to turn, when a god-awful *crack* split through the air.

Over the sound of a house being devoured, Alyssa heard a man's voice boom.

"Get out!"

The entire house seemed to shift above her.

She didn't waste any more time. Flinging the door open, she was fully planning on using the room's window as her escape when she saw another empty room.

But it wasn't empty.

"Hey!"

The room was used as an office. A large desk and computer were set up on one wall, while a small sofa was against the other. Picture frames covered the walls along with plaques and awards. However, the dog crate that sat in the corner pulled Alyssa's full attention.

A puppy with dark brown fur stood in the middle of the crate, its tiny *yaps* no match for the noise of everything else that was going on. Alyssa never would have heard him from outside.

"I'm coming," Alyssa said, running over to the crate. The puppy was yapping its head off now. She dropped to her knees, broken glass from the window scraping her bare skin, and tried to flip the lock.

It stuck.

Alyssa cursed beneath her breath. The dog kept barking. And then a sound she didn't know how to even describe drowned both of them out.

The walls shook, picture frames clattered to the floor. She whipped her head around to the open door and watched in horror as the wall of the hallway collapsed. Wall and smoke made a cloud that reached into the office like an oversize hand trying its best to grab her.

Alyssa covered her head but kept working on the latch. The sound of yelling filtered in from the broken window. She didn't care.

"Don't worry, pup, I'm not—" She cut herself off with a round of coughing. "Not leaving you."

With one hard tug the latch finally fell free. She opened the door and held her arms open wide. She wasn't about to let the dog run wild. Not when she was sure they were both on borrowed time while still inside.

The puppy stopped its barking and, thankfully, ran right up to her. Alyssa scooped him up, adrenaline surging so she barely felt the glass bite against her skin. He was heavy and would no doubt be a big dog when he grew up. But what about his owner? Alyssa shook her head, trying to ignore the fate of whoever had been on the second story.

Instead she moved to the window and stood back to kick out at the last two jagged pieces clinging to the frame. The dog squirmed as the first shattered. By the time the second fell, he was all-out trying to escape from her hold.

So Alyssa let him.

She tossed him out of the window onto the grass as another wave of coughing racked her body. The movement finally caught the attention of the man and woman she'd seen in the backyard from the laundry room.

The man started to yell and run toward them.

Alyssa didn't have time to wait and see what he was saying. Without an ounce of grace, she clambered out of the window and fell hard against the ground.

"Come on!"

The man was soon at her side. He put his arms under her

shoulders and more or less dragged her to his backyard. Alyssa didn't complain. The smoke had finally gotten to her. She didn't stop coughing until she was lying next to a vegetable garden.

"That was stupid of you. You could have been killed," the man said, standing over her. He didn't say it with any real conviction. "But I'm glad you got Sergeant out."

Alyssa was about to ask who Sergeant was when something wet ran across her face. Then it clicked. The puppy's name was Sergeant. She reached out and stroked her new buddy but felt no joy.

She knew *his* name but not his owner's.

"Please tell me—tell me no kids were in there," she managed, trying to keep from falling into another coughing fit.

"No," he said. "No kids. Just Ted."

The man's wife was all-out weeping next to them.

Then Alyssa remembered something Robbie had told her. About who lived down the street from him. Her body went numb.

"Ted Danfield?" she had to ask, even though she already knew.

The man nodded.

"The one and only."

"WHAT ABOUT THE man with the glasses?"

Caleb was looking across the desk at Captain Jones, both men frustrated.

"We already put an all-points bulletin out on him," Jones repeated. "But apart from what you and Miss Garner described, we don't have much to go on. We don't even know if he's involved, your suspicions aside."

Caleb had opened his mouth to protest that point—the man in the horn-rimmed glasses had spoken to Alyssa and even given her the keys she'd "dropped" before she found the fake bomb—when Jones held up his hand to stop him.

"Listen, I get it," he said, expression softening. But only a fraction. He still in no way had warmed to Caleb. Especially not after he'd disobeyed direct orders. "You like her and want to protect her. Hell, everyone in Carpenter does. But getting emotionally involved is dangerous." Again Caleb started to argue with that point and again the captain held up his hand to stop him. "I've seen that look," he said. "Hell, I've even seen it on our sheriff's face. And I get it. Our job is to protect people, and sometimes those people get under our skin. But you of all people should understand that letting your emotions take over on a case can make everything worse, not better."

Caleb's defense died on his tongue. He felt his jaw harden. The change in demeanor wasn't lost on the captain. He exhaled with a long breath.

"I promise you we will get to the bottom of this," Jones continued when it was clear Caleb wouldn't add in any of his own remarks. "Just try to be patient. We have good men and women out there searching for this man as well as anyone else who might have information. All we can do until then is—"

A knock sounded on the door, interrupting him. Before he could answer, it opened. Dispatcher Cassie Gates didn't look apologetic in the least.

"We just got several calls in about an explosion in a residential neighborhood," she rushed. Captain Jones and Caleb both shot out of their seats.

"Where?" Caleb asked, heart galloping.

Don't say Dresden Drive, he thought. *Don't say Dresden Drive.*

"Two-eleven Dresden Drive. We've already dispatched fire and rescue."

Caleb's stomach stopped in its descent to the floor.

"Two-eleven?" he repeated. "I dropped Alyssa off at 198 Dresden," he told the captain. "At Robbie Rickman's house."

Jones turned to the dispatcher.

"Do we know who lives at 211?"

Cassie nodded. Her face pinched in worry. He already didn't like her answer.

"Ted Danfield."

Caleb's mind raced.

"And they said there was an explosion?" Jones asked. "Not just a fire?"

"Yes, sir. All callers said the same thing. They heard a loud *boom* and when they went outside they saw Mr. Danfield's house on fire."

The captain swore.

"Ted is one of the witnesses for the Storm Chasers trial," she added, just in case they hadn't made the connection. But Caleb had. In fact, he'd made one more.

"This morning Alyssa was taken off the witness list because of the *fake* bomb," he said. "So not only is he a witness, Ted Danfield is the *first* witness."

Chapter Eleven

"She what?"

Caleb was about to blow a gasket. He'd kept the gas pedal pressed to the floorboard all the way from the department right up to Robbie and Eleanor's driveway. The rest of the street was filled with fire trucks and rescue workers frantically trying to save at least some of Ted's house plus the two neighboring houses that were close enough that the fire was threatening to spread. Caleb and Eleanor were standing in her front yard. Alone.

"She ran with Robbie toward Ted's," she repeated. "I haven't seen either of them since."

Caleb hated to admit it, but since hearing that it wasn't the Rickmans' house that had been affected, he'd felt nothing but relief. And while half of the department rushed over to Dresden Drive, Caleb had done it with only one person in mind.

And she had run *toward* the explosion.

"Stay here," he told Eleanor. "And when I mean here, I mean don't go back inside, okay?"

Eleanor wasn't a dumb woman.

"In case there's a bomb," she supplied.

He hated to do it, but he nodded. "I don't know if that's what happened to Ted, but I wouldn't take any chances."

Eleanor took a long, ragged breath but nodded.

"Go make sure they're okay," she said.

He didn't have to be told twice.

Deputies and police officers alike were trying to secure a perimeter while the firefighters did their job. Smoke was clouding half of the street. Caleb felt like he was navigating a disaster zone, weaving in between residents and responders alike, trying to find two people among a sea of strangers.

The captain's words of wisdom from earlier seemed like a lifetime ago.

Don't get too emotionally attached. That wasn't just a good rule, that was *his* rule.

Yet here he was, mentally holding his breath until he saw her.

"Caleb!"

He swung around so fast his shoes scraped.

Robbie and a man he didn't recognize were standing on the lawn across from Ted's house. The man's face was ashen. Alyssa wasn't with them.

Caleb ran over to him. "Where is she?"

Robbie held up his hands.

"She's okay," he assured him. "But she's being seen to." He pointed to one of the ambulances farther up the street.

That breath of relief hadn't released yet.

Instead of getting an explanation, Caleb was running again. He rounded the side of the ambulance, fists clenched, until finally he saw her. "Alyssa!"

Sitting on the tail of the ambulance door, Alyssa looked worse than she had when he'd pulled her from her car the day before. Once again she was wearing a blouse tucked into a nice skirt and a pair of heels, no doubt for the trial, but this time they were wrinkled and covered in soot. Across her knees and shins was blood. Her hair was disheveled and a smear of blackness bridged over her nose and to her chin.

What was perhaps the most surprising part was the puppy sitting on her lap, wrapped in her arms.

It was the only thing that stopped his impulse to wrap *his* arms around *her*.

That breath of relief finally released. It transformed into one question.

"You ran *toward* the fire?"

Alyssa averted her eyes.

Guilty.

So guilty, in fact, that Caleb took a second to really look at her again. "Alyssa, did you go *into the house*?"

She brought her baby blues up to his stare before cutting them away to the dog in her arms. The pup was panting, unaware of his anger.

Not at Alyssa, but at himself.

He should have been with her.

Caleb threw his hands up and walked around the side of the ambulance out of her view. He watched as firefighters made headway on killing the flames. It sobered him.

He walked back around to face the woman. When he spoke his voice was lighter, calmer. "Are you okay?"

Once again he looked at the blood on her legs. There wasn't a lot, but it was still more than there should have been.

"Yeah, I wasn't in the part of the house that collapsed," she said.

Caleb felt his eyes widen. It prompted her to explain her statement. "I was in the back of the house getting him out of his dog crate when that happened. Then we got out through the window. I promise I'm okay."

Caleb focused on the dog. He realized that it wasn't just sitting on her lap. She was holding him to her. It softened his anger at her for being so reckless. She'd risked her life to save a dog. Somehow, though, that didn't surprise him. It was becoming clear that Alyssa Garner had a penchant for trying to save people, dogs apparently included.

"Did they tell you who lives here?" she asked, motioning to the house.

Caleb nodded.

Alyssa's chin shook slightly as she spoke again. "Robbie said a firefighter told him they couldn't ID him for sure but they found a body. Ted lost his wife a few years back and never remarried. They never had kids either, so it's probably a safe bet that it's him." She cleared her throat and started to pet the dog absently. "So what happens now? Surely it's not a coincidence, what happened to Ted and what happened yesterday."

"No, I don't think it was a coincidence either," he agreed. He moved closer so only she would hear him. The EMT was a few steps away talking to another deputy. "I think someone might be targeting the witnesses from the trial."

Alyssa sat up straighter. "But why did I get a fake bomb that played music and Ted…" She let her words trail off. The smoke in the air around them was reminder enough that Ted had indeed gotten a different surprise than she had.

"I don't know," Caleb answered honestly. "But I intend to find out."

The trial was postponed for two months. Alyssa didn't know the reasoning behind the new time frame, but she did know it meant that the two Storm Chasers were being sent back to their respective prisons. Meanwhile their victims were scrambling to make sense of their new possible reality of being targets, yet again.

"I was supposed to take the stand first," Alyssa had explained to Captain Jones after the fire was officially put out. "Ted is—*was* second. Davis Palmer, one of the managers, was third, and Missy Grayson, one of the bank tellers, was fourth. Then one of the bank-goers, Margret Smith, and lastly Robbie."

"That's a lot of witnesses," he had remarked.

"No one wanted the possibility of them not spending the rest of their lives in prison," she had pointed out.

Just listing the witnesses, though, had made Alyssa feel like squirming. It didn't feel real. Maybe it had all been some crazy misunderstanding...

But then they confirmed it was Ted who had been killed and that some kind of explosive had done the trick. What was left of the device had gone to a lab while Captain Jones and Police Chief Hawser had met to try to figure out a plan for the witnesses who were left.

Finally, all of their houses were searched by bomb squad. Nothing was found, but that did little to ease their nerves. Missy, especially, wasn't keen on the idea of being under house arrest with a guard. Instead she told the captain in secret where she planned to hide out and then left town with her husband. Margret Smith followed their example and by that night Robbie, Eleanor, Davis and Alyssa were the only ones who opted to stay.

Although the couple tried hard to get Alyssa to leave. While she did the same with them.

"Go stay with Robert," Alyssa had pleaded, standing in the hallway at the department. "He's got that cabin on his property you two could lie low in."

Robbie shook his head. "If someone really wants to try to blow us to smithereens, then what makes you think they'll stop because we're outside Riker County?"

"That doesn't mean you have to make it *easier* on whoever is doing this by staying," Alyssa bit out.

"You're one to talk," Caleb said at her shoulder. His sudden appearance made her jump.

"But I've already been targeted," she pointed out, annoyed. "Robbie hasn't yet."

Eleanor reached for her hand.

"We aren't leaving our home," she said calmly. "And we aren't potentially putting Robert or any of our kids in danger by hiding with them." She squeezed Alyssa's hand but turned her gaze to Caleb. "We trust that the men and women of the Riker County Sheriff's Department will figure this all out and, in the meantime, keep us safe."

Caleb gave one curt nod.

Though Alyssa thought she saw an uncertainty there. Still, she already knew one thing for sure. She trusted Caleb Foster, even if he didn't trust himself.

"You're a stubborn woman," Alyssa said with a sigh.

"Takes one to know one." Eleanor winked and dropped her hand. "Now, Deputy Foster, what happens to our Alyssa when we go home?"

It was a pointed question, reminding everyone that Alyssa was indeed stubborn. They'd spent a good few minutes trying to convince her to stay with them instead of alone at her house. She'd declined. If someone was truly targeting witnesses, then having two in one house might entice their bomber to break order and try to take them all out.

Assuming the bomber wanted her dead. It shouldn't, but it bothered her that she'd gotten a fake bomb. Was it just the bomber's way of being theatrical about the start of what he was about to do to Ted?

Alyssa turned her attention back to the conversation, knowing she wouldn't suss out the motive behind the actions of a cold-blooded murderer standing in the hallway at the sheriff's department.

"Everyone will have a deputy keep watch at their residence. Including Alyssa." A muscle in Caleb's jaw jumped. He angled his body so he was mostly facing her. "Because I haven't been off the clock since yesterday morning, I've been told to take the night off to regroup."

Alyssa tried to rein in the raw panic that tore through her. Caleb might not have saved her from any danger in the past two days, but she was finding it hard to shake the idea that his companionship still helped her. It was one thing to survive an ordeal. It was another to live with it.

Caleb had helped with that part during the last two days. She didn't know why, or maybe she did but refused to think about it at length, but the idea that the deputy wasn't being forced to keep guard was more than just a disappointment. It was a fear.

"I've asked Deputy Mills to be assigned to you," Caleb added. "I've been partnered with him since I transferred. He's a good man and a good deputy. He'll make sure you're okay."

Alyssa didn't want to, but she nodded. Summoning up a smile of what she hoped resembled assurance, she skipped her gaze across Caleb and the Rickmans.

"That sounds good to me," she lied. "I just hope he doesn't mind a dog in his car."

They all cut their gaze to Sergeant at her feet. Since Ted didn't have any immediate family, that meant the Lab didn't either. The suggestion had been made to send him to the humane society, but Alyssa couldn't do that. Ted had loved the puppy, and Ted had always been nice to her. Until they could figure out a better forever home for the dog, Alyssa had offered to foster him. For a puppy he was well behaved. Plus, he seemed to have taken a liking to her. Maybe he realized what she'd done to save him or maybe it was more to do with the fact that she'd snuck into the break room at the department and fed him half of a ham sandwich. Either way he was coming home with her.

Eleanor and Robbie took turns hugging Alyssa *and* Caleb, to his obvious surprise, before wishing both of them luck. They were taken home by another longtime sheriff's department deputy who promised their safety with enthusiasm. This left Alyssa and Caleb alone for a moment while Deputy Mills collected his things.

"It's been a crazy two days, huh?" she started, avoiding any and all pleas for him to come back to her house. To what? Eat dinner and watch TV? To play with the dog?

To just sit and talk? Or not talk at all? Her face heated. There were bigger things to be concerned about. "Probably didn't think a small town like Carpenter had this kind of upset in us."

Caleb didn't smile. "Nothing about this town is what I expected." His answer was low and charged. With what, Alyssa didn't find out.

"I'm ready," Deputy Mills called from the other end of the hallway.

Alyssa nodded and gave Caleb the smallest of smiles. "Good night, Deputy."

It wasn't until she was halfway down the hall that she heard him respond.

"Good night, Miss Garner."

CALEB MIGHT HAVE gone home, but he had no intention of staying there. He stripped off his uniform, took a fast shower, and then dressed in his jeans and a plain T-shirt he'd gotten compliments for when he was in Portland. He didn't know why that thought had popped into his head when he made the decision to grab that particular shirt, but then again, maybe he did.

Alyssa Garner.

He even hung back long enough to shave his face clean. Then he was out the door with no intention of coming back until the bomber had been caught. While he had meant what he said about trusting Dante, there was a part of Caleb that he couldn't ignore. It wanted, *needed* to see this through with a front row seat. Not a spot in the balcony.

Plus, what he did on his off time was his own business, right?

Caleb spent the next half hour running around Carpenter until he got what he was looking for. Then he pointed the nose of his car in one direction. By the time he pulled into Alyssa's driveway, it was ten after seven at night.

"I was wondering when you'd show up." Deputy Mills got out of his patrol car and stretched.

Caleb figured Dante might give him some grief when he got there. Instead he rolled his eyes.

"Why don't you get back into your car and focus?" Caleb said with a snort.

Dante laughed but obliged. "I'm not doing it because you told me to, I'm doing it because your lady in there just fed me a good helping of apple pie and I really like her." He stretched one more time and got back into the car. "Just for the record," he called through the open window.

Caleb smirked and gathered the bags from his back seat. It wasn't until he was knocking on the front porch that the idea entered his mind that maybe Alyssa didn't want him there as much as he wanted to be there. He looked down at the bags and thought at the very least he could drop them off. Then maybe park down the street to help keep an eye on the house.

But then Alyssa opened the door and gave him a smile he'd never forget.

"Caleb, what are you doing here?" Her smile dissolved. "Is everything all right?"

"Yeah, everything is all right," he hurried. "I just thought you could use some backup." He shook the bags in his hand. Together they held dog food, a box with a collapsible dog crate and two chew toys in them. He dropped his voice low, serious.

"I also was wondering if you have any more pie."

Chapter Twelve

The pie was gone, the dog crate was assembled and Alyssa was yawning. As much as she wanted to pretend she wasn't tired, the fact of the matter was that the day had drained her. She hadn't had a moment to really sit and process what had happened. Let alone try to recover from it. A feat that was probably impossible. At least, until their mystery bomber was caught.

"Thank you for all of this," she said, stifling another yawn. "I'll pay you back."

Caleb waved his hand through the air.

"Don't worry about it," he said. "You ran into a burning building to save the dog. I think you've done enough for one day."

Alyssa felt her face fall before she saw Caleb's concern cross his expression. "Poor Ted. Do you know he visited me in the hospital a few times after the robbery? We weren't close—none of us really were—but afterward he made an effort to check on me. On Robbie too." A lump started to form in her throat. She swallowed and spoke around it, willing herself not to cry. "I don't know if I ever really told him thank you for that."

They were standing in the kitchen, the breakfast bar between them. Caleb's proximity wasn't helping Alyssa to control her swerving emotions. She wanted to let her grief and fear out, but her self-preservation was making a stand. Though one look at Caleb, watching her intently, and she felt every part of her waver.

Even more so when he moved around the counter and put a hand on her arm. "I'm sure he knew you appreciated it."

Alyssa was so surprised by the contact she didn't immediately respond. The heat from Caleb's hand wasn't just pressed against her skin—it felt like it was consuming it. The urge to press more of him against her flew through her mind.

"Thank you," she finally managed, breathy even by her ears.

Caleb didn't smile, but he didn't frown either. An in-between look born of thoughts she couldn't guess at. He dropped his hand and took a step back.

"I'm going to go out to the car now," he said. "I'll help Dante keep watch on the place."

"But you're off duty, I thought."

"True, but sometimes the job doesn't end after a shift." He cracked a quick smile and headed for the hallway.

"Or you could stay here," Alyssa hurried. "I mean, in the house. If you're off duty but still going to work, at least do it in comfort." Her cheeks were on fire. Still she kept on. "And it's not like you haven't done it before, right? Plus, it'll be nice to know I'm not alone."

She was telling the truth, despite the embarrassment pooling in her cheeks. It would have been nice to have anyone like Eleanor and Robbie in the house or her sister or even Deputy Mills. But if *Caleb* stayed?

Well, that would be different. It would *feel* different.

Too bad she wouldn't find out this time around.

"You're not alone," he said. "I— *We* will be right outside."

Alyssa was sure she turned as red as a stop sign, but

thankfully her head dipped low and she nodded on auto-pilot.

"You're right," she said. "Thanks again."

Caleb opened his mouth and then instantly closed it. Whatever he was going to say, he must have decided it wasn't worth saying.

"So, YOU GOT A girl back in Portland?"

Caleb was sitting shotgun in Dante's patrol car, and while they'd been shooting the breeze for almost two hours, he hadn't expected that question.

"That's one hell of a segue from talking about sports cars," Caleb pointed out.

Dante laughed. "Not when you keep looking over at the house with this expression."

Dante twisted his face into a comical version of what Caleb assumed was the deputy's attempt at trying to look "longingly" at something. Which he was not doing.

"First off, I'm doing my job by watching the house," he said. "To do that I have to, you know, *look* at the house."

"I'm looking at the house too, but not like that." Dante attached another mock expression to the end of his words. "I have to figure, if you're looking at her *house* like that, then you must look at the woman inside it with a little more intensity." He shrugged. "And if that's true, I have to also figure you don't already have a girl. Or, if you do, then maybe you shouldn't be paying as much attention to Miss Garner as you are, huh?"

Caleb didn't like the man prying into his personal life, especially in the romance department. But he really didn't like the insinuation that he was wronging another woman by being around Alyssa. He might be prickly but he was loyal.

"Not that it's any of your business, but no, I don't have

a 'girl back in Portland,'" he answered, heavy on the air quotes.

Dante snorted. "Hey, now, buddy. Remember, you're the one who wanted to sit out here with me and not in your own car. Don't be surprised if I ask a personal question or two."

Caleb rolled his eyes but knew the man was right. While he could have watched the house from his car, he hadn't wanted to be alone. And he had been truthful when he told Alyssa earlier that he thought Dante was a good man. He sighed and tried to adjust his attitude. "My sister, Kathy, likes to say the chip on my shoulder takes up too much room and no woman can get close enough to me to see that I'm not a 'complete jerk.'"

Dante was laughing again. Caleb couldn't help cracking a grin thinking about his older sister. Even if she did give him grief.

"Sounds like a woman I'd like to meet. Not afraid to call out the hard-nosed Caleb Foster."

Caleb kept his grin wide.

"She's definitely not afraid to try to tango with me," he agreed. Then something happened Caleb hadn't counted on. He kept talking. "I think she'd like Alyssa, though."

This time Dante didn't laugh.

"They broke the mold when they made her, all right," Dante agreed. "Not many people would have done what she's done in the last year *and* the last few days."

They lapsed into an agreeable silence. Then Caleb did something else he hadn't betted on doing. He asked a question he shouldn't have. "So, do you know if she's seeing anyone?"

Dante's face had lit up on his preparing to rib Caleb some more, he was sure, when his cell phone in the cup holder went off. With one look at the caller ID, any hint of humor was wiped clean from the deputy's expression.

"Mills here," he answered, tone hardened. It put Caleb on edge.

Whoever was on the other side of the phone started to talk fast. Caleb couldn't make out the topic of conversation, but the way Dante's body tensed, he doubted he'd like it.

"Yes, sir, I'm here," Dante continued. "Deputy Foster is with me." The other man said something else and ended the call before Dante could say goodbye.

"What's up?" Caleb *really* wasn't going to like the answer. He knew it in his bones.

Dante's hand flitted to his holstered gun.

"Anna Kim, the female gunwoman from the bank robbery, was just found dead along with her prisoner transport," he said, his voice grave.

Caleb's adrenaline spiked. "Was Dupree Slater with her?"

Dante shook his head. "He was on a separate transport. One that was just found back in town. All the guards were dead in the back."

"And Dupree?"

Dante shook his head again, this time with feeling. "Gone."

Caleb swore something fierce.

"I have to check on Alyssa," he said, already opening the car door. "I don't know how he's connected to what's been going on, but I do know that he's already tried to kill her before."

"Caleb," Dante said hurriedly, catching his arm to stop him.

"What?" he snapped back. He was seeing red. Red for a violent, bloodthirsty man who might or might not be coming for the witnesses.

"Get your gun," Dante ordered. "The transport was just found, but it's been out of commission since this afternoon."

Caleb's blood went cold.

"He doesn't just have minutes on us," Caleb started.

"He has hours on us," Dante finished.

Caleb reached for his gun in a holster on his hip. He'd never put too much stock in ESP or the illogical claim that sometimes you just know something is going to happen, but right then and there, Caleb felt it.

Something bad was about to happen.

"So if he was coming for Alyssa," he said, pulling his gun out and checking it, "then he could already be here."

FALLING ASLEEP WAS EASY. Staying asleep wasn't.

Alyssa wondered if it was a nightmare that had woken her. She'd already been pulled from sleep once by one filled with fire and smoke. It had spread a cold sweat across her body so badly she'd gotten frustrated and changed into the closest thing she could find: an oversize T-shirt she'd caught from a T-shirt cannon at a local football game and a pair of lacy sleep shorts in blue that couldn't be seen, hidden beneath the shirt. Normally she would have worried about the amount of leg she was showing, but then again, the only person she'd invited to stay the night had turned her down.

Alyssa sighed and rolled over. She reached for her glasses, ready to brood at her cell phone. It was only ten o'clock, yet she felt like it should have been way past midnight, creeping up on a new morning filled with the unknown.

Why had the bomber not killed her?

Why was he targeting witnesses in the first place?

What about the man in glasses?

Caleb had assured her he was still being hunted, but they were having no luck. Then again, they hadn't found a few of the courthouse-goers from the morning of the trial. Carpenter might have been small, but it was still big enough to get lost in sometimes.

Especially if that someone *wanted* to be lost.

Alyssa sighed again into the darkness of the room. The sound of stirring made her freeze. She glanced at the corner. The dog crate had been too bulky to place in the master bedroom, but then once Sergeant had gone to sleep she'd felt bad about leaving him alone. She'd snuck into the guest bedroom to sleep near him for comfort. After the nightmare, she realized maybe it hadn't been all about making the dog feel safer.

Either way, there she was, staring into the darkness and trying to push all thoughts of Caleb, the bomber and being afraid from her mind, when she heard it.

The creak.

If she had been in any other house, she might have dismissed it, but she *knew* that creak.

It was the third-step creak. The one that, regardless of a person's weight, still whined at any pressure applied to it.

The image of Caleb creeping up the stairs flashed through her mind. She couldn't deny it created a sense of excitement in her too. Late night, just the two of them, wearing what she was. Had he come to say he wanted to be closer to her? For her safety or for more?

Fantasies she hadn't thought were there before started to move through her thoughts. She sat up and swung her legs over the side of the bed. Her cheeks were already heating up. What would she say? What would she do? What—

A dull *thud* came from her bedroom.

In the opposite direction of the creak.

One unknown sound might account for the deputy, but two?

Alyssa got out of the bed, put her slippers on and tiptoed to the wall. All the lights were off—the only way to get Sergeant to sleep—but she knew the room well enough to move toward the door in the dark without a sound, unlike whoever else was moving through her house.

She hesitated in the open doorway, the hallway nightlight giving out only the faintest of illumination. Her sister had teased her about that small light, set on a timer, pointing out she wasn't a little girl. But now, trying to figure out if she was just paranoid and hearing things or if she was stuck between two people creeping around her house, she had never been more thankful for such a small material object. Ducking low, she waited to see who would step into the light first, if anyone was there at all.

Alyssa held her breath, waiting.

For one moment she believed without a doubt she'd been overreacting. That even her house could still produce noises she wasn't familiar with.

But then the unmistakable sound of footsteps padded toward her, coming from the stairs.

Her lips parted, mind already forming Caleb's name, when the small light showed her something else.

Someone else.

"Hello, Alyssa. It's nice to see you again."

Dupree Slater smiled.

Seeing him was worse than any nightmare she'd had.

Because this time she was awake.

Chapter Thirteen

Alyssa tried to slam the door shut, but the man was faster.

He closed the space between them in a flash, grabbing for her before she could scramble away. The commotion woke Sergeant from his sleep. He began barking as Alyssa began screaming.

"No need to be afraid," Dupree huffed, catching her forearm and turning on the light with the other. Like the man, his hand was large. Overpowering. It wrapped around her like a vise she couldn't escape.

She wanted to laugh at his comment, saying he'd shot her and gunned down two others and she had every right to be afraid of him. She wanted to break free from his grip, get something heavy, and make him feel at the very least an ounce of the pain he had caused her and everyone in the bank that day. She also wanted to grab her cell phone and call the cavalry in, guns blazing and ready to put down a man who seemed untouchable.

But all she could do was continue to scream in terror.

She'd spent the last year trying to overcome just the idea of the man. And now here he was, somehow managing to sneak into her house in the middle of the night.

It didn't seem real.

It didn't seem fair.

"You're coming with me," he grunted out, trying to contain her as she threw her body away from him. She tried to become deadweight in his grasp. She didn't want to make anything easier on the man. "Whether you like it or—"

Something slammed into Dupree's back so hard it caused his hold on her to break. However, the momentum of the hit sent both of them to the floor. Alyssa scurried backward until her back hit her nightstand. The lamp on it clattered to the floor just as she realized what had helped her escape Dupree's grip.

"Caleb!"

Caleb Foster, in all his beautiful glory, picked himself up and readied to take her nightmare head-on.

"Run," he managed to yell before Dupree was on his feet and in his face.

Alyssa didn't have time to examine the situation any closer. Caleb grabbed the front of Dupree's shirt and threw his weight into him again, hard. Together they went into the wall.

"Go—now!"

Alyssa didn't want to leave Caleb alone with a man like Dupree. She'd seen the evil that he created—lived through it too. She didn't want that for Caleb. She wanted to help the deputy to subdue and stop him, as a team.

"I'll still get her," Dupree growled. It was an awful sound, but it did the trick.

Thoughts of helping flew out of her mind. She got to her feet and ran for everything she was worth.

All Alyssa wanted to do in that moment was listen to Caleb and make sure Dupree never touched her again.

THE MAN WAS TALLER, more muscled, and had already found his second wind. However, Caleb had two things on him.

He put his arm up to block a punch Dupree threw and swung hard with a right cross. It connected with the man and he staggered. Angered, Dupree kicked out and flailed in his direction. Both moves Caleb avoided.

For one, Caleb had more discipline. He waited for an opening and took it, sending his fist into his chest, making Dupree wheeze. It didn't matter how big or bad your opponent was, if he didn't have patience he wasn't disciplined. In Caleb's career he had seen up close what happened to those without discipline in a fight.

They'd lost.

Caleb used Dupree's hesitation while he caught his breath to create more space between them so he could grab for his gun. He'd only holstered it for fear that he'd hit Alyssa in the scuffle. He was sure Dupree wasn't above using her as a last-second shield. Now that she was gone, though, Caleb could do some damage. He pulled out his service weapon, but before he could pull the trigger, Dupree recovered and sent him barreling back into the wall.

A *crack* sounded as the drywall broke against Caleb's back. The air was knocked clear out of him and his gun shot out from his grip away from both men. Dupree used his free hand and brought it up to his neck. It was such a sudden move that Caleb had to bring both of his hands up to keep the man from choking him. He was surprised at how strong Dupree's grip was.

"You think after everything I've been through *you* are going to stop me?" Dupree's voice had lowered to a dark, almost tangible level. Caleb peeled off his hand, but his focus faltered in doing so. Dupree delivered a knee to the groin so severe that Caleb knew he wouldn't be able to stand. He stepped away as Caleb fell to his knees, the pain nearly blinding him.

"I waited an entire year in prison for this," Dupree seethed, taking the moment to gain his own breath back. Blood dripped down his nose and fell to the carpet. He swiped at it. "And if taking her is all I have to do to finish what I started, well, then, *Deputy*, you aren't going to stop me now. No one is."

Dupree staggered toward the door to leave. Or so Caleb thought. For the first time he saw a gun, discarded near the opening. It must have fallen from Dupree's possession in the scuffle. If Dupree got the gun, Caleb had no doubt that the man would kill him. He'd already killed two guards from his transport and most likely the two guards from his partner's. Not to mention the female robber herself.

Then, once he had killed Caleb, he would find Dante, if he hadn't done so already—they had split up to search, but the deputy shouldn't have been too far behind—and then shoot him too. And if Dante couldn't best him, that left Dupree Slater to go after Alyssa.

Caleb swallowed his pain and got to his feet.

Because while Dupree had height, width and violence on his side, Caleb had something better than just discipline on his.

He had someone to fight for.

Caleb charged across the room and once again slammed into Dupree. Together they staggered out into the hallway. This time they didn't hit the floor. Dupree used the wall to keep from falling and turned with a fist ready. Caleb had one too. Neither avoided the other's attack. Pain burst bright in Caleb's right eye while Dupree made his own grunt of pain as he took a fast one to the nose. The blood already there wet Caleb's fist, but he didn't stop. Bringing his other fist around, he drilled it into the man's stomach.

Dupree lost his breath for the second time. In that moment, even in the poor hallway light, his eyes found Caleb's. Rage. Pure and simple rage. Dupree let out a thundering yell and threw his elbow so it caught Caleb against the eye that had managed to avoid all punches so far. More pain lit up his face as he stumbled backward, trying to keep from falling.

"You won't—won't stop me," Dupree said, anger funneling from his mouth and into his words, seemingly strengthening his will to take a beating and then dole one out. "He wants her, he gets her."

That surprised Caleb.

"Who wants her?" he couldn't help asking. He had put a few steps of distance between them, and now he needed a few seconds to right himself.

Dupree busted out a grin that was chilling. "What? You thought you were the only one sweet on her, Deputy?"

Caleb laughed for the sake of being more dramatic. It sounded hollow, mechanical almost. Definitely not a sound the man was used to making.

"Don't look so worried. Norman's been waiting for her for so long. He will treat her nice."

Caleb wanted to ask who Norman was and why he wanted Alyssa, but the way Dupree had said the word *nice* had put straight fire into his bones.

"No one is taking Alyssa," he seethed, a mile past defensive. A familiar anger was building within him. Last time it had consumed him and destroyed his career. His life. And now?

Now he was going to let it destroy again. And this time he wouldn't be looking for redemption for it.

He had to keep her safe at all costs.

He *had* to.

With all the silent fury created by the senseless death and violence Dupree had been responsible for, Caleb closed the space between them with a kick. It was short but not sweet, connecting with Dupree's abdomen with such force it laid the man out.

Right down the stairs.

He rolled and clattered in a heap of flailing limbs, trying to stop himself until he went stationary at the bottom. Caleb flipped the lights on, hoping to see a man so broken that he wouldn't attempt to prolong their fight. That he'd be finished with trying to resist capture. A man realizing he'd reached the end of the road and would finally, *finally* pay for everything he'd done.

Instead he saw a man sitting motionless.

And then, slowly, start to get to his feet.

"Don't you ever—" Caleb stopped midsentence as Dupree produced a gun from his waistband. There was no hesitation on his part as he pulled the trigger.

ALYSSA'S FEAR PUSHED her legs harder than they'd ever been pushed. She didn't just leave the upstairs, she left her house altogether. Later she'd wonder if her feet even touched the sidewalk as she ran full tilt toward Deputy Mills's patrol car out front. It felt like some kind of dream. No. It felt like a nightmare.

Her body was shaking, her breathing was erratic and her heart was surely about to tear itself from her chest. The situation wasn't improved by the fact that Dante was missing.

Where did he go? Was he helping Caleb?

She fumbled for the door handle, ready to attempt to use the radio to call for help, but the door didn't budge. None of them did.

Alyssa knew the Rogerses next door weren't home and didn't even bother to try her other neighbor, an older woman with a bad hip, to see if she could help. Panic was king. It ruled over her mind and replaced all rational thought with the basic need to survive kicking in. She turned tail and ran across the street to a two-acre lot covered in trees.

I'll hide in there, she thought, pain buoying up from her feet as she picked up speed. *Caleb will find me. He'll find me and we can—*

"Alyssa!"

Alyssa skidded to a halt next to the curb. She spun around, ready to ask Caleb if he was okay. Her question died on her tongue. It wasn't Caleb standing in her driveway.

"You," she exclaimed, confused. "Why are you here?"

The man wearing horn-rimmed glasses from the courthouse smiled.

"I was worried," he said, walking into the street. "I needed to make sure you were okay."

Alyssa started to back away. She didn't have to understand the entire story to know the man was someone else she needed to run from. Without asking any more questions, she turned once again and ran for the trees.

"Don't run from me," he yelled after her. A moment later footsteps sounded behind her. "I'm not going to hurt you!"

Even over the sound of her fear and panic, Alyssa heard the certainty in his words. It almost made her falter in her escape.

Was she missing something?

Was the man in the horn-rimmed glasses there to help them?

To help her?

An explosion behind her shattered her concentration. Another one followed.

Her body tried to keep running while her head turned so she could look back at the house. Before she could understand anything, her feet tucked under each other. She pitched forward. There was no stopping the impact. She let out a scream as her body crashed to the ground. A beat later and her head whiplashed against the grass.

Pain and nausea paraded to the forefront of her senses and began to cloud her vision.

Those aren't explosions, she thought, mind fogging so fast she didn't have time to fear the man chasing her. Instead darkness swam up, took her hand and dragged her down into the depths of unconsciousness.

But not before she finished her thought.

Those are gunshots.

Chapter Fourteen

Caleb dove backward and missed the bullet by inches. He got to his feet but stayed low as another gunshot cracked through the air. Dupree couldn't see him from his place at the bottom of the stairs, and Caleb wanted to keep it that way. At least until he could put his hands on his own gun.

He kept low and went into the guest bedroom. Sergeant was all-out howling from his crate. Caleb wished he could calm the pup down. Instead he picked up his gun and prepared to enter a firefight. To stop the evil that was Dupree in his tracks. He held his Glock up and out. Steady and ready. Taking a deep breath, he went back into the hallway.

No sound floated up the stairs. Had Dupree been hurt worse than he thought, or was he just waiting Caleb out?

Either way, Caleb was about to find the answer.

He aimed downward and moved into position to get the man at the bottom.

But he wasn't there.

"Dammit," Caleb said beneath his breath. He pulled his gun high again and descended the stairs.

The bottom floor was mostly dark. Alyssa had left the porch light on when she went to bed, and it alone tried to illuminate as much of the entryway as it could. It was enough to see blood on the tile but not the man who had left it.

Where had Dupree gone?

Where had Alyssa?

Caleb moved through the entryway and into the living room. He kept the lights off, his eyes adjusting to the darkness. From there he went to the kitchen.

He cursed below his breath again. The back door was open.

Dupree might have been hurt, but that didn't mean he was slow.

Caleb went down the back porch and scanned the backyard for the man. No one shot toward him, let alone moved. He kept his gaze sweeping as he rounded the side of the house. Despite the noise of gunshots, the night stayed quiet. No neighbors yelling or sirens blaring. Normally that was a good thing.

But for Caleb all it did was highlight the fact that he didn't know where Dupree, Alyssa or Dante was. It was amazing how quickly he'd lost control of the situation.

He should have stayed with her.

Why hadn't he?

Just because he was inside the house didn't mean anything other than he wanted to keep her safe.

But he'd been afraid of exactly what had happened.

Afraid he'd lose control of the situation.

For someone trying to keep from emotions getting the better of him, he sure had let fear do a number on him.

He should have stayed with her.

The outline of a body pulled his attention toward the front corner of the house. Caleb focused his gun on the man.

"Don't move," he warned. However, the man wasn't moving. He wasn't Dupree either.

Dante's face was bloody. His eyes were closed. The gun in his holster was gone along with his cuffs. Even the radio was missing.

Caleb didn't lower his gun for fear that Dupree was

near. He crouched to check for a pulse. He let out a sigh of relief as a beat pushed against his skin. It was shallow, but it was there. Feeling inside the man's pocket, Caleb was happy again for the keys the deputy had kept on him. Hopefully it meant the car was still out front. Caleb left his side to peer around the corner and confirmed the car was indeed still there.

After a quick scan for Dupree came up empty, Caleb ducked and ran for the patrol car. When no one shot at him he unlocked it and reached for a radio. He was quick to call in that a deputy was hurt and Dupree Slater was on the move. It wasn't until he put the radio down, ready to continue the search, that he noticed one detail that put ice in his stomach.

In the lot across from him, right before the tree line started, was one blue slipper, all on its own.

ALYSSA WAS LYING down when she woke up.

Had it all been a dream? she wondered.

But then the blanket of unconsciousness lifted completely, ushering in a wave of pain. It thudded along the back of her head all the way to the roots of her teeth.

Then she remembered she'd fallen and hit her head.

And then she remembered the man in the horn-rimmed glasses.

Alyssa slowly focused on her surroundings, knowing full well she wasn't in her room anymore based on the smell alone. It was a heavy musk with mildew swirled in. *Old.*

The room was dark but not to the point she couldn't see. A fluorescent light on its last legs cupped the middle of a popcorn ceiling and showed a small, faded room. Its one window was boarded up. That alone might have terrified her, but coupled with the man sitting in a corner opposite her, and her heartbeat began to pick up speed. The new surge of adrenaline made the pain in her head worsen.

Apparently it showed.

"You wouldn't have hurt your head if you hadn't run from me," he greeted. "I told you I wasn't going to hurt you, didn't I? So why did you run, Alyssa?"

The man leaned forward and put his elbows on his knees, further showing his disappointment.

And that was what it was. *Disappointment.*

Alyssa might have been confused and scared, but she read that feeling in his body language and expression as clear as day.

But who was he to be disappointed in her?

Also, *who was he*?

"You can talk to me, Alyssa," he continued in her silence. "You're safe here. So, please, feel free to say anyth—"

"Who are you?" she interrupted. "And where have you taken me?"

The man, who she placed in his thirties if not early forties, let his words hang unsaid for the moment before his smile widened. Had they been in any other setting, maybe a picnic at the park with friends or at a neighborhood barbecue, that smile would have been pleasant. Comforting and friendly. However, in the outskirts of the fluorescent lighting in the beginnings of the shadows of the room, the simple showing of mirth was downright chilling.

"You're a smart woman, Alyssa," he said. "So I won't go along with you being coy on your first question, but I will help you with the second." Before she could ask what he meant by her being coy, the man motioned to the room around them. "We needed to make a pit stop before we went home. I have some business I need to finish, and this place is safe for us until I can do that."

He got up from his chair and walked over to the couch

she was on. Alyssa scrambled to sit up. The movement made the pain in her head swim.

"Try not to hurt yourself any more than you already have," the man chided. He took a seat next to her. "Here, let me look at that."

Alyssa slapped his hand away as he reached out for her.

"I don't know who you are, where we are or why you took me," she said, voice rising despite her fear. "If you're so concerned for my well-being, then why don't you let me leave?"

A muscle in the man's jaw jumped as his teeth clenched. His smile stayed but hardened, like someone trying their hardest to pretend they were still happy with the situation when clearly they weren't. Alyssa instinctively leaned away. If he noticed he didn't show it. Instead he laughed. The sound was forced and bitter.

"I don't know what game you're playing with me, Alyssa," he said, voice eerily calm. "But I don't have the time to join in right now. I'm afraid I have more work to do before we can be together."

Alyssa felt like she was in an episode of *The Twilight Zone*. One where she'd been dropped into a world that looked like hers but was slightly off. The familiarity the man was talking to her with didn't make sense. And definitely not the being together part. She wanted more than anything to point out, again, that she had no idea who he was. Yet her instincts were yelling at her to avoid trying to remind him of that. You couldn't force a person to be stable. Sometimes you just had to try to keep from making him even more unstable.

Still, she had to try to make sense of *something*.

"Work," she said, then paused to clear her throat. It was hard to suppress her nerves. "What work are you talking about?"

The tightness around his mouth smoothed. She'd made the right call not to question his identity again.

"I was hoping you'd bring that up," he said, almost excited. "It's been quite the endeavor, but we're finally nearing the finish line. All that's left is one last wahoo. And it's a big one, Alyssa. I think you'll really like how beautiful it all will be. A great finale to a long season." He reached out and took her hand in his. She didn't dare move. "And now that we're finally together, it will be even better."

Alyssa felt her eyes widen. This man wasn't giving her anything more than vagueness and a creep factor that was off the charts. No recognition flared when she looked into his eyes. At least not before the courthouse parking lot and not with the same intensity. Yet he seemed so certain that there was a relationship between them.

"The bombs are yours," she guessed, thinking she might get more information if she didn't actually ask questions. "The one in my car and then in Ted's house. I didn't drop my keys, you took them from me at the courthouse and then gave them back when you were done placing it. Then you put one in Ted's house."

He ran his thumb across the top of her hand. It took all of Alyssa's self-control not to pull away or slap him again.

"I wasn't ever going to hurt you," he assured her. "But I couldn't abandon the plan either, not after waiting so long to put it in action. Not after all the planning. Even if I never planned for you." He sighed and then took a moment before continuing. Like some lovesick high schooler. "So I compromised. I knew I could still get everyone's attention by planting a fake one. That way I could keep you safe but still follow the correct order."

"I was the first witness for the trial," she added. "And Ted was the second." He nodded. Although Alyssa was trying to navigate the obviously unstable mind of the man in front of her, she couldn't help breaking her facade to ask a few of the questions burning in her mind. "But what's the point of all this? Why kill witnesses for the trial? Surely you have to know the Storm Chasers would still be found guilty without us. Why help Dupree and his partner?"

The man used his free hand to pat the top of hers like he was trying to placate a child. "I couldn't care less about the trial. Or the 'Storm Chasers.' My goal is and has always been bigger, the payoff much sweeter. Especially now that we're together again. But don't worry, everything will make sense soon. All you have to do is be patient and stay here, okay?"

Alyssa's focus had stuck on the "together again" portion of his answer. It kept her from responding right away. The man wasn't pleased.

The hand holding hers tightened.

"Okay, Alyssa?" he repeated. His smile skewed, no longer aligned with a pleasant mood. His grip was now tightening past annoying to painful. "You'll stay here, right?"

Tears pricked at the edges of Alyssa's eyes.

She nodded.

"Say it, Alyssa," he demanded, voice cutting low and mean. He added his other hand to the grip and squeezed so hard she couldn't keep from yelping. "Promise me that you'll stay here."

"I promise," she rushed.

"You promise *what*?" The man's intensity tripled. He was yelling now. *"What do you promise, Alyssa?"*

"I promise I'll stay here," she cried. "I promise!"

All at once the man returned to what she could only guess was his normal. He let go of her hand, and his smile brightened.

"Good," he said. "I'd hate to see you lose your way. I know you've been forced to spend some time with Deputy Foster. I'd hate for him to get into your head and mess up everything we have. Everything we could have."

At the mention of Caleb, Alyssa felt herself freeze.

Where was he?

Was he okay?

Looking into the eyes of the man in front of her, she dared not ask him.

He wasn't just a man who was unstable. He was a man filled with delusions. Ones that involved her. And her instincts warned her that if she didn't play along with her part in his daydream, they would come to a deadly end. But she couldn't police the fear that had welled up inside her. It pushed the dam to the point of extreme. The tears she'd been trying to hold back started to roll down her cheeks.

If the man saw them, he didn't seem to care.

"Well, now that we have everything settled, it's time for me to have a talk with an old acquaintance." He leaned forward and pressed his lips against Alyssa's forehead. Every part of her body felt disgust. Thankfully, he stood when he was done. "Don't worry, once this is all over we can have the life we've always wanted."

He left the room and closed the door behind him.

The sound of a dead bolt sliding into place followed.

Alyssa was glad he was gone.

At least now she could cry in peace.

Chapter Fifteen

They all looked like fireflies. Dotting the neighborhood with their flashlights, uniforms converged on Alyssa's property and then expanded out in an attempt to find Dupree and Alyssa. Guns were drawn, shouts were exchanged, neighbors were told to stay indoors, but no one set their eyes on the beautiful auburn-haired woman.

Or the beast who had managed to escape.

Hours crawled by, and with them Caleb's sanity inched further away from him. Dante had been rushed to the hospital and diagnosed with a fractured cheekbone and a nasty concussion. The doctor had refused to let him join the search on the basis of, at the very least, him being medicated out of his mind. His speech was even more impeded by the swelling around his cheek. He'd at least been able to express his guilt and anger at letting Dupree get the jump on him when they split up to check the perimeter after getting the call that he'd escaped.

But Caleb didn't hold it against the man. It had been *his* fault, not Dante's.

That fact kept becoming more pronounced as time slipped by. His darkening mood didn't go unnoticed.

"I order you to go home."

Captain Jones stood to the full of his height and pointed in any direction that was away from the department. With no new evidence, some of the men and women had regrouped for a new game plan.

"I'm not leaving until we find her," Caleb said with a hardness one wouldn't normally use with a superior. He just wanted Jones to know that it was more of a promise than a statement.

Whether the captain understood the tone or not, he also stayed firm in his decision.

"You need to get some rest," he said. "There are plenty of men and women, including the local police department, who are out there searching for both Miss Garner and Dupree." Caleb opened his mouth to protest, but Jones was quick to continue. "The dogs will get here at five and after they are done I will update you. But as of *right now* I am telling you to go home."

"I'm off the clock," Caleb pointed out, anger building inside him. It wasn't aimed at the captain but himself. "You can't order me around now. If I want to keep looking, I will."

Jones's lips narrowed and his nostrils flared. This time his anger *was* directed at Caleb. "This is a stressful situation. Never mind the emotional attachment between you and Miss Garner. So I'm going to give you a pass here and ignore that look and tone you're giving me. You're getting close to crossing that line again, Mr. Foster. Not with just me but the department as a whole. And that's not something you can afford." He took a noticeably deep breath and then let it out slowly. Like he was trying to calm down. Jones's eyes then dropped to Caleb's hands, now balled into fists, before he spoke again. "Helping people is what we do. Ensuring their safety, even when it means we lose ours. You haven't been here long, so let me make you a promise. The men and women of the Riker County Sheriff's Department are extremely capable, hardworking people. We will always be here for our community and stop at nothing to ensure their well-being."

Jones took a step closer. He lowered his volume. "Trust us and listen to me. Go home. Sleep for a few hours and then get your ass back here. Just don't waste any more of my time having to babysit you. *Go home now.* Or I'll escort you there myself."

The captain didn't budge from his new stance. Caleb didn't have to know the man well to understand exactly what his body language was saying. He meant every word, including the threat, and he wasn't going to back down in the slightest. But he was right, in part. Their conversation alone was wasting time.

Time that could be spent finding Alyssa.

Caleb gritted his teeth and gave Jones a nod. There wasn't any more to be said. The captain stayed still as Caleb turned and left the building. He walked to his car, hands still fisted.

Even if the captain was right, that he needed to trust the rest of the department, it didn't make a dent in his resolve to continue to look on his own. Trust wasn't easy for Caleb. Not after what had happened. Especially not with Alyssa on the line. He couldn't just go home, get into bed and sleep hours away.

No, not when he had no idea what she was dealing with at the moment.

If she was even still al—

Caleb slammed his hands against the steering wheel.

"Don't think like that," he yelled at himself. "She's tough."

He tried to distract his mind from looping back around to the worst possible outcome until he realized he'd disobeyed direct orders once again. He parked his car outside Alyssa's house and sank back in his seat.

Why was he even here?

Two headlights interrupted his thoughts as a pickup truck pulled up beside him. Caleb reached for his gun. It was nearly four in the morning and no one, not even him, had a reason to be there. Caleb readied to pull his gun just in case when the truck's window rolled down. He immediately dropped his hand and let out a breath he hadn't realized he'd been holding. He got out of his car and walked up to the window.

"What are you doing here?"

Robbie was alone in the truck and looked ready. For what, though?

"I've been looking for you," the man said back, hurried. Impatient. The tone put Caleb on alert. "I thought you might be here."

"Why? What's up?"

Robbie's face hardened. "Do you have any leads on Alyssa or Dupree?"

Caleb didn't like to, but he shook his head. "No, everyone is still looking."

"And you?"

"I was told to go home." Caleb motioned back to the house. "But I wound up here."

Robbie lowered his voice.

"Do you have your gun with you?" he asked. It surprised Caleb, but he answered without skipping a beat.

"Yeah, why?"

Robbie leaned out of the window. "Because I think I know where Alyssa might be."

ALYSSA'S FINGERS WERE bloody and her shoulder and head ached.

While her captor was gone she'd spent the last hour trying to actively escape her makeshift prison.

The boards on the window wouldn't budge. They were held together by so many nails that not even one shifted as she pulled with all her might. Not that it would have made much of a difference if she managed to pull one off. Through the gap in the top layer of boards, she saw that on the other side of the glass was another layer. Still, she kept her focus on that window long enough to make her fingers rub raw at the attempt.

Once that route was proven to be a dead end, she'd gotten a little desperate. Trying to pick the lock was impossible thanks to having no tools of any kind, not even a bobby pin, never mind the skills or knowledge to do it. So she'd sucked in a deep breath, pulled herself together and then charged the door like a bull at a red flag. However, the door wasn't as worn as the rest of the room. It creaked but didn't budge. By the third attempt, all she was doing was breaking herself down, not the door. And she wanted to be the best she could be when the man returned.

She took a seat on the couch and tried to focus on anything she could turn into a weapon. Had the man had a gun when he was in the room with her? Alyssa tried to remember, but all thinking about him did was send a chill down her spine.

The way he talked to her.

The way he *looked* at her.

Was she missing something?

Did she know the man?

Footsteps sounded in the hall outside the door. Alyssa scrambled to her feet and looked around one last time in the hope that she'd missed some glaringly obvious pipe or baseball bat or vase—*anything*—but she knew she hadn't. The dead bolt slid open. Maybe if she treated the man like she had treated the door she could buy herself a window of escape.

She readied herself, bending slightly, ready to go, but the door didn't open.

Instead she heard the man from before talking to someone else. She moved a step closer to try to make out what they were saying.

"It's my choice. Not yours." Another chill ran down her spine. That was definitely the man in the horn-rimmed glasses. And he was angry.

"This isn't part of the plan," the second voice said even louder than the first. There was no chill cold or deep enough that could fully express her feelings for that voice. It was Dupree Slater's. "*She* isn't a part of this plan and never was. Get rid of her."

Alyssa took an involuntary step backward.

Her panic levels had been holding steady the last few hours. Now they were increasing at an alarming rate. She almost didn't hear the other man's response.

"There will be *no* plan if you touch her," he yelled, volume going from zero to a hundred in a second flat. Dupree reacted in kind, his voice more an extended boom than words.

"This connection you think you have with her isn't real. *She doesn't remember you.* And do you want to know why?"

Alyssa jumped as the sound of a tussle bled through the door. Muttered cursing followed and then Dupree had the door open. Alyssa let out a shriek as he moved toward her with startling speed. Her back slammed the wall just as he reached for her head. Out of terror she closed her eyes, waiting for what she thought was a punch to her face. Instead something unexpected happened.

She felt her glasses slide through her hair and across her skin. Dupree pulled them off her face and whirled around to the other man. He held her glasses up and shook them. Then he dropped them to the floor.

And stomped on them.

"*This* is why," Dupree bit out.

He walked over to the door and stopped. Alyssa blinked a few times to focus, but he was still a blur.

"How many fingers am I holding up?" he asked.

"Wh-what?"

Of all the things he could have said, that hadn't even made her list of possibilities.

"How many fingers am I holding up?" he repeated, raising his voice.

Alyssa knew that there was no way other than to wear her glasses to answer him correctly. Still, she squinted and tried.

"I'm nothing but a blur, right?" he added.

Alyssa nodded.

What did it matter that she couldn't see?

"That's what I thought." Dupree must have looked at the other man. His tone changed into a smugness that made the situation even more confusing for Alyssa. "She might have looked at you, but she didn't *really* see you. And if she didn't see you, Norman, then how did that connection happen?"

Alyssa didn't understand what was going on, but now at least she had a name to give the man in the horn-rimmed glasses. *Norman.* Though that wasn't the best feeling, considering the name brought her no recognition.

"That's enough," Norman growled. There was undeniable authority thronging through his voice. Dupree had hit a nerve. A big one. "We have work to do."

The blur that was Dupree didn't leave right away. Instead he stood next to Norman with a look Alyssa guessed wasn't polite in the least. Then, without another word, he left them alone.

Alyssa felt her body relax a fraction. While she had no love for Norman, in her book, he was better to be with in close proximity than the man who had shot her the year before. But no sooner than she'd had that thought did it change.

Norman closed the space between them. His face swam into focus when he was an inch or two in front of her nose. He put his hands on the tops of her arms. She couldn't move away. He smiled.

"Don't worry," he whispered. "He just doesn't understand what we have. But you do, don't you?"

Alyssa felt frozen. Not even fear could unthaw her this time to play along with him.

However, Norman didn't seem to care. He kept smiling. "When I found out you had survived... Well, I knew what you gave me was more than a look. It was a promise." He reached up and tucked a strand of hair behind her ear. "One that said we'd be together when all this was over."

He stepped away and blurred.

"And we will," he finished. "Just one last step."

Alyssa's fear gave way long enough to ask one question. "And what *is* that step?"

"Revenge," he said, matter-of-factly. "Sweet, sweet revenge."

Chapter Sixteen

"Are you sure about this?"

Caleb and Robbie were parked at the mouth of a street lined with abandoned houses just outside downtown Carpenter. Two lone streetlights were the only things that seemed to be in order in the one-block stretch. Aside from the electrical buzz, nothing and no one else stirred.

At least not outside.

Robbie rubbed his hands together, tense.

"I don't know how much Alyssa has told you about it, but during our recovery we spent a lot of time together," he started, eyes never leaving the house in the middle of the block. "She's a strong cookie, but anyone in her position would have had a difficult time. And she did. One day her physical therapist suggested she find something else to focus on like reading or a hobby. Basically anything that would help her cope and work through what had happened. So she focused on the one part of her life that she couldn't make sense of."

He nodded in the direction of the houses. "She couldn't understand why Dupree Slater did what he did. So she spent most of her recovery trying to figure out who he was." He shrugged. "She thought if she knew about his life she could find out how he ticked, and if she knew why he'd shot her, then everything would hurt less."

Caleb felt an ache in his chest. He could imagine Alyssa

pretending everything was all right while trying to desperately make sense out of senseless violence. In that way he could relate to her without hesitation. His career—his past—had proven to him that sometimes there just was no answer.

"Did she ever figure it out?" Caleb asked anyway.

Robbie shook his head. "Eventually her sister, Gabby, Eleanor and I sat her down and convinced her that some people are just bad and do bad things and that it was time for her to move on." Robbie gave a small smile. "And she did, but not before she got a little backstory on Dupree." He pointed to the houses. "Or his brother, who lived in town before his house and his neighbors' were abandoned after a fire broke out and made them unlivable. No one had insurance and the city hasn't been able to touch them. That house is the only tie Alyssa ever found between Dupree and Carpenter."

Caleb sat up straighter. "And you wanted to find me and not tell another deputy because…"

"The last time the cops were called in, Dupree killed two people, and almost took another," Robbie answered, solemn. "I figured Alyssa has a chance of living through this if we do it quick and quiet. And try not to anger the beast that is Dupree any more than he already is. There's no telling what he might try to do."

Logically, it might have made more sense to call in backup. More manpower, more coverage. But part of Caleb—the part that cared for Alyssa more than it should have—didn't want to risk a team of people going in either. But he also didn't want to risk Robbie going in too. He had a pretty good suspicion that Alyssa would never forgive him if he let something happen to one part of her favorite couple. And, he had to admit, the old man and his wife had grown on him in the short time since he'd met them.

"Okay, here's the plan," Caleb said, pulling his gun out and checking the chamber. "I need you to do exactly as I say."

THE LIGHTS WENT out right as Norman was leaving the room. It was a nightmare within a nightmare for Alyssa. Now her last hope of seeing anything without her glasses was gone. She hugged the wall as Norman cussed. At least he wasn't as enthusiastic as he had been before.

Footsteps hurried toward their room. A small flashlight bounced down the hallway. By the blur's shape it was easy to guess it was Dupree.

"A truck is parked on the other side of the street," he said, clearly angry. "The security guard from the bank is inside and he's talking on the phone. That can't be a co-incidence."

Why was Robbie outside? And just like that, worry clenched her chest. But so did hope. Surely he wouldn't have come alone.

"Don't make a scene," Norman advised. "But take care of it. I'd like to stay under the radar as long as possible."

"So otherwise, be quiet when I kill him," Dupree said. "You got it."

Alyssa's fear turned a corner and ran smack-dab into anger. Like a bucket of ice water to the face, she felt a jolt. She had to warn Robbie.

"Norman," she called into the darkness after the bounce of Dupree's flashlight retreated away from them. She tried to soften her voice, showing affection. Even if he'd just ordered her friend to be killed.

Norman must not have had a light on him. He answered her in the darkness.

"Don't tell me you're afraid of the dark?" he said. "After everything you've been through already."

For the first time Alyssa heard a Southern drawl.

"I'm afraid of Dupree," she said, voice not as steady as she liked. "I don't trust him." Alyssa took an uncertain step forward. The darkness was near debilitating. But she had to do *something*. "And neither should you. He could—he could hurt you, Norman. He could kill you."

Again Alyssa took a step forward. It was small and her slipper shuffled at the movement. There was no sound in return. Norman must still be in the doorway. Trying to watch her.

"You don't have to worry about that," he said, a degree less harsh than when he'd been speaking to his partner.

"He shot me in the back!" Alyssa's voice broke, but from anger, not pain. "I wasn't a threat and he shot me. What's stopping him from doing it again to both of us?"

This time there was a sound in the darkness as Norman's shoes moved across the floor. Alyssa fought the urge to flinch away from it.

"Dupree helped prove we were meant to be together," he said, getting closer. "When you survived, I knew it was a sign. And for that I'm grateful. But now that I know, *he* knows the limits and he'll respect them." The heat of another body radiated out to her. She felt his breath when he spoke. "As long as you stay by my side, Alyssa, I won't let anyone hurt you." She nearly screamed when his hands grabbed the tops of her arms again, holding her in place.

It made her wonder how he even knew where to grab in the dark. Even if she'd had her glasses on, the boarded-up window didn't allow any outside light in. He should have been as blind as she.

Which gave Alyssa an idea.

One that might possibly have been terrible.

Knowing exactly where his hands were and that they were occupied, Alyssa took a risk. With all her might she kneed Norman as hard as she could where the sun didn't shine.

His pain was instantaneous. He let go of her arms and wailed. As soon as their connection was broken, Alyssa pushed forward until the man sounded like he'd fallen over. She moved as quickly as if her life depended on it. Which she was sure it did.

Alyssa outstretched her arms until she felt the opened door. Without Norman blocking the entrance she could just make out light in the distance. Which could be Dupree. Either way she had to get out of that room.

Because while Norman had seemed sincere in his words, the only promise of protection she believed in had been from a man named Caleb Foster.

Dupree took the bait.

Caleb watched as the man left through the back door and disappeared around the side of the house. He was cautious, trying to scope out his surroundings to make sure Robbie was alone. And that was exactly what Caleb had wanted him to do.

As soon as Dupree disappeared, he hurried to the back door, clicked on his flashlight and entered the house. While he wanted more than anything to bring a world of justice down on Dupree Slater's head, he had to make sure Alyssa was in the house. If he apprehended the man or had a shoot-out and won and Alyssa was hidden somewhere else? Well, that wasn't something he wanted.

No. First he had to find her. Then he'd deal with Slater.

Even without the fire and water damage, the house was old. Caleb slightly regretted turning the breaker off. His small beam of light couldn't show him every part of the playing field. He just hoped he wasn't about to step into a hole in the floor.

He had navigated halfway through the house when he finally heard movement. Hope and relief welled up inside him so fast he was seconds away from calling Alyssa's name when those footsteps were coming fast toward him. He moved the beam of light to the source.

"Alyssa?"

Her eyes met his. They were wide, terrified.

"Caleb?"

She collided into his arms, but the embrace lasted only a second. The flashlight beam skittered to the wall. For that one moment there was only the two of them, holding on to each other in the darkness. Then it was gone, and Alyssa was pulling back. Still, it was long enough for Caleb to be surprised at how badly he'd wanted to feel her in his arms.

"We have to hurry," Alyssa rasped. "He's behind me."

"Dupree is outside. I need you to stay here until I can—"

"Norman is the boss," she interrupted. "*He's* behind me."

That new piece of news was followed by the grunting of someone in pain at the end of the hallway. Caleb's plan certainly hadn't accounted for another man. Who was Norman?

"We have to go," Alyssa added, grabbing his hand and tugging. The warmth of her hand put him into gear. He turned around and whispered back to her to keep quiet. The last thing he needed was to be caught between an unknown man and Dupree. Even with a gun, that was one too many variables for his comfort.

Caleb cut his flashlight off and navigated the path back out of the house with relative ease. Dupree hadn't come back, and Norman had started to make more noise. Which meant their window to get away from both men was closing.

"We need to run," he rushed, turning them toward the back fence. If they could get on the other side and keep going, then Robbie could get Alyssa and take her to safety before Dupree realized which direction they'd gone. Then Caleb could fight. He could end this.

Caleb stopped just short of the fence. It was chain link and showed that the backyard of the house next door was just as desolate as the one they were currently in. Alyssa hesitated in front of it.

"Don't worry, I'm here. I have you," Caleb assured her. He moved aside to help her climb the fence, giving her a push up until she was on the other side. He followed, but not before a sound he was hoping not to hear yet rang through the air.

It was a gunshot, but it wasn't directed toward them.

"Go, go, go," Caleb yelled, grabbing Alyssa's hand again.

If he was right, then Dupree had just shot at Robbie. Which meant the distraction had reached its end and soon all hell would break out. Caleb just hoped he could get Alyssa clear beforehand.

They ran around to the corner of the new house, jumped one more fence and then paused in the side yard. It had less damage than the other two on the street but was boarded up tight. They weren't getting inside any time soon if they needed to hide.

"We need to get to the end of the street," Caleb whispered, dropping her hand. "I have to call Robbie."

Alyssa didn't comment. Her breathing was heavy, erratic. Like it had been in the car when she thought the bomb beneath her seat was real. Panic verging on an attack or hyperventilation. Neither ideal for their current situation. Even more of a reason to put urgency into his every action. She knotted her fist on the back of his shirt and followed along without complaint as they hurried into the next house's side yard. He used his free hand to fish out his cell phone and call his now number one contact.

It rang twice, but thankfully Robbie answered.

"Did you find her?" the older man greeted. He too sounded geared up.

"Yeah, and another man," Caleb said, still keeping his

voice low. "We're running toward the end of the street, trying to stay out of sight. Pick us up at the corner."

"I don't know if I can," Robbie hurried, adding in a stream of nasty, heated words. "After I drove off, Dupree jumped into a car and peeled out after me. He's on my tail and shooting."

Caleb in turn cursed beneath his breath.

Their backup wasn't able to help them.

"Drive straight to the sheriff's department," Caleb said, waiting for Alyssa to come around him and open the gate to the backyard. "Call them and tell them the situation. Drive smart and fast."

"Keep her safe," Robbie answered.

Caleb ended the call.

"What's happening?" Alyssa's voice had a tremor running through it.

"A change of plans," he answered honestly. "But nothing we can't handle. We just need to put distance between us and them."

Caleb reached for her hand, ready to run, but Alyssa pulled away.

"I—I can't," she whispered. "I—I just can't."

Even in the poor light around them, he could see she was freezing up. It caught him off guard. It was the first time he'd seen such a strong reaction from her. Eyes wide, breathing erratic, lips trembling. She wasn't beginning to panic; she was beginning to lose it.

"You can," he said, squeezing her hand to try to assure her. "All you have to do is hold on to me and I'll get us out of this."

Alyssa shook her head, her blue eyes still wide.

"He broke my glasses," she said, voice going hollow. As if she was trying to distance herself from her fear. "Dupree broke my glasses. And it's dark."

It finally clicked in place. He should have realized she

wasn't wearing them. And why she was so terrified. She really couldn't because she was blind without her glasses. The extreme vulnerability now fit. And it made Caleb pause.

An overwhelming wave of feeling surged through him.

Without a second thought he grabbed her chin and angled her face up. Then he met her mouth with his own.

The kiss was meant to distract Alyssa from her fear. To give her something else to focus on. Something, he hoped, that was good. He also hoped it reminded her that he was there. Down in the trenches with her. Not going to move an inch unless she did too. That, no matter what, he'd get her to safety.

Yet all thoughts and intentions fell away as the warmth of her lips pressed against his. Those pink, pink lips aroused something almost primal in him. He wanted it to last. He wanted it to evolve.

He wanted her.

But he had to get her to safety first.

Caleb pulled away, breaking the kiss.

"Listen to me," he said. "You are one of the strongest people I know, and I'm right here with you. Together we can do this. You just have to trust me. Please."

Once again he reached for her hand.

This time she didn't back away.

Instead she slipped her hand in his. "I trust you."

Chapter Seventeen

They made it around another house before their mystery man named Norman started to shout. Caleb didn't like how close his words were. Or the gunshot that exploded in the early morning air right after them.

Caleb yelled out as a searing pain cut through his left arm. He backtracked hard, guiding Alyssa to the side yard of the last house they needed to get on the other side of before they were at the end of the street. Not that he had a great plan for when that happened. He'd been hoping the other man would stay off their trail so Caleb had more time to figure out an escape. Or at least had time to wait out help.

"Were you hit?" Alyssa yelled, clutching his hand.

Before he could answer, another shot sounded. Dupree wouldn't have had the time to double back and be on them. It had to be Norman.

"We need to run around the front while he's shooting over here," he said, already picking up speed. Alyssa didn't argue.

"She's mine," the man yelled. The voice carried to them with an ease it shouldn't have because of their distance. Which meant there wasn't much of it between them anymore. That fact alone tainted their victory of finally getting to the end of the street. Their last obstacle.

"What now?" Alyssa asked, breathless.

The street they were on intersected with one that had seen better days. It led to a network of other neglected streets that dumped into more-used routes. According to Robbie, before the fire that effectively made the houses behind them uninhabitable, the surrounding areas had been more used. But after the fire, a lot of Carpenter had somehow all decided to steer clear for one reason or the other.

So, expecting someone to drive by the exact area they were in, especially so early in the morning, was a very, *very* long shot.

As for hiding until they could call someone in?

A field of green stretched out beyond them on the other side of the street. Trees were in the distance, but there was no way they could make it to them without being exposed for several minutes.

"Alyssa!"

Norman sounded enraged as he yelled her name. Caleb didn't like how close the sound was either. He looked at the house behind them.

"I need you to stay here," he ordered, pointing Alyssa toward a gap between two bushes still miraculously alive against the back end of the house. "Stay low and don't come out until I say."

"But what about you?" she rushed.

It was endearing, he had to admit. Even with some madman yelling her name and chasing them with a gun, she was still worried about him.

"I'm going to stop this man named Norman," he promised. "Because you are *not* his."

He could tell Alyssa didn't like the idea, her brow drawn in as a look of concern clung to her expression. Still, she did as she was told and crouched down in the gap.

"Be careful," she whispered. "That's an order."

Caleb couldn't help smiling.

"Yes, ma'am."

He pulled his gun high and crept around the front of the house. There was a fifty-fifty chance Norman was making his way toward them through the front yards, while there was also a fifty-fifty chance he was going around the back. Caleb kept his breathing as steady as he could and hoped he'd chosen the right direction.

When he'd planned on going toe-to-toe with the man responsible for taking Alyssa, he'd hoped that he'd have her well hidden or out of danger altogether. And that he'd be dealing with Dupree. Not some mystery man. Now Alyssa was hiding in the bushes while he was making decisions that could easily backfire.

Which was exactly what happened.

No sooner was he aiming his gun out around what used to be the front porch than Alyssa let out a gasp loud enough that it drew his attention backward. Caleb spun around, gun ready, and felt his stomach plummet.

A man was standing next to Alyssa, his own gun pointed at her head. He was panting but in no way looked any less dangerous. And it wasn't just any man.

"You," Caleb bit out. "I knew you had something to do with all this."

The man with horn-rimmed glasses managed a quick grin.

"You really *are* good with faces, but don't feel bad, *Deputy*," Norman said in between catching his breath. "I've fooled smarter people than you."

Norman was a few feet from Alyssa, but that didn't comfort Caleb in the least. Even if the man was a poor shot, the chances of him hitting her if he pulled the trigger were too high.

"What do you want?" Caleb asked, his own gun aimed forward. He could hit Norman if he wanted to, but what if the man pulled the trigger before he could stop him?

There were too many variables.

And none of them were good.

"I want you to leave us alone," Norman practically growled. His demeanor shifted into what Caleb could only describe as disgusted. "Stop trying to save her when she isn't yours to save!" Spit flew out of his mouth as he yelled. His face turned red.

Caleb didn't have time to be confused. His attention listed over Norman's shoulder to a pair of headlights in the distance. Caleb hoped beyond all hope that it wasn't Dupree making his way back.

"You should mind your own business," Norman added, unaware of the car. He shook the gun. Caleb realized it wasn't because he was trying to appear more threatening. Instead it was the man's emotions bleeding through. He was angry.

Really angry.

Reckless.

"You put a bomb in her car," Caleb pointed out, trying to buy time to devise a plan that wouldn't risk Alyssa getting shot or caught in the cross fire. "She needed help, so I helped."

Norman shook his head with fervor.

"It wouldn't have hurt her," he defended. "She didn't need you or your help. She still doesn't. She needs *me*. Not you confusing her."

The car was close enough that Caleb could see it wasn't a car at all but a four-door Bronco.

One he'd seen before.

"Then let her stand up," Caleb said, thinking fast. "You have a weird way of showing you want to protect her if you won't even let her *stand up*."

It was a weird thing to say, he knew, but Caleb hoped it would do the trick.

"Of course she can stand up," Norman answered.

"Then let her!"

Norman's nostrils flared, but he addressed Alyssa directly. "Show him, Alyssa. Stand up!"

Alyssa followed the order without comment. She might have been unable to see the Bronco barreling toward them, but now, Caleb hoped, the driver could see her.

Thankfully, he did.

The driver changed course just in time to jump the curb.

"Run," Caleb yelled.

Alyssa's sight might have been compromised, but her legs didn't have any trouble moving. Norman whirled around but didn't act like a deer in headlights. What he had in anger he also had in speed. He dove out of the way as the Bronco hit the side of the house, separating Caleb and Alyssa from the rage-filled Norman.

The driver's door swung open, but the man inside didn't make it out before gunshots slammed into the other side.

"Get in," the driver yelled.

Caleb didn't need to be told twice. He ran to Alyssa's side and helped her into the back seat floorboard. When he shut the door he lay on top of her, elbows on either side of her body, shielding her from any bullets that made it through. "We're in!"

Metal scraped against wood as the Bronco floored it in Reverse. Glass shattered overhead.

"Backup's behind me, but we're going to get you two out of here first," the driver yelled. "Hold on!"

Caleb kept his gaze down, eyes only for the woman staring up at him. The motion of going backward shifted his body against hers. It was a welcomed feeling. Concrete proof that she was with him.

"Are you okay?" he asked. The Bronco swerved to the side and then shifted into Drive. "Did he—did they do anything to you?" He moved the hair out of her face, more to check her skin for any signs she'd been touched. It was as clear as it had been the night before.

A wild expression crossed Alyssa's face. It was one Caleb couldn't place. He opened his mouth to repeat his question with more force, already getting angry at the possible answer, but she was faster.

Alyssa threw her arms around his neck, pulled him against her and kissed him hard. Unlike the kiss he'd given her minutes before to help focus her attention, this one was rough and hungry. It pulled his breath from him and begged for more.

And he wanted that.

Parting her lips with his tongue, he finally was able to taste her, returning the kiss with equal force. After days of danger and uncertainty, Caleb answered a longing he'd been trying to deny.

An attraction he'd tried to ignore. To distance himself from. A woman who had invaded his thoughts from the get-go, thoughts he was unable to shake free from since.

He shifted his weight enough so that his hand was free to grab her. To feel her. His fingers wrapped around her hip. He pulled her up against him and felt her breath hitch against his lips.

Caleb wanted to deepen the kiss. He wanted to explore more of her.

But he also knew it wasn't the time.

With more self-control than he thought he had, he gently pulled away.

Alyssa was trying to catch her breath, her pink, pink lips darkened from the contact and her blue eyes focusing on him.

"You two okay back there?" called their driver, foot still pressed hard on the gas pedal.

"I'm okay," Alyssa finally answered for the both of them. Her voice was ragged but stronger than it had been.

Caleb waited a beat, still caught in her blue-eyed stare, before he answered, "I'm okay too." Finally he tore his gaze from the woman and focused on the driver in the front seat. "Thanks for the save, Sheriff."

Sheriff Reed didn't take his attention off the street, but when he answered there was no doubt in Caleb's mind that the man was smiling.

"It's what I do."

IT WAS LIKE her life was now made up of moments that were either on the extreme side of the danger spectrum or floundering in a deep calm. Though, sitting in the conference room at the sheriff's department, trying to make out the blurs on the whiteboard across from her, Alyssa thought maybe calm wasn't the right choice of words.

She let a sigh out that no one heard. It was the first time she'd been alone since the sheriff rescued them. Even though he'd brought deputies on his tail, they still hadn't been able to capture Norman. Or Dupree, for that matter. Which was the main reason it was now seven in the morning and she was still at the department. Everyone on the force seemed to be out on the streets, hunting down the two men. Dupree they knew, but his connection with Norman and who Norman was, well, that was the mystery. One that she wished she could help solve.

Another sigh climbed out of her mouth and through her lips. She traced them with the tips of her fingers.

In all the madness that had happened, how did she always come back to a kiss?

Two kisses, actually, she thought, cheeks heating while somewhere lower warmed. She couldn't forget that one she'd planted on the unsuspecting deputy. No, she definitely couldn't forget that.

Or the fact that he'd responded.

In more ways than one.

If it had been up to her, she would have let the deputy take her right then and there, sheriff in the front seat and all. She'd been so relieved and happy to see him in the house. That enthusiasm had waited until she felt even a small amount of safety.

And then she had needed to let him know how she felt about it.

"More important things," Alyssa whispered to the empty room. "Focus."

"What was that?"

Alyssa jumped and looked at the new body in the room. The image might be blurry, but Alyssa knew it was the dispatcher, Cassie. The woman had already stopped by when she first came in to work to check on her. Thanks to her, Alyssa was also wearing a pair of exercise pants and not her sleep shorts. Which somehow had made her feel better. Or, at the very least, a little more in control of the situation.

"Oh, nothing," Alyssa hurried, the heat of her blush getting a little hotter. "Just, you know, talking to myself to keep awake."

"Well, I think I might be able to help with that!"

Alyssa smelled the coffee before she even saw the cup.

"The perk of being across the street from a coffee shop," Cassie added. She leaned against the table's edge, closer than if she'd taken the seat next to Alyssa. Which was probably on purpose so she wasn't a blur in her vision.

Alyssa hoped after all this was over that she'd become friends with the dispatcher.

If Alyssa survived the madness.

"I know this is a weird thing to bring up right now," Alyssa started. "But I wanted to thank you for the advice." Cassie raised her eyebrow in question. "For telling me to request Caleb for protection. I, well, I don't know how everything would have played out otherwise."

Cassie's lips curved up into a small smile. "I'm glad he's worked out for you. He seems to be a good guy." Her expression dampened. "It'll be a shame when he goes back to Portland. The department will suffer for it."

Alyssa had spent the last few days stumbling upon realizations that had turned her blood cold. However, Cassie had just shared information that had a parallel, if not equal, effect on her. More than anything she'd bet that Eleanor had been trying to tell her the same thing she'd just learned before the explosion that had killed Ted happened.

That Caleb didn't plan on staying in Carpenter.

And why would he?

Feeling her face harden into what she hoped was a normal smile, Alyssa nodded.

Voices floating down the hallway toward the conference room saved Alyssa from having to pretend she wasn't upset. Disappointed was not a strong enough word.

"Well, speak of the devil," Cassie greeted Caleb. He was holding a duffel bag and looked as tightly wound as could be. Alyssa couldn't blame him for that. But she also couldn't meet his eye at the moment. Not when the news of him eventually leaving hurt more than she was comfortable with. Instead she deferred her attention to Captain Jones behind him.

"Anything?"

The captain shook his head. Despite his earlier grievances with Caleb, he didn't seem to have any undue anger radiating off him. Instead there was an intense focus that Alyssa was finding synonymous with the Riker County Sheriff's Department.

"Nothing concrete," he answered. "And not Norman or Dupree. We've even looked everywhere you suggested that you found Dupree frequented when looking into him last year."

"Maybe they've left Carpenter altogether," Alyssa pointed out. Though she didn't want to see either man again, she realized the danger of them possibly never being caught would increase if they left town.

It was Caleb's turn to shake his head.

"There's a reason Dupree didn't leave when he had the chance," he said. "Whatever plan Norman was talking to you about must be keeping them here until it's finished."

"Not to mention Norman—" the captain started, but he cut himself off right after.

Alyssa let out her third sigh in a handful of minutes.

"Norman seems to want me," she finished for him.

"Which might be a good thing," Captain Jones said. "It could keep them in town, which gives us the time to complete our search and find them. It's not ideal, but none of this is."

"Captain." A female deputy stopped in the doorway. "Sorry to interrupt, but Chief Hawser would like a word with you. He's on hold in your office."

"Okay, thank you." Jones turned to Caleb. "If you need anything, don't hesitate to let me know. The sheriff too."

Caleb nodded. A look passed between the men, but without her glasses Alyssa couldn't tell if it was a good one or not.

"I also need to get back to it," Cassie said at her elbow. "I just wanted to make sure you had some caffeine in you."

Alyssa smiled.

"And I thank you for that," she said. "And the pants."

Cassie patted her shoulder and followed the captain out. Then it was just the two of them.

Alyssa couldn't avoid the deputy anymore. "So, what now?"

Chapter Eighteen

If you had told Alyssa the week before that she'd be naked in Deputy Caleb Foster's house, she would have laughed. Not to mention ask who Caleb Foster was. Staring at her reflection in his bathroom mirror, she marveled at the fact that she'd never even known he had existed until a few days ago. Now there she was, freshly showered and contemplating her relationship with the man a few rooms over.

That was one of many curveballs she hadn't been prepared for in the slightest. The others being the still unknown man who was Norman, her nightmare incarnate Dupree and their joint, mystery plan that either did or did not involve her. All during a week that should have been spent putting away the Storm Chasers once and for all.

Alyssa hoped she'd eventually be able to hit all those life curveballs.

In the distance the *clink* of dishes broke her out of her reverie. She grabbed the towel and dried the rest of the way off before diving into the duffel bag Caleb had packed while she was at the department. At the time she hadn't known the deputy was going to her house but was grateful he had. Along with clothes, toiletries and a pair of shoes, he'd managed to find her spare set of glasses, beneath the couch of all places.

Slipping them on had reduced her anxiety by half. It

was one thing to be scared. It was another to be blind *and* scared.

Alyssa changed into a pair of sports shorts and a plain T-shirt. She might have gotten a few hours of sleep the night before, but it hadn't been enough to replenish any exhaustion caused by the chaos that had come after. Unless it was absolutely necessary, she planned on staying put for the time being. Caleb had assured her that the captain and sheriff had assured *him* that they would be the first to know if any break in the case happened. On the off chance Dupree and Norman tried to track Alyssa down again, there was an undercover black-and-white car outside on high alert. So, until that break came, all they had to do was wait.

Which made her anxious for another reason.

Alyssa sucked on her lip and exited the bathroom.

"Thanks again for letting me stay here," she greeted the deputy when she got enough courage to walk into the living room. He was settled on the couch, so she took the chair at his side. Close but not too close.

"I'm just returning the favor," he said with a shrug. "You opened your home to me more than once already."

Alyssa's face began to heat at the thought of his hand gripping her body, feeling the beginnings of his arousal pressing against the thin material of her sleep shorts.

But then just as quickly she remembered Cassie's words.

He was leaving Carpenter.

He was leaving her.

"So, what did Deputy Mills have to say?" she asked, trying to curb her hurt before he could see he'd caused it. He'd taken a call from the man just before she excused herself to go shower.

"It was actually from his father, but he said Dante will be fine." He pointed to his cheek. "He has a hairline fracture but nothing permanent. When he was awake he told the captain that Dupree used the butt of his gun to knock him out. He didn't even hear the man coming."

"It's a good thing he did that instead of shoot," she pointed out. The spot on her back that was puckered from her scar tingled. "He hasn't always been reserved about doing that."

Caleb nodded. She noticed his jaw hardened.

"I can only assume he decided against it so he could try to sneak around me. It was bad and good timing he got to your house when he did. Otherwise he might have taken you before we even realized he had escaped the transport."

"That should be a silver lining to look at, but when it comes to Dupree, I'm not too thrilled about it," she admitted. "But I am glad you were there. I'd much rather have been grabbed by Norman than Dupree. As weird as *that* sounds."

Alyssa tried on her best "I'm all right" smile, but Caleb already looked like he wasn't buying it. She let a sigh drag her body down. "The way Norman talked to me... I don't think he would have hurt me. I mean, he could have done whatever he wanted with me, but he didn't."

Caleb puffed up as if he had an air pump attached to him. "Just because he didn't do anything to you doesn't mean he's a good guy. You *were* kidnapped."

Alyssa couldn't help giving a small eye roll. "I know, I know." She dropped her gaze to the coffee table. Sports magazines were stacked on top of it, being one of the few bits of proof someone inhabited the rental house. It only reminded Alyssa that Caleb's stay wasn't permanent. Which made her feel somehow awkward when she continued, "It's just that, well, Norman seems to be in love with me. Or, at least, *thinks* he is. Which is another thing I don't understand at all."

From her periphery she watched Caleb loosen a little.

"I don't think it's that hard to grasp that a man fell for you," he said, voice serious.

Her cheeks heated for the umpteenth time. She started to open her mouth to stop him.

"You're brave and smart," he continued, cutting her off. "You took a bullet trying to save a man you hardly knew. You ran into a burning building to try to save someone who *might* have still been alive. You blindly fought your captor to escape without any help from me. You did all that and still took the time to show concern about Robbie and Eleanor and the rest of the witnesses before showing concern about yourself." Caleb moved to the edge of the couch, teetering on standing or, in her mind, reaching out to her. But he kept the distance as he finished. "I might not know you like the rest of this town does, but I *do* understand how easy it would be to fall for you."

Alyssa's lips froze. What she had been about to say stalled. The heat of her blush wasn't raging. Instead it moved across her body as a slow burn. It reminded her not of embarrassment but of something else. Something she'd felt when Caleb kissed her. Something she'd felt when she kissed him back in the sheriff's Bronco.

It was longing. Plain and simple.

There was no denying its place anymore. To pretend she didn't want the man in front of her was too much of a pain. He was right. She'd been through her own version of hell and back in the last year and week. Admitting she had kissed Caleb in the Bronco because she'd been so terrified she had lost him that when he was there, staring down at her, she'd realized how happy the sight had made her... Well, that didn't seem so scary now.

Still, she managed to hold back enough to correct him. With a small smile, she tucked her head a little but not her gaze. It stayed right with his mesmerizing green eyes. "I meant I don't understand why he's in love with me, considering I've never met him before."

Caleb's eyes widened a fraction. For one tense moment Alyssa thought she'd offended him by pointing out he'd given her a world of compliments because of a misunderstanding. But then a slow grin pulled up the corners of his lips.

"Ah," he said with a little laugh. "Well, I've already said what I think and I'm not going to take that back."

It was Alyssa's turn to laugh.

"I wasn't going to ask you to," she said. "It was a really nice compliment."

Caleb's grin faltered. "It's the truth."

The distance between them felt unbearably vast. Somehow the foot or two seemed almost cruel.

"You know, the past few days have put us in intense situations, and sometimes those can lead to emotions running high," Alyssa said, voice going softer the more she spoke. Was it her imagination or was the deputy leaning closer? And was she responding in the same way? "It can confuse the way people think and feel. Especially when the rush is over and everything gets back to being quiet."

Caleb leaned forward, like Alyssa was attached to him by an invisible string, and she mimicked him. The impossibly large space between them shrank until it was nonexistent. Slowly, or maybe cautiously, Caleb reached out and tucked a strand of her wet hair behind her ear. When he was done he let his knuckles brush along her jaw. His skin was warm and perfect.

"But it's in the quiet times like right now that I find you the most fascinating." Caleb grabbed her by the chin, holding her steady. Holding all of her.

And in the next second, his lips brushed against hers.

Electricity. She could have sworn she felt it between them. Alyssa was ready for its current to carry them further, but once again, Caleb pulled away. Their kiss broke. With hooded eyes she watched as his lips parted to talk.

"I—I'm sorry," he said, pulling farther back. "I shouldn't have—"

Alyssa watched as the certainty of his actions fell away. It created such strong disappointment within her that Alyssa jumped up off the chair.

"It's fine," she interrupted, the heat in her cheeks now complete embarrassment. It prompted her to blurt out the first thing that popped into her head. "We can count it as a goodbye kiss."

Whatever Caleb was about to say caught in his throat. He raised an eyebrow but couldn't hide a look she knew well.

Guilt.

"Cassie told me that you're going back to Portland," she explained. The look of guilt worsened.

"Eventually," he finally said. "That's the plan."

Never had she disliked four words more.

She took a deep breath and mustered up a smile.

"Then I guess it's good we went ahead and got that out of the way," she said, already angling her body to head to the guest bedroom. It was set up as an office, but there was a couch inside. That was all she needed to lick her wounds in private. "You know, I'm pretty beat anyways. I think I'm going to lie down for a little bit, if that's okay."

She was already walking away, but Caleb still answered. "Maybe it's a good idea if we both get a little sleep."

Alyssa nodded, felt stupid for nodding and fled to the bedroom. There she shut the door and put her back against it.

It's for the best, she thought.

She pushed herself off the door but didn't make it two steps before it opened again. Alyssa turned, confused.

Caleb's eyes were wide, his chest heaving. He looked

every bit like a man trying to restrain himself. From what, though, was something Alyssa wanted—*needed*—to know. She felt her eyebrow rise.

"The other day you said that not everyone stays," he started. "Yeah, that might be true. People leave for all kinds of reasons. And I might not have known you that long, but—" he took a step forward "—no matter what happens, I want you to know that you are one of the only reasons that I'd ever stay."

Caleb's hands found their way across the space between them and into her hair. They pulled her face to him again. Just like he had done after escaping the house. Just like she had done to him after getting away from Norman.

His tongue parted her lips and this time around neither pulled away after a few seconds.

Caleb moved his hands down her sides and then pulled her against him in an embrace that put her flush against him. Alyssa wrapped her arms around him as the kiss deepened. Her body began to thrum at every movement. It was a feeling that she wanted to add fire to, so when he used his embrace to lift her off the floor, she wrapped her legs around his waist.

Alyssa had thought there was nothing more the man could say or do to make her want him more. But, somehow, Caleb Foster did it.

He walked them to his bedroom, put her on the bed and broke their kiss. Through hooded lashes Alyssa watched as the man smiled a smile that sealed her fate.

"Oh boy," she whispered.

Caleb's smile widened. He kicked off his shoes and threw his shirt to the floor. Alyssa didn't even pretend she wasn't checking the man out. His finely toned chest dipped into abs that didn't seem real before a light dusting of golden hair headed south to the hem of his jeans.

"Well, *hello*, Deputy Foster," she breathed.

Caleb's smile turned mischievous. She answered his with an offer of her own. Without hesitation Alyssa pulled her shirt over her head and threw it. Caleb also wasn't for pretending he wasn't tracing her body with his eyes. Belatedly she realized that the red-and-black-lace bra she had on was one that he himself had packed for her earlier that morning.

"Well, hello, Miss Garner."

Alyssa's heart was thumping against her chest as Caleb took charge. He moved onto the bed with purpose until he was hovering over her. Then his mouth was on her lips. Then on her shoulder. Then her collarbone.

His lips left a trail of raised flesh as they moved across her skin. She arced upward, moaning as they reached her cleavage. He used the arc to his advantage and slipped his hand behind her back. She was too aroused to care at how easily he unclipped her bra. All she knew was that she was grateful when it loosened. It gave Caleb enough room to move one cup aside. He chafed his thumb over her nipple in a tantalizing rhythm.

Alyssa couldn't take it any longer. She pulled his lips back up to hers and moaned. Of its own accord her body began to pulse against his, wanting—needing—more. If the hardness pressing against her was any indication, she wasn't the only one who was hungry.

She had moved her hands from around his neck, down the sides of his arms, more than ready to rid the man of his pants, when her fingers ran over something she didn't expect. Confused, she pulled away.

He hovered above her, eyebrow raised.

"What happened here?" she whispered, eyes tracing over his bare biceps. Two butterfly bandages were over a deep cut. It was covered in dried blood.

Caleb managed to shrug.

"Caleb?" she prodded.

He sighed.

"A bullet grazed me earlier," he admitted. "When we were running from the house."

Alyssa felt her eyes widen.

"It's just a graze and I'm okay. The most it will do is scar."

Alyssa felt a heaviness in her chest.

"You were shot because of me," she said, her mood darkening despite a body strung out with pure arousal. "You could have been really hurt, or worse."

Caleb's expression softened. He lowered his lips and brushed them gently across hers. He pulled back to meet her gaze again.

"But I wasn't," he whispered. He lowered himself again, but this time his lips trailed down to her hardened nipple. She tried to restrain a moan as he kissed the tip. When he looked up at her and spoke, his breath against her skin sent a chill across her body. It made her ache in all the best ways. "And right now, Miss Garner, I'm here. With you."

The space between them dissolved, replaced by a desire neither could ignore. Caleb resumed kissing every part of her before each had found a way to undress the other. Alyssa opened herself to the man, and Caleb pressed against her until both were caught in a whirlwind of heat and friction and pleasure.

Lust, longing and something undefinable created a dance between them that kept all thoughts and emotions occupied.

Norman, Dupree Slater and Carpenter became distant memories.

All that was left was this one room.

Chapter Nineteen

Warm.

Quiet.

Blurry.

Alyssa's world might have been filled with fear and danger and so much uncertainty it should have had her locked in constant panic, but the moment she woke up in Caleb's bed, all she could feel was contentment.

She rolled over, trying to be as quiet as possible. Even without her glasses she was surprised to be able to make out Caleb's face in detail.

A smile split her lips. It was because he was so close to her. Within the small bubble that was her field of good vision. Alyssa couldn't remember the last time someone had been that close to her, especially in bed.

That thought prompted a rush of heat to move up from below her waistline. It settled in her neck and cheeks. She'd known the man entangled with her beneath his sheets for a handful of days and yet...

She searched his slack face, knowing she shouldn't feel what she did. While awake his expression so often switched between a quiet burden and a loud concern, but the sleeping man she was looking at now had found peace. It might not extend past his eyes being opened, but for the moment, he seemed to have found it.

Alyssa chanced stroking his cheek. Lying on his stomach, arm tossed over her middle and legs tangled with hers, he didn't move an inch as she did so. She absently wondered when the last time he'd gotten good sleep was.

A loud series of beeping snuffed out her current thoughts. Caleb's body went from relaxed and comfortable to coiled and tense all within one moment. Two green eyes, perfectly rimmed with gold, found hers.

"I think it's your phone," she said, nodding to the other side of the bed.

Where she'd thrown his pants.

Right next to where he'd thrown her shorts.

She had no idea where her undergarments had wound up.

Alyssa's cheeks heated again as Caleb pulled his arm off her bare skin and moved his attention to the other side of the bed. His phone belted out another series of high-pitched beeps. He muttered under his breath and pitched over the side to swat for his phone. In the process the sheets shifted and Alyssa was presented with an unobstructed view of the man's very bare backside. It was slightly blurry but still just as perfect as it had been a few hours before.

"Foster," he grunted, pulling his upper body back onto the bed. It shifted the sheets again and exposed Alyssa's naked chest. There was a soreness around her nipples, but she in no way disliked it. Still, she hurried to cover herself, suddenly uncertain. They'd both melted into the heat of passion. Skin on skin, heat with heat, lust and hunger and a singular attention only for each other... But now their fire had had time to cool. What if it never happened again? What if this was the first and last time she ever felt him?

Alyssa tamped down her worries while the man on the other end of the phone rattled off information with alarming speed.

"Got it," Caleb finally said, voice tight. "No, no problem. Thank you."

He ended the call.

"Did they find Norman or Dupree?" Alyssa asked, hopeful.

Caleb turned to face her, keeping on his stomach. She fought the urge to blush again.

"No," he said. "But the sheriff promised me he'd let me know when Robbie and Eleanor made it to their son's house. And they did and are fine."

Alyssa let out a sigh of relief. While Robbie had been quick to refuse leaving town, Dupree's escape had put pressure on his decision to stay. Especially since Dupree had chased Robbie most of the way to the police station, shooting up his truck as they went. Together Alyssa and Caleb had been able to persuade both Rickmans that maybe out of town *was* the safest option for them. And, to both their surprise, Cassie had been given orders to drive them to their son's when they'd agreed. However, before they'd left, Eleanor tried her best to sway Alyssa into going with them, but everyone knew that was a pointless fight.

Whoever Norman was he clearly wanted Alyssa. Their best bet of capturing him was to stay in Carpenter. If she left, Alyssa had no doubt that Norman would follow. At least in Carpenter they were on her home turf. It was easier to look over your shoulder while navigating the familiar. Plus, there was no denying she felt safer with the naked deputy next to her.

"I didn't mean to sleep this long," Caleb said, jumping topics. His gaze went back to his phone, but she caught his grin. "I didn't mean to sleep at all, to be honest."

"My guess is that you needed to recharge."

Just as quickly as Alyssa said it, she felt her cheeks flame. She wanted to stick her head in the sand like the awkward woman she was. "Because, you know, you haven't slept in a while. That's why you needed the recharge."

Caleb's grin widened.

"I definitely got a charge of something," he said with a wink.

More heat thrummed through her from below her stomach. The sheets covering them seemed impossibly thin and yet cumbersome. She resisted the urge to throw them off, waiting to see what the deputy would do next.

She wasn't disappointed.

Pushing himself up on his forearms, he met her stare easily enough. So close she could feel his breath against her. The same breath that had trailed across her body. His lips, soft when needed and hard when wanted, pulled up out of a grin and into a smirk. It exuded nothing but an exciting mischievousness. She saw it in wonderful detail. It prompted another unfiltered response from her. "I like when you're this close so you're not a blur."

Caleb moved in until his lips were over hers.

Soft. Warm. Brimming with promise she didn't know she'd wanted. Her body started to arc up, responding to the hope that the kiss would extend past just one kiss when a foreign noise cut through the air.

Caleb laughed against her as another growl sounded.

"Sorry," he said. "I guess sleep wasn't the only thing I was lacking." He pulled away and rolled over, tapping his stomach. "I think the last good meal I had was Eleanor's leftover pie."

Slightly disappointed, Alyssa realized she hadn't eaten in a while either. But watching Caleb untangle himself from the sheets, she pondered the importance of eating versus the desire to keep the deputy naked.

"How about I go make us some food?" he asked, picking up his jeans and shimmying back into them. His shirt remained off. She wasn't about to complain.

"You won't hear me arguing," she said. "Especially if by food you also mean coffee?"

The cup she'd gotten from Cassie in the early morning hours hadn't dented her exhaustion. Even the sleep she'd just woken from hadn't relieved her of the desire to lie back down.

Caleb laughed again.

"Not only do I have coffee," he said, his smile slightly blurred. "But I have some of the best you'll ever taste. Thanks to my old chief, it's straight from Portland."

Alyssa felt her stomach drop.

She tried to keep her expression from going down with it.

"Great," she exclaimed, attempting to recover and be convincing. "Sounds great!" Trying to pretend that the mention of Portland alone hadn't thrust her back into a reality she didn't want to be a part of at all. One where Caleb was only a temporary resident in Carpenter. "I'm going to go freshen up and then take Sergeant out to stretch," she added when Caleb seemed to have stalled beside the bed.

If he was going to say something, Alyssa didn't give him the chance. Without asking, she wrapped the sheet around herself, grabbed her bag and hurried into the bathroom. Once the door was closed she immediately went to turn on the shower. It muffled any sounds that were outside the room.

Alyssa waited to see if the deputy would come for her like he had before. To try to comfort the part of her that was hurt by the idea that he would leave her, eventually. But he never did. So she did as she said and freshened up, changed into jeans and a shirt, and tried to see the poetry of having at least known what being with the deputy was like. Even if it might never happen again.

It took a little time, but she felt she was starting to convince herself that it was fine in her book when she got up to the mirror to brush out her hair. She took a towel and tried to un-fog a circle of space so she could see her reflection. It was an action she was used to handling when it came to her glasses and the often humid weather of Alabama. Something so natural to her that she often did it on autopilot whether she was at home or out and about.

Alyssa froze midwipe.

An idea grew louder in her head. It was attached to a memory. One she hadn't thought was important.

Until now.

CALEB LOOKED AT the plate across the counter from his own. It was small and chipped and a part of a set he'd had for years... Yet somehow that plate looked different now.

Holding eggs, bacon and toast, it was a sight that he hadn't expected to make him contemplate his life. But that was what he was doing. Because he knew it wasn't the plate that had changed all of a sudden. It was who the plate was meant for that had cracked his plan for an ideal future.

He saw the plate.

He saw the woman meant to eat off it.

Caleb exhaled above his coffee.

Yet another small detail that had changed the way he thought.

He replayed Alyssa's reaction to when he'd mentioned Portland. Even in the smallest way. The way her face had fallen for a second as she, no doubt, was reminded that he was going to leave. He didn't know what bothered him more after seeing that. Hurting her with the truth of going back or the idea of going back itself.

A series of memories reminded him of a night he never wished to relive again. A darkness he hoped to keep buried for life. His hands fisted.

He knew it wasn't that easy.

If he stayed he'd have to tell Alyssa what had happened. He'd have to show her he wasn't the man she thought she knew. But if he left?

She'd never know.

Blue eyes, soft skin, hair that smelled like citrus.

Caleb opened his hands back up.

If he left, he'd be leaving behind every part of the woman he'd gotten to know in the last week. The strength and humor and compassion. The quiet contemplation, the way her brow creased in worry and the blushes that colored her cheeks that he seemed to have a skill to incite.

The way her skin felt against his. Their bodies moving together and against each other at the same time. The soft moans. The eventual release.

He might have been uncertain about a lot of things in life, but Caleb knew, without a doubt, that if he left he'd never find another woman like Alyssa Garner again.

And he wouldn't want to.

Footsteps made him turn around. Alyssa was dressed again and also wearing a look that worried him.

"What's wrong?"

Alyssa's eyebrows were drawn together, her forehead creased in thought, but her expression was hard. And oddly energetic.

"Stand here," she hurried, grabbing his hand and pulling him to the middle of the room. "I want to try something."

Caleb obeyed and watched as she took her glasses off. Without explanation, Alyssa moved a few steps backward and then walked forward again. She bumped into his shoulder but kept on walking past him. Curious, he turned his head to look at her. She stopped a foot away from him, brows drawn even tighter together.

She squinted.

"Alyssa?" he prodded. "What's wrong?"

For a moment she didn't speak.

And then she said something that changed everything. "I think I *have* met Norman before. He was there, Caleb."

He turned to face her head-on.

"There?" he asked, already hoping for information that could help them close the case once and for all.

Alyssa gave one, decisive nod. As if she was confirming her hunch with herself before letting him in on it.

"He was at the bank," she said. "The day of the robbery, Norman was there."

Chapter Twenty

"Just tell them what you told me."

Caleb's hand touched the top of hers with reassurance. No one else in the conference room at the sheriff's department could see the contact beneath the table. But it helped steady her all the same.

Alyssa straightened her back and cleared her throat. "Before the robbery took place, when I was first going into the bank, my glasses fogged up." As if the sheriff and captain needed help understanding the information, she motioned to her glasses. "It was raining and so humid I knew it was pointless to try to wipe them off until I was inside. So I took them off and held them at my side so no one would see me looking clumsily around while I waited for the fog to disappear. I was so focused on trying to look like I wasn't blind that before I put them back on I ran into a man in the lobby. He was leaving, but we hit each other hard enough that we both turned to look at one another." This time she took her glasses off and returned her gaze to the two men on the other side of the table. "You two are blurs right now. Even if you pointed a gun to my head, without having seen you before *with* my glasses on, I couldn't for the life of me describe what you look like. Other than with descriptions like tall, brown hair and wearing a suit, I wouldn't be able to recognize you later either."

Alyssa put her glasses back on just in time to watch Sheriff Reed catch on.

"And you think it was Norman that you ran into," he guessed. "In the bank."

Alyssa nodded.

"It would explain why Dupree came into the room she was being held in and broke her glasses," Caleb interjected. "He was trying to prove to Norman that even though she might have looked at him, she didn't really see him. Which is in line with the conversation between him and Norman she heard."

The captain was already standing.

"I have a copy of the security footage from the bank in my office," he said to the sheriff. "I'll go see if I can find this man."

Sheriff Reed nodded but didn't split his attention. He kept it right on Alyssa.

"If it is the same man, that still doesn't fill in all the blanks," he said. "So let's say Norman did bump into you at the bank and it was the first time you two met... What he said to you when you were at that house sounds like he's in love with you. *And* he seems to be under the impression that you are in love with him too. Or at least in the same reality together. Now, I'm not one to discount the notion of love at first sight, believe you me—I was knocked on my backside when I first saw my wife—but what Norman seems to be feeling might be something a great deal more dangerous."

"Obsession," Caleb jumped in.

The sheriff nodded, grave.

"Obsession, especially within the walls of an unstable mind, can be even more dangerous than someone who is just mad at the world or, as Norman told you, out for revenge," Sheriff Reed said. He put his hands together in a show of binding two objects. "But put those two together?"

He whistled and shook his head.

Alyssa cleared her throat. While she'd given the two men in the room with her a breakdown of everything both Dupree and Norman had said to and in front of her, she had sidestepped one particular statement. In hindsight she realized it was to try to keep the then-angry Caleb from getting even more angry. Now, though, it felt pertinent.

"Norman said Dupree helped prove we were meant to be together," she began, already feeling uncomfortable. "I don't think he became obsessed with me until he realized I survived."

Caleb squeezed her hand. Whether it was meant to calm her or protect her she didn't know.

"Okay, so let's say you bump into Norman, make eye contact—which starts this crazy notion you two should be together—and then you get...well, you know."

"Hospitalized," Caleb offered. In a different situation Alyssa might have thought it was cute how both men were trying to sidestep the gritty facts of that day for her benefit.

"Yeah, so you get hospitalized and Norman realizes that you've survived," the sheriff continued. "In his mind that means you two are meant for each other, creating an obsession that he adds into his plans for, as he said it, his revenge."

"That would explain why Dupree seemed so mad," she added. "Maybe it's affecting their partnership."

"Which in itself is another set of questions we don't have answers for," Caleb pointed out. "If Norman was at the bank, then why didn't he help rob it? For that matter, why did he go in at all beforehand and without a mask?"

"And why is he blowing people up?" Alyssa tacked on.

"And what revenge is he talking about?" the sheriff asked. "His partners being killed and caught?"

"That's a lot of questions, but I think I can at least answer one for you."

In unison the three of them turned to Captain Jones in the doorway.

"I found the man who bumped into you on the tape. It's Norman," he confirmed. "From your descriptions of him now, he appears to be more cleanly cut from the footage, but it's him. Glasses and everything."

Alyssa didn't know if that should have made her happy, but in a small way it did. Better to know what was going on than be in the dark any longer.

"But—" the captain started. What small amount of happiness had cropped up within Alyssa disappeared. Apparently she wasn't the only one. Caleb let go of her hand.

"We may have another problem," Jones finished.

Without saying a word, they followed the man back to his office and crowded around him as he sat in front of his computer. Alyssa sucked in a breath.

It wasn't that she saw herself on the monitor, frozen in time right in front of an also-paused Norman, that caught her off guard.

"We had no idea what was about to happen," she whispered. An old pain ached within her. This time Caleb didn't hide his attempt to make her feel better. He put his hand on the small of her back. The pressure was comforting. She took a deep breath.

"But that's him, right?" the captain asked to make sure.

It was Caleb who nodded. "That's him."

"And that must be the look he was talking about," the sheriff jumped in. He pointed to the screen. Alyssa tried to focus on it and not the dam that kept her memories at bay starting to crack.

"You can see my glasses in my hand," she said after a tiny head shake to help get her back into a more stable mind-set. Past Alyssa was a good two feet away from Past Norman. "If I'd only left them on instead of worrying about how I looked, I would never have bumped into him in the first place. And y'all wouldn't be in harm's way because of me."

"Don't blame yourself for the crazy in others," Sheriff Reed said. "Plus, I don't think his obsession for you is what made him start making bombs and using them. It also doesn't explain what his connection with Dupree is."

Captain Jones held up his index finger. "I have a theory."

The captain hit a few keys on the keyboard until the security footage rewound. Alyssa watched her past self, as well as Norman, leave the bank in reverse until he hit Play.

"You see this is when Norman enters," he said, letting his finger trail the man on the screen. "He doesn't hesitate or break his stride as he goes to talk to one of the tellers. He has a plan."

"That's Larissa," Alyssa realized. A lump started to form in her throat as she watched Norman and Larissa talk. The teller was smiling wide, polite. Alyssa tried to ignore the sorrow while pointing out the teller to Caleb. "She didn't survive the robbery."

No one said anything for a moment. Alyssa took the time to say a silent prayer for the woman and those she left behind.

"Okay, so what's the theory?" Sheriff Reed finally asked.

There was no denying that a new thread of anger had woven itself into the fabric of the room. Caleb's hand was still on the small of her back, but the gentle nature had taken on more of an edge. The other two had shoulders lined with tension.

Captain Jones rewound the tape and pointed to Norman. Or, rather, the briefcase in his hand.

"You see this?" Jones asked. "He walks in with it." He fast-forwarded the footage and hit Pause again. It was right before Alyssa had bumped into him. "But now…"

Alyssa watched as Past Norman left Larissa's line and headed to the hallway that led to the bathroom. The captain moved the footage along until Norman reappeared in the lobby.

Without his briefcase.

"So he left the case in the bathroom," Caleb said. "And I'm guessing he doesn't go back for it?"

Captain Jones shook his head. He'd let the security footage continue to play. Alyssa watched as another bank-goer caught Norman's eye and started a conversation with the man. It wasn't a long conversation but seemed pleasant if their easy smiles were any indication of the mood.

Currently, Alyssa's own mood was nose-diving.

"That's Carl," she said, cutting off whatever Captain Jones was about to say. "He's talking to Carl Redford." Alyssa's gut turned cold.

"Carl also didn't make it," Sheriff Reed explained to, she assumed, Caleb. The deputy opened his mouth to say something, but Alyssa cut him off.

"Does he talk to anyone else before leaving?" she asked, heartbeat speeding up.

The captain fast-forwarded the footage again in answer. He stopped it when Alyssa showed up on the screen. "Just you."

Caleb's hand dropped from her back. They shared a look.

"The only three people Norman talked to were shot by Dupree during the robbery," he said, voice steel. "That can't be a coincidence."

"I *knew* it wasn't an accident that he shot Larissa and Carl," Alyssa agreed.

"He could have been acting under orders from Norman to take out anyone who might be able to remember him inside the bank," Caleb added.

Sheriff Reed cursed beneath his breath.

"But why go through all that trouble when we can just look at the security footage?" Alyssa asked. "Why walk into the bank without a mask on at all?" None of what they were finding was making complete sense. They were only getting pieces that weren't quite fitting together.

"It was such a cut-and-dry case that we didn't pore over the security footage with the same attention to detail we would have if the robbers hadn't been caught," the sheriff admitted. "Dupree claimed leadership for the crew and took responsibility for creating the plan to rob the bank and executing it. We had no reason to suspect there was another party to contend with." He motioned to the monitor with an angry enthusiasm. "Norman might as well have been invisible."

"But his briefcase isn't," Caleb interjected. "Maybe if we can find out where it went, we can—"

"We can figure out why he was there in the first place," Sheriff Reed continued.

Caleb nodded.

"Am I the only one who thinks the bank robbery might not have been a normal bank robbery?" Alyssa couldn't help asking. Norman just didn't *fit* into the situation. It didn't make sense.

"Whatever is going on, we'll get to the bottom of it," the sheriff assured her. He patted Jones's shoulder once. "Can you keep going through the footage? Now that we have a new perspective, maybe there's more we missed originally."

"Sure thing." Captain Jones rewound the footage again. This time Alyssa didn't want to watch. It all made her stomach turn.

"As much as I want to dig into this, I need to focus on the present," Sheriff Reed continued, walking them out. "I'm going to go back to heading up the search for Dupree and Norman. I'll be damned if I'm going to let the two of them run wild in my town."

Chapter Twenty-One

Alyssa stopped the sheriff before he headed out to try to save the day. Caleb kept to her side. She doubted she'd be able to shake him again until Dupree and Norman were caught. Not that she was particularly excited to do that.

"I thought you were working a case out of town?"

She remembered what Cassie had told her in the hospital and couldn't help asking the man about it. She felt obligated to check in with him, considering he'd saved her and Caleb's backsides earlier. "Did you finish it up already?"

A shadow of emotion crossed the sheriff's face. It made her wish she hadn't asked at all. He shook his head.

"My chief deputy and lead detective are still working it," he said. "It's an old case, but we're hoping to wrap it up sooner rather than later."

Caleb perked up at that. "I thought you were done with it and that's why you came back to town."

Sheriff Reed smiled. It was a sad look. "No matter where I am or what I'm doing, you just don't get away with attacking my home. It's as simple as that. After I heard what had happened, nothing could have kept me from coming back. Plus, I had a hunch you wouldn't listen to Jones's telling you to go home and rest. I figured backup was just the thing you might need. As long as you're a part of my team, that's the very least I can offer you."

Alyssa felt a genuine smile spring to her lips. An infusion of pride blossomed inside her chest at the conviction behind his words.

"Now, I need you two to keep a low profile until we get a break in this case."

Caleb opened his mouth to, she assumed, protest, but the sheriff cut him off. "Before you say anything, I want you to know I'm not benching you because of protocol. I'm just asking you to keep her out of the sights of two unstable men while we work the case. Okay? That's not the same thing. She's a part of this wild web, an important part that we can't afford to let go."

Caleb shut his mouth. He gave a curt nod.

"Let me know if you need anything," the sheriff said, turning to her. "And I'm sorry this is all happening. I know from experience it's not fun to be this close to a case like this. We'll catch them and make sure they pay for everything they've done. Sheriff's honor."

"Thank you," Alyssa said, sincere.

The sheriff gave a parting nod and walked deeper into the department. The badge on his belt shone as the light caught it when he turned. Alyssa followed Caleb out into the lobby, still smiling.

"You know, I voted for him," she whispered at his shoulder, the feeling of pride for the sheriff carrying into her words. "He's a good man."

Caleb made a show of looking back to the hallway. He shrugged.

"I guess he's okay. You know, if you're into that tall, dark and rugged thing," Caleb deadpanned. It made Alyssa laugh.

"Is that jealousy I hear?" she teased, walking out the door he was holding open. She caught his grin.

"What do I have to be jealous about? I mean, have you seen these guns?" He made an exaggerated show of flexing his arms. Alyssa had to admit she liked seeing a more playful side of him. It was a nice break from the somberness that came from being in constant danger.

"Of course I've seen them. I'm betting on those things to keep me safe," she joked. It made the deputy's grin widen. Another welcome sight.

"You're about to see them drive us right back on to my place, where they'll then shovel some kind of food into my mouth." He grasped his stomach in exaggerated pain. She laughed.

"You were the one who threw out our breakfast when I had the Norman epiphany," she pointed out.

He shrugged.

"I got excited," he defended. His smile dropped. "Well, you know what I mean. Not *excited.*"

"I knew what you meant," she assured him. Still, she felt slightly guilty for his hungry gut. Before she walked around to the passenger side of the car, she paused at his side. "How about *I* make us something when we get back? I don't want to brag, but while I'm sure your eggs and bacon were great, I can make a mean breakfast casserole. As long as you have some biscuits, that is."

His grin broke out into a full-on smile. It made an already attractive man that much more delicious. On reflex she began to lean in closer to him. She smelled his cologne. Had he always worn it? Or was it something new? Either way she had to actively try to keep her eyelids from closing as she savored the crisp scent.

"I guess it's lucky for me that I do."

Alyssa knew they were talking about breakfast and food, but suddenly the air between them felt charged. She imagined the body of the man in front of her sans clothes. The way he had touched her, held her. The memory alone started to heat her up.

Maybe she wasn't the only one.

Caleb's eyes moved to her lips.

And they looked just as hungry.

Just like that, a switch seemed to flip beneath Caleb's exterior. She didn't have time to be concerned about it before he bent down and pressed his lips against hers. The kiss didn't last long, but it was enough to make her desire for him burn bright. "But first, I need to tell you something. Something about my past I should have told you already."

Guilt.

Alyssa read that emotion as if a sky writer had flown it across the sky.

It sounded an alarm bell in her mind so loudly that she took a small step back.

Which gave her the perfect vantage point to see Norman walking up behind the deputy.

And he was smiling.

It only took a second for Caleb to know Norman was behind him. Alyssa's face became a mirror, showing him a look of surprise that wasn't at all a happy one. Fear was there too, but not nearly as much as if Dupree had been the culprit. Caleb reached for his gun and whirled around, careful to keep Alyssa behind him.

The bastard was showing teeth.

"Shoot and they die," he greeted the end of Caleb's gun. The man didn't even flinch at its presence. Alyssa did, judging by the small intake of breath Caleb heard. He guessed it was more for the vague threat than the tool that could end Norman's attempts to take her.

"Who dies?" she asked.

Norman tilted his head to the side to see Alyssa better. Caleb's finger itched. Only a few feet separated him and Norman. How easy it would be to end the man wasn't lost on him.

"Do you know that bombers usually only stick to one method when it comes to setting off their handiwork?

Using pressure-plated bombs, for instance, has an entirely different pathology behind it than using a bomb with, say, a detonator." Norman shook his right hand at his side. There was an old flip phone open in it. "*Usually* a bomber will stick with only one method versus switching between the two." He shook his hand again. "*But* since I'm new to this I decided to try my hand at both."

He let that sink in a moment.

Caleb used that lapse to hope that whoever manned their security cameras for the department would see what was happening. They were in the side parking lot, away from the sight line to the main street and on the opposite side from the courthouse next door.

"Who dies?" Alyssa repeated. Her voice was cold but steady. Caleb wished he knew what she was thinking.

"The witnesses, of course."

Caleb's blood went cold. Surely the man was bluffing. Still, Caleb had to test him.

"You're lying," he said, gun arm not wavering. "They're all safe."

Norman bit out a chuckle.

"Why?" he asked, amused. "Because the fine Riker County law enforcement officers got them to do exactly like I wanted to do by leaving town?" Norman's laugh wasn't clipped this time. "It's easy to finish the puzzle when you can finally get to all the pieces." He shook the phone again. "But if you don't believe me I guess I could prove myself and my intentions. Who should go first, Alyssa? Missy Grayson in South Carolina with her husband? Or should I use the Rickmans' cabin in Tennessee as an example? I believe it's technically owned by their son Robert, but really, he's a Rickman too, so I suppose it's all the same."

"Why are you doing this?" Alyssa yelled. "Why continue to hurt all of us if your partner is already out of custody? *What's the point?*"

Norman was nonplussed by the emotion leaking into Alyssa's words.

"Because you care about them, Alyssa," he said simply. "And that's how I'm going to get you to come with me."

Caleb tightened the hold on his gun. "I don't think so, buddy. The lady stays with me."

Norman's humor vanished.

"She isn't meant for you," he said, voice pitching low. Threatening.

"And if she was meant for you, you wouldn't have to threaten her into leaving with you," Caleb countered. It clearly angered the man. Caleb realized he should probably tread lightly. It was hard if not downright impossible to read an unstable man. He couldn't tell if Norman was telling the truth or not. "Listen, why don't you disarm your bombs and then we'll talk with Alyssa about leaving with you? I'll even lower my gun."

Norman scrunched up his nose. He made a noise of disgust.

"I'm not falling for any of your tricks," he said. "I know what kind of man you are, Deputy Foster, and I don't trust you." Norman's gaze shifted to Alyssa. "He's a bad man, Alyssa. He's done bad things. You're safer with me."

Caleb clenched his teeth together. Hard. He'd been about to tell Alyssa *everything* a minute before, and now Norman was there ready to spill the beans. How had everything gotten so off track? And where was a deputy or staff member on a smoke break when you needed one?

"If you disarm your bombs, or at the very least let me warn them, I'll come with you."

Caleb kept his hands around the gun but chanced a look at Alyssa.

"I don't think—" he started, but the woman put a hand

on his shoulder and squeezed to silence him. She kept her gaze on Norman.

"Do we have a deal?"

The man adjusted his glasses with his free hand, as if he was thinking. He shook his head.

"You come with me and Mr. Foster here can warn whoever he sees fit to warn once we're gone. I won't detonate any of the bombs, but I won't disarm them either. That's not my job," he said. "That's my only offer."

To show he meant it he lifted the phone. His thumb hovered above its keys.

"And where is Dupree?" Alyssa said, no doubt hedging her answer. Though in hindsight Caleb would realize later that, at that moment, she'd already decided. "*I* don't trust him."

"Don't worry about him. He has his orders." Norman returned his gaze to Caleb, but not before checking the watch he was wearing. "Part of those being that he'll use a second detonator if he doesn't hear from me in the next two minutes. So, even if you decided to be a fool and shoot me, the damage would already be done."

"I'll go," Alyssa rushed. "I'll go!"

Caleb was trying his best to figure out a different solution and coming up blank. Or, rather, ending with a *boom*. He'd seen firsthand the destruction left in the wake of Norman's handiwork at Ted's house. So had Alyssa. She wouldn't want that for Robbie and Eleanor.

And neither would Caleb.

But to let Alyssa go with Norman?

"He won't hurt me," Alyssa whispered at his side. "Please, let me go." He was sure Norman heard it, but the man didn't comment. Caleb didn't lower his gun. He looked at Alyssa.

"I don't want to," he said, honestly. He wanted to point out that just because Norman was obsessed with her didn't mean he wouldn't hurt her.

Her blue eyes were an ocean of feeling when she responded.

"We have to protect them. They'd do the same for us." Alyssa gave him the smallest of smiles.

He didn't return it.

"I'll find you," he said instead. Then said to Norman, "And I'll make you pay."

Norman laughed before taking Alyssa's hand. Caleb felt like his heart was burning through his chest as he watched them walk behind the building to the back parking lot. The moment they were out of eyesight, Caleb grabbed his phone and readied to follow them while warning Missy and the Rickmans.

But then he heard a truly chilling sound.

It was Alyssa. And she was screaming. What, he couldn't understand.

Every part of Caleb's body propelled him forward, following the intangible connection between him and Alyssa that had formed over the last few days.

But he didn't make it two steps.

The parking lot exploded around him.

Chapter Twenty-Two

There were no clouds in the sky. Just an endless sea of blue. It reminded him of something, but he couldn't put his finger on it. So he just kept looking up, waiting to remember.

But it never came.

Instead something blocked his view.

It was a man and he was yelling something.

That was when he noticed the ringing in his ears.

And the pain. And the heat. And that the man looking down at him was the sheriff.

And then everything else filtered back in.

"Where's Alyssa?" Caleb yelled, his words a warbling sound. He struggled to get up off the asphalt. Sheriff Reed helped by putting himself under his arm. Caleb let out a howl of pain he didn't have to hear to know. The sheriff in turn quickly switched sides.

"Alyssa?" he repeated as they began to walk.

It was harder than it should have been.

The sheriff's mouth moved, but Caleb couldn't make out any sound that made sense. There was too much ringing and something else.

Caleb turned to look over his shoulder. The side parking lot was engulfed in a blanket of smoke, metal and fire. His car was among them but still recognizable. The car two down, however, was a twist of metal and paint. As far as he could tell, two others in the lot were the same.

Norman hadn't blown up the entire parking lot, just some of the cars.

And it would have been enough to take him out too, if Alyssa had not screamed. But she had, and that was all he'd needed to start running to her.

Even when she was being kidnapped, she'd managed to save him.

The ringing in his head worsened and his vision started to spin. Throbbing pain lit up his shoulder. Maybe he wasn't as good as he had hoped. The world tilted and swayed, but the sheriff guided him inside through the back of the department before his legs gave way.

The sheriff yelled something that sounded like an order. Seconds later a deputy named Brant appeared. He helped walk Caleb to the break room two doors down. It was already filled with people, all sporting varying looks of concern and fear. Cassie was among them. She made her way through the group and pointed toward the couch. The sheriff and Brant dropped him as best they could onto it.

The ringing in Caleb's ears lessened enough to finally make out what the sheriff was trying to ask.

"Where does it hurt?"

Caleb couldn't have thought of a more idiotic question, but in the back of his mind, he knew the man was only trying to help. Still, he had better things to worry about.

"Everywhere," he said, assuming it was more of a yell than anything. "Where's Alyssa?"

The ringing could have been turned on loud and Caleb still wouldn't be distracted from the face the sheriff was making.

"You don't know," Caleb answered himself.

Sheriff Reed shook his head.

"But we'll find her," he promised with a raised voice. "But first—"

He pointed to Caleb's shoulder. Cassie's face pinched. Brant's did too.

"It's dislocated," Caleb guessed. The pain he was feeling was a familiar one, he realized. He'd dislocated it before.

The sheriff nodded. He picked up Caleb's wrist and arm.

"Brace yourself," he yelled. "This is going to hurt."

THE HOUSE WAS MASSIVE, but it was also a shell.

Alyssa felt empty too.

"Stop your whining and pick up the pace," Dupree said at her elbow. "This detour to grab you already wasted enough of my time."

After the explosions, Alyssa had turned into a violent, violent woman. She'd lashed out at her captor as Norman tried his best to push her into the back seat of a car. Dupree had been there, ready. He'd put his hand around her throat and held her until he could slip a pair of handcuffs on her.

Then, when she'd tried to fight again, he'd told her in no uncertain terms that while the bombs with the witnesses had been a bluff, that didn't mean he personally couldn't go out and kill every single one of them.

It was a threat that pierced through her grief and made her quiet. Still, the drive out to the country had become a blank space in her memory. All she could think about was Caleb.

And how she should never have left him.

Dupree pushed her through the main floor, up a set of grand stairs, and stopped at a room with only two chairs inside.

"Where are we?" she had to ask. Her throat hurt, but she'd managed to stop crying. If only for the sheer bizarre situation she was currently in.

"Your house," he said, pushing her farther into the room. He pointed to one of the chairs. It was facing a large unobstructed window. Green grass and trees stretched out as far as she could see while an enormous deck pushed out from the first floor. It looked over a good-sized swimming pool, covered with a pool tarp.

"I don't understand," she said. "It doesn't look like *anyone* lives here."

"Not yet."

Alyssa felt her skin crawl as Norman's voice entered the room.

"But today we start."

"FOUND IT! MY GOD, I finally found it."

Caleb looked up from his computer as Captain Jones ran into the bull pen. He didn't slow as he made his way through to the conference room where the sheriff had made the base of operations since the station had gone into lockdown three hours beforehand. Just thinking about the time that had gone by and they still didn't have a lead on Norman or Alyssa made Caleb's stomach twist.

But he was starting to like the enthusiasm in the captain's voice.

"What did you find?" the sheriff was already asking by the time he made it into the room. While Caleb's shoulder had been popped back into place, the explosions had covered his body in cuts, burns and pain. All minor compared to what could have been. Still, he'd spent a useless amount of time trying to fend off the advice of the EMTs. He'd go get seen about after he found Alyssa. And only then.

"The briefcase," Jones exclaimed. "And damn if it wasn't hard to track down. But, thanks to the current manager of the bank and the shop across from it, I found the sucker."

He bent over the table to an open laptop. His fingers danced across the keyboard and mouse until he was satisfied. Caleb waited. It was a hard feat.

"Norman goes back to pick it up three weeks after the robbery." He stepped back so they could crowd around the laptop's screen. It was a picture of Norman holding the case they'd seen him enter the bank with earlier. "No one paid him much mind, since no one from the original robbery was actually there that day. Which means not only did he hide the briefcase before the robbery, he waited until he knew he could go back and get it without being recognized."

"Which means whatever was in that briefcase was extremely important to him," Caleb concluded.

Jones nodded. He held up his index finger.

"But that's not the exciting part," he said. "All the witnesses inside the bank during the robbery told authorities that Dupree and Anna disappeared into the back to go to the vault to fill their bags with money. Even the manager at the time, Davis Palmer, corroborated that story. However, after we made the discovery about the briefcase, I decided to give Davis a call to just go over everything one more time." He smiled. The gesture wasn't born of happiness but excitement. He'd found something. Something important. "While Anna shoveled money into her bag, she ordered Davis to get on his hands and knees and face the corner. He assumed Dupree was always there in the vault with them because a few minutes later he walked Davis and Anna out."

Jones held his finger up again to tell the room to hold on. He moved quickly to the whiteboard and wiped a space clear. He started to draw as he spoke.

"Two days after the robbery the bank owner took stock of all the damage done, making a list to turn over to CSU to add to their findings as well as a copy for insurance."

Caleb took a step closer as the man's drawing began to look like rough floor plans. The bank's floor plan, to be more precise.

"Two of those items included a busted lock on one door and another door off its hinges." Jones circled two spots on the drawing. According to the floor plan, those doors were separated by a hallway that ran parallel to what Caleb assumed was the vault.

"The owner admitted to the head of CSU that he'd already been having issues with one of the doors being loose." Jones pointed to the one closest to him. "So it wasn't flagged as something suspicious. Just as the busted lock wasn't either, since they'd also had some problems with it sticking before. Plus, it was assumed that Dupree never left the vault until now. The owner and CSU had bigger fish to fry and chalked it up to a coincidence or just moved past it altogether."

Captain Jones tapped the vault, moved his marker to the hallway next to it and moved past another hallway's intersection all the way until he made it to the circle he'd drawn for the busted lock.

"This leads into the safe-deposit room," he said. Before anyone could comment, he ran the marker back down the hallway to the intercepting one. He tapped the second dot he'd drawn for the door off its hinges. "And this is the employees'-only entrance next to the bathrooms and lobby. It's usually always locked."

The captain capped his marker.

Caleb's mind was racing.

"The robbery *was* just a distraction," he said, already going through the implications in his head. "Dupree slips out while Anna keeps the manager occupied. There's no one to stop him from going to the safe-deposit boxes, so he gets something out of one of them and goes into the bathroom, where he stashes whatever it was into the hidden briefcase. He gets caught, but Norman has no issues coming back a few weeks later and getting it."

"He could easily have hidden it behind a ceiling tile,"

the captain added. "No one would have looked up there unless there was a reason to. And there's already no cameras in front of the bathrooms."

"But what about the cameras outside the safe-deposit room or in the hallways?" the sheriff asked. "And, for that matter, what about the two keys needed to open one of those boxes?"

The captain didn't look as excited as he once had.

"The cameras covering both had been down a week and a half," he answered. "The owner had called for a technician, but he never showed up. After the robbery he called a different company and they came out to fix it. Again everyone thought these were separate issues."

"But together they're making a brand-new picture of what happened," Caleb finished. "The sheriff's right though. Let's say Dupree had one of the keys to get into the box. He still needs the manager's—" The captain's expression stopped Caleb's thoughts. "Let me guess, a set of his keys went missing and no one thought to add that into any kind of report."

Captain Jones nodded.

"Davis admitted he thought he lost his keys during his attempt to escape when the shooting started." Jones's expression softened a fraction. "Not that I give in to rumors around here, but Cassie heard that Davis had been sweet on Larissa Colt. He was with her when she died."

They all silenced.

If Caleb had been in the bank manager's position, holding on to Alyssa while she… Well, he also wouldn't think twice about lost keys. Especially when they didn't appear to have any bearing for what happened.

"Okay," Caleb said, breaking the silence. "If all this is true, then we know *why* the robbery happened but not *what* was taken. Is there any way to find out which box he might have opened?"

Sheriff Reed's expression scrunched in thought. Then he was jumping up out of his chair. "I have an idea."

Caleb listened to the plan with optimism as the sheriff explained it to a roomful of deputies before disappearing altogether. That feeling, however, started to dwindle as another half hour went by. By the time it turned into an hour, he was ready to throw in the towel and start to search all of Riker County inch by inch until he found Alyssa.

But then they finally got something they'd been lacking in the last week.

A good lead.

"We have a caller who claims a file of his is missing from his safe-deposit box," a deputy named Patty said, rushing into the conference room. Caleb jumped up, body stringing up with an adrenaline boost. The sheriff was on her heels.

"Dean Cranston."

No sooner had he read the name out loud than Reed's expression darkened.

"Who's Dean Cranston?" Caleb asked, annoyed he was new to town. "And what's missing?"

"Dean Cranston owns a processing plant on the outskirts of town," Cassie answered. The sheriff cursed beneath his breath. "He isn't the most liked man in Riker County."

"Why?" Caleb once again was in the dark. He didn't like it one bit.

"He inherited the plant when his father passed away a few years ago and decided to make a few changes the county didn't agree with," Patty answered.

"And by changes she means he started outsourcing almost everything he could to cut costs," the sheriff said, clearly angry. "He laid off more than three hundred people and then dumped the extra savings into building a fancy hotel in the city of Kipsy. He's always been in love with his own name and thinks he's some kind of celebrity when really most people just despise him for the greedy man he is. His layoffs forced a lot of longtime residents to move out of the county just to find a job. It ruined a lot of families. It wasn't pretty."

"So this guy is scum," Caleb said. "But what is his connection to Norman and—" He stopped himself and changed gears. A hunch began to yell so loudly he couldn't help blurting it out. "What if Norman was one of those families? What if he was laid off?"

"He said he was out for revenge," the sheriff said, eyes widening. They were finally getting some traction.

"What better target is there than a scumbag employer who took away your livelihood?" Caleb added. The sheriff snapped his fingers.

"But what did he take from the safe-deposit box?" Cassie asked Patty.

The deputy's lips had stretched into a grim line.

"Detailed blueprints to the Cranston Hotel in Kipsy," she said. "And Cranston's secretary relayed this information to me because Cranston was getting ready for a party being thrown tonight in his honor…at the Cranston."

The sheriff and Caleb shared a look.

"It's a lot easier to destroy a building if you know just where to put the bombs," Caleb pointed out.

"And that's one hell of a way to get revenge."

Chapter Twenty-Three

The sunset was beautiful, all things considered.

Alyssa watched through the window as violet, red and orange faded into darkness with a weird sense of calm. Or shock. She didn't care which. All she knew was that she was stranded in a place where fear and anger and anguish had become a constant. And, in that way, they had canceled each other out.

Now she was waiting for an opening.

One she hadn't been able to get, since Norman hadn't left her side in hours. She'd tried to talk to him, to understand what was going on, but he'd told her on repeat to wait for the sunset. She'd contemplated running but knew Dupree was near. She could hear his heavy steps echoing.

"Did you enjoy it?" Norman asked once they were staring at darkness through the window. It made her jump. When she didn't answer he continued, unperturbed. "When I built this house, that's what made me choose this room as my favorite. Sure, all the other views are nice, but there's something about *this* spot that makes it feel magical." He let out a long sigh. His tone changed. "This was supposed to be my castle. I was going to be the king."

He reached over and, as if her hands weren't cuffed behind her, patted the top of the armrest.

"I'm glad you stayed," he said, stronger. "It would have

been a shame had you left too. I might be forgiving, but I'm not that forgiving."

Alyssa's emotions were starting to pick up traction again, a slimy feeling along with them. It was like Norman was and wasn't there. Like he was and also wasn't talking to her. She wondered if she could use his struggle with reality to her advantage.

"Who else left?" she asked, careful to keep a soothing tone. Even if she wanted nothing more than to cause his pain. "Norman?"

He lazily moved his gaze to hers.

"She said if I couldn't have a castle, then I couldn't be a king. And she deserved more than someone like me."

His words were low and hollowing out. Alyssa's muscles started to tense. Readying. To run or fight, she didn't know.

"And why could you not have a castle?" she asked, matching his volume. "Isn't that where we are right now?"

A faint smile crossed his lips.

Then it twisted.

"These are just walls," he snarled, getting to his feet. "They don't mean anything, Barbara!" Norman's eyes were crazed when they met hers. Alyssa didn't move an inch. He rounded the chairs and stopped in front of her, grabbing the armrests. Who was Barbara? "We could have been happy, but you left me! Why?"

Alyssa yelled out in surprise as Norman lunged at the chair. Together she flipped over with it. Pain lit up her back as it connected with the hardwood.

"It wasn't my fault he took it all away from us," Norman roared, still rooted in his own world. He turned around and punched the window. Not hard enough to shatter it, but Alyssa didn't miss the blood that blossomed across his knuckles. He paid it no mind. "If you'd just given me some time…"

He sighed and looked down at her. "But *we* can be happy here."

Norman lowered himself into a crouch.

To her surprise, he gave her a smile. It was off, but Alyssa was starting to believe that Norman had finally reached a point of constant unraveling. She just hoped she wasn't with him when he finally went over the edge. He reached out and brushed his knuckles along her cheek. His blood was wet against her skin. She fought the urge to shudder.

"We'll be happy here now that you're mine and not some lowly deputy's. You'll see."

In that moment all Alyssa saw was red.

"I am not yours," she said, teeth bared. "I am not his. I. Am. Mine."

Alyssa swung her left hip around and up, her leg with it. The kick caught Norman off guard. He didn't have time to block as her shoe connected with the side of his head. He let out a strangled yell of pain and fell backward. Alyssa knew an opening when she saw one.

She rolled off the chair and managed to get into a sitting position. From there she got to her feet. The movement was hampered by her cuffed hands, but she wasn't about to let that slow her down. Not wanting to chance Norman getting the upper hand again, Alyssa ran straight for the open door. She paused for a second, trying to listen for a clue as to where Dupree was, but Norman's yell of pain changed to one filled with cursing. She decided she was just going to have to chance it.

Unimaginably glad she'd worn good shoes, Alyssa tore down the hallway toward the stairs. Halfway down them, though, a gunshot over her head made her nearly trip.

"What a pain in the ass," Dupree yelled behind her.

Alyssa screamed as another shot sounded. By the time

she hit the first floor, her heart was hammering in her chest.

Run, her mind yelled. *Run!*

She wanted to go down the only familiar path she knew of the house, but it was too long and open for her liking. Instead Alyssa ran through the kitchen and toward the back door.

"Don't shoot her!"

Norman's voice carried through the house just as Alyssa made it to a set of French doors. The seconds it took her to turn around and grab the knob with her bound hands were excruciating.

"I'm done playing these games," Dupree yelled back. He was too close for her comfort. "If you don't want me to kill her, *then stop me*."

Alyssa got the door open and ran outside. She was on the deck that overlooked the sloping yard and the pool. It reminded her of Gabby's giant deck in Colorado. Which gave her the hope that maybe it was built the same way with an access door at its front used for storage.

Norman and Dupree were still yelling behind her.

She didn't waste any more time.

Trying to run as fast and quietly as she could, Alyssa took the side stairs that ran alongside the deck until she was on a concrete patio that surrounded the pool.

"No," she breathed, rounding the front part of the deck. There was no door. Just stained wood and a life preserver placed in the middle.

"You should have hidden," Dupree yelled into the night air, tearing her own thoughts from her mind. "There's nowhere to do that out here."

Alyssa froze up as footsteps thundered toward her.

"You are not worth this effort." Dupree's face swam into view as he peered over the deck and down at her. He was angry, very much the man she'd seen before he'd shot her in the bank. He lowered his gun. "And I have to say, I'm going to really enjoy repeating history."

The shot exploded through the quiet of the night.

Alyssa braced herself for the end.

But it didn't come. At least, not for her.

Dupree dropped his gun and tipped forward. His weight carried him over the railing so fast that Alyssa hurried backward to get out of the way.

Expecting to find solid ground, she yelled in surprise when she started to fall.

Right into the pool.

Cold water rushed over her as the tarp wrapped around her body. Panic exploded in Alyssa's chest. She tried to move upward, but with her hands behind her back, she floundered. She kicked out viciously, but the tarp countered every move she made to try to make it back to the surface. In the movement her glasses fell off her face.

The already dark world blurred.

A muffled shot sounded overhead, but she didn't have the focus to wonder about it. Not while her lungs were starting to burn.

She was suffocating.

Something hit the water next to her. The chlorine burned her eyes as she tried to focus on what it was, but the tarp created a barrier she couldn't see past.

But then, out of that darkness, a hand found her side. Then another.

She stilled as the tarp was pulled away, lungs on fire.

Then she was being pushed to the surface.

"Breathe," a man commanded at her side as soon as she began to cough and sputter. He repeated his order while moving them to the shallow end of the pool. Alyssa did as she was told, turning her gaze to the blur next to her.

But he was too close to be a blur.

"Caleb!"

The deputy gave her a smile that reached into every part of her body and warmed it. His golden hair was in tangles and he looked a little worse for the wear, but there he was. Alive.

"I thought you were—" she started, already fighting tears. Caleb closed the space between them, interrupting her with a kiss.

"But I'm not," he said after they parted. "I'm right here with you."

Alyssa wanted to stay within the warmth that Caleb seemed to always make her feel, but the reality of where they were set back in.

"You shot Dupree before he could kill me," she realized.

Caleb's expression pinched. "Not exactly."

He guided her to the steps of the pool and waited to explain when they were out of the water. The night air made her cold, but she didn't care. Not when Caleb was with her.

"I heard the gunshots in the house, but I got out here too late," he admitted.

"Then who shot Dupree?"

"Norman did." He walked them onto the grass, away from the pool and deck. Away from Dupree's body. Voices sounded from the house. Caleb didn't flinch, which made her assume he'd had backup this time around. "It's not that surprising if you think about it," he continued. "He wanted to protect you."

A range of emotions crossed Caleb's expression. Some were a mystery. Others weren't.

"And I can't blame him for that," he said with the smallest of smiles.

That warmth within her heated, but she still needed to know what had happened while she was underwater. "Where is he now?"

On cue Norman's wail carried over to them. It was followed by a voice she recognized as the sheriff's.

"After he shot Dupree he turned on me," Caleb explained. "I was able to get his gun away without killing him. Then I went in after you."

That sobered Alyssa.

"Good," she said. "I want him to be able to pay for what he's done."

Caleb nodded. "And he will. Of that the sheriff will make sure."

Alyssa might have been cuffed, soaking wet and mostly blind, but in that moment she felt something she never thought she'd feel.

Closure.

ALYSSA HAD HER head hung over one of the biggest cups of coffee Caleb had ever seen. He watched her from the door of the conference room for a few seconds, marveling at how beautiful she was, before he took a deep breath and sat down next to her.

"I need to tell you something," he jumped in. "Something I should have told you a lot sooner." Alyssa turned to him, eyes widened in surprise. He hoped they wouldn't turn away from him completely when he was done.

"I was a beat cop in Portland when my current partner and I got a call to a town house in the suburbs," he started. "When we got there a neighbor said that he'd called because he had heard this man beating his wife almost every night and couldn't take it anymore. He said the screaming was so loud it woke him up. So we investigated." Normally just thinking about that night would awaken a new surge of anger, but somehow looking into Alyssa's eyes made him feel calm. "Long story short, the wife was pretty bad off but didn't want to press charges. I tried my best to convince her to at least leave for the night, but she kept looking back at her husband, clearly terrified. And that's when he looked at me and said, 'She knows she deserved it.'"

Alyssa sucked in a breath. Caleb took one of his own. "Something in me snapped," he admitted. "I threw one punch and before I knew it my partner was pulling me off the man and he was going to the hospital. And *that's* why I was transferred here. I lost control."

Caleb averted his gaze. He thought he could handle it if Alyssa realized she'd made a mistake in getting close to him, but now the thought wasn't one he wanted to face.

"Caleb, look at me."

A warm hand guided his chin to turn toward her.

"I can't pretend to know what it's like being in law enforcement. To go into dangerous and occasionally heartbreaking situations, forced to see the world at its worst sometimes. But what I do know is that you had the chance to kill a very bad man tonight and no one would have blamed you, and yet you didn't." A small smile pulled up the corners of her lips. It was soft and sweet. Just like her. "You wanted him to face justice, the right way. And because of that decision, that's exactly what's going to happen. What you did in the past is already done. All you can do now is move on and become better for it."

She moved closer, and that smile grew. He welcomed her lips, once more, against his. "Plus, I'm here to tell you that if you were looking for some kind of redemption, I think you more than found it here."

Epilogue

"So, everyone has a pool going on you."

Caleb looked up from his desk and couldn't help grinning. Sheriff Reed had once been a man he didn't understand, but after what they'd been through he was a man Caleb not only respected, but liked. "Oh yeah? What kind of pool?"

"On whether or not you'll stay."

Caleb eyed the clock over the man's shoulder, still grinning.

"I actually just ended my shift," he answered, closing the file on his desk and standing. "So technically I'm leaving."

Reed laughed and followed him as he made his way out to the lobby. His blazer was slung over his shoulder. "How convenient. I'm on my way out too."

It had been three weeks since the night Caleb had thought he'd lost Alyssa. And he hated to think it, but he realized he would have, had Dean Cranston not grown a conscience. He'd sent a list of every employee laid off from his plant, and thankfully Norman Calloway had been the only Norman on the list. From there it had been easy to look up his address out on the cusp of Carpenter. The house he'd built for his wife, Barbara. The house he couldn't afford when he'd been laid off. The sheriff had had the pleasure of talking to Barbara after the arrest. She'd admitted to leaving Norman high and dry when he couldn't accommodate her lifestyle and she never looked back.

According to the psychologist assigned to his case, that was when Norman decided he wanted to gain back the control he'd lost. One night he approached an angry man at the bar and promised him revenge if he helped him steal blueprints from a safe-deposit box Norman knew Cranston used. Dupree had agreed easily. While he wasn't an employee of the plant, his father had been. Their family, like Norman's, was shattered because of it.

However, when he'd bumped into Alyssa at the bank, all the stress of what he was doing finally pushed him into a new reality. One where a woman loved him so much that she cheated death just to stay with him. In the year that followed he worked on his plan, believing it was the last obstacle between them, but at the same time began to devolve. His stability took more hits as parts of his plans backfired.

The sheriff believed that if Norman didn't spend his life in prison, he'd at least spend it in an institution. Far, far away from Riker County.

"What's your bet?" Caleb finally had to ask Reed as they walked out of the building.

"You mean do I think you'll stay in Riker County or go back to Portland?"

"Yeah. Will I stay or go?"

The sheriff was already grinning. They paused on the sidewalk.

"First, answer me this," he said. "What are your plans tonight?"

Caleb felt his eyebrow rise. "Alyssa wants to try out the new Chinese place that opened up off Main. We're meeting Robbie and Eleanor there. Why?"

Reed let out a laugh. "That's why I think you'll stay."

Caleb snorted.

"Because of Chinese food?" he hedged, already knowing exactly what the sheriff meant. However, the man didn't answer. Instead he turned his attention over Caleb's shoulder with a look that was nothing but glee.

"Well, hello, Miss Garner! I do believe that you're going to help me win a bet."

Caleb turned in time to see Alyssa confused. She looked between them.

"A bet?" she repeated.

"Don't worry about it," Caleb jumped in, trying not to laugh. "The sheriff just had too much coffee today."

"Speaking of coffee," she started. "I was hoping to grab a cup from the café before we take Sergeant to the dog park, if that's okay with you?"

"Sounds great to me."

Alyssa beamed.

They said goodbye to the sheriff and parted ways in the parking lot. Caleb slipped his hand in hers as they walked. It was warm and perfect.

While the danger had ceased in the last few weeks, his feelings for the woman next to him hadn't. So, while the department might be taking guesses at whether or not he was going to stay, Caleb already knew the answer.

"Hey, Reed," he called across the lot, stopping the man before he got into his Bronco. "You've already won the bet!"

The sheriff just laughed.

* * * * *

Look for more books in Tyler Anne Snell's
THE PROTECTORS OF RIKER COUNTY
series in 2018.

And don't miss the previous title in
THE PROTECTORS OF RIKER COUNTY *series:*

SMALL-TOWN FACE-OFF

Available now from Mills & Boon Intrigue!

Sheriff Flint Cahill can and will endure elements far worse than the coming winter storm to hunt down Maggie Thompson and her abductor.

Read on for a sneak preview of
COWBOY'S LEGACY,
A CAHILL RANCH NOVEL *from*
New York Times *bestselling author*
B.J. Daniels!

SHE WAS IN so fast that she didn't have a chance to scream. The icy cold water stole her breath away. Her eyes flew open as she hit. Because of the way she fell, she had no sense of up or down for a few moments.

Panicked, she flailed in the water until a light flickered above her. She tried to swim toward it, but something was holding her down. The harder she fought, the more it seemed to push her deeper and deeper, the light fading.

Her lungs burned. She had to breathe. The dim light wavered above her through the rippling water. She clawed at it as her breath gave out. She could see the surface just inches above her. Air! She needed oxygen. Now!

The rippling water distorted the face that suddenly appeared above her. The mouth twisted in a grotesque smile. She screamed, only to have her throat fill with the putrid dark water. She choked, sucking in even more water. She was drowning, and the person who'd done this to her was watching her die and smiling.

Maggie Thompson shot upright in bed, gasping for air and swinging her arms frantically toward the faint light coming through the window. Panic had her perspiration-soaked nightgown sticking to her skin. Trembling, she clutched the bedcovers as she gasped for breath.

The nightmare had been so real this time that she thought she was going to drown before she could come out of it. Her chest ached, her throat feeling raw as tears burned her eyes. It had been too real. She couldn't shake the feeling that she'd almost died this time. Next time...

She snapped on the bedside lamp to chase away the dark shadows hunkered in the corners of the room. If only Flint had been here instead of on an all-night stakeout. She needed Sheriff Flint Cahill's strong arms around her. Not that he stayed most nights. They hadn't been intimate that long.

Often, he had to work or was called out in the middle of the night. He'd asked her to move in with him months ago, but she'd declined. He'd asked her after one of his ex-wife's nasty tricks. Maggie hadn't wanted to make a decision like that based on Flint's ex.

While his ex hadn't done anything in months to keep them apart, Maggie couldn't rest easy. Flint was hoping Celeste had grown tired of her tricks. Maggie wasn't that naive. Celeste Duma was one of those women who played on every man's weakness to get what she wanted—and she wanted not just the rich, powerful man she'd left Flint for. She wanted to keep her ex on the string, as well.

Maggie's breathing slowed a little. She pulled the covers up to her chin, still shivering, but she didn't turn off the light. Sleep was out of the question for a while. She told herself that she wasn't going to let Celeste scare her. She wasn't going to give the woman the satisfaction.

Unfortunately, it was just bravado. Flint's ex was obsessed with him. Obsessed with keeping them apart. And since the woman had nothing else to do...

As the images of the nightmare faded, she reminded herself that the dream made no sense. It never had. She was a good swimmer. Loved water. Had never nearly drowned. Nor had anyone ever tried to drown her.

Shuddering, she thought of the face she'd seen through the rippling water. Not Celeste's. More like a Halloween mask. A distorted smiling face, neither male nor female. Just the memory sent her heart racing again.

What bothered her most was that dream kept reoccurring. After the first time, she'd mentioned it to her friend Belle Delaney.

"A drowning dream?" Belle had asked with the arch of her eyebrow. "Do you feel that in waking life you're being sucked into' something you'd rather not be a part of?"

Maggie had groaned inwardly. Belle had never kept it a secret that she thought Maggie was making a mistake when it came to Flint. Too much baggage, she always said of the sheriff. His "baggage" came in the shape of his spoiled, probably psychopathic, petite, green-eyed, blonde ex.

"I have my own skeletons." Maggie had laughed, although she'd never shared her past—even with Belle—before moving to Gilt Edge, Montana, and opening her beauty shop, Just Hair. She feared it was her own baggage that scared her the most.

"If you're holding anything back," Belle had said, eyeing her closely, "you need to let it out. Men hate surprises after they tie the knot."

"Guess I don't have to worry about that because Flint hasn't said anything about marriage." But she knew Belle was right. She'd even come close to telling him several times about her past. Something had always stopped her. The truth was, she feared if he found out her reasons for coming to Gilt Edge he wouldn't want her anymore.

"The dream isn't about Flint," she'd argued that day with Belle, but she couldn't shake the feeling that it was a warning.

"Well, from what I know about dreams," Belle had said, "if in the dream you survive the drowning, it means that a waking relationship will ultimately survive the turmoil. At least, that is one interpretation. But I'd say the nightmare definitely indicates that you are going into unknown wa-

ters and something is making you leery of where you're
headed." She'd cocked an eyebrow at her. "If you have the
dream again, I'd suggest that you ask yourself what it is
you're so afraid of."

"I'm sure it's just about his ex, Celeste," she'd lied. Or
was she afraid that she wasn't good enough for Flint—just
as his ex had warned her. Just as she feared in her heart.

THE WIND LAY over the tall dried grass and kicked up dust
as Sheriff Flint Cahill stood on the hillside. He shoved his
Stetson down on his head of thick dark hair, squinting in
the distance at the clouds to the west. Sure as the devil, it
was going to snow before the day was out.

In the distance, he could see a large star made out of
red and green lights on the side of a barn, a reminder that
Christmas was coming. Flint thought he might even get a
tree this year, go up in the mountains and cut it himself.
He hadn't had a tree at Christmas in years. Not since…

At the sound of a pickup horn, he turned, shielding
his eyes from the low winter sun. He could smell snow in
the air, feel it deep in his bones. This storm was going to
dump a good foot on them, according to the latest news.
They were going to have a white Christmas.

Most years he wasn't ready for the holiday season any
more than he was ready for a snow that wouldn't melt until
spring. But this year was different. He felt energized. This was
the year his life would change. He thought of the small velvet box in his jacket pocket. He'd been carrying it around for
months. Just the thought of it made him smile to himself. He
was in love and he was finally going to do something about it.

The pickup rumbled to a stop a few yards from him. He
took a deep breath of the mountain air and, telling himself he was ready for whatever Mother Nature wanted to
throw at him, he headed for the truck.

"Are you all right?" his sister asked as he slid into the

passenger seat. In the cab out of the wind, it was nice and warm. He rubbed his bare hands together, wishing he hadn't forgotten his gloves earlier. But when he'd headed out, he'd had too much on his mind. He still did.

Lillie looked out at the dull brown of the landscape and the chain-link fence that surrounded the missile silo. "What were you doing out here?"

He chuckled. "Looking for aliens. What else?" This was the spot that their father swore aliens hadn't just landed on one night back in 1967. Nope, according to Ely Cahill, the aliens had abducted him, taken him aboard their spaceship and done experiments on him. Not that anyone believed it in the county. Everyone just assumed that Ely had a screw loose. Or two.

It didn't help that their father spent most of the year up in the mountains as a recluse trapping and panning for gold.

"Aliens. Funny," Lillie said, making a face at him.

He smiled over at her. "Actually, I was on an all-night stakeout. The cattle rustlers didn't show up." He shrugged.

She glanced around. "Where's your patrol SUV?"

"Axle deep in a muddy creek back toward Grass Range. I'll have to get it pulled out. After I called you, I started walking and I ended up here. Wish I'd grabbed my gloves, though."

"You're scaring me," she said, studying him openly. "You're starting to act like Dad."

He laughed at that, wondering how far from the truth it was. "At least I didn't see any aliens near the missile silo."

She groaned. Being the butt of jokes in the county because of their father got old for all of them.

Flint glanced at the fenced-in area. There was nothing visible behind the chain link but tumbleweeds. He turned back to her. "I didn't pull you away from anything important, I hope? Since you were close by, I thought you wouldn't mind giving me a ride. I've had enough walking for one day. Or thinking, for that matter."

She shook her head. "What's going on, Flint?"

He looked out at the country that ran to the mountains, Cahill Ranch. His grandfather had started it, his father had worked it, and now two of his brothers ran the cattle part of it to keep the place going while he and his sister, Lillie, and brother Darby had taken other paths. Not to mention their oldest brother, Tucker, who'd struck out at seventeen and hadn't been seen or heard from since.

Flint had been scared after his marriage and divorce. But Maggie was nothing like Celeste, who was small, blonde, green-eyed and crazy. Maggie was tall with big brown eyes and long auburn hair. His heart beat faster at the thought of her smile, at her laugh.

"I'm going to ask Maggie to marry me," Flint said and nodded as if reassuring himself.

When Lillie didn't reply, he glanced over at her. It wasn't like her not to have something to say. "Well?"

"What has taken you so long?"

He sighed. "Well, you know after Celeste…"

"Say no more," his sister said, raising a hand to stop him. "Anyone would be gun-shy after being married to her."

"I'm hoping she won't be a problem."

Lillie laughed. "Short of killing your ex-wife, she is always going to be a problem. You just have to decide if you're going to let her run your life. Or if you're going to live it—in spite of her."

So easy for her to say. He smiled, though. "You're right. Anyway, Maggie and I have been dating for a while now and there haven't been any…incidents in months."

Lillie shook her head. "You know Celeste was the one who vandalized Maggie's beauty shop—just as you know she started that fire at Maggie's house."

"Too bad there wasn't any proof so I could have arrested her. But since there wasn't and no one was hurt and it was months ago…"

"I'd love to see Celeste behind bars, though I think prison is too good for her. I can understand why you would be worried about what she will do next. She's psychopathic."

He feared that that maybe was close to the case. "Do you want to see the ring?" He knew she did, so he fished it out of his pocket. He'd been carrying it around for quite a while now. Getting up his courage? He knew what was holding him back. Celeste. He couldn't be sure how she would take it—or what she might do. His ex-wife seemed determined that he and Maggie shouldn't be together, even though she was apparently happily married to local wealthy businessman Wayne Duma.

Handing his sister the small black velvet box, he waited as she slowly opened it.

A small gasp escaped her lips. "It's beautiful. *Really* beautiful." She shot him a look. "I thought sheriffs didn't make much money?"

"I've been saving for a long while now. Unlike my sister, I live pretty simply."

She laughed. "Simply? Prisoners have more in their cells than you do. You aren't thinking of living in that small house of yours after you're married, are you?"

"For a while. It's not that bad. Not all of us have huge new houses like you and Trask."

"We need the room for all the kids we're going to have," she said. "But it is wonderful, isn't it? Trask is determined that I have everything I ever wanted." Her gaze softened as the newlywed thought of her husband.

"I keep thinking of your wedding." There'd been a double wedding, with both Lillie and her twin, Darby, getting married to the loves of their lives only months ago. "It's great to see you and Trask so happy. And Darby and Mariah... I don't think Darby is ever going to come off that cloud he's on."

Lillie smiled. "I'm so happy for him. And I'm happy

for you. You know I really like Maggie. So do it. Don'
worry about Celeste. Once you're married, there's noth
ing she can do."

He told himself she was right, and yet in the back of hi:
mind, he feared that his ex-wife would do something to ruir
it—just as she had done to some of his dates with Maggie

"I don't understand Celeste," Lillie was saying as she
shifted into Drive and started toward the small Western
town of Gilt Edge. "She's the one who dumped you fo:
Wayne Duma. So what is her problem?"

"I'm worried that she is having second thoughts abou
her marriage to Duma. Or maybe she's bored and has noth
ing better to do than concern herself with my life. Maybe
she just doesn't want me to be happy."

"Or she is just plain malicious," Lillie said. "If she isn'
happy, she doesn't want you to be, either."

A shaft of sunlight came through the cab window
warming him against the chill that came with even talk
ing about Celeste. He leaned back, content as Lillie drove

He was going to ask Maggie to marry him. He wa:
going to do it this weekend. He'd already made a dinne:
reservation at the local steak house. He had the ring in hi:
pocket. Now it was just a matter of popping the questior
and hoping she said yes. If she did… Well, then, this wa:
going to be the best Christmas ever, he thought and smiled

* * * * *

*COWBOY'S LEGACY, available
wherever Mills and Boon Books and
ebooks are sold.*

www.millsandboon.co.uk

Copyright © 2017 by Barbara Heinlein

MILLS & BOON®

INTRIGUE
Romantic Suspense

A SEDUCTIVE COMBINATION OF DANGER AND DESIRE

1217/46